Niche

Jane Ireland

THE CRYING TREE SERIES BOOK 2

Niche © 2022 Jane Ireland.

All Rights Reserved.

No part of this book may be reproduced in any form or by any electronic or mechanical means including information storage and retrieval systems, without permission in writing from the author. The only exception is by a reviewer, who may quote short excerpts in a review.

This book is a work of fiction. Names, characters, places, and incidents either are products of the author's imagination or are used fictitiously. Any resemblance to actual persons, living or dead, events, or locales is entirely coincidental.

Cover by Melinda Childs @studioorchard

Internal design by Book Burrow www.bookburrow.com.au

Printed in Australia

First Printing: November 2022

Second Edition: January 2025

Published by Wild Magenta Books

Paperback ISBN 978-1-7637599-2-3

eBook ISBN 978-1-7637599-3-0

Hardback ISBN 978-1-7637599-5-4

 A catalogue record for this work is available from the National Library of Australia

*For those who fan my love of nature,
and anyone in need of a little magic.*

The Crying Tree Series

Book 1: *Emigree*
Book 2: *Niche*

The Crying Tree Series

Book 1: *Emigree*
Book 2: *Niche*

*For those who fan my love of nature,
and anyone in need of a little magic.*

*Welcome the nudge of tiny fae wings skimming your cheek.
Unfurl your own, beloved. Prepare to be spirited away.*

'And into the forest I go, to lose my mind and find my soul.'

— *John Muir*

Chapter One

Pig Peak, New South Wales, Australia, May 1968

Ferocious autumn winds pummel an old eucalypt on the Alton property. Within its bark, it writhes and wavers. Should it cower? Or attempt a rebellious stretch? Wild westerlies never untangle contorted limbs, they whip away branches.

The gales intensify. They howl and rumble. The tree shudders violently, swaying, creaking. A stinging rip assails an upper branch, leaving an injury the tree will eventually heal over with another burl.

As if suddenly deciduous, a flurry of leaves erupts from the canopy, dancing away in a pretty show to sprinkle down upon the homestead roof like holy water. A sigh of dull relief. It will lose more of itself, and its loss will be felt somehow in all other living things—the way since time immemorial. Here, now, it remains stuck in its mortal coil, beseeching the stubbornly clear blue sky for life.

Irrespective of the weather, far beneath any light of hope, it toils deep within the parched earth. As it weaves tenacious new roots, it butts against the hard ground in search of elusive water.

No less profound is the suffering of the property's current custodians, who reveal their pain in rash actions, endure harsh consequences. One female here hides marks she has cut into her skin in a misguided attempt to reach her torment. She will need her strength if she is to heal her gashes, slay those encroaching dragons.

The tree will suffer further, yet it still warns the family of danger.

Beyond the sensibilities of many humans—yet not all—the tree taps into ancient vibrations and frequencies, their messages integral to Mother Nature's order, her synergy.

One woman here was gifted such heightened intuition—which another will receive, too, in her time of need. The sacred signs that the universe reveals—the inexplicable, the sometimes incorporeal—will throw them into a spin. Yet they can grow, give themselves over to wonder, realise their potential through their joy and their pain.

The crying tree understands the ways of the universe and its place within it. Deep inside the tree's core, a subtle tide is on the rise, preparing for the time when its true purpose will be served.

Craving comfort, Fleur Alton is back doing a sneaky nose about in Teddy's bedroom. She finds solace amongst his things—his precious things, her mother Grace calls them—despite this quiet room now being so grossly at odds with her animated brother.

An indignant huff escapes Fleur as she pictures her mother pinning down her wild boy to his room, keeping him neat and precious like her memories of him. Guilt surges through Fleur's body, as unavoidable as her flow of blood, unseen yet heard in her mournful gasp, as she imagines Grace's unspeakable agony when she packed everything of Teddy's away. Instinctively Fleur crosses her arms. None of her pitiful self-ministrations ever touch her pain, let alone stop it. Is this what it is like for her mother?

Fleur scans the room. Here's Freddy, her brother's teddy bear, poised in a half-sit on the bed, sensing Fleur is about to spring into action and wishing he could too. Irresistibly, Fleur catches Freddy's contained excitement. His one eye watches her as she flings open cupboard doors and dresser drawers, in her contained madness, giving air to Teddy's life things her mother has tried to preserve in situ, like limp fruit in jars no-one will ever savour. Fleur sees embryos in formaldehyde, because untouched they are in danger of becoming dead things. It's enough to give you the creeps. Teddy would hate that.

She relishes her disturbance here, inviting some to-the-rest-of-the-world-unseen part of her brother—the best part of him, the wild part—to come play with her. Each time, when the games are over, she restores Teddy and his things to their nice, neat, precious state—her mother none the wiser—with a sleight of hand and swing of a door. Today, to enliven her brother, Fleur sings a Beatles song as she practises a new dance for him, twisting and shaking her hips. She wraps up by placing one hand on her stomach, the other on her lower back, before giving her brother a deep, reverent bow—despite sensing that both Teddy and Freddy would laugh at her antics. Imagine if Tripp could see her now. Oh no!

Fleur sits down cross-legged on the prickly Axminster carpet in front of the open wardrobe's dark cavity. She gives her nose a frantic rub; her allergies, at least, are coming alive. Although her mother now keeps the room spotless, in a futile quest for soft pale Teddy hairs Fleur picks at the carpet pile, before craning her neck to see what lurks at the back of the cupboard. From behind two pairs of small, scruffy shoes, she yanks out his xylophone which lost its mallet about a year ago. Hoping to set the room alight in musical notes, she runs her fingertip and nail over the cold tone plates and taps them. Nothing. She chucks the mute instrument back into its cupboard cage, hears it clang in protest because she has not bothered to think of something inventive to use in place of the stick. The momentum has caused something cylindrical to roll out onto the carpet and bump her shins. Teddy's kaleidoscope. It gave him colours, he said.

Fleur scoops it up, rushes to open the window and pauses in a beam of sunlight, absorbing its nourishing warmth. Positioning the end of the instrument against one eye, screwing up the other, she aims the kaleidoscope towards the sun-drenched yard. She twists the wheel of the short tube, enabling the mirrors, glass, and beads, to form a myriad of colourful symmetrical patterns. With a small flick of the wrist, everything changes in an instant…

… and turns blue, as a tiny Matchbox toy car appears at the end of the tube. Teddy's little blue Maserati—the one he took everywhere;

the one Fleur has been searching so hard for on the riverbank since the day she lost her brother—is caught in a spotlight at the end of his magic colour tube. Unexpected. Beautiful in its presentation.

'See Teddy? I told you I'd find it!' Her fingers tremble as she turns the tube this way and that, testing the credibility of an image which makes no sense, yet perfect sense. She even gives the toy an almighty shake before checking again, wanting the magic to stay, but it won't because magic is always short-lived. Sure enough, when she looks again, the image has gone. Pulled back to her dull world, she flounders in a sea of tears.

Everything changes in an instant.

As she wipes her eyes with her blouse, she admonishes Teddy with authority. 'You know I've been using your red hat as a signpost at the river. Now you've shown me your car. You want it back here, don't you? Yes, because you hate the river now. But surely you must realise I've been searching for it everywhere, Teddy!'

She peers outside across the acres of bleached pastures, wondering if anything will ever colour them again. Good things change to bad, never the other way around—that trick can't work.

Chapter Two

Saturday night at the local, a seventeen-and-a-half-year-old woman exhales a white cloud in vaporous tendrils, which is swiftly lost to the night like a soul delivered into the brisk air. Fleur wonders if it was a soul escaping Earth. Was it doomed? It may have been hers, surely now a mere scrap of a thing. Lately, she has felt the urge to leave, and with all the ugliness here, who could blame it for fleeing? If the universe were to dispense some looming perdition for her soul's breakout, it could almost be worth it. If she were to lose her part-soul, no-one would even notice it...

Gone.

A head shake fails to shake life into her, but a yawn suggests that most of her seems intact. She hates it here; perhaps she could feel wanted here. No, she *deserves* to be here. Leaning back against the Criterion Hotel's convict-era brick façade she forms another point of contact with the sole of one shoe, as if doing so will keep her propped upright, keep her from collapsing. She hangs on the wall: a tattered, filth-infused old coat.

Meat on a hook. On the turn.

A backfiring car startles her. A sudden childhood memory: hefty double bunger fireworks exploding on Cracker Night. Ignited Catherine Wheels spinning round, shooting circles of incandescent surprises, lighting up the black canvas—such excitement! Tonight, though, she is St Catherine of Alexandria lashed to a wooden torture wheel. But unlike that Christian activist, no angel intervenes and tears the wheel to pieces to save Fleur. She could almost suck her thumb right about now.

What has become of her? She wants to go back to when she was her father's 'firecracker': sparkly, carefree, unpredictable in her old cheeky ways. She wants to hunt for treasure with her brother again, to feel his chubby fingers give her palm squeezes of anticipation.

Scratching an itchy leg causes a sudden rip to one of Fleur's fishnet stockings. The shock of white knee—like a miniature skull demanding attention—causes her to laugh. She grabs handfuls of flouncy red dress and hitches the material over her patent leather belt to expose a pair of crisscrossed thighs. She wears heavy make-up she thinks makes her appear older, and curls of thick eyeliner rise from her outer eyes towards her eyebrows like a broken Dali moustache. Inside those black lids her liquid-amber eyes are beginning to smart; she closes them for a moment, crushing her dress with her fists.

She opens her eyes to the Italian shopkeeper from the deli next door channelling Dean Martin's velvety tones, singing 'O Sole Mio' in tenor. The music gives her a momentary lift. She would waltz down the street if she could without looking stupid, but she simply hums along and watches him hose the public's visible smut from his footpath. An unusual task for night-time, yet she reasons that it is filthy. As water hits the oily gutter, plays of colour skim upon its surface. Rainbows encircle a mass of soggy cigarette butts, inflating their ignoble status. A whirlpool of opalescent flashes forms above the stormwater drain grate, and dallies, before getting sucked into dark tunnels underground.

Why is magic so fleeting? Things always end badly.

Fleur herself is not immune to forced and unwelcome changes, and she knows there are oily men here who would drag her down and suck her dry. Her now electric eyes—ignited by the headlights of slow cars—catch in the eyes of the oily drivers who check her out. What if they stopped? She wants them to hit the gas at breakneck speed and leave her the hell alone. Time to move.

Sauntering inside the hotel, Fleur is hit with the gag-inducing miasma of cigarettes, hoppy beer, the beeps from back-room poker machines. Eyes to the floor. Tonight, she refuses to let the cedar-clad walls suffocate her with their darkness. Digging her stiletto heels into the musty purple carpet gouges out fibres to leave in her wake: her little marks of destruction.

She raises her gaze to a line of patrons sitting at the public bar who have all turned to the centre of the room, watching as a man dangles a treat above an irritated white miniature poodle in a pink netting skirt. The dog is urged on by his mates as it simultaneously dances on its hind legs whilst growling and snapping at the air. After circling a bit, it gets rewarded with the treat and a saucer of beer. At the bar, a cockatiel eats peanuts from a bowl and craps on the bar runner.

Fleur strolls into the pool room. Seeing two guys she met the last time she was here—she's only been here twice before now—she watches them a little before swiping a pool stick from one and breaking into their game.

A relieved looking Jacko retreats to a seat. 'Ya'd better keep up me brilliant shots, Fleur.' His little billiard balls far outnumber the big ones left on the table.

'Couldn't do much worser now, could she?' says the more arrogant, good-looking Trevor. 'Hey, Fleur, why doncha take over and play for both of us? That way we can just sit back and watch that pretty skirt of yours ride up with every shot.' He winks at her.

'Sounds like you're feeling threatened, Trev,' says Fleur. 'Besides, where's my fun in having no-one to make look even more stupid than they are? Prepare for defeat.'

Over-chalking a cue stick, Fleur blows a dusting of blue powder over Trev's face. In a melodramatic production of rubbing his eyes with fists like a toddler would, Trev blinks manically and then beams at her; she can do what she wants. She bends over the table in a straddle, aims her stick, then in a decisive move sinks three little balls into three separate pockets. Jacko shrieks with joy. A small crowd has now gathered, and they cheer her on—rah, rah. Fleur tosses her cue stick onto the pool table, scratching its green felt to a near rip. 'Whoops.' She shrugs her shoulders, and bows.

She turns away and inserts coins into the jukebox, selecting The Doors. The boys buy her a few drinks from the public bar—she hopes enough drinks—while they make small talk. Then they lead her towards the stairs. Getting caught in the mix of aftershave and body odour trailing behind them, she hangs back. Sudden recognition causes Fleur to attempt to blot the line of sight of a woman in the adjoining room.

'I'll be upstairs shortly,' says Fleur to the boys as she slips away to a hidey hole.

'You don't even know the room. 205. Don't back out again.'

Unavoidable eye-contact causes the woman sitting in cigarette haze to cringe and duck. She lets the poker machine she uses block her as she wills her voluminous cats-eye sunglasses to swallow her up in shadow. Fleur imagines the woman is thinking: *Oh no, not the sister of my son's girlfriend. She won't recognise me, and she'll move on, leave. How the hell could I explain being here, alone?*

Hiding behind another machine, Fleur watches as the woman gives a hacking smoker's cough before rising to scan corridor and stairwell. Back in her seat, the woman jiggles one leg, glancing up at the wall as though searching for a missing wall clock. Fleur understands hotels keep time blurred so gamblers stay longer, sink more coins into the ravenous machines. The woman mouths, 'Ouch,' as she shakes an arm, the one-armed bandit having probably hurt her own. Just minor ailments. Fleur knows this woman's mindset: she is willing the bright lights, bells and sirens to do their work, to seduce her once again to the thrill, that addictive anticipation of a windfall.

The woman rummages around in her handbag and pulls out a coin purse, shaking her head at the insubstantial weight of it. Stumbling a little on her way to the bar—diminishing the gravitas she may have been trying to present—she gets another drink and breaks a large note into the change she requires. As far as having the *best pokies in all New South Wales,* as the sign outside boasts, Fleur can only imagine what constitutes *best*—it sure has nothing to do with winning money. The woman stuffs the cash into her purse, collects her drink, and grumbles as she sees a man has claimed her seat. Such inconvenience, such gall.

Growling, she waylays the hotel manager and instructs him to move the intruder on. He knows her—of course he knows her—and understands as she slips him ten quid for his efforts. He grins, nods, then strides across to the man, where a word in his ear is all that is required for him to apologise to her and move on to another machine.

Fleur wonders when this woman's secrets will unravel.

Tentatively, Fleur taps at the door to the 'expensive' room Trev says he has booked for the night. It opens on two shirtless young men grinning back at her. She exhales shakily and turns away, repelled by ugly lines of curly hair snaking down under their belts.

'At last, she shows. We were startin' to worry ya weren't comin',' says Trev.

'I'm still unsure...' Fleur crosses her arms, her eyes magnetised to the double bed looming large and ominous, taking prime position in the room. Her lips wobble like they do before she cries.

'Here, have one of these—compliments of management.' Trev unwraps a gourmet chocolate and shoves it into her mouth. Unprepared, she almost chokes. In another situation she would savour its rich bittersweetness.

'Where's my treat? Come here.' Trev draws her to him and feasts on her neck, which stings with his mauling. Why can't she just dance like the dog downstairs?

Fleur sees Jacko wearing a slack smile, like he's just been caught perving in the girls' changeroom.

'Enough. It hurts.' Her words ride on a dribble of chocolatey saliva as she pulls away.

Trev draws back and shoots her a look of disgust. 'Yuk. Hey Jacko, she's gonna need a bib.' The men exchange knowing winks.

'I, I need to go downstairs to the toilet.' Fleur rushes away, wiping her mouth to expunge the experience.

If Fleur's secrets are to unravel one day, she doesn't want anything or anyone here to be part of them.

Hunched inside a locked cubicle, swallowing against waves of nausea, Fleur closes her eyes and chews the inside of her cheek until she tastes blood. She will splash her face at the washbasin then make a quick exit from the hotel.

In a *whoosh* of cold air, the bathroom door flies open as two giggling young women enter, hearing two types of shoes hitting the tiled floor. Alcohol permeates the air.

'...wrapped around her finger. Can you believe it?' Excitement in one voice. 'They went upstairs, and she followed later in those ripped fishnets. What a tart.'

Two doors bang shut and lock either side of Fleur. Afraid to escape her cubicle, mortified of the dreaded conversation she fears is not over, her heart pounds. She grips her stomach because their stabbing words could well pierce right through her.

'What do they see in her? I guess she's pretty in a scrawny way, but she's stuck up. And she's weird, the way she always clutches at her clothes like she's covering something nasty. Wonder what's underneath them.'

'I'd say they're finding out upstairs right now.'

'Probably pimples and blackheads.'

'And blonde hair everywhere. Like an Afghan hound.'

'White pussy.'

They snigger.

Fleur sits tight—unable to move anyway—caught in the roar of toilets flushing. She hears them wash and then disappear as quickly as they arrived, leaving behind their cheap perfume pong.

Fleur stays put as her tears build; her foggy eyes locked on the big hand of her watch as it creeps five minutes. Avoiding the mirror, her own hands tremble as she washes them at the basin.

She hurries home, concentrating on the changing ground surfaces, wishing fallen tears were her only evidence of being at the hotel this night, because she knows they will soon evaporate.

Chapter Three

As gentle dawn light entices Fleur towards her bed, she detours to the bathroom for the previous night's ritual she did not get to do—the ritual she has been practising since Teddy left her. Using sharp nail scissors and tweezers, she makes stinging attacks on body parts she trusts no-one need see. She has been trying to get to the gruesome place where her pain lurks, to release her poison, but its exact whereabouts eludes her.

But is she venturing too far? She must be stealthier. Her world would end if anyone discovered her secret. Some people might not care but she would, too acutely.

She dabs foundation and face powder over her fresh wounds—then wonders why she bothers to cover her tracks, before retiring. Pops her contraceptive pill—always, just in case. Furtively, woozy, she moves into her bedroom so as not to wake her sister, unwilling to share anything personal with Erin, especially now. But Fleur doesn't manage to stifle a loud cough, nor the knee-jerk swear word which tumbles out with surprising relief.

'Fleur?'

Fleur's reply is shaky. 'It's the nemesis of Santa Claus, with nothing but coal, I'm afraid. And it's probably for myself.'

Erin scratches her head.

She could have nits, Fleur imagines, but she's too upset to mention that. 'I just, just…'

'What time is it? Where have you been? Again.' Erin's voice is groggy as she fumbles for her clock on the side table and sits up.

'Please stop mothering me. You're only two minutes older, not twenty years.' Fleur sighs. 'Typing class, then pub. What else is there to do in a prosaic dump like Pig Peak? Satisfied?'

'I'm concerned, that's all.'

'Which always seems to put you in a good light, not that you're selling me with it.'

Fleur's heart rate intensifies as she rams her trapped head through the small neck hole of her nightie in a struggle for freedom. She pictures her knee emerging from her holey fishnet stocking last night outside the hotel, but she is past being amused.

'Speaking of a good light, is that awful red welt on your neck a love bite?'

'Mind your own bloody business.' Fleur grabs the first thing she finds in her drawer—she thinks it's a scarf—and wraps it around her neck. 'And go bite your bum.'

'Oh, Fleur, forever the uptight child.'

'I'm exhausted. What time did you go to bed? 6 o'clock? Or did Mum let you stay up for Disneyland? You'd like me to feel guilty, wouldn't you?'

Erin sighs. 'No. Because I've seen what it does to you.'

Fleur throws herself onto the bed, spreadeagle on her back. 'From now on, I'll shield you from my misery.'

'I do care, Fleur.'

'I know you do; you can't help it. But practise on Scott. He could use some mothering.' The unattractively handsome redhead with a crooked smile, eyes the colour of lime cordial straight from the bottle—the kind they were never allowed. 'Then again, how will you deal with Cappi?'

Cappi: brother to Mario and Paolo, son of Marco. The Italian farmhands have been with the Altons since the late 1940s when Marco's children were only small boys. Those small boys grew into strong and handsome men. Erin still visibly lusts after one of them.

'Cappi is kind to me, and I won't apologise for that. As for Scott, I barely know him, really.' Erin's face glows red in the low light.

'Really? Scott has been sniffing around here for months. I have no idea why.'

'Obviously he likes me, Fleur. Perhaps if you were nicer, you could get someone.'

'I never want a boyfriend, especially not a husband.' *It would ache too much to lose him.*

'You might just get your wish.'

As Fleur stares her sister down, Erin's expression softens.

'No matter what you say, I'll always worry about you, Fleur.'

'Yes. Concern. Thanks. Listen, I just need privacy. Let me get some sleep. Please.' Her voice catches. She turns to the wall, takes a deep breath. 'Here's an idea: elope with Scott and you'll never have to worry about me again.'

'You're just jealous.'

Silence.

'Not that you'd ever admit it, especially to me. Go on, say it.'

Fleur rolls as far away from Erin as she can manage, searching the plasterboard for a hole to magically open for her escape. She hears her sister lie back down. Fleur sneaks a smug smile. Give Erin something to fret about? Mission accomplished. But then comes the thud, as her heart sinks remembering what had just happened at the hotel.

Erin's exaggerated sigh provokes Fleur to bark back with another louder—gagging—cough. Too much cigarette smoke tonight; she wonders why Erin has neither mentioned it nor started wheezing.

Smarmy Scott. The dinner party was the trigger. Organised by his father Dukie at his Harris family's art deco mansion—as everyone pompously calls it—Scott has been obsessively pursuing Erin and the entire family at the farm ever since. Fleur cannot stand it—all that mournful fussing over her sister, especially when she has an asthma attack. He thinks she's dying with every wheeze, like she's never had asthma in her life! The best Fleur can do is to try ignoring them both.

So, while Fleur imagines Erin pondering her magnificent future with Scott, Fleur keeps doing the only thing expected of a lonely girl disinterested in study, marriage, babies, life: she goes to secretarial college. That part of what she told Erin wasn't a lie, but she only attends during the day, on weekdays. She hates its drudgery, but it helps distract her a bit. Erin and Scott are getting awfully close. Fleur suspects the time is coming soon to move into Teddy's old room. She will find some peace there.

In her blanket cocoon, she envisions never waking again, or metamorphosising in a new form like a butterfly. She thinks these things whenever she remembers last night. Because if Tripp were to hear the rumours those cruel girls will probably spread about her, she will lose all consciousness forever.

Drifting off to sleep, Fleur is thrust into a fury of fire. Immobile, she stands in tacit realisation she has no need to panic or escape; no harm will come of this. As the blaze engulfs the scene—she can view this as both an observer and from within herself—with wide-eyed curiosity and nonchalance, she peels large, mottled sheets of skin from her arms. She examines each piece of herself against the orange flame light as though inspecting strange maps, searching for answers of crucial importance always out of range. Nearby, someone shrieks and gurgles in agony, melting as she continues her task.

When Fleur awakens, reflexively she thrusts her thumb into her mouth, wishing time could go backwards and she could start all over again with everything.

Chapter Four

As if time is mocking her aim to sleep the day away, Fleur finds herself stuck wide awake Sunday afternoon. And if the day is not going anywhere, she must. Not bothering to shower, she moves to the lounge room, relieved to find it empty—especially of Erin and Grace. Her mother's odd behaviour: is she really going crazy? Perhaps Fleur is plummeting down the same hole. God no, she doesn't want anything of her mother's, except the one thing she is not willing to give her, and she wants that desperately.

Plonking down on one end of the old Genoa lounge disrupts dust motes which float around her like live things, causing an immediate itch to her nose and throat. Her stomach rumbles, awaiting the boiled egg she'll soon force herself to eat. She thumbs through her mother's *Woman's Day* magazine. With the spirited gossip comes tears which wet the pages, sticking them together all pulpy. Her body is, evidently, functioning.

A pungent odour of something oily and piny wafts through the air. Aftershave. Her father's? No, not his usual brand anyway. The bathroom door closes quietly as Tripp's tall frame appears in shadow above her, covered in apparent clean shirt and trousers. Her heart comes alive again. She's intrigued by the way the outside light from an open window hits his wavy black hair in vivid gold and purple hues. With a shy nod and a barely-there smile, Tripp positions himself on the other end of the lounge. As Fleur continues her blurry 'reading', she glances sideways to see him fiddling with his fingers. Why is he sitting near her now? She wants to be alone and even Tripp amounts to a nuisance today.

She gives two distasteful sniffs as she scans his body. 'Going somewhere?' Her voice disappoints her: loud with impatience, deep, mucous-thick nasty.

'Hah!' Attempted nonchalance? 'Nuh, just trying to kill the stench of sheep on me. Lately, Mum's been telling me I smell like a big jar of lanolin.'

'Well, Izzie is right. You reek of greasy sheep, so whatever you did, it didn't work and you still pong.' Noticing his distress, she adds, 'At least you look alright.'

Fleur surveys her flannelette pyjamas, embarrassing enough. But when she lifts her scarf to her eyes she really heats up. Why hadn't she checked it? A forest of tinselled Christmas trees grows on her. Tripp appears puzzled—rightly.

'Anything Yuletide is all the rage now, haven't you heard?' Fleur's voice comes out as a squeak. 'Anyway, why are you all dressed up like Hong Kong at night yourself?'

'Okay. Can we drop this now?' Tripp munches on his bottom lip.

'Shouldn't you be outside with Dad? You'd have to watch those rams though, in your alluring condition. Seriously, why aren't you helping the others muster?'

'I was, but they're almost done with the last of the shearing, and your drover said they could finish without me. I started earlier than usual this morning, too. Lawd, you should've seen Ringo and Butch, I swear they have more discipline than the lot of us. And pace, they've been rounding up the flocks beautifully. Good sheepdogs, those two.'

She scowls and says with spite, 'My drover? Marco isn't my drover. He has nothing to do with me, none of this does.' She wishes she could indicate the whole world with the arc of her arms, because right now she could easily hate being anywhere, even somewhere exotic. When did she last dream of somewhere exotic?

Tripp's pained yet earnest grin shows he's oblivious to her anger and the enormity of his gaffe.

Don't associate me with this place, with these people.

But look at yourself, Fleur. The on-edge one. No self-control, no temper control, withdrawing...

She squints back her tears, determined that Tripp won't detect her latest weakness and note another reason to judge her. As she presents him with her best nonchalant face—which she fears must appear dolorous—he turns to stare straight ahead, dead still.

'You know, your dad told me recently that you used to love helping with mustering and stuff,' says Tripp, still alive.

'In the past,' says Fleur.

'Fleur, I—' He turns to her.

'There's nothing you can do. It's all been done.'

'The mustering?' He squints and scratches his head like Stan from Laurel and Hardy. Ridiculous.

'Why would I care about stupid mustering?'

'Okay, dumb comment.' Tripp's laugh is brittle as he whacks his head. 'Is it Erin and Scott?' He rubs the area he hit, messing up his hair. Fleur wants to run.

'No! I'm almost happy for them. Almost.' She gives a derisive smile. Her shaky hand reaches for her décolletage, mind of its own. Oh, what she would do to separate herself from her body these days!

Tripp squirms on his seat. 'I'm not doing well, am I? It must be Teddy, then.'

'He was just so, so bloody funny and cute and little, and he was my friend. It was like the world ended. How long ago was it? Months? If only I could revisit that day and look after him better. Why did I suggest going to a flooded river in all its fury, imagining it would be safe for a seven-year-old? What the hell was I thinking? I can't stand it, Tripp. And the worst part is that there's absolutely nothing I can ever do to repair what happened. There's nothing left.'

She has chest-tapped to the rhythm of the words, because rhythm is safe and predictable in a good way. Her mother taps her own chest and Fleur thinks she does it for safety reasons. In such moments, Fleur wonders if she is becoming her mother. As a toddler Grace patted Fleur's back to the beat of a silent tune in a futile attempt to quieten her, to still her enough to nap. Grace may have wanted to slap

Fleur during those frustrating episodes, yet her mother was gracious enough to never show anger. But Fleur has never felt gracious.

'You have so much left,' offers Tripp, 'people who love you.'

She places a hand on each thigh.

'Family. Your friends.'

'Friends? Come on.'

'Anyhow, open up to me when you want, okay? I know what it's like to lose someone you love, having no-one to confide in. Hell, Fleur, I've spent over half my life feeling that way.'

Tripp looks her straight in the eye. She understands this may be new to him, having spent so many years slaving away with refugees and Aboriginal workers—all men—at the wheat farm of their former cruel neighbour, Len Robinson. But why should Tripp care for her? Perhaps he really considers her a friend, even though their palpable chemistry always demands more. How can he stand her pallor? She turns her ugliness from his gaze.

'I know. Thank you. Yes, wonderful Izzie. You lost your mother for many years, but you got her back, didn't you?' says Fleur.

Her words sound bitter, accusing, and they punched her in the stomach. She sneaks a look at Tripp. 'I didn't mean that. I know you've had years of hurt. I don't want to sound harsh but it keeps on happening anyway. You caught me at a bad time. I'm sorry for my lack of tact.'

An almost-smile. 'Well, that makes two of us. But if you go through bad times, there's no need to think you're alone, to suffer alone.'

'Thanks, Tripp. You don't deserve me.'

'Well, I'll have to work harder.'

'No, that's not what I meant. You deserve more.' She levels her eyes on his. 'You would have liked me before.'

He shakes his head. 'You're a silly duffer.'

Kindness. When Tripp isn't stumbling, his depth attracts her. Her feelings, although powerful, are confused. She thinks about him a lot. Heat emanates from his hot hand, which hovers close above hers as if awaiting the all-clear to land. Her fair arm hairs wave about excitedly; he must see them too. She flattens those revealing hairs to cover her nakedness. They have touched one another before, so why does he still scare her like this every time he is near? Through the windows she studies the most boring view on earth when all she can think about is the power of Tripp's hand. Her wet eyelash windscreen wipers could clean those windows of the greasy smudge, the dead fly. She doesn't mind sitting with Tripp now—his presence is comforting. Once again, he is making something come alive that she can't quite believe is in her, because it's something good. Agony and ecstasy, paradoxically like the title of her current reading material.

Without fuss, she pulls away and wipes her leaky face. His eyes are two deep indigo seas with stars floating upon their surface, urging her to dive in. (So maybe there are some places she would like to visit.) Is this all a trick, a foil for her bleakness?

Her words come before she can stop them. 'Your eyes. I wish you could see them now. Do you wonder at them in the mirror? Were those stars always with you or did they go away when you were separated from your mother?'

She knows the precise time all traces of life disappeared from hers: *What have you done to my children?* Her mother's words of hate: the barrier she erected, the acute gap that persists— putting Fleur more on the outer than ever before. As if she hadn't been through enough that day...

'Stars? You funny thing. I rarely look at myself in a mirror. It's counterproductive. Everything fell apart when I lost my mother, so then I'm sure my eyes looked gloomy, like this.' He knots his brow, fattens his bottom lip in a mock sulk, eyes a constant sparkle of magic seas.

She wants to flip that silly frown. 'And when you found her, no more stars fell. Will I ever get mine back?'

'You haven't lost them.' Tripp's voice is trembling. 'Didn't Keats say something about beauty being everlasting?'

'I love that you read, and all the books you have read! No. He recommended finding joy in the enduring beauty of nature and other comforting stuff because people have no hope, they just get old and ugly. Listening to you, apparently beauty is also found in the eyes of beholders in obvious need of glasses, but I don't think Margaret

Hungerford said that last bit.'

'I don't need glasses,' says Tripp, his voice now husky.

'I'm not so sure.' Her smile tugs at her lips until the truth hits her and she frowns. 'My stars have disappeared.'

'Well, someone will just have to coax them back to their shiny best.'

'You make them sound like car headlights.' She shudders, remembering the cars outside the hotel and their ugly contents. 'How can you trust that I still have something alive in me?'

'It's there alright, that spark. It comes out to play when it wants to.'

'I thought only Teddy...' If only she could ask Tripp to play with her now. But when she looks at him this time, his eyes are, once again, averted. How confusing.

Fleur often considers the universe, the transience of living creatures. Tripp's stars are caused by something older than him, something deep and indefinable; she knows this much. And their word play... Has she subconsciously been trying to bait him into flattering her? For him to do that would be lying. She can barely recall when her eyes lit up over anything of note; they reflect what is inside her now and it is nothing but pain.

'Does going out at night help?'

She digs her nails into her palms. 'What? So, you're keeping tabs on me now, too? That's perfect.'

'I'm not, I just notice. Can't help it. I live in the same house.'

'Well, if you don't like it...' She fixes him with a harsh look.

'Listen, what you do is probably none of my business.'

'If you believe that, why do you keep bringing things up that are personal to me and my family?'

'But maybe it *should* be my business, after what we've shared together.'

She ignores him. 'Why do I only seem to make an impact when I'm not here? Perhaps I shouldn't even be talking to you—on such intimate terms, I mean—let alone "sharing" anything else. You're the son of our housekeeper, and yes, she's a wonder, you both... But you've just about overstepped the mark. Let's forget this conversation ever happened.'

Fleur throws down the soggy magazine. 'By the way, I'm not about to hang any hopes on stars of any kind. They're insubstantial. And they have a habit of falling.'

He grumbles, 'And falling stars don't always grant wishes.' He stands, eyeing her now. 'Especially when they're blown off course.' He stomps outside in a blind rage.

Alone in bed, she chastises herself. 'Fleur, you're a bloody, bloody bitch.'

Once again, waves of tears come, having held back pain for too long. Just like those of the crying tree.

Chapter Five

After an hour of aimless walking around the property, the chilly late-autumn evening urges Tripp towards the shelter and privacy of the shearing shed. The farm workers have shorn near one thousand sheep, in an arduous task, taking several weeks. They miss the efficacy of the two Romanian workers brought over from Robinson's former property, who are providing urgent assistance at a nearby wheat farm.

Rather than solace, Tripp discovers his two Italian co-workers, Bene and Luca—men he had also worked with at Robinson's—finishing up the last of the day's shearing. Tripp hoped the men would be relaxing in their quarters by now, having spent much of today mustering, but these two are tireless.

Tripp balks when he finds Scott working at the skirting table. Charlie wisely keeps Scott and Tripp separated when they work, whenever possible. Today, Scott hardly glances at Tripp.

'Look what the cat dragged in. And what's that stinky stink?' says Bene, giving a hearty belly laugh.

'It's called eau de cologne, you uncultured drongo.'

'More like eau de try too hard. And all done up like a movie star. Who are you trying to impress? Daisy here?' says Luca.

Springing from his grasp, a naked Daisy bleats her jumbuck response. Bene steps back from the released animal as Luca curses and tosses the ewe's entire fleece onto the large table.

'No, wait on, he's just come from the big house. All the fussy fuss must be for one of the Alton girls. Now, which one could it be? Hmm.' Bene taps his chin. 'If I had money, I'd put all my hard earnt lira on the one they call Fleur—she makes him all gooey. But I'll bet she'd cost you pretty penny, Tripp. Or maybe not... From what I hear at the pub, she's getting a reputation with boys in town, no?'

Instead of strangling Bene, Tripp grinds his teeth, while Luca scans nervously from one man to the other. In the awkward silence, Tripp's deep breaths fail to cool him down. The men stay stuck in their moment; an amplifying rhythmic rustle and crunch of straw—the noise halting at the open sliding tin doorway—ushers no interest within them.

Bene will not let it go. 'Go find flirty Fleur at the pub.'

'I might just do that. You know, mate, sometimes I wonder why we even bothered with you, why we didn't just let you stay and rot at Robinson's.' Tripp glares at Bene. 'I swear you'd still be festering away there like a dog turd if we hadn't saved you.'

'Why do you say "we" like you're one of those Altons? You and all your reading. You're as low as us, Tripp, remember?'

'Never! And I'll do anything to prove it. And one day you'll be polishing the shit off my work boots and wondering why you ever thought Len Robinson was a tyrant.'

The unmistakable pit-a-pat of someone running away alerts the men. Bene pushes past Tripp, races outside into the darkening day, and bellows, 'Who's there? Show yourself now,' in a deep angry tone intended for no-one but Tripp.

The only response is from the crickets.

What does Bene mean by suggesting Fleur is promiscuous? Tripp knows Bene's reaction was out of character but spreading rumours like that about her is unconscionable. Tripp's stomach churns. He does not want to imagine Fleur sleeping around. The thought of her getting hurt makes him shudder; she has been through too much already. But why should it worry him now? She has made her position clear, put him firmly in his—lowly—place.

'Think it's time I took my leave,' says Tripp. 'See you in the morning, gents.'

'Huh, not if we see you first!' says Bene, as Tripp disappears into the night.

Lying in bed, Tripp's earlier dressing down by Fleur resurfaces in the darkness. Vivid, angry thoughts become nightmares disturbing his fitful sleep.

Why is it that the one person he wants to impress most is the one he inevitably inflames and pushes away? He would do anything for that girl.

Tripp knows the next few days—working with Bene and Luca, handling, skirting, and classing the wool from the previous days' shearing—will be unbearable. Charlie and Grace will then check the grade before the wool is pressed, baled, and sent off for auction.

On the first day of working side by side at the skirting table, the three men remove the fleeces' edges, necks and pieces, and any soiled wool. A few hours into work, the only words to have punctuated the silence have been swear words.

Luca wipes his nose. 'So much shit and piss! Seems like only yesterday we crutched 'em, but it's probably been months.'

Bene's far-away eyes hint at better times. 'When everything around here dies, wool keeps growing, like my *madre's* belly with her dozen *bambini*.'

'Like your tall tales,' says Tripp, glaring at Bene.

Bene turns his head to check his backside. 'Eh, Luca, do you see a tail growing on me?'

Luca remains silent, scanning the two men.

'What, Tripp, you think I'm a lizard or something? Growing a big, long tail?'

Tripp frowns. 'When are you dagos going to learn how to speak English?'

'What? When will you learn how to speak Italian, mate?'

'Hey, boys, let's try getting on, okay?' says Luca.

'I was gonna say sorry, then Tripp here called me a lizard.'

'I didn't call you a lizard. If I was to call you anything, it'd be a snake.'

'And what you think I call a little boy who thinks he's a big man?'

Ignoring Bene's last comment, Tripp says what he's been wanting to say from the moment he saw Bene this morning. 'How come you know so much about what Fleur is up to?'

'You're still thinking about that, mate? Just forget about it. Just a joke.'

'But it's not a joke, don't you see? I respect the Altons and don't want you spreading rumours about any of them.'

Bene bangs his fists on the table. 'Rumours? Why don't you go to the pub yourself? You will find out the truth of Fleur then. Hang on, you never go there, do you, Tripp? Why is that? Don't you drink, now?' Bene casts his eyes to the ceiling before lowering them to drill Tripp's. 'Yes, now I know. That must be because no children are allowed in the pub.'

'Come on, boys, you two used to get on. Real buddies,' pleads Luca, his palms open in supplication.

'Before Tripp here got too big for his shoes, shoes he wants us to clean.'

Tripp clenches his jaw. 'You know I didn't mean that.'

'Okay, so that's your sorry?'

'That's my sorry.' Best he can do.

'Good. Listen, that Fleur, she's a nice girl, a cheeky girl, but she plays up, like she's always at a party. I see it with my own eyes.'

Tripp's skin prickles, hoping what Bene said is all either he or Fleur have been doing. 'Stop it now! Here's some advice: keep your big mouth shut about Fleur. You're not even fit to say her name.'

'Okay, mate, back to work. Too much shit here on the table.' Bene's best conciliatory attempts hold no quarter.

'Too much shit coming from around the table, too—especially from you, Bene. Let's get rid of it all, eh?' Tripp shouts.

Bene rolls his eyes at Luca, then snorts like a bull at a red rag. Tripp lifts the heavy fleece he had been examining and dumps it back down on the table, throwing up a cloud of dust which settles to reveal the bewildered stares of the two coughing men.

Chapter Six

Saturday night. Tripp stands shuffling his feet for several minutes at the Criterion Hotel doorway, the loose drivel of plastered patrons doing nothing to entice him inside. Yet he opens the door on the oppressive smoke-filled air. Cutting through it, sweet, yeasty smells of beer, the hay-like aroma of whiskey. The latter: the stench of Len Robinson. Beer: his workmates at the end of a long day. For a short time, Tripp was a heavy drinker, when life without love became too much to deal with in the glaring light of overly long working days. The mere thought of grog turns his stomach now, and this fills him with a sense of irony, having come tonight to the alcohol-pedalling establishment.

Sitting at the bar, three old blokes with puffed-up plaid chests and beards as frothy white as the heads of their beers, exude self-proclaimed swagger, as they attempt to outdo one another with bravado and bullshit: Tripp detects something about sheilas and cows, and a local performing poodle mauling its owner. As he skirts them, they quieten, raising their eyes to assess the newcomer. Their perfunctory stares heat Tripp's face as he gives them an awkward nod before moving to the far end of the bar, far enough away from their mindless rabble for some solitude if not silence. He may want peace, but when the men resume their slurred chatter, their clatter, removing their focus from him, he is relieved.

He will avoid anyone familiar except the one person he has come to see. Will she be here tonight? Is she a regular at the pub, just as

Bene had said? It is not a safe environment. She has not even reached drinking age, and someone could easily take advantage of her if she were drunk. The thought causes angst, just as someone smashes a glass and a roar goes up, fraying Tripp's nerves even more.

He wants a chance to explain himself to Fleur without the prying eyes of family or farm workers. As he sits sipping a ginger beer—now *that* order raised eyebrows—he recalls with shame the debacle of the recent clumsy conversation he guesses she is still upset about, judging by her frosty reaction to him in recent days. As he rehashes every cringey detail, he gets stuck on Fleur's accusation about him checking up on her. From somewhere in the back of his mind he has a dull thought that she would be correct in her accusations.

Suddenly he has a target on his back and wonders why he ever came here. *Idiot!* If Fleur is here, she will think he is spying on her, giving her further ammunition. Perhaps he really intends to catch her out. Doing what? No, surely not Fleur. He shivers, aware that he must take stock.

After ordering himself a real beer he takes a tentative sip, then a long, cold slurp. Rather than making him sick, the alcohol immediately fills him with a surge of euphoria, each gulp relaxing him further. *What have you driven me to, Fleur?* He orders another and sits mulling over it as he glances up and sees her.

She has her back to him, but he recognises her flaxen hair, slender body, her clothes: she wears her trademark night-time black miniskirt. A table hides her lower half. Probably in high heels, as she looks taller tonight.

He sinks the second schooner. Bolstered by the grog, he moves towards her, vaguely aware of another girl at the billiard table but not worried enough to stop himself from barging in on a private game in play. As Fleur bends over, cue stick poised to shoot, he taps her on the shoulder.

'What are you doing here?' Tripp's controlled voice emerges as something less. And what a stupid moment he has chosen to interrupt her.

'Shit!' she cries, dropping the stick and wheeling around to face him. 'I could ask you the same question.'

Tripp jolts back. 'I'm really sorry. I just wanted to say—'

'I know, I'm positively the sexiest babe you've ever laid eyes on.' She gives a cutesy shrug of one shoulder—any anger dissolving in a total about-face and dramatic flutter of false eyelashes. Somehow, she is so familiar. Yet this woman looks nothing like Fleur. Her eyes are not pale amber but coal-black and her skin is olive, unlike Fleur's porcelain-pale complexion. Her hair is bleached. She is also older—he glimpses her low heels—and taller.

'I apologise. I thought you were someone else.' His face may have turned a telling shade of magenta.

'Hmm. I don't think you're sorry at all, not in the slightest.' She appraises him with a head-to-toe scan. 'And I could almost forgive you. I'm Cathy.'

'Tripp.' Why did he tell her his name?

'Funny name. Then again, so is Matt, or Doug, or Neil. Basic words. Names even a dog could learn, don't you think? No offense, but it's all so unimaginable. Then again, so are most males.'

'I think you mean unimaginative.'

'Whatever. So, Tripp,' her lips make a popping sound, 'haven't I seen you working around the Alton farm?' She shortens the distance between them.

'How would you know that? If I was, I mean.'

'How do I know? Because I get around.'

'Well, so do I.' He grins at her, then regrets suggesting he is a skylarker.

'I've seen Scott Harris working over there, too. The well-off posh one. Not too shabby, if you've noticed.'

'I haven't. What are you, a spy?'

'Just observant.'

'Do you know him?'

'Not yet. Anyhow, say hello to him from me—if you can remember my name, that is.'

'Sure, I can, *Karen*.' Tripp releases a wink and a toothy grin, relieved to discover her interest lies elsewhere. Her message would worry

Erin, so he will not pass it on to Scott. 'Seriously, how do you know we, ah, work at the farm? I haven't seen you around.'

'Aha, at last he admits the connection.'

'Got me there.'

'Let's just say it's all part of my mystique, knowing things. Right. So, can you see her?' Cathy scans the room.

'Who?' Tripp hardly remembers who he has come to see. There is no doubt Cathy's attraction is magnetic, and he understands it is largely because she is bold like Fleur. Yet this girl is a poor imitation; anyone would be. He gives another cursory look around. 'No, I don't think so.'

She cocks an eyebrow at him. 'Whoever she is, she's a lucky girl.'

'Uh, thanks,' says Tripp.

He should get his bearings and leave. Cathy's friend grins maniacally, giving her a nudge, which spills wine from her glass onto the carpet. Cathy glares at her.

'What's her name?' Cathy asks Tripp, who frowns in response. 'I may know her, that's all.'

'Don't worry about it. I should get going. Nice to meet you, Cathy.'

'Yes, it was, wasn't it,' she declares. She cackles—her gape exposing horsey gums and mercury-covered molars. She must have some rich dentist. 'Before you go, can you show me how to set the balls up properly? We're new to this game—or, rather, the boys we play with usually set them up.'

Tripp's inexorable stupidity is about to show itself, having never played pool in his life. He sees another game about to start, noting the triangular configuration of the balls on the table. If their layout has anything to do with colours or numbers, he knows he's in trouble. But then, in his struggle to leave the pub now, he is beyond caring about looking like an imposter.

He places a triangular rack onto the table, fills it with balls. Cathy moves close behind him, exuding seductive 'oohs' and 'ahs' at his non-existent prowess.

He plans his exit strategy. As his eyes locate the open doorway beyond the crowd, he realises Fleur has found it too, and she has found him as she walks inside. Her face registers shock as she catches Tripp with Cathy draped over him like a shroud. She turns and flees.

※

Fleur feels like an awry red whirlwind as she flounders in high heels along the dirt road, trying to get far away from the pub. Angry at herself—she wasn't ever going there again! Until the recent shed incident when she overheard Tripp's furious tirade he unleashed on Bene and Luca. She hears Tripp zooming up behind her, his long stride, his breath.

'Stop,' he calls, almost at her heels.

A sudden clasp to her shoulder causes her to spin around.

'Fleur, I...'

She flicks her head away. 'You've got a cheek. I just want to go home.' Fleur's little big words, dark as night, pathetic as her tears. She starts to move from him as he grabs her hand.

'Wait. Just stop and listen to what I have to say.'

She yanks free. 'I don't want to hear your empty words.'

'That woman back there, she just wanted my help.'

'Your excuse is as lame as any help you could have been to her, Tripp. Who was helping who?'

'I thought... I thought she was—'

'A slut? Because that's what she is. Her name is Cathy. She prowls around the bar and schemes. She pinches things that aren't glued down. I haven't yet told the manager, but I just might.'

'Listen, I couldn't care less about Cathy's antics. You, I thought she was you.'

'Same thing, isn't it? You see me as a slut, don't you, Tripp?'

'Whatever are you talking about? You'll never be like that. You don't understand, she had her back to me. She looked like you, that's all.' He shakes his head. 'This is madness.'

'It's not only tonight. I heard what you said to the men in the shearing shed about wanting them to clean shit from your boots, saying if pushed you could be as much of a tyrant as Len Robinson! Len Robinson the murderer? The cruellest man that ever lived?' Her voice is pure vitriol.

'You were there?' Under the streetlights, Tripp's face pales. 'I didn't know. Did you hear the rest of the conversation? Because if you did, you'd know why I said those things. And no, I didn't mean them. It was the heat of the moment.' His words catch.

'So, what was the rest of the conversation?'

'You just need to trust that they deserved what they got, especially Bene.'

'I don't understand. My father, mother—everyone, it seems—thinks you are a wonderful man who could save the world if he had half the chance. If that's true, why do you keep showing your darker side? I'm sure my parents haven't seen it, yet.'

'I don't have a dark side, Fleur.'

'Then what is this I am seeing from you so much lately, and why are we always fighting?' She doesn't leave him time to answer. 'Why were you at the pub?'

'Because I didn't know where you were and I thought, on the off chance, you might be there. And you were which, let me tell you, I'm not happy about. I went there because I wanted... I wanted—'

'To check up on me.'

'No. Yes. I don't know. I do know that I just want what is best for you.'

'You have a funny way of showing it. But, I guess, for so many years you didn't have a good role model, so it would be illogical to think some of the muck wouldn't have rubbed off on you.'

'You are wrong but, well, what's your excuse?'

'Me? I'm just no good.' Fleur's unnerving resignation almost scares her.

'I meant, what's your excuse for being at the pub? Never mind. All this—,' he points to her minuscule, flimsy red outfit anyone could rip off in a heartbeat, '—and all your tough talk doesn't faze me, and it doesn't fool me either, Fleur. I know you, and I know you belong with and—'

'What? With you? Are you drunk? You have so much to prove to me before I can trust you again.'

'So be it.'

'I'm a wreck! I want to laugh and cry only happy tears and joke around like any normal person my age, but I don't deserve to. I'm so overwhelmed by life. And us—we're both so far down I fear we'll never have the strength to lift one another again.'

'Try me then.'

Before she can react, he grabs and kisses her with gentle reverence. When they separate, like her, Tripp is crying.

'Oh, Tripp.' The cut of sorrow in her voice. 'I'd better go. You exhaust me.'

As Fleur walks off, this time he does not try to stop her. As much as she wants to, she does not glance back at him. Fleur knows he won't be looking back for her, either.

Chapter Seven

Grace Alton lies in bed clawing the walls, craving the sleep her overactive mind denies. As late autumn pulls the temperature down outside, she pulls the bedclothes up—ironically setting her bottom lip aquiver—against the rude chill permeating her bedroom.

A breath kisses her ear: just a feather-light 'Mummy?' so as not to startle.

'Hello?' she replies.

Where is he? Here, there, or in between?

She opens her eyes—smile, heart—to find him standing beside her in the moonlight. He is here. Teddy is barefoot; he must be cold. Yet his touch to her hand heats her entire body.

Together they open the sash window. She encircles his hand as he leads her up onto the ledge where they inhale the icy air. Like birds, they leap and dodge around tree canopies. They soar high then higher still to wheel through a rainbow's iridescent arc in a secret playground sky—both now weightless, warm against the wind.

The colours! Bursts of familiar and otherworldly hues dazzle like silent fireworks. She finds it curious how a rainbow can appear after dark without sunlight or water. But Teddy's golden glow—one perfect light amid the chaos—pales the celestial show around them.

'I kept my promise to fly with you, Mummy.' Teddy's voice of reassurance to Grace in the silent night, making everything, once again, good.

Yet this episode is surely fleeting because good things never last.

As she considers this impermanence, clumsily she falls back onto her bed, face up—Grace and mattress bouncing with the momentum. Colours shatter then disappear. Her beautiful son… gone.

In glaring morning sunlight, Grace cringes at the sight of her calloused hands: signs of hectic, physical weeks on the farm. Had Teddy felt their nasty roughness? In or out of bed she knows her thoughts won't settle, so she slides out and stretches to the click of her arthritic shoulders protesting. She drops her arms: dead weights, aging bones, aging everything that holds them together. But when…

… she watched *Romper Room* on the family's new television set with Teddy, both bending, stretching, reaching for the stars to the music, her body was agile.

Sometimes she can also escape her flesh and blood during trauma. Not today. Today she will focus only on good things. Alone with her thoughts, Grace feels more together than she has in months, especially when she notices a sprinkling of glittery stardust (pixie dust?) on her pillow—mystical evidence of the night before.

She lets it dance on her fingertips, then leans out the still open window, where a welcome swallow makes eye contact from its nest on the rafters. She marvels at the slick blue-black sheen of its top feathers, its rusty little head and throat suggestive of red ochre.

Grace gushes, 'Good morning! It's magic today, isn't it?' Then she whispers, 'Yes, I've seen your funny dance.'

The normally skittish creature focuses on the woman's subtle smile, so Grace cuts the air with her pointer finger—up down across, up down across—the beady avian eyes follow her every move. Her finger mimics the bird's recent circumnavigation of the iconic gnarly old eucalypt on the property—a little too close to the house for Grace's liking. The tree's roots may threaten the foundations, yet she admires its crippled reach. All who live here call it 'the crying tree', commenting on the odd occasions it drops water from its canopy, rainy days or dry. She lets them delight in its reputation, their misguided sentiments. She knows it is sentient.

Studying the tree, she marvels at its intuitive mystique disguised in an almost anodyne structure. Why, on a day like today when it is not crying, does it look sadder than ever?

Surely the swallow will help cleanse Grace's thoughts. Its black eyes, redolent of paw-paw seeds, study her. 'What are you trying to tell me, little bird?'

A soft chirp. A baby chick must have hatched. A heralder of new life: nature at its nascent best. Exhilarated, Grace mounts a footstool, gripping the window's architrave to steady herself. She peeks inside the nest. Sure enough, perched between two unhatched eggs sits a wet and bedraggled new chick.

She could weep for the fragility of its skin: all pink translucence, peppered grey in parts where immature feathers lie in wait. Its sharp beak widens towards its mother, ready for a feed. Nature enlightens, and we must listen and attune to the moment—she knows this. Nature also rides with us through our wonderful experiences, dying a little, on some level, with every dire one.

She flops back down onto the double bed, closes her eyes. The chirping continues and Grace's hammering heart ignites with the jolt of an exceedingly rare, recent memory. She grins, her eyes flying open. Last night was real! And he was okay, wasn't he? Her protracted sigh becomes a jolly laugh as she jumps up from the bed, somehow lighter. She has seen her son!

For Grace, her world shines again with a little promise. Now is the time for a new start.

For the crying tree, its tears are quietly building.

Chapter Eight

With a thump, Fleur plonks down at the kitchen table, causing Grace to spring back from dark cupboards refusing to give up their secrets. She turns to face her daughter. 'Oh, it's only you. I mean, you startled me.'

Fleur fixes her mother with a look of distaste as she points above her own eyebrow. 'Yes, only me. You have flour here.'

'I'm not surprised.' Grace runs a dismissive finger across her forehead. 'Gone?' Fleur nods, scans, sniffs the air. 'Did you burn something?'

'Give me a break, daughter dear. I haven't even started cooking.' Chuckling, Grace turns back to the cupboards. 'How does Izzie find anything in here? I'm intending to make biscuits. Want some late breakfast?'

'I'll get myself something soon.'

When my mother leaves me alone, Grace understands. 'I met a new welcome swallow this morning.'

'Congratulations on making an actual friend.' Fleur's cruel words.

Hurt, Grace looks around at what she is doing, her basic task, her isolated existence…

Fleur's face wears a strange mix of embarrassment and shame. 'Sorry, that was unkind. I know it's not your fault…'

'One of three eggs hatched this morning. Maybe more by now. Isn't that wonderful? New life, new hope?' Grace grabs a tea towel. Her momentary urge to do a dance of scarves is dashed by imagining her daughter's reaction.

'New life doesn't always mean new hope. You of all people should know that.'

'No, it brings hope, Fleur. Hold onto it.' Grace's face flushes.

'And where there's death, there's hopelessness, Mother. We know that.' Her daughter's cutting words appear to come from something almost dead.

'Fleur, just let me help.'

'I don't think you can.'

Grace dies a little hearing Fleur give a feeble cry of suffering on her walk back to her room.

Grace listens to Izzie singing a Greek lullaby from the yard, which cheers her a little. Failing to locate the recipe book, Grace works from memory alone.

Using a wooden spoon, she scoops the dough from the bowl into a shallow cake tin because she can't find the biscuit cutters. It will be a crunchy biscuit cake. She pops the sticky goo into the oven.

She trots outside to give Izzie a hand in the garden, closing the kitchen door behind her. Grace finds Izzie's tiny frame crouching down over the vegetable patch, grunting with each yank of a fat carrot which refuses to budge from the parched earth. Her voice is less sweet now.

'*Fattyu!* Fuck!' Izabella snarls, mixing Hungarian with English. She turns, sees Grace nearby, and sighs. 'Sorry I swear.'

Grace laughs, knowing Izzie must have heard such profanity from the farm workers. 'Come on. Let me help?'

'No, no. Just let me get this.' Izzie continues to battle the stubborn vegetable.

'Silly me,' Grace says, 'I've forgotten to turn on the oven. But what's that burning smell?'

She about-faces towards the house and watches as charcoal-grey licks of smoke sneak out from the door's perimeter. In a languid dance, they twist and turn like a helix, hinting at calamity in the kitchen. She coughs.

'Help.' Grace's small, disquieted voice.

Izzie jerks. 'What's happening?'

'The kitchen. Fire.' Grace remains rigid on her starting block.

'What do you mean? There's no fire. Look, I show you.' Izzie rights her body and heads towards the kitchen door.

'Stop. We shouldn't open it. It's too dangerous. We'll only fuel it.'

But Grace pushes Izzie aside in her dash to the house. With one hand Grace holds her apron over her nose to filter the fumes, with the other, she twists the doorknob and pushes the door open.

A powerful blaze of bright angry colours billows from oven to ceiling. Grace's body again succumbs to inertia while her head tries to make sense of this. She squints and concentrates on what appears to be a diorama of sorts amidst the flames: a miniature timber structure perched in the middle of bushland. A lean-to perhaps? Suddenly, the burning support logs tumble like dominoes, coughing up embers in their wake, trapping a little person underneath. Grace blows a thick blonde tress from her stinging eyes, flummoxed at the sight of the victim's two tiny flapping arms. Her heart races. If she wanted, she could so easily reach right in there, right into that fire and... She doesn't want to.

Izzie's voice, panicky now, niggles from somewhere far away or right beside her, as Grace chants her pathetic plea. 'Help,' the word is more instructive than Grace's ridiculously hushed voice. Not knowing what she is summoning, she makes balls of her fists and shoots death rays from her eyes at the bush scene until the surrounding fire envelops it.

'What do you think happened to the little person, Izzie?' Grace's voice singsongs like a kindergarten teacher.

'What little person?'

Barely hearing Izzie's question, Grace raises her arms. Energised, she fixes her gaze at the top of the flames, urging them down—instructing with open hands—back into the oven. Her strategy works—the flames retreat until extinguished, leaving her arms flaccid by her sides. She is spent, vulnerable, anything but threatening now. Trembling, she inches her way over to the appliance, expecting the worst as she assesses the oven. She was right, she had not turned it on.

'What just happened?' Izzie whimpers, hands clasped to her breast.

'I'm not sure.' Grace's voice is, once again, small.

'Why were you acting like that, saying *fire*? You scare me.' Izzie tugs at her frizzy black curls.

'Because there was a fire inside the oven, but somehow it was reaching out of the oven, and there was a little person in the flames. Didn't you see it?'

'No. By crikey, Grace, what has happened to you?' Izzie has been practising her Aussie slang.

Studying the little lady's terrified face, Grace feels Izzie gently patting her arm. Will Izzie now fear her?

'What's going on? All that shouting, Izzie!' Erin arrives in the kitchen, shadowed by Fleur.

Grace's voice is monotone. 'There was a fire. It was as if a house was burning down, and someone was trapped.'

'She see a little man in fire,' offers Izzie.

'Our house?' Erin's eyes dart. 'Oh, Mummy, someone trapped? What? Where? There isn't even any smoke.'

'But I smelt smoke before,' offers Fleur.

'I didn't,' states Erin.

'It's out now.' Grace's head feels light. She finds the back of a chair to steady her. Catching Izzie's attention, Grace upturns her palms, and shrugs. She studies the dishevelled state of the usually striking diminutive woman of Greek/Hungarian descent: her disordered hair sticks out at all angles around a face paled to biscuit batter beige. Izzie backs out through the kitchen door, collapsing onto a wrought-iron bench in the yard, all rag-doll-floppy and defeated. Grace closes the door quietly on her.

When the girls leave—shaking their heads, leaving Grace to her lunacy—she opens the oven to remove the mess. Twelve perfectly rounded, crispy brown biscuits sit separately in the tin, proud as punch.

What is *beyond* trying to tell her? A raging fire from an inert source. And the little scene within the flames, the falling logs, the person trapped. A warning? A fire has happened or will happen somewhere. But why so short-lived? And why would something so vicious create rather than destroy?

Beyond: Grace's silent provocateur, unpredictable confidant, omniscient harbinger of wonderful times and—she now knows, to her horror—bad. This power can gently lead or come pounding on her door in the guise of a cryptic stranger. Once again, she has experienced its strange mystery, but this time she has had company—a witness to her follies, her madness. She has done wrong by sharing it with Izzie, but how could she have hidden it from someone standing right beside her? There are dire consequences to not following *beyond*'s unwritten rules, of not heeding its warnings...

Sitting at the table, Grace mindlessly gobbles up four biscuits. Considers her limited options. No, there is nothing for it, she must eat the evidence. They're even better than she remembers.

Chapter Nine

Seeing Teddy last night did not ring in the beautiful morning Grace had envisaged. Yet another spat with Fleur whose suffering she cannot seem to touch. Then, the strange apparition of a destructive fire. Now more than ever, Grace suspects she needs guidance from the mystical force of *beyond*. Or does she?

She steers her mind away from her biscuit-induced tummy ache to the monotony of farm life. Only routine will temper the morning's confusing magic.

So many changes since her arrival in Pig Peak as a newlywed in 1950. Yet battling the weather has remained one unwelcome constant. Suffocating dust storms and years of drought have desolated most of New South Wales—including the Alton's several thousand acres of property. Despite sporadic violent storms of the water variety, many formerly lush paddocks have become cracked-earth barren.

On her husband Charlie's instruction—doing what he can—the farm workers plant grass seed then move the flocks to other arable pastures before the sheep can eat the seeds. Trouble is, more relocation means more supplementation with grains, which costs money, and that, too, is dwindling. So far, her husband has avoided shooting stock. Charlie—of all people—doing that would disturb everyone at the farm.

The days may be cooling but the workers cannot afford to. When not spending leisure time with Erin, Scott has become a farmhand, helping with odd jobs such as providing fresh water, hay, and grain to stock on overcrowded paddocks. Scott has also learnt to hoof trim the sheep when required.

Although she has her doubts about Scott, Grace must admit that his work is always shipshape, and he has appeared at just the right time to help Charlie. Both Scott and Tripp have shown themselves to be quick learners with competitive natures. She knows Charlie can hardly keep up with them.

Charlie recently gave the go-ahead to put the more robust rams and ewes together over a five-week mating period, giving Marco, the farm's drover, charge for monitoring the joining process. Now big and bold enough to handle the rams' mood swings, Marco's three sons helped stop them from hurting the ewes. Charlie, Grace, and Erin—Fleur when she begrudgingly bothers—will be busy providing grain to supplement the nutrition of the pregnant ewes. Work around the farm never wanes, especially in this drought when every stressor seems to mushroom relentlessly.

Today, as usual, Charlie rose early and left the house before Grace woke, so they've neither seen nor spoken to one another since going to bed last night. She has plenty to share with her husband: Teddy, the new chick, the troubling kitchen 'fire'. She probably should keep quiet about her visions, understanding its unwritten rule.

Despite the crazy morning, Grace is determined to revisit the river where they lost their precious Teddy, her Treasure—a place now forever tainted for the family—but she won't go without Charlie. Yet, when she finishes donning her boots, overcoat, and wide-brimmed bush hat, she's unsure if she can do it even with her husband's calm presence. She sits on her chair like a reluctant bushranger, cradling her covered head against her fears, failing to still her mind.

Inexplicably, unseen things had rattled Grace the day she lost Teddy. Then blatantly worrying signs occurred: a dead bird smashed against a window; Erin's asthma worse than ever before. A sheep mangled by fallen branches left Grace and Charlie too distraught to worry about hastening dramas unfolding elsewhere. Afterwards, Fleur lumbering home alone from a forbidden place in shock and shame. Erin appearing later still, looking like a pale corpse. Teddy not returning. The cruel climax came after a day of warnings from Nature which Grace had not heeded.

She should have known better—her failure to read the signs, her inaction in response to *beyond*'s portents, was a dreadful misreading. By doing so, she let everyone in her family down, especially her son. In a blind response, she let Fleur down, too, blaming her for what happened to Teddy and failing since that awful day to apologise to her. This excruciating fact hangs thick like stagnant air whenever mother and daughter are together. But Grace will not let her fears dictate her future. She belches, makes a quick toilet stop. She pulls the hat's toggle too tight in a purging sting, and leaves the house, slamming the door behind her.

In determined stomps, Grace traverses three paddocks to locate her husband. She checks the ground for pitfalls, having stumbled previously on the uneven, lumpy pastures. The sparse brown grass cracks with each assault of her boots. How can anything this broken ever regenerate? Perhaps it won't. But somehow their sheep will remain well cared for. On another farm livestock may suffer, but not on the Alton's. Today Grace will find Charlie once again supplementing their food to ensure good nutrition in these arid conditions.

Spying him, she picks up pace. When she reaches him, she must take some deep, deliberately discreet breaths to regain her composure. Charlie can't think her out of shape; she needs to appear, and remain, strong. Together now, Grace relaxes.

Several shorn sheep crowd Charlie as he fills their food troughs. The workers usually shear before the cooler weather sets in, but this year's early autumn clipping stalled because of other family dramas. Without their coats, the sheep look smaller, whiter; clean but cold. She reasons that at least they won't get wet, or freeze.

Her husband's tractor sits nearby, empty of the hay bales he has dropped into the tubs. She watches as he uses a bucket to scoop a pre-mix of a protein meal, sorghum, molasses, corn, and minerals from a potato sack into the bales. He then mixes it through the hay while trying to keep the hungry animals at bay. They are impatient, bleating up a storm, shoving him out of the way.

'Get back, ya bastards!' Charlie is getting impatient too.

Grace picks up the only other bucket, suspecting Charlie has left it there for her. She may be late but she's here now.

'That last trough,' Charlie instructs his wife as she moves bucket from sack to trough, adding the supplement to the hay. Some sheep have followed Grace's lead; two give her gentle nudges.

Grace backs away from the racket to stand with her husband. 'Sorry I wasn't here earlier. I was trying my hand at cooking again.'

'Really? I guess it has been a while. Can't wait to find out what's in store.' He rubs his hands together.

The morning's events, and their consequences, continue to unnerve her. 'It wasn't what I expected, had to get rid of it.' Her voice trembles.

'Sounds ominous. Although I appreciate you saving me from eating something unfit for human consumption.'

If you hint that it's bad, it must really be bad, Grace understands his meaning. If he knew she had eaten all twelve biscuits!

'Anyhow, thanks, love, for your attempt at cooking, and for helping me with this.' He chuckles as he wraps her in a smelly hug, his body now free to move again.

'Both pitiful, meagre attempts.'

'It's difficult. Someone's gotta put up with you and it may as well be me.'

'Gee, thanks. You always know how to make me feel special.' She pulls away and wipes herself down, wanting to move on, having serious issues to discuss with her husband. 'We need to talk.'

Charlie flicks a finger at the tractor. 'Hop on with me. You can sit on my lap. I could use a cuppa, especially since it seems to be the only thing on offer.'

Grace winces, notices Charlie catch her irritation.

He adds, 'I'm sure we can rustle up something to eat, Gracie. Or Izzie might have done some cooking.'

'Yes, I know, good old Izzie.' Grace imagines Izzie is now anywhere but in the haunted kitchen. 'Listen, can we go back later? Walk with me.'

Charlie frowns as she takes his hand, and moving in the direction of the river, Grace near drags him. She knows his trepidation comes less from his grumbling stomach and more due to where they're headed.

'Charlie, come with me to the river. Please.'

He shoots her a look of concern. 'Only if you think you're up to it. I know you haven't been there since—'

'Have you been there?' Grace interrupts, refusing to hear his sad words.

'No.' His tone is brusque as though it is a given.

'I think I can do it now. Can you, Charlie?'

'I can't let you go alone, can I? But why now? What's changed your mind?'

'I'll tell you about it, but let's get to the bank first.'

Grace has resolved to make peace with the Europa River, but how that looks and whether they can bring themselves to do it, she is not sure. As they traverse more paddocks in their gentle decline, Charlie steadies his wife, steering her around the proliferation of sheep droppings.

The place of former family adventures and joy has become nothing more than calculated seduction and a scheming magnetic pull. Grace shivers. Is it trickery that brings them towards the river now? She knows today is strange and will do with them what it wants. But in her core, in her heart, she understands this quest with her husband is for Teddy. They couldn't turn back if they tried.

The grasses are becoming taller, the shrubs bushier. Grace and Charlie shrink amongst palms with majestic fanning leaves, black she-oaks, mulga, saltbush, the proliferation of Xanthorrhoea. Sticky paspalum weed seeds and barbed cobblers' pegs cling to their hair and clothing. It will be an effort removing them one at a time, a worry for later. In a futile attempt she shakes herself off—like a mangy dog.

They push on. The river's sudden burble causes them to wobble on their feet. How silly to be shocked; they know it's nearby. In tandem, they turn their heads towards its source with the precision of sunflowers called to the sun. Like standing at a portal to a grand orchestral concert, Grace used to be excited to hear the running water, to discover the river's mood of the day. Today its instruments grate in flat, clashing notes.

How can a river in drought be flowing, even barely? But were they really expecting the beast to lie low until it died? It didn't go away when Teddy did, the way Teddy did—a river can't do that. It merely cowers in bush camouflage. Coward.

Lost in nervous silence, they rest in a sunlit clearing about fifty feet from the riverbank, grimacing as they force stiff joints to sitting positions. A rustling in bushes has them turning towards an industrious scrub turkey threshing about, claw-raking to clear for its nest, apparently oblivious to its human company. But Charlie is focussed on something else.

'What's that red thing?' He points. 'Is it caught up in a grass tree?'

Half-heartedly, Grace shades her eyes to peer at something peculiar, something more out of place than they are.

Teddy.

Chapter Ten

Teddy shouldn't be here; he should be at home where he belongs, thinks Grace.

Charlie mutters, 'Ya wouldn't credit it.'

As Grace's mothering instincts kick in, she rolls onto her knees, jumps up and lurches towards the object, bellowing out her son's name. She hears Charlie yelling out her own name, senses his bulk moving to stand behind her, his hot breath on her sweaty neck.

Teddy's body has turned to straw. *Has it?* She squints against the sun, focusing carefully. *No, it's not him, not him, not him... It's only his hat.* Grace gives a heaving moan and collapses back against Charlie.

In a small voice she says, 'Things have been happening. Now this.' Aware of her husband's eyes on her, she reaches up and yanks the faded material from the top of the grass tree's spike before screwing it up and pocketing it.

Charlie turns Grace around to face him. 'Settle down, love. Listen, it was an understandable mistake, especially in your emotional state.' His glance checks his last comment hasn't offended, but she has other things on her mind.

'Last night made me believe anything was possible. Let's have that talk.'

They sit back down upon their grassy spot.

'I wonder where his little blue car ended up, Charlie. Fleur told me it got stuck in the mud somewhere on the riverbank. It would be good to find that too, put it in Teddy's room with his other precious things.

His hat, though! How could I imagine...? Here she goes again with her madness, you must think.' She wipes her brow.

'Never madness. Visionary,' says Charlie. 'Like saving Tripp from bloody Len Robinson because of a vision you saw. Our boy Teddy found that scarf. Our boy. He must've known one day it would help bring that tyrant down.'

'We crushed that monster, didn't we?'

'We did indeed. Together. But you, Gracie, have a gift. That's what we call it, what we'll always call it. You can tell me anything.'

'And I do, but probably too much!' Her 'gift' wasn't new for Grace but telling anyone about it was. 'After Teddy left us, I told you about *beyond* because I had nothing left to lose. Do you even know that I call it *beyond*? Anyhow, it was a relief to finally share my strange secret with you. But you must have thought me an idiot because you hardly believed my crazy words. You still don't understand how it works and if I'm honest, neither do I. But I seem to keep breaking its rules. Even talking like this to you could be dangerous.'

'Since when do you call intuition dangerous?'

'You know exactly when, but it's more than that. Does intuition cause those visions, make people fly?'

'Make people fly?' Charlie looks at her with the mixed emotions of someone catching a monkey masturbating at the zoo.

She won't elaborate, some things she will keep to herself. 'Intuitively I understood its unwritten rule: never tell another person of its power. I suspect I did the wrong thing in telling you about *beyond*. I became flippant because it had become nothing but an isolating curse, and it had betrayed me, betrayed all of us. All that time of remaining quiet and it still took Teddy!' Or was it her irresponsibility that took Teddy? 'But it redeemed itself a little with Tripp.'

Grace fears she may have another price to pay for confiding about something so powerful, so personal yet elemental. And that price may be losing *beyond*. Will that be the penalty? Would it be such a bad thing?

'What's this about last night?'

'I saw Teddy.' Why can't she just shut up?

Charlie sucks in a deep breath. 'Where?' Exhaling the word in a heavy sigh.

'We flew through a rainbow together. And, Charlie, somehow, I felt his warmth.'

He nods. 'Did he have a message?'

'I think he was trying to let us know he is alright.' She lightens with every word.

'If you say he is, he is.'

'And that's why I wanted you to bring me here, because seeing Teddy has made me believe we should make our peace with the river. But his hat has thrown me, appearing like that after months. I really thought we'd find Teddy underneath it. But I understand, I do. Nothing can hurt him anymore.' She juts her chin to indicate the sky. 'He's with the colours now. Let's get down to the river.'

Grace considers the chaos of the storm's rare deluge months ago, the velocity and turbulence of water roused by that event. Reminders are visible around them: stray branches, large and small; trees displaying silty tide lines half-way up their trunks with random tatters of sun-bleached debris hanging from their branches spiderweb-creepy. Evidence of a cantankerous, swollen river, so different to what they know they will encounter today. What horror had their children experienced here? The thought of their son floundering in this environment leaves her cold. Life doesn't always dance lightly; on some people it tramples. Grace knows this first-hand.

They stare down at what remains of this section of river; the shallowest Charlie has seen it, he comments. What an awful sight!

Black oily water oozes along like a slow python caught in a ravine; sporadic bursts of activity belie its near lifeless state. Grace is reminded of the sometimes-violent death throes of her patients from her nursing days, reassured only by knowing the pain would not last long. This river appears sluggish, but she understands how potent, how sinister it can be in its return to life.

'Something else happened this morning.'

'Apart from your chaotic cooking?'

'You could say that, yes. There was a fire in the oven.'

As expected, Charlie's jaw drops. 'WHAT?' Reactively, a magpie warbles and launches from an ironbark tree. 'Is everyone alright?'

Grace sighs. 'Yes, yes, we are all fine.'

'What the bejesus are we doing here then? And how on earth did it happen?'

'Let me try to explain.' She can't explain, shouldn't. 'I don't know how it started. Izzie was with me.'

'How did you put it out? Was there damage? Was there—'

'I saw flames coming out of the oven. Fleur smelt smoke.' *What was that all about?* 'Izzie saw nothing.'

'I thought you said she was with you.'

'She was.'

'Right. Why is it that every time you open your mouth, I get worried?'

She wonders that Charlie doesn't accuse her of having hit the sherry bottle this morning, wonders if the roles were reversed…

'It was obviously a vision. I shouldn't have shared it with Izzie! I told her exactly what I saw, and now she thinks I'm a stark raving loony.'

'Understandable.' His sideways grin doesn't quite make it to his eyes.

'Shut up. There's something else.'

'Here we go.' He clasps his hands behind his neck and groans.

'Charlie!' Sometimes they can have a good old laugh, but the mood now is grim.

'Sorry. Go on.' He clenches his hands by his side.

'I saw a scene within the fire. And there was a little house falling around a little person waving its little arms at me, like it was trying to call for help.'

'What's that, Grace? Someone stuck in the oven? A tiny person?'

Charlie's words are suddenly matter of fact. He sounds like a character interpreting the all-knowing Skippy the bush kangaroo, from their new favourite television program. She is relieved because he wants her to elaborate, he understands her. How can he?

'Yes, a person, but this was all happening above the oven, outside of it. Charlie, my vision, the whole scenario, it definitely had something to do with a fire.'

'So, what are you asking from me?'

'Why would I want you to do something?'

He rolls his eyes at her, no doubt recalling the Robinson caper. 'Because I know from experience how these things start.'

'I just wanted you to know, that's all. And I think we should take care, because I hope what I saw wasn't telling us something, a warning about a fire.'

He stares at her as if awaiting a crack in her story, but she doesn't flinch.

'What you saw was just a little morning glitch.'

'Remember, Charlie, it took only one day for our world to collapse. I know, everything will always go back to Teddy, but it must, you see. Before our tragedy, I'd foolishly thought the signs shown just to me by the universe could signal only good outcomes. I'd been lax the day we lost him, thinking if I kept quiet about my niggling visions, my sentience, prescience, whatever, we'd be protected. But, even in my staunch silence it didn't protect me, or any of us. I was wrong not heeding *beyond*'s warnings, and there were many that day. I'll never take them lightly again. But I also know that I can't keep *beyond* to myself any longer.'

'Alright, we'll stay alert. We can't go back in time, but we can go back home now. It's been an exhausting morning for both of us. Come now, your husband needs feeding.'

Hunger always makes him prickly. Such a basic need, but she won't let it undo her plans, even if vague.

'Not yet. We're here to make peace with the river. Please.'

'What do you expect us to do here? Sing? Swim? Tap dance?'

'Don't make fun! I'm not sure what we should do. Just don't leave.' She lowers her head like a despondent animal.

What can she do? Squinting against sunlight, she begs for divine guidance, something from *beyond*, perhaps. Suddenly, pointing to the opposite bank, 'Look, Charlie.'

The scenery glows, and something grows from within it. Two

distinct patches of rainbow colours flare within the canopies of two separate trees. Rooted to their hosts, they elongate, gravitating towards one another, tapering as they move, reminding Grace of sucked rock candy. She darts a look at Charlie as he instinctively grabs her hand. Why wouldn't he be confused? A rainbow in this drought? Spanning the distance between them, the colours join and flare in a small fully formed arc. Together, Grace and Charlie watch the quiet performance; motionless, entranced, oblivious to time yet understanding one thing with certainty: that they must wait and observe until the colours fade away. And they do.

'Why are we standing here like this?'

'The rainbow, of course. Didn't you see it forming? Shining between those two trees?' She points to the site of the phenomenon.

'No.'

'What?' Suddenly she understands, it was not for him this time. 'Never mind.'

'Well, if you say it was there, I believe you.' He looks hurt. 'And how could a rainbow foretell anything but good news? Good luck for us.'

A shadow crosses her eyes. She thinks of the rainbow she flew through with Teddy the previous night: the magic of it. The new chick this morning. And now the rainbow: the stunning intensity of each hue, its strange formation appearing just for her while here with Charlie. Despite the best thing that has happened to Grace for months—seeing her son—her skin crawls.

She fiddles with Teddy's hat on the walk back to the tractor, trying to rouse her son from his resting place, hoping that like a genie he will magically spring out, granting their wish.

When they reach home, and Teddy has still not appeared, Grace carefully places the hat in a drawer in his room—the room now empty of inhabitants—with his other precious things. She reflects on her now dismal mood, reasoning the fire (was there a fire?) and her consequent bad vibes about the river rainbow have halted the magic, at least for today.

Chapter Eleven

Fleur went deep last night. Trembling and faint by the time she collapsed into bed at around ten, wracked with exhaustion, sleep eluded her. She lay awake in throbbing pain in those long pre-slumber hours, which was nothing new. She obsessed about that elusive toy car of Teddy's she knows is somewhere in the vicinity of the river. And why did she smell smoke in the kitchen when her mother had another conniption? Her main thoughts were of Tripp: fretting for him, regretting the pub debacle, the blundering conversations. Fleur's pain intensified in a mind/body battle before she finally nodded off.

Today, lying on her bed, she remains unconvinced of her sanity. She takes her mind to somewhere dark and icy, somewhere like Alaska at night, where giant ice chunks break from glacial cliffs and crash into the ocean. The scene is real but as much as she tries, she cannot hear their whip-like cracks and thunderous booms upon their collapse. If they are in her mind, they must be real, mustn't they? Because sometimes it is like her mind is more real than her body, even though it is unstable. She does not want to think about her soul. She needs *Tripp*.

Why can't she hear what is happening within her during pivotal moments either? She wonders at her body—scrawny and scarred now—the science of it, its silence. Her first orgasm, mighty enough to shift tectonic plates. Tripp. The reverse of pleasure: encountering her brother's body in the river. The wavy water flowed tannin-dark, not in the red hues she thought it should have turned. Because his life-colour had to go somewhere, didn't it? She remembers later (was it that day?) watching some dark-suited man (was there even a man?) prodding him with a stick before flipping him over like a fried fish—insensitive bastard. Her body was quiet and still at those times, too. Yet in its inertia, her mind quietly fell to ruination.

If only she could sense Teddy's true presence, it would give her solace. She tries to tap into his spirit by surrounding herself with his things, in the room that will one day be hers. The lunacy of the vision of his little blue car through his kaleidoscope, her fruitless searches for the damn thing on the muddy riverbank, because he wants her to find it. But why not leave it outside in the elements rather than pack it away with his other dead things? She can barely understand his preference to bring it back to the house; if she were in the same position, she'd rather everything of hers, including her body, be left out in the wild.

She looks down at her useless body, clothed in a pretty nightie like a doll worth showing. But those horrible girls at the pub were right about the ugliness underneath. Cotton with intricate patterns of lace overlay covers the messy truth.

Whatever is inside Fleur causing pain must lurk about amongst her disgusting internal organs—surely not in her mind—because that is where it hurts most. She wants to ignore it but cannot. She has been trying to get to it—the pain—to evoke something profound, something noisy, to show she is near the source because she imagines it would not go quietly. But her body remains silent, despite the metal assaults from tweezers and sharp nail scissors. The weapons sting her, but the hurt deep inside her is like no other and it is somehow linked to her heart. She wonders if she will ever reach its source to cut it away. What would it look, feel like? Or is her turmoil just like her now: silent, invisible. Nothing. She must prove it is inside her because that is all she can do. Fleur and her body are like two enemies fated to live their entire lives together.

She and her mother cannot manage to work things out. But what is said is said, done is done. Would Fleur even give Grace a chance to apologise?

Fleur and her sister do not belong together. And that boyfriend of Erin's, ugh, he gives her chills. Recently, she pulled Grace up about Scott 'co-incidentally' being the son of Charlie's rich best friend. Her mother had snapped, saying she preferred to judge people by their benevolence, their fortitude, once again leaving Fleur feeling like dirt.

Fleur and the farm don't belong together. Everything at Pig Peak is slow and excruciatingly sad.

Fleur and Tripp will never belong together. They will! They won't... *Tripp*.

The other night she almost felt sorry for him—his pains to explain himself, to make her believe him. She knows he is not a bad man, but she is overthinking. Perhaps she is the irrational one. But why did Tripp speak so harshly to Bene as though he holds such wild, ruthless ambition? Tripp's bellowing words—even his voice that night—sounded different, cruel, so unlike the man she has grown to know and respect. Although everyone has a dark side; Fleur is living proof of that. It's just that she foolishly thought Tripp did not. She even thought that he may bring himself to care for someone broken like her. Everything she loves gets taken away from her.

Fleur crushes the material of the nightie she wears to every inch of its life, then splays her fingers and crosses her arms over her chest. She cannot let herself become insane. With a groan, she covers her head with her arms and weeps. Who is this confused, unrecognisable girl? Where does she belong? Hating the horror of her body, hating what is inside her. Hating the way her thirst for life was ripped from her on a rushing river wave that should have been red, as it swiftly swallowed up Teddy's life colour. Hating the supressed guilt that rises through her core whenever she thinks about her brother. Hating this place.

She craves renewal. Is new life hiding somewhere here, out of reach, waiting to be birthed? Yet, how could it, in this barren landscape?

Fleur: knowing nothing else and terrified there may *be* nothing else.

Chapter Twelve

When Erin and Scott announce their engagement at the Alton's homestead after dinner, Fleur is speechless as she watches her mother wrap Erin in a teary hug.

'Remember, we'll always be here for you,' Grace says, as though her daughter is marching off to war. Fleur waits for someone to play, 'We'll Meet Again'.

Her father appears the most excited, until one night when they all get dragged over to the Harris's white stucco behemoth of a house in eastern Pig Peak.

'Congratulations! This is marvellous, just marvellous,' chortles Scott's father, Dukie, flapping his arms about like a scarecrow on a windy day. He lights a cigar and offers another to Charlie who declines.

'We plan to wed late September, if that suits everyone,' says Scott in pacification, no doubt having pre-empted the inevitable bamboozled reactions: How can they possibly organise a wedding in two months? So soon! Surely Erin can't be...?

The silence is awkward.

'Oh, I'm positively chuffed, aren't we, Dukie?' states Scott's snooty mother, Carmen. 'We're so pleased you've set the date. Late September, eh? It will be a sumptuous spring affair. And afterwards, the darling couple will naturally move in here to this.' Beaming victoriously, Carmen wiggles her pointer finger around all 'this' as though crossing off a shopping list, claiming Erin as her own. Poor Dukie, with that pushy wife.

Fleur sights Erin trying to catch her mother's attention in quiet alarm, but Grace decides instead to examine her shoes, and Fleur joins her, noticing one has a hole.

Erin, whose face has turned the colour of the flame trees outside, at last breaks the stunned silence. 'Well, um, there's plenty of time for that. We have a wedding to plan!'

'Give me strength,' Grace mumbles, and Charlie shoots her a look of reproach.

For once, I agree with you, Mum. Fleur catches her mother's eye, then looks down, unable to supress her giggle at the preposterous Carmen.

Charlie's friend Marmaduke Harris—Dukie—the epitome of a well-worn dog, wears a Band-Aid under his right eye. It moves slightly whenever he blinks—which is often—highlighting an underlying bruise. He and Charlie prance around like uncoordinated ballroom dancers with invisible partners. They should get together, Fleur thinks glumly.

'Well, this calls for champagne! Sidney, Sidney!' Dukie yells while chomping on his cigar.

Beckoned, a strangely square, compact elderly man with pink skin marches into the room. 'Yes, Sir?'

'Crack open a bottle of our best champagne,' orders Dukie. 'Our boy is engaged!' Sidney looks stunned—Fleur imagines Dukie has never been one to share family business with the help—as he fills four glasses as steadily as he can manage.

'One for you too, Sidney! Yes, good fellow.' Dukie flushes as he ushers the butler into gear, who promptly takes his block body to the cabinet for another glass, and another bottle. Sidney fills his to the brim.

'A toast: to the soon-to-be Mr and Mrs Harris!' roars Dukie.

As they clash their delicate flutes together, one smashes. Fleur cannot tell whose it was, as people jump back and banish theirs to the nearest surface. A little assemblage of splinters falls onto the exquisite Persian rug which guzzles up their finest. All eyes drop to the shattered glass which takes on baby pastel colours, birthed by the crystal prisms of the chandelier above.

The beautiful deadly show leaves everyone mesmerised, except for Sidney. He takes a substantial swig of his intact drink then rushes about shouting, 'Stay still!' before crawling around collecting glass shards from around everyone's shoes. No gloves, silly man. Fleur sees blood trickle from his fingertips onto the rug. It will dry to the colour of Scott's hair.

The Altons gratefully call it a night. Sitting in the back seat of the family car, its engine running erratically, Fleur cringes, realising she has left her beret hanging on the hat rack in the entryway.

'I'll go get it,' says her father.

'No, no. My mistake, my task.' She couldn't bear for her father to get chatting again.

With luck, the front door is ajar. She edges it open further, tiptoes towards the object hanging on a hallstand hook, reaches up and retrieves it.

Loud voices from the loungeroom reverberate around the large entryway. Fleur hides behind the hallstand, wondering why it isn't flush against the wall, until she sees the wall has a small door built into it. A secret compartment? Could she fit?

'Well now, that went spiffingly, don't you think?' says Scott's father, his tone still rousing. 'You've done well, Son, done us all proud.'

'Thank you, Dad. I've only ever wanted to do the right thing by you, by you both, although I never realised I'd be changing my whole life for the family.'

'She's the first-born, Scott. It had to be her.' His mother's adamant voice.

Fleur swallows at a lump wedged in her throat.

'And from what we've seen, she's the more stable one,' adds the unstable Carmen.

'Yes, sensible future planning all round, just as you suggested.' Scott's flat voice.

'Don't make it sound so dire, Son, she's a lovely girl,' reassures his forever-optimistic father.

'Yes, she is, and with strong moral fibre. Erin comes from an honourable family; I'm committed to making it work, and the last thing I want to do is hurt her.'

Carmen chirps, 'You won't hurt her, Scott. You are exactly what that girl needs: a reliable and, fair enough, handsome man who will give her a wonderful future.'

'What kind of future can I give her now, with our situation?'

'One you're both entitled to, darling,' says Carmen.

Fleur pictures it: Scott's mother proffering a chorus line of lipstick-smudged chalky teeth, gripping her son's shoulders, trying to shake some sense into him, as she pierces his shirt with her purple fingernail hooks. About to face ten bouts with the favourite, the odds aren't good.

'You'll have a son, an heir to our dynasty, ensuring our name rightly lives on forever. Those Altons... they're a penny-pinching lot, worth a fortune yet they live like paupers. Never mind, at least you won't have to live there and grovel in their muck.'

Heat moves through Fleur's body as her heartrate accelerates. She cannot bring herself to budge.

'I can't imagine I'd ever grovel, Mother, no matter where I was. Living at the Alton property wouldn't be so bad. I don't know why you suggested Erin and I move in here, with everything going on.'

His mother emits a 'tut-tut'.

'I agree, best idea would be to live at the Alton farm,' says Dukie, 'despite it being riddled with penny-pinchers, according to your mother.'

'I just thought Scott and Erin might like to stay here and look after us as we grow old and infirm, for as long as we can stay...' warbles his left-out mother. Fleur imagines she is twirling her skeletal hand before placing it delicately across her cold heart.

'Listen, you know I adore you, Mother. Wherever I live I'll always look after you—both of you. And you're probably right, perhaps I do need a push into marriage. I feel I'm going stale here.' A pause. 'Isn't there anything the lawyers can do, Dad?'

'Precious little. We really need you to pull something out of the bag, and fast.' Dukie's voice sounds anything but convincing, and

Fleur wonders if it has to do with his lack of faith in his boy, or merely his own resignation of life being a bitch.

'I'll do whatever I can to build a solid future for us all,' says Scott.

Fleur pulls free and escapes to the car, making herself as tiny as possible, pleased she didn't try to creep into the secret compartment because once in there she doesn't think she would have the strength to escape.

'You took your time. All good?' asks her mother.

'I... got my beret.'

What has she heard? Will her sister's intended marriage be nothing but one of convenience for the Harrises? Although Scott did say nice things about Erin and promised to make a go of their future. Are the Harrises going broke? Fleur is not surprised; she knows Carmen is racking up bills at the pub.

The achingly long driveway their car chugs down is bordered by huge Illawarra flame trees. Either side of the car, their red blossoms pulsate and glow in the dark like lights warning of imminent attack. Fleur sniffs and rubs her nose, assaulted by the smoke emanating from the many chimneys of the Harris 'mansion'. Yet, there had been no fires burning in the fireplaces; everything and everyone seemed cold. She gazes back to the house and wonders if they're burning bodies of former—slow, fat—snoopers they discovered wedged in other secret compartments. As Fleur's alarm grows, the stench of smoke lingers in the car, but no-one comments on it.

Her heart sinks as those dreadful words ring around her head: *It had to be her...*

Chapter Thirteen

Two days after the engagement announcement, Charlie and Scott tell Grace they have faced a harrowing day replacing eighty feet of rotted timber fence palings and posts. Despite having the correct equipment, despite their spirit, the day-long job has left them spent, and injured.

After sending the men away to clean up, Grace sets two beers, and a shandy for herself, upon the coffee table. Sitting on the lounge chairs, the men cradle their arms in protective hugs. Grace lights a match, burns the tops of two of her sewing needles for disinfecting. She wipes them on a clean linen serviette, then passes them to the men as they settle into the grim task of removing splinters from their hands.

She watches Charlie stop to take a sip of his drink while they both study their future son-in-law. A patchy pink pallor makes Scott look like an unappetising roll of Windsor sausage. A bruise—about two days old by the look of it—encircles his right eye in shades of purples and greens.

Charlie breaks the ice. 'Jeez, mate, I hadn't even noticed your shiner. What happened?'

'This?' Scott points to his eye. 'I was under the car and stuck my head up. Forgot I had the door open.' He gives a slow *silly me* head shake.

'Doesn't look too flash.' Charlie widens his eyes at Grace. He has told her of other bruises he has noted on Dukie. Are he and his son having punch-ups?

'It's true what they say: what hurts most gets all the attention. Right now, those splinters are crying out to me.'

'That's the way of it, Son. Chin up, we'd better get stuck in.'

As Grace sips her beverage, she notices blisters covering Scott's palms, but she won't mention them. She has something more important to discuss. 'Scott, about your future living arrangements…'

He takes a long drink. 'Has Erin spoken with you about this, Sir?' He asks Charlie earnestly, as though Grace doesn't exist. Swallowing hard, he continues, 'I know it was a bit awkward, the way Mother assumed Erin and I would live at the Harris mansion and all.'

Grace now rolls her eyes at three things: the memory of Carmen's ostentatious performance following the engagement announcement; Scott's stuck-up bullshit use of the word Sir; and his casual use of the pretentious title of 'mansion' for where he grew up in eastern Pig Peak. Grace knows where he must have gotten that word, and it is not from Scott's father, down-to-earth Dukie.

Failing to stop herself, she says, 'Yes Scott, it was awkward because we know our daughter, and—'

'Frankly, mate, she's been at her wits' end about the whole thing,' interrupts Charlie. 'She doesn't want to leave the farm. Tell me straight, could you live here?'

'Erin wants to, and I'll do whatever she wishes. She says she feels a great responsibility to you and Mum.' The weight of his words…

Charlie—smile plastered across his face—mouths 'Mum' towards his wife, and Grace does all she can not to gag. Yet she is relieved about Erin. Of course, she wants to stay at their property, and she has had the guts to tell Scott.

'That's my girl alright.' Charlie claps his hands. Catching Scott's quizzical look, he reverts to his surgery. 'Ouch, damn it! These things are in deep.' He angles his widened hand towards the window light to hit the right areas.

Grace sees little red spots spreading across Scott's serviette like wildfire.

'Excellent news,' says Charlie. 'You can both move into the empty blue workers' cottage after the big day. It's a family tradition.'

Wincing, Scott does not look up, immersed in the horror of his blood.

'But hang on, Scott, you're sounding serious. About Erin and her "responsibility", I hope you're not suggesting she thinks it's a burden for her here, because by crikey, our girl loves this place something fierce.'

'I know, Sir. I agree that we should live here. Erin's such a family girl, and she credits you—both—with her farming education. It's her passion, what she was born to do. I've never known a girl to like that sort of thing, but I'm more than willing to sacrifice—no, that's the wrong word—to leave my life with my parents.'

Sacrifice? Is that how he looks at it? The reassurance Grace craves regarding Scott is not forthcoming.

'Well, that's just bonza. You can join Erin getting your hands filthy here. It used to be Fleur doing the hard yards around the farm, but, well, things change.' Charlie's voice has faded. 'To tell you the truth, Erin's been worried, thinking she's leaving here. Have you told her she's not going anywhere?'

'No, not yet. Wanted to run it by you—both—first. But now I can't wait to tell her. In the meantime, before we marry, I'll divide my time between here and helping my parents, if that is suitable. Can I stay overnight in the workers' cottage sometimes?'

'Sure, you can. And for God's sake, put Erin out of her misery and tell her you'll be living here after the wedding. She'll be sitting pretty, then.' He stares Scott in the eye. 'I'm sure you and your family would provide well for our daughter wherever you pair were living. But this farm is Erin's entire life, hence her passion for the place. Also, you've got to admit, I'd be a miserly bastard if I deprived my flesh and blood of the chance to live on the property that they'll one day inherit. That includes you Scott, naturally.'

'Very kind of you, Dad. I'll work, day and night, as much as it takes to provide well for my family. And by the way, I'm quite used to getting my hands dirty.'

Judging by those blisters Grace doubts it.

'I've been thinking about Izzie and Tripp and their living

arrangements and how it's been incredibly generous of you to provide them with a room at the homestead for so long,' Scott says in one breath, losing it with each word.

'Bullshit!' says Charlie gruffly, stifling a grin. 'Jesus me beads, I sound exactly like Grace's father, George. Must be getting old. Not generous, common sense really. We like them living here.'

'It's true, Scott,' Grace interjects. 'Sometimes I think they've given more to us than we have given them.'

'You should've seen 'em when they first got together,' says Charlie. 'We could hear the chatting—yakkety-yak—day and night coming from their room. But it was all good, you know? Grace reckoned it was like listening to sweet music, didn't you, Love? Until Izzie started up her singing.' He chortles.

Grace chastises her husband, 'Stop it. You know Izzie has a lovely voice.'

'They had years to catch up on, didn't they?' Scott's smile looks painted on. 'I don't know the details, but it's really something seeing them back together again. Must be darned amazing the way they got together. Seems a bit weird from my perspective. Perhaps it was more a miracle rescue?'

'You have no idea, mate.' At Charlie's words, Grace gives her husband a sign of slitting a throat, willing him to keep his big mouth shut.

'I'd like to hear all about it.' Scott's look is imploring.

'Um,' says Charlie ineffectually. Grace now angles her neck towards one shoulder, making a hangman's noose with her raised fist, her tongue lolling.

'Long story and not for today, mate. Perhaps some other time.' Charlie flickers his eyes at Grace expectantly as she frowns back at him.

'Fair enough.' Scott raises his eyebrows. 'Anyhow, I have an idea. What would you think if I built them their own little workers' cottage on the property? There's some flat land east of the homestead that would do nicely. I'll cut and prepare all the timber myself.'

'What? Why would you do that?' asks Charlie.

Grace is flummoxed. 'Let's be honest, Scott, you've shown little regard for either of them. If you do care about them, you have a funny way of showing it.'

'My lack of articulation doesn't mean I don't feel for their situation. I'm simply… reserved. I believe they have earnt the right to a new home. While I certainly don't know their full story, Erin's told me they've been through hell, which makes me want to do something positive for them. Also, it would create some privacy for you all.'

'You're not like your father in that respect, are you?' says Charlie.

'What do you mean?' Scott snaps back.

'Your dad has no trouble in the feelings department, that's all I meant.' He gives Scott a measured look.

Grace wonders why he is so uptight; it seems more than the predictable pre-nuptial jitters.

'The idea may be noble, but I smell a few problems,' says Charlie. 'You're not a builder, Scott, and you're up against two other issues: time and money.'

'Oh, but you're wrong about your first roadblock. I did two years of structural engineering at Sydney University before turning my hand to mechanics.'

Charlie almost roars with joy. 'What? Well, blow me down, you *are* a little ripper! Anything else in your past you'd like to enlighten me with?'

Scott beams. 'I like to remain a man of surprises.' He gives his soon-to-be old man a wink.

'Well, you can floor me with surprises like that any day.'

'Thanks, Charlie. Listen, if I can sort out my roster, please tell me you'll consider my offer about the house. It really is the least I can do.'

'I'll give some thought to it.'

'Sometimes I wonder why I spread myself so thin. But then I recall the reasons behind my assiduity, and I relax a little. Sir, I'll do whatever it takes to prove myself to your family.'

Charlie looks impressed. Grace wonders if he'll check the meaning of the word *assiduity* while he still remembers it.

Chapter Fourteen

Arriving home from secretarial college, Fleur performs a giggly pirouette down the hallway to her and Erin's bedroom, hoping no-one has caught her. She could have been a dancer, she muses, but tomboys aren't taken to ballet classes. Sharing a room with her sister has been hell, but yesterday Erin—noisily, angrily—moved some of her things into the blue workers' cottage, saying she intended to set it up for after the wedding. The thought of Scott's presence permanently at the farm fills Fleur with dread, but she reasons that at least he won't be sleeping in the main house.

When she asked Erin last night who, exactly, decided Erin and Scott wouldn't live in that monstrosity of the Harrises, Erin told her, 'That's just the way it will be. I have nothing more to say on the matter.'

Fleur knows Carmen is an absolute bitch and will be furious she won't be able to control them. Living like royalty would probably have suited Erin; she's always been a princess.

Scanning the bedroom now, Erin has her stamp on everything: musk-stick-pink paint, borders of girly floral wallpaper. Erin's bed—perhaps it could be moved? Fleur fears her sister's curse may linger no matter what changes are made. Hurriedly, she moves back down the hallway.

Entering Teddy's bedroom she feels an immediate sense of home, belonging, connection, because the room is unchanged from the time a little boy lived so large in it. Some facades don't change.

Freddy lies quietly on the bed now his, gazing up at her, threadbare but loved. With a grin Fleur pulls him to her and plants a firm kiss on his fusty face. 'Oh, come here. You're lonely, aren't you?' She appraises him. He smiles with glee in her company, as always. His one brown bead eye jiggles precariously on a cotton strand as Fleur gently lies him back onto the bed. If his eye were to fall off, she would have to leave him blind which would be cruel but sewing it back on would be crueller still. *She* couldn't do it anyway. 'I understand, you lovely little moulting thing.'

With a decisive yank of swollen timber, she opens Teddy's top drawer. Books, comics. Shuts it with as much trouble. Second drawer: his little clothes, how sweet! Fleur closes her eyes and inhales the soapy scent of his shirt before returning it. So sad. Guilt adds to her dampening mood.

Rummaging around, she's slapped with sudden shock at what lies underneath Teddy's clothes. His red hat! Faded now. Ever since that fateful day at the river, Fleur has seen it perched up on the same tangle of reeds as it was on the day of the storm. A shrine to her brother, at least a marker to show her where she was. Did someone locate it through Teddy's kaleidoscope? No, she knows instinctively who the culprit is. She lifts the hat from its grave.

'Mum!'

Fleur hears the patter of feet down the hallway, her mother arriving, panting, bunging it on.

'There's no need to shout. The house isn't that big, you know.'

'I didn't realise you were nearby. Why are you breathing so hard? Never mind.' Fleur dangles the hat accusingly towards her mother. 'How did this get here?'

Grace plonks down upon Teddy's bed as though it is hers. 'Oh, Fleur dear. Dad and I found it on the riverbank the other day, caught up in vegetation. It was quite a surprise.'

'Yes, I know where it was. I've been noting its location when I go to the river, or I did. It's been there ever since… But now you've broken the spell.' She tosses the hat onto the foot of Teddy's bed.

'When you go to the river? I didn't know you did now.'

'Well, I do. If you really want to know, I've been searching for his little blue car which I'd planned to bring back here. But now you've moved his hat, you've spoiled it, you've taken away my signpost, so perhaps I won't be going there again. You didn't happen to find his car and not tell me about that too, did you?'

'No.'

'If you do, *don't move it!*' Fleur must be the one to do that.

'Alright. Calm down, darling. Does it matter so much that we moved the hat?'

Fleur shuffles on the spot, head averted towards the window, mouth set tight. Calm down? How can her mother possibly understand? 'Yes, it matters, because I like to think of Teddy being under that hat, safe on shore instead of where he ended up.' Her stupid bottom lip wobbles, her bite doing little to stop it. 'It's time you told me what happened. We need a heart-to-heart.'

With a pleading look Grace pats the spot beside her. Begrudgingly, Fleur obeys and there they sit, shags on a rock.

'You've made your feelings perfectly clear about how you think I failed everyone that day. Do you even remember your words? Do you realise how much they hurt me?'

'Oh, Fleur, I do, I really do.' Grace cups her forehead in her hand, waits a little. 'When I was a teenager, someone I trusted hurt me, with actions and words that have haunted me for years.'

What exactly had happened to her mother? Something inside Fleur wants to break out and demand answers, wants retribution for her mother's perpetrator, wants to grab hold of her mother and comfort her, but... Why can't she focus on Fleur for once, on her broken feelings?

'So what? You want me to suffer the way you did?' Why does her mother draw out from her things she doesn't mean? 'How could you be so cold? Didn't you realise the effect of your horrible words? And after what I'd just been through...'

'Please, darling. Tell me what happened.' Grace's face breaks out in the tell-tale rash she gets when uncomfortable.

Fair enough, but Fleur suspects her mother will not understand. 'If you want to keep this going, you can hear my side of it. I tried so hard to keep track of Teddy. After the storm, when I saw his hat above the tall reeds, I thought he was standing underneath.'

'Just like I did recently,' says Grace.

Fleur barely hears her mother's words, let alone her own hushed ones: 'But a little later he was still there, and I wondered why. But it wasn't Teddy at all, was it? He'd gone. He'd left his hat there to follow something. Teddy was chasing a rainbow when he went away, Mum. It piqued his interest more than any storm damage.'

'A rainbow? He was chasing?' Grace loses her colour to the notion. Her arthritic fingers cover her twitchy mouth. *Is the wobbly lip affliction hereditary?* Her mother takes a deep breath as if she is about to dive into deep water. 'I need to tell you something too, Fleur. When I saw the hat at the river the other day—all faded and tattered, but Teddy's for sure—I thought he was underneath it, too. I even ran to it and your dad had to comfort me. And then the strangest thing happened. Two rainbows formed in opposite trees, joining to form one magnificent arc. Without any rain. Isn't that wonderful?'

'It was Teddy's rainbow.' Fleur's words are flat. Why should she celebrate her mother's magic?

'Little rascal. Before that awful day, I dreamed of Teddy painting a rainbow. He invited me to hop on and ride it with him. That exact dream happened in real life! I'll show you that painting one day. One night recently I rode a rainbow with Teddy. I know all this must sound like stuff and nonsense to you, but I was awake when it happened, I really was.'

Fleur simply feels sadness. Why should her mother's magic eclipse hers, now that a little magic has entered her own life with a vision of Teddy's car? Was it simply her imagination? She hopes all the smoke she has encountered lately is just imagination. A tear cuts a cold line down her cheek.

'I wish it had been me, Mum. I've been searching everywhere for some trace, some sign to say that Teddy is alright, but perhaps I'm not worthy to find it. There. I've said it. Are you happy now?'

'Oh darling, you are worthy! How could you not know that? You were probably the most important person in Teddy's life. He poured all his love into you. He would have followed you anywhere.'

'And look where it led him.'

'Don't say that. He would hate for you to hold onto any guilt about that day.'

Hold onto guilt? Guilt means wrongdoing. I did wrong.

'But look at us. We are talking about Teddy together and not fighting. Could this be a message, a sign for us?' says Grace.

'Just because we're talking doesn't mean we're not fighting. I don't know what you want. What do you want me to say to you?' Fleur's anger subsides, just a little.

'Nothing.' Her mother appears to muse before widening her eyes at her. 'Teddy has used his hat to bring us together, just as he used the scarf to reunite Izzie and Tripp.'

'Perhaps.'

'Believe it, Fleur, he's waiting for your trust. Follow your intuition, it will encourage Teddy to show more of himself to you. Then exciting things can happen to you like rainbows and flying!'

What can she say to this? She wants to believe her mother's words but wishes Teddy could tell her himself. She wants to fly so much! And she wants her mother to say sorry. A twinge of *deja vu*, as—

Her mother speaks. 'It's my turn to ask you to forgive me for my selfish accusations. I've made no room for you, have I? I've wanted to apologise to you for so long; knowing I should have has been eating away at me. I understand how you lost track of your brother that day. Even if you hadn't just told me about the hat on the reeds, you weren't responsible for him, I was. It's a mother's duty! I was the one who failed. I've seen—we've all seen—what this has done to you. Your hurt, your pain; it's crushed us all. What I'm about to say has nothing to do with forgiveness.'

Her mother is reaching out, taking Fleur's hands. Four joined hands make for one hot, sweaty bundle of awkwardness. Is her mother really apologising?

'I don't forgive you—'

'There it is.' She feared her mother could not do it and she was right all along.

'Stop. Listen to me!' Her mother's hands now lock around hers. 'I don't forgive you because there is nothing to forgive. You did nothing wrong, Fleur. I'm so sorry if I've made you carry this around like a dead weight. And please, don't think the lateness of my apology in any way lessens its sincerity, because it's heartfelt. I can only hope that one day you'll forgive me.'

Curiously, as her mother's tears brim, her mouth hints at a smile. Her piercing eyes leave Fleur embarrassed, and all this contact makes her want to flee, at least break away. But an apology, at last! Her fingers tickle. She senses a shift of some sort is about to happen.

A gob-smacking surge—tingling with life and secrets—shoots from Grace's hands into Fleur's and spreads throughout her entire body, setting her alight in power, swiping everything else away, leaving no room for anything but awe.

Fleur finds her voice. 'Do you feel that, Mum? It's like electricity, like the zap I get from the outside tap, but nice and warm, comforting somehow.' Her pitch escalates to a near-squeal. 'What, what's happening to me?'

Fleur must wear possum eyes; it is just the effects of this extraordinary power surge. Although it cannot last. *Snap out of it.* Gasping with the effort, she tries to yank her hands away and it takes some clout but, finally, she is free. Fleur brims with fresh vigour.

'That weird feeling—it came from you, Mum. What is this all about?' *What just happened?*

'*Beyond.* I don't control it. I think it may have just chosen you, Fleur.'

'Now you're frightening me.'

'Don't be frightened. It's complicated. Things may now change for you, dear. My heart hopes you will tell me if you start experiencing things like predictions or flashbacks or visions, but my head warns me that you must keep things to yourself, or *beyond* may punish you. But take heed of what it shows you; do what it tells you to do. It's an unpredictable force.'

Fleur wonders if she should reveal to her mother about the smoke in the kitchen and at the Harris's, or if she will be 'punished' for doing so. Then again, Fleur is used to keeping secrets. She would act upon its predictions if only she knew what to do, and what they meant.

'And your explanation is practically incoherent, Mum. When did you get it, this *beyond* thing?'

'When my trust had been broken as a teenager. *Beyond* can cause good things as well as bad, believe me. But please, you must act on its warnings.'

Appearing clammy and pale, Grace touches her own forehead.

'Are you alright?'

'I think I just need a little lie down,' says her mother, in halting words as tiny as she has—curiously—now become.

Grace can barely rouse herself. If her head feels so light, why can't she lift it from her pillow? In fact, her entire body has become weak, which is why she harbours no guilt about remaining in bed all afternoon.

She switches on her bedside lamp, watching her china ornaments on the dressing table opposite the bed: tiger, bear, dog, rabbit. She wills them to talk to her as they once did in Brisbane, to give her advice, yet all she gets in return here is silence, stillness. They need someone to bring them back to life.

How will her daughter react to her newly acquired power? Fright, fascination, anger? Grace considers the irony that Fleur wouldn't have wanted anything from her mother other than an apology—certainly not her weirdness—but now Fleur has been struck by *beyond*.

Her weird mother, still weird but losing power.

As the sun sinks behind Pig Peak, Grace hears a knock at her bedroom door. Throat clearing. 'Can I come in?' Fleur's voice is tentative.

'Please do.' Grace sits up, her head now surprisingly weightless. She rubs her eyes, adjusts her hair and clothes.

Fleur enters and sits beside her on the bed. 'You can't just leave me like that. Tell me about this *beyond* thing.' Panic in her daughter's voice.

'Your dad calls it a gift, you know. I meant it when I said it could do good. *Beyond* caused me to see a vision of Tripp in Izzie's scarf. And when you told us where Teddy had found it... Well, it helped Izzie and Tripp come to us.'

'Then Teddy helped, too.'

'Yes, he did. What happened in Teddy's room earlier today was strange, wasn't it?' That stunning, definitive energy exchange from mother to daughter was not random or without meaning. 'I don't imagine it will do you harm.'

'Well, that's not at all reassuring.'

'You almost glowed, Fleur, like you were ignited by a new rush of verve. You didn't fear what happened, did you? I could see it in your eyes.'

Grace had seen another emotion reflected in her daughter's eyes: compassion—she doesn't think it was pity. A rare thing, especially lately, and Grace couldn't have been happier. She prays the episode was a forerunner to reconciliation. Its origins are clearer. What else could have caused such power, such catharsis, if not *beyond*?

'But why me?'

'Because you could use a little magic.' Grace tries for her best reassuring face. Surely no cruel act has been committed against Fleur as it had to Grace when she received *beyond*?

Yet, she suspects there is a fragility one must have—or attain—for *beyond* to attach itself to someone. Fleur is a fragile soul, despite her cantankerous carry-on.

Intuitively, Grace should know the root cause of her daughter's pain. Perhaps she does. Teddy was Fleur's rock, her anchor; they ran riot, yet he grounded her somehow, too. Now what good is freedom with no-one to share it with? Perhaps Tripp can fit the bill for Fleur. Grace hopes his calming influence will do her good.

'I suspect my mother, Connie—your Brisbane grandma—had *beyond*.'

'I suppose it's a good thing I'm not planning to have children.'

Grace balks.

'So,' Fleur continues, 'what if I don't want to be part of this family line of lunacy?'

'Sorry, darling, I don't think you have a choice. But don't worry, things will reveal themselves when the time is right.'

'I didn't choose this!' Fleur's irate voice. 'I don't need anything else to deal with now. Life for me is unpredictable enough.'

'I know you're struggling. Trust that all will improve.'

Grace rises from her bed and opens the curtains. 'Goodness, it's almost dark. I'd better get moving.'

As Fleur begins to leave first, Grace says firmly, 'Please understand, you should always come to me for advice or reassurance.'

Her daughter simply nods.

As Grace moves towards the kitchen her thoughts run amuck. That recent ferocious kitchen 'fire'... What was the significance of the little man waving his hands about before being pinned down under burning logs? Fleur said she could smell smoke that day, too, so why didn't Grace take that further, at least acknowledge her words? She should have realised Fleur was hinting at strange times coming, even if her daughter didn't realise it herself.

Grace is caught between mothering and walking *beyond*'s slippery track.

What lies on Fleur's cryptic horizon? How will she handle her journey?

Chapter Fifteen

June 1968

Charlie returns home from the post office with a large envelope. Delving inside, he lifts out and presents Grace with a postcard from Port Douglas showing white beaches, huge paperbark trees, clear sun-kissed water. There are also two brightly coloured photographs of his parents: Edith and Al.

'Nice to know they're still alive,' Charlie tells her, his smile bursting with relief because he has not heard from them for months. It is quietly understood his parents will not be returning to the farm, having been away for years.

For Grace, the mail is a welcome distraction from her concerns for Fleur. She snatches a photo from his hand. 'Wow! Look at that catch.'

'What a whopper,' says Charlie, also impressed by the huge cod Al presents to the camera.

In another shot, Charlie's mother wears a dress of the same blue as the hydrangeas behind her, hands clasped in front like the Queen of England, wearing an appropriate subtle, regal smile.

Al writes that the caravan is holding up beautifully, *and your Mum's not even complaining!* He tells Charlie he is officially letting go of managing the farm, trusts his son is doing a splendid job of it, and at last suggests they may never return to Pig Peak. He sends greetings to the family and workers, along with their contact details, and mentions that Charlie's sister Kitty is now working as a nursing sister, just like Grace did in Brisbane—which they already knew—having eloped to Oxford in England to live with her doctor husband, Oliver Godfrey. The latter they did not know.

Grace wishes she would hear more from her own parents, Connie and George. She communicates with them in letters, learning of her mother's worsening arthritis, her father's gout—a possible legacy of his generous daily beer habit. Having never visited Pig Peak, she fears they may never see where their daughter lives.

Lying in bed that night, she reminisces about her arrival with Charlie at the Alton's family farm as a newlywed almost two decades ago. Even the first day cast its spell. Pig Peak's rural landscape and uninterrupted skies were unique and strange to her. Grace's patch of earth had suddenly become panoramic, and it *felt* wider. Out here, one could almost believe that the planet was flat, and she could almost have embraced the notion herself. But she didn't feel agoraphobic, didn't want to hide away. In order not to jinx the landscape's steadfast constancy, she moulded herself to it. No effort, she embraced her new home with devotion. On the then-fertile land, she thrived and reproduced, working as hard as any man on their wool-supplying sheep property.

It had been such a relief to escape Brisbane, where masked danger lurked in the guise of order, charm, convention. The person her childish mind labelled Plasticine Man—Grace's godfather. She has never spoken of him to Charlie, let alone given details to her children or Izzie. They have had enough burdens without having to deal with more of hers.

Grace's new life with Charlie at Pig Peak had held such promise. But then came trauma and heartache—one ghost multiplied and assumed new locales, new identities—and the urge struck Grace to flee the farm too, just as she had ached to leave her old house in Brisbane. No fault of Charlie's, but she had almost given up then, unable to comprehend the devastation that should never have happened to her and her beautiful family.

Now, especially now, Grace feels a tugging, missing her mother's innate ability to make everything better. Is a husband's love enough for her mother? Does she ever crave her daughter's presence as Grace craves hers, or even think about her now?

What of Izzie? When the family first brought her to the farm as their housekeeper, she was such a mystery. Every day for years she quietly went about her work, never revealing a clue about her history. Yet, within Izzie's staunch silence, Grace recognised she, too, must harbour ghosts of the past. Only recently Grace helped Izzie face some of them. But Grace cannot relax, knowing there may be more to confront. From what she has hinted at, Izzie's dark entity assumes the shape of her own father. What would happen if they met up again?

How could Izzie have endured years without her family? Being such a sensitive soul, Izzie would surely miss her mother, but who and where she is now, even if she is still alive, remains a mystery.

Grace fears opening old wounds, but she knows what she must do. With the sudden clarity of these autumn mornings, Grace knows she can do something to help. Perhaps she will even find a little space to heal herself.

Grace considers the strange events of late. A day beginning with such promise in the shape of a baby bird, the menace of a 'fire', a rainbow which defied the rules of nature. She has had enough experience with her confidant—her messenger of good and bad, *beyond*—to know that strange events are not without meaning. She must trust that secrets will unfold when the time is right. She hates *beyond*'s trickery, the way it can foretell the worst in life, but she knows there is nothing she can do about it, just as her mother must have known this too. Will Fleur learn this in time? *In time.* Grace shudders and admonishes herself.

Right, Grace, show some of that fortitude and benevolence you assured Fleur you admire over wealth and position. Those words have niggled Grace for weeks since she remonstrated Fleur for having a go at Scott. Despite Grace's bravado, she is unsure if she demonstrates such strengths herself.

Today she will focus on Izzie's needs and broach a subject of concern she has dared not raise with her, for fear of digging up a past Izzie has spent so long trying to keep buried.

Grace sits beside her at the newspaper-covered kitchen table. Upon it, a small collection of family silver lies under a layer of Silvo polishing liquid. Only one tarnished bowl awaits its smothering fate. Grace notices Izzie's fingertips are powder white against her olive skin, rare physical evidence of the tireless work she does around the house and garden. Static hums, American twangs, and laughter emanate from the television set Grace has left on in the adjoining lounge room.

'Want a hand with that?' Grace blushes, knowing she is too late.

'No, almost done, thank you.'

'Can we have a little chat? You never seem to have a break, dear Izzie.'

'Always much to do, Grace.' Using a rag, she gives the remaining bowl a thick film of Silvo.

'Charlie received some photographs from his parents the other day, which got me thinking about my mother. You must wonder where your mother is, what she's doing. I miss mine all the time.' She tries to keep her voice calm and matter of fact, knowing the intensity of the subject matter.

Izzie gazes up at the ceiling, as if searching for an answer on its flyspecked surface.

'I give you truth, Grace. Every day she's in my thoughts. Every day.'

'And Tripp? Does he remember her?'

'Yes, yes!' Her voice raises. 'He loves her. He tells me he remembers times she washed him in the tub with the yellow soap. Times she took him on walks, read to him, made him big Hungarian goulash, or stew as you Aussies call it. Not as good as at home in Budapest. Australia has no flavour.'

Grace beams. 'Maybe none of us have any taste?'

'Pardon?' Izzie fails to recognise the double entendre.

'Never mind, Izzie. I'm just concerned for you and your family. When Tripp was young and someone took him away, it must have been so shocking, terrible.'

'You don't know. Worse than guns in my home country. We escaped those.'

A surge of guilt rushes through Grace, for how Izzie has been treated in her new 'free' country. She curses herself for turning this into a negative conversation, broaching sensitive topics, bringing bleak memories to the surface.

'You must have happy memories of the three of you together.'

'Yes, yes. Good memories. Bonza.' Izzie's words belie her tone.

'Before we brought Tripp to the farm, you stayed put here, you never tried to find your family.'

'I told you before! I not because I thought I look like, er, *tolvaj*—person who takes.' Her English always falters a little more when she is worked up. 'Bloody English! Sorry.'

Grace is upset too. She watches Izzie's small hands snatching at the air in quick succession before grabbing the rag and rubbing the life out of the last bowl.

'Don't be sorry. Were you afraid of the authorities?'

'Afraid of father of Tripp! Afraid of friends of my *apa*—my father. Afraid I not know where I am here.'

'But Tripp was missing, away from you for so many years.'

'What? You think I not care about my own son?' Her voice is vehement as she scowls at Grace.

'No dear. I, we—Charlie and I—don't think that at all. I'm talking about feeling heartbroken, but trapped and helpless. Have you ever felt trapped here on the farm, like you couldn't escape? Because if that were true, we would feel terribly guilty about keeping you here against your will.'

'What is guilty?'

'Bad, as if we had done wrong.'

'I had so many years of... how do you say... guilty? But trapped? When animal lives in cage, like a wolf, it wants escape. But then, wolf gets fed and warm, gets good care from people, so it stays.'

'So, you feel like a caged animal?' Have they done this to her?

'Cage is only in my head, Grace. You Altons, you are so very kind to me, very kind...' She trails off.

'If you ever want to leave us, even for a little while, especially now you have Tripp back, although we would be sad, we'd understand. We Altons can learn to make our own Hungarian goulash, no?' Grace tries for her best cheeky face.

Straight-faced, Izzie says, 'With no taste.'

'No taste, that's right, yes.'

'So, it is stew.' The sides of Izzie's mouth lift a little.

Grace exhales in relief. 'Of course.' She smiles.

'Travel to Budapest for good food one day. Have real Hungarian goulash.' A sun-gold wide smile catches on Izzie's pretty face.

'One day, perhaps.'

'I must ask you one thing too, Grace. It is very important, too very important.' Her words are almost a whisper.

'What is it?'

'Please, you never tell Tripp who his father is! I hardly remember his other name. What did he call himself?'

'Len Robinson.' Bile rises from Grace's stomach at the taint of his name on his tongue.

'Yes, that bad man. The man I call Joe. How did I ever think he was good?' She lowers her head, shakes it slowly.

'Charlie and I won't say anything, Izzie. We understand. It must have been a terrible shock for you to discover he lived on a neighbouring property with Tripp for years.'

'Oh, Grace, you do not know how bad. When I was pregnant, Joe went away. So, the man who took Tripp was stranger to him, you see. Joe was a stranger to me then, too, in different way. When Tripp ask me about his father, I told him he changed for bad. He *reszeg*,'—she lifts an imaginary bottle to her lips. 'Joe hit me, like my *apa*, my father, do to me too, and I was so glad Tripp never knew that. But my son, he tells me his boss treated him bad. If he finds out his boss was his father, we will both die in tears.'

Grace rubs Izzie's arm. 'You don't have to worry; your secret is safe with us. And Izzie, just remember, you have no-one to fear anymore. Len Robinson, or Joe as he called himself to you, is dead now.'

'But my father may not be, Grace. I am afraid of him too. He is evil man like Joe. Sometimes I think I should find *Anya* and take her from him. Tripp could help me search but she may be dead now.'

'Hopefully she's alive. And surely your father wouldn't want to harm you now? If he saw his daughter again, met his grandson, he would be happy, wouldn't he?'

'No, you not know my *apa*. He only thinks of what he lost—money from friend for no baby.'

'But your mother...'

'She will be like broken window. Little bits cannot get put back together the right way. Hurts me too much to think this. But then I think, perhaps Tripp and I can help fix her. Perhaps, bits can go together a new way, eh?'

Grace senses a shadow cross Izzie's vision as her eyes glaze over. What is she planning?

'And I can break my father like he broke us. Tell me, Grace, where do we start?' A glint now shines in Izzie's eyes, rare and blinding like a diamond.

Chapter Sixteen

July 1968

Izzie and Tripp lie parallel on their narrow beds. Tripp's bed is too short for his tall frame; Izzie's is too long. They have known this for months, yet tonight as Tripp's feet hang over the end of his mattress it strikes him like a new fact. No matter, they are settled and safe which is all they need. Having both suffered years of insecurity and separation, they have no embarrassment about sharing a room together.

'You awake, Mummy?'

'Huh? What's wrong?' A panicky voice, her inherent survival skills always on alert.

Tripp switches on the bedside light. 'Nothing. Can we talk?'

'Yes, son, anytime.' She stretches languidly.

'I was thinking of the little song you used to sing to me.'

'*Nani, nani*, my sweet baby *nani*.'

'That's it.'

'I can sing to you now.'

Tripp imagines the words catching the melody in his mother's mind, threatening to croon from her throat, but it would probably make her cry. 'No! I can't seem to get it out of my head. Did your mother sing that to you when you were a child?'

'Yes, she did. A Greek song of love. And now you remember how your mother sing it to you. One day you will sing the song to your *baba*.'

'We'll see about that, Mummy.' He gives a little chuckle. 'I might have been young, but I remember her, my *nagymama*.'

'You and me, we live with her near five big years.'

'Do you miss her? I do.'

'Yes!' The forceful word fills the air, taking up more space than he thought possible for her.

'I don't want to upset you, but why didn't you ever leave here and try to find her?'

'What?'

Tripp wonders why she would not think he would ask this. Tripp was young when the three of them were torn apart, just a *fiu*, a boy, but even young children have memories. Why wouldn't he want to find his grandmother? Why haven't they spoken about this before? *Hulye*. Stupid.

'I couldn't. My... father.' A catch in her voice.

'Yes, my grandfather. What about him?'

'He was a cruel man.'

'You've told me that. But it shouldn't have stopped you from trying, for your mother's sake.'

Izzie can't seem to find a response. Perhaps it's hiding under her bedclothes? Cowering under her sheet and woollen blanket, she appears to be trying to vanish in a magic trick.

Tripp ignores her fumbling distraction. 'You said he thought you'd bring shame on your family if you didn't give me up, yet you still kept me. And I guess that was, well, very brave of you. But how did you hide me as a baby? How did you keep me safe?'

She pokes her head out. '*Anya*—your *nagymama*—and me, we good for keeping you a secret. But we wanted to shout it to the world about you, the beautiful boy so full of joy, *szeretet*.' She presses a hand over her heart. 'Tripp, the traveller. I name you that because I want you to travel the world. But if I know where you'd be going, to an evil man, travelling away from us... Even in your sleep clothes, you look important like a businessman, Tripp.' She turns to the wall. 'I am becoming *baba* and want to sleep now.'

'Wait! Not long after I arrived here, you said you were pleased my boss hadn't been a Hungarian friend of your father. What did you mean by that? And Mummy?'

'Yes?'

'Sit up and look at me,' Tripp growls, surprised by the rare anger in his voice.

Izzie moves to dangle her legs over the side of the bed, her feet hanging mid-air. Tripp sits up too, his long feet confidently flat against the floor.

'When you were in my tummy, I tell your *nagyapa*—'

'My grandfather.'

'Yes, yes. Bloody English.' She fusses about, straightening the sheets, trying to collect herself. 'I not married then, so he think I shame family. He sent me away to hospital to have you, give you away, but I not let that. My father went away for work at that time. He wanted me to give you to his friends, Hungarians.' She raises her voice, her hands curled into fists. 'But I could not, ever, because they may have been like him and hurt you like my father hurt me and my mother.'

'So, you finally discovered it was Robinson and not the friends of your father who took me. But why was I taken there to live with Robinson at his farm? I... I never understood.'

His mother appears deflated, sad. 'I think Robinson had bad friends to help him get workers. You know Bene and Luca, they are Italian.'

'Yes, but they came to work for Robinson as adults. I was only a boy.'

'I'm sorry. I don't know, Tripp.' She turns away, fluffs up her pillow.

He sharpens his piercing stare. Izzie's breathing is shallow, and when she turns back, he almost sees the pulse of her heartbeat under her nightie. Why does this talk terrify her?

He sighs. 'Well, I wish I could find out. And one day I would like to see every person who has ever stolen a child from its parents punished. I'm only pleased Robinson didn't have children of his own; society doesn't need his evil spreading.'

'What you mean?'

'I mean it is good that Robinson died. He was evil. If he had children, they could inherit his genes.'

'Trousers?'

Another time, Tripp would laugh, but not tonight. 'Genes are things that make a person like their parents, like being mean and cruel.'

'But you will never be mean and cruel, like your...' She swallows hard. 'Like Robinson, just because you live with him. Please always believe. I'm so sorry for what you went through, my good boy. I wish everything had been better for you.'

'What about my grandmother? We're together now. I could help you find her. Besides, I could use some time away from here.'

Silence.

'Mummy?'

'Alright, Tripp. I will not be afraid. Perhaps it will be good for you and *Anya*. Even myself. We will go look for *Anya*, your *nagymama*. But you will miss Fleur, no?'

He will, more than either she or Fleur will know.

Chapter Seventeen

Nerve-wracked yet pensive, mother and son grip the curved arms of their chairs as they sit opposite Grace and Charlie on the lounge room sofa. Sensing their hesitation to share with Charlie what they had previously discussed with her, Grace makes the first move.

'Charlie, we are all gathered here today—'

'To join this man and this woman.' He chuckles.

Grace drops her shoulders, relaxing a little. 'Be serious. Izzie and Tripp are excited about something.'

'They look about as excited as if we'd just given them the death penalty.'

'Hush, Charlie. Tripp, can you please take over?' Surely, he will be sensible.

Tripp makes eye contact with Charlie. 'Now Mum and I are back together, thanks to you and Grace, we've been talking about lost time. We both think we should find Izzie's mother, my grandmother.'

'I said I'd help them,' Grace interjects.

'Did you just? Well then, let me see.' Charlie studies the ceiling fan, his circling eyes lost in its rhythm. Finally, 'How do you propose to undertake this little adventure? I mean, do you even know where she lives?'

'I know I walked for two days and two nights before here,' says Izzie, leaning forward expectantly.

'And look what happened: a snake bit you,' says Charlie.

Izzie slumps back and wrings her hands. *Poor Izzie!*

'And knowing how long it took doesn't help much. Your old place could be in any direction.' Picking up on Izzie's frayed nerves, Charlie's face softens.

'I know the name of town in the bush where we lived.' Izzie brightens again.

Grace finds her smile. 'That's a great start. I can take you to the post office and look through the telephone books for an address.'

'Yes, that all sounds logical, I guess. But there could be problems.'

Grace wishes Charlie would crack. She can't stop jiggling her leg—taking on Charlie's nervous habit—in impatience and frustration.

'But, Izzie, could you pull off organising our girls to cook and clean around here while you're away? And Grace's cooking? Wouldn't trust it for *quids*.'

Grace elbows her husband. Izzie appears puzzled, her mouth forming the word quids over and over.

'Now, Tripp, spring will soon be on our doorstep along with hundreds of new lambs. You may think you're busy now, but just you wait. We'll need everyone on board when the births get underway. I'll especially need your help if anything goes wrong with the lambing in the night.'

'Yes, I realise that. It's why we want to get going soon before the start of the season. If you say no, we won't go, but if you can manage without us for a short time, I'll work for half pay for as long as you want when I return.'

'Don't talk like that. I won't be docking your pay. You've worked harder than any other farmhand around here. Except for old Gracie, naturally. Difference is, she does it all for love.'

'Don't know where you got that idea.' Grace smiles, warming to her husband again.

'Who could resist this face, eh?' Charlie frames it with his hands, grinning manically. His words and gestures are becoming so like those of Grace's father, which always causes her to miss him.

'Typical!' Grace shakes her head, chuckling. 'So, what do you say, darling? Show us all what *you* will do for love.'

'Enough drivel for now. Just promise you'll get back to us soon.'

Charlie looks almost reflective as he eyes the pair.

'Within a month, two at the most,' says Tripp, now smiling with relief.

'One month it is, then. We want you here for the births, mate! Now, how do you propose to get to this place in the middle of nowhere?'

Grace assesses her husband; he has grown in confidence lately and she approves. But now she feels the eyes of Izzie and Tripp turning to her for guidance. It's obvious they hadn't considered the logistics of the trip.

'Depends on the location. There are probably buses, but what do you think, Charlie?' Grace prods, passing the baton to him.

'Buses? Bullshit. You're a good driver, Tripp. Granted, I've only seen you work the property, but it's easier driving on roads than rough-as-buggery paddocks, and—'

'Fair enough. I know a safe driver, and I see one in you, Tripp. You can take the old Holden ute I bought after... after I lost the Dodge. I won't be needing it now Scott's offered to help me get new wheels.'

'You would really entrust me with your car?'

Certainly—more than that scoundrel, Scott, any day, thinks Grace. *What is this about a new car?*

'Drive it to your heart's content. I'd trust you behind the wheel over anyone else.'

Grace relaxes, exhaling lungs full of pent-up doubt.

'That old bomb, it's like me: it has age but it's reliable.' Charlie frames his face again, smiling at his wife like a funny flower in full bloom.

'Okay, righto, so where do we start?' Tripp leans forward in his chair, blows on his hands, and rubs them together, determined to get moving with the search. Grace has never seen him more confident. Where is her bravery?

She wonders what secrets mother and son will uncover. Will there be some they'll wish they hadn't disturbed? She will fight her fears and try to remain optimistic, for all their sakes. With a quick head shake for clarity, Grace pipes up. 'I'll show you.'

'Righto, bonza!' says Izzie, glints of expectation and mischief in her eyes. How could anyone not love her?

It surprises Grace that Izzie didn't say *fuck*, the little expressive word she's been practising lately that Grace hasn't had the heart to correct.

Chapter Eighteen

Izzie has prepared a favourite dinner of corned beef with mustard sauce and vegetables; the sweet aroma of caramelised onions makes Fleur's mouth water. The family has gathered at the table where they sit impatiently awaiting the meal, especially her father who follows Izzie's movements with keen eyes, his back ramrod straight. Everyone seems to be shooting one another sly glances, and Fleur acknowledges that she, too, is tense.

'And biggest one is for Mr Charlie. Big food for the man with the big heart.' Izzie presents him with a piled-high plate.

'Thanks, Izzie. How will we get by without you?'

Something sinks in Fleur. 'Whatever are you talking about?'

'I mean that, by the time Izzie and Tripp return to us, we will all be skinny, like POWs.'

'Oh, good grief, Charlie, don't exaggerate,' says her mother. 'You know we'll all manage perfectly without them, even though they are our star workers. And don't you ever speak about the horrors of war, things you're ignorant about—especially with Izzie here who has in fact been through it! You were never a prisoner of war, and you escaped serving in either world wars. We haven't even told the girls yet.' She turns to her daughters. 'Sorry, darlings, this has all happened so quickly. Izzie and Tripp are going away to—'

'I asked Dad the question,' hisses Fleur. *Bloody ignorant.* 'Where? For how long?' Fleur keeps her voice controlled. She glares at Tripp who eyes his food as though filling his stomach was the only thing to worry about. Why hasn't he told her about this?

'They're going on a journey,' says Grace.

'Right. Where and for how long? Why do you both ignore my specific questions?' Fleur screeches. Her fork chinks as it hits the plate while she shoots her mother an accusing look.

'Don't fret,' soothes Charlie. 'They'll be leaving within the week and be back before you know it, in a month or so.'

'I'm not fretting, not fretting...' says Fleur, her breath catching as she inhales, exhales. She bunches the material of her dress over her decolletage. She wishes she could burn this night away.

'Fleur.' Her mother's soft voice, her caring look.

'I'll tell you what, Tripp,' says her father. 'The workers aren't too keen on you going. I mean, they can cope—they always do—but...'

Tripp makes swirly artwork of his potato and peas. 'Thought they'd think otherwise,' he murmurs, shuffling in his seat.

'True, they might get some peace at last.' Fleur now glares at him, but the vegetable artist is absorbed in his creation.

'Fleur! What an insensitive comment!' Grace chastises. 'Neither polite nor generous.'

'It's okay, Grace.' Tripp's face darkens.

Fleur wonders if her mother was aware of Tripp's harsh dealings with the workers, would she change her tune?

Charlie squirms and blushes, joining his wife to cast Fleur furious looks. 'Tripp is a wonderful worker. Those boys out there think the world of him. They told me.'

Although Fleur sits in shock, she is heartened by her father's words. Did she get that conversation in the shearing shed all wrong?

'Said they fear they might have caused him to want to leave. I spent ages getting them to understand the journey has nothing to do with them and Tripp will return before they know it. Strange, eh? Some foreign thing, I expect. No offence to Tripp or Izzie.'

Grace says, 'No offence? They are offended, and it's not only about that word *foreign!* You can speak *to* them, Charlie, rather than *about* them. They're right here, see.' She extends her arm towards the pair.

'Where are they going?' Erin asks Grace.

'To search for Izzie's mother.'

'And that was my earlier question as well!' exclaims Fleur, her eyes to the ceiling hoping gravity will defy her building tears. She sneaks Tripp a furtive glance. Finally, he returns a look that appears pleading, placating.

A knock. The door opens to Scott before anyone can rise. *Now this!* The family falls silent. Scott flattens his hair, guided by the wall mirror. Turning to see the reality of the group gathered at the table, he gives a wide-eyed double-take.

'Ah, this is cosy. Sorry to disturb. I didn't realise you'd still be eating dinner... all of you.' He inspects each person with the compassion of an army general with a toothache. Laughing now, he plants a kiss on Erin's cheek who indulges him with a quick smile.

'Quite alright. Come in, come on in, mate. Grab a seat. Didn't expect you. Izzie, this fine specimen of manhood looks hungry,' says Charlie, flushing as he rises like a Jack-in-the-box Fleur wishes she could close the lid on.

'Oh, my God,' Fleur mumbles into her serviette. *Not him, not now.*

'Sit back down,' mutters Grace. Her father complies, having once again been embarrassed by his wife, yet Fleur wishes she could have said it.

'Yes, Charlie. Can do. Bonza,' says Izzie, ever the peacemaker. She rises, heaps food onto a plate and sets it in front of Scott before returning to her chair.

'We're glad you're here.' Her father beams. He wipes sauce from his chin with his serviette, another stain for Izzie to try to remove.

'Again,' says Fleur as her sister shoots her a look.

'He *is* part of our family, Fleur,' Erin retorts as Fleur presents her sister with an indulgent smile. *Does she know she's just spoken for Scott? Hah!*

'We were just talking about these two.' Charlie indicates Izzie and Tripp to Scott. 'Do you want to tell him?'

'Not really,' says Tripp. Izzie joins her son to turn away.

Charlie says, 'They'll shortly be leaving us for a few weeks to search for Izzie's mother. Frankly, the men worry about the excess work that will be caused by Tripp's absence.'

'Oh really?' Scott's eyes widen. 'Well, I'm always at your service. I didn't even know they were going.'

'We only just found out about it ourselves,' says Fleur, eyes to the ceiling. Scott beams at her which makes her respond with a blank stare, then a palm to her open mouth in a mock yawn for his boring presence.

'You know I'm more than happy to put in extra work while Tripp's away, mate,' Scott says to Charlie. 'It'll be as though he never left.'

Now it's Scott's turn to speak about people in their presence as he cements the fact he is threatened by Tripp.

'But what about your mechanical work at your parents' house, Scott?' asks Grace.

'No worries. I am working on a long job with a car, but it's a side job.' His eyes focus on Charlie.

'Now see, everyone, that's what I mean when I say this boy's a genius. He can do two jobs at once.' Fleur's father fawns as Erin beams approval.

'Three, as a matter of fact. That other job I asked you about completing, it would be the perfect time to get cracking with it.' He winks at Charlie. *Winks!* 'I'm quite capable, you understand, Sir.'

'Yes, you would be. Well, it's up to you. I'm here for advice and help if you need it. You'll be mighty busy, that's for sure. I'll get Marco and the lads working overtime on farm matters. We'll get some wigging and crutching done while Tripp is away, filling the lag as productively as we can before the births start.'

Fleur feels her mother's gaze upon her, watching her daughter about to explode. 'I can't imagine Scott completing any job on a car safely. At least it's not ours. Look at—'

'Give the man some respect, Fleur. Scott is a mechanic and engineer. He's even going to build a house for Izzie and Tripp while they're away. That's the mark of a good man, one who does things generously, graciously. I mean, we could get a builder in, but that would cost money which we don't have much of anymore.' Charlie shovels food into his gob.

'Surely not!' blurts Scott before clearing his throat. 'I mean, I can do all the building.'

Whatever next? So, her father has finally admitted to Scott about their struggles. Fleur knows he won't be at all happy about this, which makes her very happy indeed. She wonders if he'll even marry Erin now. And what's this rubbish about building a house?

Everyone except Charlie has stopped eating. All mute, stupefied.

Tripp glances at Izzie who shrinks, her head coming to rest just above the tabletop. Inhaling deeply, Tripp faces Scott and says steadily, 'My mother and I will discuss our living arrangements with Charlie at another time, when we get back.'

Fleur senses Tripp's embarrassment, his shame. What a horrible way to learn of this.

'You mean to say that you, Scott, organised this with Dad before even discussing it with Izzie and Tripp?' says Fleur. 'I can't take this anymore.'

With Scott's eyes burning her flesh, she rises, scraping the chair across the floor, and stomps from the room to escape the stifling heat.

Fleur remains leaning against the hallway wall, waiting for Tripp, missing him before he even leaves the farm, practising the awful drill. She catches him on his way to his room.

'Why didn't you tell me you were going away? I had to sit there like a stupid person, pretending all was fine when it wasn't.'

'I'm really sorry. I wanted to tell you myself, but I hope you can understand why we are going.'

'Like I was saying, it wasn't fine until hearing from Mum and Dad in their ridiculous way that you and Izzie would be searching for your grandmother. I'm happy about it, Tripp, you're both doing the right thing. And, you know, she'll be delighted to see you both, she really will. She'll be excited about her family returning to her after so long, even if it's only for a visit.'

'You have no idea how much your support means. This is big for us, you know.' He looks a tad embarrassed. It is big—huge in fact—especially for Tripp who has never travelled far.

'What will finding your grandmother mean for you?'

'It's not really about me; it's more for my mother. It's like she has a piece missing.'

'You do too, Tripp. Someone needs to coax you back to your shiny best.' She tries to crinkle her nose at him in a cutesy way, but she fears it looks like a grimace.

He colours up before ruffling his hair. 'You may be right. But what of my grandfather? I've never even met the guy but from what my mother tells me, he's no good and could react violently. As a baby, I was meant to be adopted by his Hungarian friends while he was away working. My mother was against it from the start, fearing they must be bad if they were friends of his. So, she fled hospital to give birth to me, then returned to her mother where they both looked after me. I wasn't even five when someone stole me from my mother. Have I told you this?'

'Mostly. Well, I know some bloke on horseback took you from your mother to Robinson's, where he treated you like dirt. But I know no further details.'

'It wasn't just me; Robinson abused all his workers. I try to spare Mum the details, she feels bad enough about being separated from me for all those years.'

'I remember another part of our conversation. You told me you wanted to be a teacher some day? Is that really on the cards?'

Tripp eyes her eagerly. 'What do you think about it?'

'Does it really matter so much what I think?'

'I value your opinion, more than anyone else's, Fleur.'

'Even more than your mother's?'

'Well, on even par with my mother's.' Bright smile, merry eyes. 'I guess the answer is yes, I would still love to be a teacher. Although I'm unsure if dreams like that fit with people like me.'

Her carefree voice belies her pain. 'You can do anything.' *Not me.* The weight of her thoughts causes her to droop her head, eyes to the floor.

'Look at me, Fleur, and listen.'

She lifts her chin and shows him her bravest face.

'I know you don't like some of the confusing messages you've had regarding me. But please believe that there were reasons behind my actions and words. You need to consider what *you* want. Use the month I'm away to think about us. More importantly, I want you to stay safe and healthy. People do love you, Fleur. You just need to trust that things will improve.'

'Right. Sure. I'll try.' She sounds like a robot.

She will try to hold on while he is away, try to regain some trust. She wants to be strong and stoic, but she will have things to share with him! *Change the subject.*

'What was that about Scott building a house for you and Izzie? Don't let him do it, Tripp.'

'I'll tell you straight, my mother and I will never live in any structure built by that man.'

'No, you won't. Shouldn't you say something before you leave?'

'Probably. I don't know. We haven't even been asked about it. I only hope Scott doesn't really build the thing.'

'He's sneaky, he might do it while you're away.'

'True. But it doesn't mean we have to live in it. I'll try to catch him before we leave, although the thought of being anywhere near that leech leaves me cold.'

'Even if you try to stop him, he probably won't listen. It's all about impressing my father. If Scott does build it, I hope it near kills him. I hope the whole bloody thing collapses.'

'With no-one inside, of course.'

'I wouldn't go that far.'

As Fleur flashes Tripp a sly smile, he winces a little, causing her to shrink in guilt for her sick humour. It's only a joke, isn't it?

Chapter Nineteen

Grace's mind won't settle, leaving her body in sleepless limbo. She keeps recalling Scott during the last part of the evening's dinner: his eyes alert, mouth open in a half-smile, his rubicund face inflamed, as Fleur left the table. He watched her legs as she tugged down her short skirt which had ridden up while she was sitting. Fleur glowering at Scott because he had ogled her. Tripp seeing all this too. But granted, the sight of Fleur's bare thighs was difficult for anyone at the table not to notice.

'I hope I haven't offended anyone,' said Scott to the rest of the group after Fleur had gone.

Charlie was quick to reply. 'Don't be ridiculous, son. She's just been going through a bit of a hard time, that's all, since losing her brother. And if anyone has overstepped the mark, that would be me.'

Grace still hears his silly comments about the war, blurting out about the house Scott intends to build.

When Tripp excused himself from the table he appeared to Grace as ghostly as *beyond*.

And now there is nothing subtle about the way her husband is squirming about in their double bed, turning his pillow, thumping his big body from side to side, followed by a 'bugger', loud cough, heavy sigh. Such a rigmarole! His wayward cry for attention. Between his latest *bugger* and cough, she pounces.

'Want to talk or are you going to keep this up all night?' Grace's words drip with fatigue and impatience. She should be angry: her husband's lack of decorum, the bloody Scott house.

Charlie coughs. 'Don't think it will do much good, but rightio.' His wide-awake voice proves he is obviously relieved for her invitation. On cue comes his heavy sigh. 'Guess I'm just a bit worried about Tripp leaving us. I know it sounds selfish but he's worth his weight in gold around here.'

'True, but you managed perfectly well for years without him.'

'I was also young and fit then.'

Charlie turns his pillow, rolls towards his wife. 'At least Scott will be with us. Good on him for offering to spend time working hard here before the marriage.'

Grace stiffens. The sight of Scott practically leering over Fleur has had her ropeable since dinner. That, and Fleur's car comment. She could think of more upsets.

'Do you realise that Scott didn't even ask permission for our daughter's hand in marriage? That hurts. Have times changed so much that this lack of respect is now commonplace? Does it worry you too, or are you too blindsided by the Harris family?'

'Times have changed, love.'

'I still have my concerns about that fellow, Charlie.'

'He's just become engaged to our daughter!'

'I can't help it. All my reasoning tells me Scott and his family are bad seeds.'

'So, the whole Harris mob now? You just cast your—'

'Aspersions. Okay, fair enough. Not Dukie. He seems like a decent man.' *Although he is a bit of a wimp.*

'He is a good man, and a bloody loyal friend of mine. I know you and Carmen don't see eye to eye, but you haven't exactly gone overboard to welcome her into our family. And as for Scott...'

'Carmen is priggish. I know Scott seems to be doing all the right things.'

'Seems to be? He plans to build Tripp and Izzie a new house, and while they're away would be the perfect time. He'll chop all the wood himself! He's done university studies in structural engineering, so he knows what he's doing.'

'Yes, I've heard. It would have been nice if everyone had been told of this before dinner.' She is not impressed about Scott having studied towards some probably incomplete degree she imagines was paid for by his father.

'I'm sorry about that. It was all getting a bit rowdy. Honestly, I hadn't even decided if I'd give him the go ahead about building the house.'

'So, Scott just assumed you agreed and will build the thing irrespective of what everyone wants? What of Izzie and Tripp? They may even think we want them gone from our home, which is certainly not true for me. As if they'd want this! Imagine how they must feel now, just before they set out on the trip, on their huge leap of faith. Like charity cases, probably.'

Grace feels like a charity case herself, embarrassed about Charlie having disclosed their family's money woes over dinner.

'I don't want them to go either. But, rationally, moving out may not be such a bad thing. They can finally get some space for themselves.'

'I know there's nothing rational about how Scott works.' Stewing, she adds, 'It sounds like Scott wants to get Tripp out of the house and away from the family.'

'And what benefit would that be for him? If Scott is so paranoid about Tripp getting too close to us or whatever, he could easily just have it out with him. They're simply sparring partners keen to impress, each trying to get one up on the other. Of course, there's a little unavoidable jealousy and rivalry. Scott says he's building the house because of all the pain Tripp and Izzie have endured over the years. I think it's mighty good of him. Besides, it's a bloody big backbreaking job for Scott to take on with no reward except feeling good for lending a helping hand.'

'Goodwill? I hope that's all it is, I really do.'

Grace searches Charlie's face, but she knows she won't find anything accusatory in his stance on his future son-in-law.

'Love, I'm also worried about what Fleur hinted at during dinner. Perhaps Scott really did do something to your ute. I warned you back then and it's still on my mind.'

'So now you're saying he's an attempted murderer? You saw the way old bastard Robinson took off in it that day.'

'And it could have been you.'

Lying on his back now, Charlie gives a flabbergasted slow head shake, enough to flatten his pillow, turn it over, turn away from her, say 'bugger', cough, then give an extraordinarily drawn-out sigh. 'You know, Grace, sometimes I wonder if anyone would be good enough for your beloved Erin.'

She pokes his back. 'Look at me, please.' He rolls over, head inclined towards her. 'That's unfair and you know it is. Don't you turn this around. I keep wondering what the police would find if they ever managed to get that car out—'

'Stop being paranoid. You know the cops did what they could to investigate it. Isn't the fact that we are rid of the old mongrel enough for you? Put it to bed.'

'Paranoid? I'd call it rightly questioning unfinished business. The authorities haven't effectively put it to bed. It's difficult for me, and I wish it were a little less easy for you to simply discount all the red flags.'

'I hate to say it, Grace, but in terms of Scott I think your powers of deduction are fading fast.'

Does Charlie recognise her fading power of *beyond* too?

'I hope you're right about Scott, I really do,' says Grace. 'At least you call my powers deductive, what's left of them.' Even saying it hurts. 'I've always thought of them as intuitive, somehow psychic. I can't even be angry about your criticism, because just lately, despite flying with Teddy, the fire in the oven thing, and the rainbow, I've felt that my time with my 'gift' is coming to an end. I'm just getting old, and it's time for me to let it go—if it will let go of me, that is.' *Fleur has it now. What will that mean for the poor girl?*

'You'll get no argument from me, Gracie. Life without surprises, I can't wait. But can you just manage to give Scott a chance, for me? He's trying so hard to do everything right by us, by Tripp and Izzie, by Erin. He comes from a good family. What more could you want? He's not Satan. Let's try to get some sleep, eh?'

'I will if you promise to stop your pre-sleep repertoire.' She coughs and sighs dramatically, raises an eyebrow at him.

'I will if you stop your accusations about Scott.'

'Don't discount my concerns, Charlie. You know I've been right in the past. I hope something isn't lying in wait ready to attack.'

'In terms of your intuition, if you opened your eyes, I think you'd catch it limping away into the distance like a dying animal. You're way off with this one.'

His words stab at her heart. 'We'll see. Goodnight, husband.' Her jolly words reveal nothing of the determination she has to set Charlie straight about Scott.

'Right. Goodnight, wife.'

She did not even get to apologise to him for being snappy at dinner, which had been her intention, but now she certainly does not want to.

Scott. Satan. *Satan*.

She is back in church, years ago, staring at an uncontrollable child with penetrative eyes, running ragged around the pews like something possessed.

Months ago, on the family's worst day ever, she saw him again. Defying her wishes, until now only the catastrophic, dark events of that day have remained as surprisingly intact memories. Was seeing Scott a less painful part of that fateful day when Teddy died? She is not sure. It certainly shocked her at the time. Perhaps the girls have developed some form of amnesia and blocked the day's entire events. Because otherwise how could they not recognise the young man who in different ways made such an impression on them in church? Especially Erin—she's now engaged to him, for goodness' sake! Neither Erin nor Fleur has since mentioned the church episode. Such must be the spell he casts over his prey.

Grace sees it clearly: the eerie illuminated visage of a teenage altar boy—around the same age as her daughters—with incandescent red candle horns sprouting from his head. Eyes ablaze like the devil himself. In her motherly knowhow, Grace could see that Scott's effect on herself and her daughters in church was instantaneous. She remembers avidly distracting the girls with the sternest looks she could muster, tearing them away because she thought either the eerie vision or its embodiment would affect them badly. But the girls were all blushes and giggles, so obviously his effect upon them was more intoxicating than shocking; they hadn't seen Scott cloaked in evil as Grace had.

Lit up like Lucifer in a house of the holy. A warning. If she had trusted her instincts—the brevity of her gut feeling, of *beyond*—there is no way Erin would be engaged to him now. She may be losing *beyond*'s power, but she has not lost her memory, nor the ability to put pieces together. She hopes Fleur will use her power to help as needed, to do the right thing, whatever that means.

How could Grace have blocked the connection she formed that day: boy and Lucifer? But will this change anything, make any difference at all? Perhaps the connection has been in her subconscious all along, leaving no room for anything but for Grace to hate Scott. Surely her fears about Scott cannot be unfounded or just plain mean. She saw him as a bad omen that day. Now—she concedes—how could he prove himself to be otherwise? Grace will try to be charitable and open-minded, but with that man it is so damn hard.

Now she is losing *beyond*, can she really trust what she is doing or thinking anymore? Then again, could Grace trust herself before? There may be hope for Fleur. *Beyond* could give her the strength and clarity of thought Grace so sorely lacks.

She and her younger daughter both need help. And healing.

Chapter Twenty

Grace sits in the back loungeroom listening to her regular radio serial, *Blue Hills*, while Charlie and Scott share an afternoon beer at the kitchen table. She overhears Scott persuading Charlie to buy another car, reminding him he has been without a reliable vehicle since the Robinson incident. Before long, Charlie takes Scott's advice for a car search tomorrow. Charlie promises Scott that he will buy him a beer or three at the pub tomorrow night. They move rooms to hover about where Grace is sitting.

She will need to keep an eye on this purchase. 'I heard what you were talking about. I'm sure you won't mind if I come along too?' Grace flashes the men her prettiest smile, which doesn't seem to work on Scott, who appears alarmed. She furrows her brow at Charlie. Like it or not, she is coming.

'Of course, love,' he says.

The next morning, they collect Scott from the Harris property. Charlie promises Dukie a viewing of the new purchase when they return his son later in the day.

At the new car dealership in Pig Peak, Scott's smooth talk helps secure Charlie a great deal for a slightly used race-car red 1968 Holden Monaro. Scott checks every nook and cranny before agreeing for his future father-in-law to sign off on the purchase. Grace is riled about Scott taking charge yet is pleased for Charlie.

Scott climbs into the back seat of the shiny V8. As the trio get driving, he sits forward and admires the rig's instrument panel.

Grace notices his hand stroking the backing of the leather seats, before getting serious.

'I would hate the thought of my family being in a car accident,' Scott says. 'I have no idea how the brakes on your Dodge ute failed, having given it such a thorough check-over. But you never told me how the whole scenario came about, Charlie. I can't imagine you would have been pleased about that terrible Len Robinson driving your car?'

Charlie casts Scott a measured look. Grace is relieved that Scott's questioning has been met with stony silence. The look her husband now gives her is hard to interpret, but it's certainly a little offensive.

He averts his head towards Scott. 'I'll take you to the pub tomorrow night, mate. We can have a good yarn then.'

Grace sucks in a sharp breath, dreading Charlie might not keep quiet about Izzie's nor Tripp's backgrounds, especially after a few beers.

High on the new purchase, as the shiny red Monaro rumbles along the Harris driveway, Charlie says he feels he could line this beast up on the start line of the upcoming great Hardie-Ferodo 500 car race in Bathurst. He gives it a revving—looking out for Dukie expectantly—before turning the engine off. When Dukie doesn't arrive, Scott slides out of the car and invites Grace and Charlie inside.

They enter through the grand glass doorway. As Scott paces the downstairs rooms, calling for his father with restraint, the Altons twiddle thumbs, admiring the soft green glass of the Lalique ceiling lamp.

'Duke!' Carmen's voice bellows from the floor above. Footsteps cause them to look towards the coiling staircase, but she does not appear.

'Scott should worry about his own car,' they hear her say. 'You can bloody well tell him, Duke. When that manager fellow, Potter, coerced Scott to bring me home from the pub the other night—how humiliating, they must've been wanting to close early—I told Scott to enjoy the Jag while it lasts, and all he did was laugh it off. So, I laughed along too with the nerves because we were hitting potholes. He said my smile was exquisite. Loves his mummy, he does. Anyhow, then he started on my ciggies, blowing high smoke rings like old Puffing Billy. And as for Grace Alton, she, she and that daughter of hers refuse to even see me about organising things. Me! Well, if that's the way she wants to play it, I'll let her. Reverse snobbery, that's what it is.'

Grace shudders and looks to Charlie who is studying the floor, fidgeting with his car keys.

They barely hear Dukie's response. 'You know Erin has said she wants it to be kept small.'

'Like her, yes,' Carmen scoffs, slurring a little, causing Grace's gut to twist. 'This wedding *will reflect us*. Are they going to pay for anything or remain as parsim... parsimonious as ever? Doesn't it matter what *I* want? Do you care what I want, Duke? Because right now I think you care more about your precious future outlaws than you do about your own family.'

Scott, too, is rooted to the spot, fists clenched, tongue darting out to occasionally lick his lips. Now he shakes his head, as though bringing himself back to the unfortunate moment. Fixing his eyes on the Alton couple, he extends an arm towards the door. 'It would be best...'

Yet they cannot find their feet, all three stand stock-still.

'For heaven's sake, Carmen,' growls Dukie, 'you know that's not true.'

'Well, prove it!' she screams. 'Tell those simple Altons that I'm going to plan the whole affair and have it here. I won't lower myself to beg for my only chance of a proper wedding. And it will be sumptuous, to mirror my status. They might be taking away my son, but, but they won't take that from me.'

'You know Erin's wishes, and having spoken with Scott, I can tell you that he also wants something restrained. And you're not being realistic, dear. You do understand... we're no longer able to... have anything big, don't you?' Scott's father's voice is low, breathless.

'I'll. Do. What. I. Damn. Well. Want.' Each of Carmen's words seems to elicit a tiny cry from Dukie. *Is he being poked?* He murmurs something else before a commotion: loud slaps, groans, the repetitive brush of two hands like self-congratulatory applause—

Silence.

Wide eyed with cheeks flushed—obviously mortified—Scott grabs his Jaguar keys and jacket from the hallstand and ushers the Altons out the front door. Grace and Charlie rush towards their car.

Gripping the passenger door handle and hearing voices, Grace turns back to see Carmen in the doorway, calmly straightening the felted wool shoulders of her son's jacket as he pushes her away. She is stunned at Carmen's appearance: she wears a dirty, tattered dress, her faded strawberry blonde hair showing inches of greasy ginger regrowth. What a sorry sight.

'Where the hell do you think you're going?' she demands of Scott, apparently oblivious to the former visitors in the driveway.

He brushes her hand away. 'Anywhere but here. Shaming me in front of my future parents. Pull yourself together.'

Grace keeps her eyes fixed on the action at the entryway. *Future parents. What has Scott endured over the years?*

Carmen holds her fist under Scott's chin. 'Don't be impudent.' I've just had your father to deal with. Pick us up some bottles of Scotch—the good kind—and a few cartons of Virginia Slims for me, honey? Don't you let me down, too!'

Scott pulls the door shut on her and rushes past Grace and Charlie to his vehicle, his breath catching.

'Remember: tomorrow night at the pub,' Charlie calls through the open car window. 'I'll pick you up at six. My shout.'

Scott's Jag speeds down the driveway. The shiny Monaro follows the dust cloud, while a white cockatoo flies overhead and releases a copious dollop of white mess onto the windscreen. Charlie hits the wipers which only smears it.

On the silent trip home, Grace doesn't know where to look.

She cannot see where they are heading.

Chapter Twenty-One

Grace takes Izzie and Tripp on a half-hour drive to Pig Peak's post office in Charlie's new purchase. Even though untrustworthy Scott helped him choose the car, Grace could not wait to get behind its steering wheel. She loves the roar of the car's V8 engine, and Charlie's buying it reassures her that they still have some hope financially.

She's pleased for today after fretting overnight on how or if to deal with the recent embarrassing encounter over at the Harrises. Grace has not dared ask Charlie if he and Scott somehow managed to bond at the pub last night. Also, she suspects her husband is hungover.

Grace makes random checks on Izzie in the rear-vision mirror, whose face suggests no apprehension or fear at the speed they are travelling, just sheer bliss. Sometimes she sticks her head out the window, the wind's assault on her black curls making her giggle.

'How are you doing, Izzie?' As if Grace doesn't know.

'Go faster, Grace!'

'*Anya!*' shouts Tripp, smiling, pretending to be thunderstruck.

In town, Grace parks the car outside the post office. They clamber out. A bell announces their entry. Tripp leans an elbow on the counter, bunging on the nonchalance. A man with incomplete facial features—like they've eroded away or never fully emerged—comes from a room out the back. White powder covers what there is of his face, catching on his eyelashes like the tiny scales that coat moth wings.

Izzie clams up at the ghost man, cowering directly behind Grace. Grace does a little sideways shuffle to test Izzie, and, like a shadow, she mimics her moves. Grace could have some fun with this, but now is not the time. Standing still, she wills that they get down to business.

'Good morning and welcome,' the man says lifelessly, insincerity oozing from his thin lips.

Grace takes a deep breath. 'Good morning. We have come here today'—*To join this man and this woman. No, stop*—'to locate a woman who I once knew.'

A gasp from behind her: Izzie knows Grace and her mother have never met. Too late to discuss now, she fixes Izzie with a work-with-me stare.

'May we search through your telephone books for her address?'

A loud whistle pierces the air. 'Kettle. Will youse excuse me while I make meself a tea?' He backs away, pointing to a shelf. 'Just find the book catering to the area where yer friend lives.'

'Thank…' Grace tracks the disappearing powder-puff. The whistle hisses before fading away to silence.

'Alright. Now, Izzie, tell me where you lived.' Grace hopes the man takes his time.

'My *anya* said Bounty Bay.'

Grace nods. 'I think it's south of here.'

In a flash, Tripp has located the correct book and thumps it onto the counter.

'Now, Izzie, your mother's last name.'

'Papp.' She spits it out like something nasty.

Tripp appears startled to hear the word on his mother's lips. *What is my surname, Mummy?*

Chills surge through Grace. *Has Tripp ever asked his mother this? What if he had his grandfather's surname? Papp? Tripp Papp. Tripp Trapp. Trap. Trapped.*

Izzie wipes away a tear.

'What was N*agyapa's* first name?' asks Tripp.

'Your grandfather is Marcel. Marcel Papp.' Izzie's words are stilted, they don't come easy. 'My *anya's* first name is Cora.'

Having flicked through many pages, Tripp wears a look of dismay. 'I can't find any Papps in Bounty Bay.'

'Are you sure you've looked carefully? Here, another pair of eyes.' Grace runs a slow finger down the page. 'You're right. Nothing.'

'Oh no, have they moved?' asks Izzie.

'Not necessarily. The books only list people with telephones. Is it possible your parents don't have a phone?' asks Grace.

'Okay, bonza.' Izzie flaps her hands. 'My father left us in a half-house for years. Why would he get a telephone?'

'Well then, I'm silly, aren't I? I should have asked that first. Can you remember the names of anyone who lived near you? Neighbours?'

'There was a little shop—the only shop—near our half-house. I knew the lady there: Mrs Rose Leighton.'

Without hesitation, Grace searches and locates what she is looking for. 'This could be her husband, I. Leighton. It's the only Leighton in the area.'

'What now?' asks Tripp.

'You could just turn up there, but it would be more polite to let her know you were coming. Will you call her, Izzie? We can help,' offers Grace. Is she game enough?

The diminutive woman blinks back. 'Why would we call her Izzie?'

Grace and Tripp exchange grins.

'No, no, that's not what I mean, silly moo cow. I mean it would be good if you rang her on the telephone.'

Izzie chews on her bottom lip. 'I'll do it, before I can't.' She takes an audible breath.

'Only if you are sure.'

Izzie appears far from sure, as does Tripp. Izzie pushes back her shoulders, grips the countertop staring straight ahead at the wall.

'Mummy? Are you alright?'

'I am good because I am not afraid of that thing anymore. Put her voice on the telephone, Tripp. I'll tell her we are coming to see Cora Papp.'

After instructions, Izzie does it herself then waits for a reply.

'Hello, Mrs Leighton?' And surely before the person on the line can respond, Izzie exclaims, 'We live on big sheep station in Pig Peak. We are coming. To see. She is C-c-Cora P-p-Papp. Oh fuck, sorry.'

Izzie throws the handset back down onto its base. It doesn't go on properly, the long beep, beep tone from the receiver telling them so. Her hands flap again, this time at invisible wasps. Someone, get rid of this strange thing!

Tripp snatches up the handset and with a decisive click places it correctly upon its cradle.

Izzie gives a weighted sigh. 'So sorry. I too nervous. Can we try again?'

Tripp opens his palms to Grace—who cannot stop her smile—in confusion, near supplication. 'No, Mummy. That may not be a good idea.'

'I fear she may not answer now, Izzie,' Grace says, patting her shoulder. 'Never mind, dear. Perhaps you and Tripp should just go there instead.'

From the service station they buy a road map and make plans to leave the Alton farm, in search of Cora Papp, within two days.

Chapter Twenty-Two

Departure day. Tripp could not bring himself to waylay Scott and ward him off building the house. He'd tried to stand his ground at the recent dinner, but it was difficult knowing the way Charlie admires Scott. Surely Charlie wouldn't push Izzie into another half-house? His mother doesn't deserve that mortification.

Equipped with the large map, Izabella and Tripp travel south. Even with having to negotiate unsealed sections of road, Tripp finds driving on open roads—rather than navigating through bumpy pastures—easy, even in an old wreck of a ute like Charlie's.

His mother's nerves are picking up. She prattles on, turns the map this way and that, often obstructing Tripp's driving view. He secretly wishes he had driven solo—the scenery would provide a relaxing distraction from his worrying thoughts about Fleur. Or would silence have exacerbated his fears? In any case, Izzie's fumbling and constant talking make the trip anything but relaxing, leaving him flabbergasted by the time they arrive at the town of Bounty Bay—a mere handful of houses, shops, a pub, and post office.

His mother says that, although changed, the street they drive down is familiar. As Tripp pulls up to parallel park, the irony of lines of grandiose palm trees planted along the main street of a poky town in drought rather than somewhere like Hawaii is not lost on him. Although geographically not far from the ocean, this drab town couldn't feel further from it.

Izzie says she recognises the little shop from her past but doesn't want to go in until she finds where she lived with her mother. Tripp understands the half-house would hold dark memories of frightening times with her father before Tripp was born. Best get it over with. Using the shop as a reference point, mother and son walk the few sad streets, Izzie counting every step she takes. Two scruffy boys on dragster bikes—the type he has seen used by Marco's youngest son, Paolo—ring bells on their high handlebars as they pass by yelling, 'Boo', making Izzie jump and grab onto her son's arm.

Becoming breathless, Izzie slows her pace; the journey is both physically and emotionally tiring for his mother. This is a mammoth task for Izzie, returning to the place where she fled her own mother in search of Tripp so many years ago, leaving Cora in what must have been agonising limbo for near fifteen years. And poor Izzie, she must fear her father could still inhabit the half-house she has often mentioned to Tripp in disparaging terms. Although Tripp has never met his grandfather, his mother has told him enough to know he is, or was, big trouble. Big trouble. A sudden shudder grips him at the possibility of soon meeting the man who brought his mother and grandmother such trauma and heartache.

A scattering of small cream-coloured weatherboard houses lines the street, as though unimaginative neighbours had shared paint. Izzie stops out front of a block of elevated land strewn with pieces of old timber, tin, shattered glass, and rubbish. The stiff sea breeze—unsuccessfully clearing the stink of something rotten—tangles her dark curls.

'I not understand.' Izzie swipes hair tendrils from her forehead. 'The half-house is gone.'

'Are you sure this is the right place?' Tripp raises his voice against the wind.

'For sure. One thousand, two-hundred-and-five steps from shop.'

'Could it be you were smaller, and your footsteps were shorter back then?'

'*Nem*, no way, of course not! I was woman with big legs when I left here in search of you, silly sausages.'

Tripp glances down at his mother's spindly, short, legs. 'Let's just go back to the shop and see if we can find Mrs Leighton. She should be able to give us some answers.'

'Bonza.' Izzie about-faces and stomps back towards the shop.

Is his mother pleased about the missing house? Her smile may just be a trick of the head-on breeze. She must want answers, but she would have deep trepidation too. Whatever her motives and intentions—if she has any—curiosity is giving her an apparent boost.

Surprisingly, Izzie enters first through the front door of the old red-brick building. In a corner cage a moulting blue budgerigar sits chewing the underside of its wing before flicking its head up with a squawk too loud for its little body. As silence settles, Izzie reverts to her uncertain state and turns to high tail it out the door.

'Can I help you?' an elderly woman calls, striding in from out the back, her hair wrapped in rollers. Tripp cannot tell if she has been caught off-guard or wears this look proudly. The budgie turns its attention to its mirror.

Izzie spins around, face ashen, Tripp noticing that nerves have indeed claimed his mother.

'Hello, Mmm, Mrs Llleighton,' stutters Izzie.

'How do you know my... Hold on, are you the woman who rang about Cora Papp?' Her blue eyes—naturally bulgy—have attained further roundness due to one tight roller pulling hair savagely back from her forehead. They could be on stalks.

'Yes. Izzie is my name, sometimes Izabella. Cora my mother.'

'Izzie, child, of course it's you! I used to call you by both names too, remember? It's been so long. I'm awfully sorry.' With eyes now fit to detach, she lifts open the countertop, rushes over, and gives Izzie a hug.

Wriggling out of the woman's tight grasp, Izzie redirects attention, saying, 'I'm alright, really. See, here is my big handsome son, Tripp!'

'Yes, hello Tripp. You've come here about your grandparents? But haven't you heard?' The woman seems concerned. 'About the fire.'

'Fire?' His mother's tiny voice. She steadies herself against the counter.

Tripp produces words he suspects his mother cannot. 'Is that what happened? The house my mother says she lived in is no longer there.'

'Yes, the building was gutted.'

'What happened to my grandparents?'

'*Anyam es apama,*' Izzie whispers.

'Izzie, your mother and I were very close,' murmurs Mrs Leighton.

'Were? What do you mean?' asks Izzie.

'She used to confide in me her deepest secrets. I suspect she really had no-one else to turn to.'

Tripp's mother turns away, her worried face suggesting a great lump of guilt has seized her because she had deserted her mother.

'Izzie, she understood you had to go find your son after he was taken. Yes, I knew about Tripp here even though we'd never met. She loved you both dearly. What she couldn't cope with was the loss, not knowing where you both were.'

'For all these years, all I want to do was see her, to speak with her.' Izzie fixes Mrs Leighton with a direct stare.

'Don't worry. She understood why you hesitated in making contact.'

Tripp cocks his head. 'Was it to do with my grandfather? How much did Cora tell you?'

'Cora told me all about her husband's intentions after you were born.'

'His evil plan.' Izzie nods. 'So, you know he wanted me to give Tripp to his friends?'

'Yes, Cora told me... eventually, and I know that plan didn't succeed. And I also know that you, Izzie, secretly came back to Cora with your new baby when your father was away working. She said she couldn't tell anyone else outside the family that you'd been living there.'

'At half-house,' whispers Izzie.

'Why?' asks Tripp.

'Because of what she feared on his return,' says Mrs Leighton.

Izzie nods. 'Same as my fear.'

Tripp wants the truth articulated. 'Because my grandfather was violent?'

'I saw Cora's bruises, the injuries. Even before you two left her I saw them,' Mrs Leighton says steadily, eyeing them both. 'You, Izzie, would know all about that, wouldn't you, poor child?'

Izzie dabs her tears with a handkerchief. 'Tell me what happen when my father come from work to half-house and I not there.'

'Alright, if that's what you really want. Cora told me he became furious when he arrived home from working away. Marcel contacted his friends who had no explanation about why the deal hadn't transpired. And neither did Marcel, because Cora refused to talk about you both with him.'

'Don't call my son a deal! He's not part of some stupid game.'

Even in her most challenging moments, Tripp's mother's fighting spirit remains with her, having had years to harness it. His does too.

'I apologise, Izzie. Poor choice of words. Cora did eventually tell your father about Tripp being taken from you.'

'What was his reaction?' asks Tripp.

'I'm not comfortable telling you what he said.'

'Please, we've had enough of lying.'

'Alright. He said that for all he cared you could both rot in hell. I'm sorry.'

'His friends must have been really angry,' is all his mother comes out with, hard to read.

'And Cora bore the brunt of his anger, Izzie. For many years, I saw her almost every day. I witnessed her steady decline, especially after you left. I'm sorry to have to tell you this, but by the time of the fire, your mother was little more than skin and bone.'

'*Jezus*, what have I done?' cries Izzie.

'No, dear child, you have done nothing wrong, and you probably couldn't have helped anyway. The question for you to ask is: What did *she* do?'

'I don't understand.'

'Izzie, you need to know the truth. Your mother triggered the house catching on fire, and the blaze was fatal.'

Izzie turns to Tripp. 'What does that mean?'

'It means lives were lost,' he answers with sorrow, gently placing a hand on his mother's shoulder.

'True,' says the woman.

What next? 'What lives?' asks Izzie.

'One life. Your father cannot hurt anyone anymore, dear. He perished in the fire.'

'My father is dead? *Anya!* My mother! Is she locked up in cage?'

'No, no child. The police released your mother, my dearest friend Cora, on compassionate grounds.'

'But where is she?'

'When the police learnt Cora's story—and I helped show them the full picture—they came to understand the mental and physical torment that had led her to such an act. On the night of the fire, Marcel had left a cigar burning in an ash tray on his chair. Cora was nursing a deep cut to her head caused by him that night. As she brushed past him on her way to bed, she tipped the container over. Marcel grabbed her arm, but she fought him off and went to the bedroom. Cora said she thought he would pick up the cigar butt, yet he didn't. He was so drunk. She said she had not intended for your father to die; she was simply angry at him. When she saw the fire take hold, she tried but didn't have the strength to pull him outside. He just stood there amongst the flames waving his arms about and raving about losing the house. She ran out, suffering some burns herself.'

'Oh *Jezus*, the little person in the fire!' says Izzie.

Tripp stares at her, wondering what on earth she is talking about.

'I guess he wasn't very tall, that's correct.' Mrs Leighton wears her own quizzical expression.

'Where is my mother? I want to see her.'

'She got work counselling new Australians at the migrant centre you went to when you first arrived in the country. In Victoria.'

'In Wagtail?'

'Yes, Wagtail.'

'Is she trapped there?'

'No, I'm sure she isn't. She is helping people.'

Izzie had told Tripp that, with all the drama surrounding her since Wagtail, she had barely thought twice about the busy, confusing place that was her family's first introduction to Australia: the great southern land. Izzie hated life at the complex, but her mother loved it, befriending other Hungarian women, often meeting up with them for an afternoon tea chat. Together they compared stories of the war, their losses, small joys. Cora sometimes attended dances there, celebrating triumphs they hoped would come. Tripp doubts Marcel would have joined in.

'So far away,' muses Izzie. 'I remember we took a train from our Italian ship in Melbourne to Wagtail. When we moved from there to here in Bounty Bay; it took so long by bus on bad roads.'

'There are good roads now. Is that your ute outside?' asks Mrs Leighton with a look of wariness.

'Yes,' answers Tripp.

'At a pinch, you could do the drive in a day, but considering the state of that rig, I'd suggest drawing it out to two. You could still get a few hours in today, but you should leave now and be done by sunset because if the roos hit your car, you're goners. I know of a decent place to stay the night. Nothing flash, but they do top pies, beers if that takes your fancy. Sheila who owns it is a friend of mine.'

Tripp wonders if the hotel owner's name is Sheila, or if Mrs Leighton has simply used a slang term for woman.

'You must forgive me; I'm running away with myself. I've pictured this scenario so many times. I'm sure Cora would love to see you both, no matter where she is. I talk to her on the telephone sometimes. I can phone to tell her you are both coming. She'll be so excited!'

Tripp hopes the sheila woman is more stable than this woman's eyeballs. 'What do you think, Mum?'

'Let's get two of those pies, eh?'

'Beer for you too, Mum?'

Mrs Leighton wills Tripp on with a nod, as if to agree that Izzie needs a salubrious stiff drink.

'Yes, that might be good.' Izzie's smile is now so much fainter than the one the wind stamped on her earlier.

Tripp suspects his mother will indeed need alcohol with what they've just discovered. With what he needs to talk to her about.

Chapter Twenty-Three

They stayed overnight at the place Mrs Leighton recommended, discovering there was nothing much 'decent' about it. At first sighting of the decrepit building, Tripp wanted to run but it was too late in the day to continue driving safely. In the near darkness he couldn't help but laugh at the sign for The Midass Touch Hotel; neither the name, nor surely the establishment, could bring any traveller in their right mind good fortune. Not only was the spelling incorrect, but the red flashing light bulbs intended to form the letters had blown over the M, i, and d. When Tripp explained what the words now spelt—and meant—to his mother, she laughed until she cried, begging for a toilet. They met the owner whose name was, indeed, Sheila.

Izzie did have that beer, and a pie, downstairs in the bar—they both did—and she was very talkative by the time they went to bed in their hot, stuffy little room, which they thought unfair with cool air outside. Tripp decided not to broach any more sensitive topics; his mother had experienced more than enough surprises for one day. So, they settled in and watched hours of mindless television with Izzie prattling on in the background. By ten o'clock they were dog-tired, but the rock-hard beds didn't deliver a good night's sleep for either of them.

Around six in the morning a knock on the wall causes Tripp to open the door to no-one. He smells breakfast. Guided by his nose, he finds a surprising little door on the inside wall. Inside he discovers a tray of piping-hot bacon, eggs, sausages, toast, coffee, and little pots of condiments, just as he'd ordered on the paper that he'd left dangling on the doorknob before they went to sleep. He felt Izzie needed a treat after learning the terrible news of her parents yesterday. Seeing her relaxed and excited about the little pleasures resting on their beds before them is priceless.

At nine, they bundle up their meagre belongings and begin the drive to Wagtail. Although nearing winter, the temperature outside is pleasant. Inside the car, however—especially at first—it is stifling, necessitating that they buffer the hot leather seats with clothing. They are heading south-west now, and when they reach Wagtail, they will have crossed the Victorian border. Izzie hangs her head out her window to catch the breeze.

'*Anya*, can we talk about yesterday?' says Tripp. 'You never told me your last name had been Papp.'

'Oh, Tripp, Papp left with my old life.'

'Did you change your last name when you married?'

'What?' His mother retracts her head, suddenly highly interested in her shoes.

He pushes on. 'What is my father's name?'

A sneak-peak reveals his mother as ashen and vacuous as the clouds above them.

'Joe. Haven't I told you?'

'No, you haven't. I just know him as evil or bad or despicable. Nothing I would ever aspire to.'

'What is dispic—'

'Never mind. What is my last name, Mummy?'

'Papp.'

'But you married Joe, didn't you?'

'We had pretend wedding.'

He would drag his mother's voice—faint and feeble—screaming from her if he could.

'So, not a real wedding. I didn't know that.'

'Sorry, Son.'

'What is Joe's last name?

'What?' Izzie braces herself by gripping her hot car seat.

What is she hiding? 'What is his last name, his surname.'

'I, I don't know, Tripp.'

'Wow.' Tripp scratches his head. 'You sure didn't know much about him, did you?' He can't help his sarcasm. 'You know, whenever I brought up the topic of the name of my father or mother, or even my full name, with Robinson, he changed the subject. One time, just to shut me up I guess, he told me that my surname—my last name—was Tooheys. It was only when he left me with an empty beer bottle and I read its label, that I realised he'd lied. The bastard.'

'I not understand, but please stop now, Tripp. I am tired already and want to think of my mother. What will we say to her? What she say to us? I'm so nervous.'

'Well, if she's your mother, I probably won't get any more from her than I have from you, will I?'

Izzie fixes him with a look that seems remorseful; Tripp repays it by casting her an angry one. So much of his life doesn't make sense to him. So many gaps of years and people and events. He needs someone to break through the lies, because he doesn't have the information to even begin to do it himself. Even now, surrounded by people he loves, he knows some are not being honest about what they know. He doesn't believe their words. He knows he has trust issues. Only when people start being honest with him can he allow himself to relax in his skin.

Tripp remembers his mother telling him about the first time she and her parents came to Wagtail Migrant Centre. It was late 1948. They had arrived by train from a ship docked in Melbourne which they had boarded from an Italian port, having fled the siege in Budapest as displaced persons.

On the train that first day in Australia, as the countryside whooshed by in a clatter of depressing murky browns and greens with occasional splashes of yellows, Izzie wondered if all the continent was as dry and brittle as her first impressions suggested. Things did not improve: Izzie's first Australian home looked as tired and sick as many of the train passengers. She had been right about the sickness; some children later died of malnutrition at the centre.

But now as mother and son approach the entrance to Wagtail, despite the cloudy weather and the humidity, despite Izzie's—she swears near-fatal—nerves, she and Tripp are struck by the complex's now positive mood created by lush greenery. So many plants in different varieties, shapes and colours. A feast of vegetation, some of the plants Izzie says she remembers from Europe. Tripp wonders if the seeds were brought over in luggage, the owners determined to create a little piece of home in Australia. From what he has heard, if any people can grow plants, it is the Europeans.

Tripp has read that years ago there were precious few gardens here, just a series of washed-out grey buildings. Many buildings were required because of all the people-separating they did: pulled apart by nationality, women from men. With his grandmother living here now, his mother must surely experience some relief for Wagtail's greenery. What are the people like here today? Izzie tells Tripp that if anyone here is nasty to her mother, she hopes they are locked up far away from her. Tripp agrees.

'So nervous.' As Izzie grips her tummy, Tripp imagines her enduring butterflies must be near drowned by now. Tripp feels her eyes upon him as he sits straight-backed in the driver's seat, his posture belying his own unease.

'You are important driver, Tripp.'

'Thanks, Mummy.'

Pulling up to park, he realises that due to their exchange which left Tripp in a bad mood, they haven't spoken of how to approach the topic of Cora and Marcel.

As if reading her son's thoughts, '*Jezus*, Mary and Joseph, how can we speak about Marcel? And, Son, she may not understand our words. My English is now too much better than Hungarian. Can she speak English?'

'It's a bit late to think about that now, Mummy. Let's just go in. Don't worry.'

He takes her hand and rubs her thumb. He has forgiven her; he must, today. She seems to find his kindness painful because Tripp catches his mother wiping away a tear.

'Come on. Out we go,' he encourages.

Tripp opens Izzie's car door and helps her out. Together they walk towards a sign reading *Office* placed above a door to a small wooden building. They peek through a window as the door creaks open to a little woman who strides towards them. Tripp could be watching an older version of his mother; the woman even wears her black wavy hair in a bun just as Izzie does. This is indeed his grandmother.

'Izabella? Izzie? Tripp?' Cora's voice is thick with emotion, her movements suddenly neither fluid nor confident. 'Rose told me you were coming.'

Tripp speaks for his mother, 'She was helpful. We've thought of you often. We've been waiting for this opportunity.'

Izzie nods.

Cora says, 'So have I. You both are always in my thoughts, and now that you are really here, well...' She gives a self-conscious, 'Here you are!'

For what feels like many minutes, the three generations huddle amid sighs and copious tears.

In concert, they ask the same question, 'Are you well?' They respond with enthusiastic affirmations and nods.

'Tripp!' Cora stands back and looks him up and down. '*Magas es jokepu.*' At Tripp's puzzled expression, she says, 'You are tall and good looking.'

He flushes.

'*Anya?*' asks Izzie.

'*Igen.* Do you speak much English?'

'Yes! We speak plenty English, not much Hungarian now.'

'Ah, good, good. So do I. I cannot believe you found one another and are together!' Cora's arms cross at her breast, her little head sinking into its centre.

'Oh, Mummy, so much to tell you.' Izzie must be braver because her mother seems approachable.

'Come,' says Cora, 'sit with me.'

She leads them into the office where they sit around a table displaying a vase of golden wattle blossoms, their honey perfume filling the air. Some pollen seems to tickle his mother's nose; she gives it a wipe. On the walls are signs in English about care and safety accompanied by drawings of hands and water taps. Tripp knows the wording would wash over Izzie in a fog. It is very quiet.

'Where is everyone?' asks Tripp.

'When I saw you outside, I told my staff I needed time alone with you both. They understand.'

'Mummy, when Mrs Leighton say you were here, I not believe it. Will you go back to Budapest?'

Cora gives a hearty laugh as Izzie bites her bottom lip and looks down to her lap.

'No. Australia is my home now. Why would you say that?'

'I thought people stop here in Wagtail on way to other places.' His poor mother, her silly thoughts, her silly English.

'I see. Of course. What are your memories of this place, darling?'

'I made no friends. I wanted to be Australian, live like Australian, not with Europeans. I wonder if I was wrong.'

'Why do you say that?'

'Because some Australians here have hurt me. Not different or better.'

'People are the same the world over. If we'd become separated in Budapest during the siege, do you believe we would ever have met again?' says Cora.

'I don't know, Mummy. No, not in the war. But we were not separated there.'

'No. But we so easily could have been. We are alive today because we came here. But enough about our home country for now. Rose told me you both work on a grand sheep station!'

'Yes, we do,' Tripp and Izzie say together, their eyes meeting.

Izzie continues. 'We were apart for many years but have found each other again. We work with Altons who say we are like family to them.'

Now Cora's face has turned a flustery red. 'Well, I'm happy you've found a safe place.'

'What do you do here, *Nagymama?*'

'Ah, still speaking some Hungarian, Tripp?'

'Yes. And I read lots of English books, some literature. And I speak some Greek, too.' He gives Cora and Izzie a grin, knowing his grandmother was originally from Greece.

'How wonderful! I teach English. Wagtail could use you, Tripp, plus your language skills. Perhaps one day you might consider it? You'd be an asset here.'

'I would love that. Is that why you remain here: to teach English?'

'More, much more. I help people when they arrive here from Europe. I'm afraid there's still so much unrest over there. Right now, we are welcoming to Wagtail trauma-struck victims of the Sicily earthquakes which happened earlier this year. People are often in shock when they arrive here, and I try to help them deal with it. I also teach a little English to them, which they will need. You see, I reconnected with a friend I met here on our arrival years ago, and she invited me back to Wagtail. She said they could teach me better English and give me a job here after... what happened.'

His grandmother's hands tremble as she turns to peer out the window.

'We know about the fire, Grandma,' Tripp says, raising the topic because he fears his mother could not.

'Yes, Rose mentioned what she told you in Bounty Bay. I am so sorry. After all you've both lost, and now you learn this! I never wanted to take more from you, please believe me.'

'You haven't taken, you've given us freedom.' Izzie's words flow strong and free. 'My *apa* took from you, *Anya*. My father wanted to steal my baby. What kind of man does that?'

If Marcel had still been alive and living in Wagtail with Cora, somehow, Tripp and Izzie would have ensured it would not have been for much longer.

Awaiting an answer from Cora that does not come, mother and son sit fidgeting.

'Do you want something to eat and drink?' Cora eventually suggests.

The shake their heads.

'How about a walk outside, then? We are in drought here, but there is a chance it may even rain! It takes a lot of water and hard work for our gardens to look as lush as they do. We use bore water on them.'

'Rain? We haven't seen rain since...' Izzie halts. Tripp assumes she is recalling the freak storm that blew away the rain forever. Remembering Teddy. Thinking of Fleur missing Teddy. *Fleur.*

'How long can you stay? I've organised a nice room for you both. You'll have good food, and you may even get to know some people from Europe. You could help them, teach them about Australian farm life. Can you stay a few weeks, a month? Please, we have years to catch up on, my two little chickens.'

Little chickens? Tripp is practically twice her size. Izzie giggles. How can they refuse her?

As they saunter around the picturesque gardens—so welcoming, verdant, and lush—Tripp reflects on how much Fleur would love all these signs of life.

When night arrives, he telephones Charlie and tells him they will be staying in Wagtail for several weeks helping Cora and people new to Australia. Another month away from the farm. Being away from Fleur for longer will be the worst thing for Tripp. The best: they will spend precious time with their dear Cora.

Chapter Twenty-Four

August 1968

Fleur has moved herself and her possessions into Teddy's room, knowing there will be more chance of connecting with him there. Plus, she has had about as much as she can take of her sister, and the bedroom they have shared for far too long.

Erin will soon marry Scott—poor dumb thing. They will move to the blue workers' cottage—where Tripp and Izzie were planning to live before learning of the engagement—leaving the main house free of them both.

They are not the only ones changing scenery. Fleur's dad told her Tripp had phoned, saying he and Izzie plan to stay with his grandmother, Cora, in Wagtail—further away, and longer than first stated—helping orient new Australians to their new way of life. At least Fleur is now aware of where they are; knowing they are within a vague driving distance has not been enough information for her.

The fear that Scott may have fiddled with the ute Tripp is driving dissipates for Fleur with each passing day. Although Scott is jealous of Tripp, he would not risk his future marriage to Erin by doing something that stupid, again, would he? Paranoia remains Fleur's constant, unwanted, and—she hopes like hell—unreliable companion.

Missing Tripp and Izzie terribly, she wishes she could have tagged along. She would have been their *reliable* companion, kept them safe, warm, well fed. She understands the irony of her thoughts: she cannot even look after herself. But what a joy it would be to see them reunited with their beloved *nagymama*. If Fleur had her own driver's license—which one day she's determined to get—she would have driven some of the way. Wouldn't Tripp be impressed with her then!

Steering to logic, she reluctantly acknowledges that a little distance between herself and Tripp will do them both good. Too many mishaps, misunderstandings, too much trust broken. Only time away will put things in perspective, one way or another. *Stay positive.*

Today, Fleur is searching for a new, clearer perspective on something that involves Teddy. She has come down to the river this bright chilly morning to search for his little blue car once again. She feels intrepid, yet fragile as she scurries, trying to declutter her mind of Tripp.

Although the property is bone dry, in need of soaking rain, Fleur finds today's unblemished blue dome above her just right for a girl on a mission, and the sunshine keeps her pleasantly warm.

A thrumming of bees. Glossy fan-like fronds of cabbage tree palms spread high above Fleur's head. She's a dignified lady—now that's a rarity—shrouded in a shelter of umbrellas held aloft by her debonair protectors. Plants in hues of upcoming spring exude scent redolent of new beginnings. Gaudy rainbow lorikeets stumble drunk across the ground, having feasted on end-of-season, overripe mangoes that have dropped there. The invincible birds turn wattle branches into trapezes in a comic display of the sated. Their screeching! Fleur is relieved to be in a remote location. Who could ignore it?

She sits cross-legged in a comforting patch of midday sun on the riverbank. It is not perfect. The stink—caused by the river below oozing slimy detritus—gives her the willies, makes her almost gag. But today she can't be deterred by human frailties; today is for Teddy. If she can entice him, he will help get her what she needs, what he needs her to have.

'Teddy. Are you here?'

Is that a faint reply? A male eastern whipbird gives its *ee-whip* call. Sure enough, comes the call of the female: *chew-chew*. Not Teddy, but a welcome performance none-the-less. She adjusts the faded red hat on her head. Teddy's head was smaller than hers but somehow the hat has stayed put for the entire walk. She calls to him again. No response.

Despite her instincts, she breathes deeply and reverently to exorcise all that stench and renew the air. Unless she's just gotten used to it, her trick has worked. Satisfied with this new mood, with Tchaikovsky's 'Dance of the Sugar Plum Fairy' planted in her head, Fleur removes Teddy's mouth organ from her backpack, brings it to her lips and blows, trying to replicate the famous piece of work. A few pure notes emerge like something holy—better, at least, than Ethel the organist's pitiful attempts in church. Inhale. Exhale. With strenuous breaths, she rubs the instrument back and forth across her lips. A nervous look around suggests no-one heard. She giggles with her bold childishness, the volume of her mostly-out-of-tune performance. Collapsing onto the ground, spreadeagle to the sky, she is an open target for predatory birds. *Come get me, I dare you!* She wipes drool from her mouth then sits up picking clingy bits of dead grass stalks from her hair. Places the mouth organ by her side. The smell of toffee apples fills the air.

A gentle fissle. Faint tittering. She scans the area in expectation of the company she knows to have conjured, knows has always been here. The world suddenly awakens as Fleur, too, senses the assurance of something more than the usual native flora and fauna. Little gingerly-executed movements kiss the atmosphere as if to herald nobility. Fleur understands the instigators of this quiet commotion would never willingly disturb a thing here; they know that humans— being the master pillagers—do the bad business of impacting habitat in much more reckless ways than Nature would ever contemplate. Fleur watches on with intrigue as bushes spread their branches; small rocks tumble like marbles along the ground towards her; flowers unfurl tender petals; tall grasses open.

Oh look, the city is thriving!

And its inhabitants are moving. Little creatures—seen, or unseen yet sensed—untangle then stretch tiny limbs as they emerge from their posts to scamper or glide or fly towards a wide-eyed and welcoming Fleur. She appreciates their splendid quirkiness: an odd bulbous nose, flashes of tiny misshapen teeth. Gossamer-thin iridescent wings become a whir of crystal colours as dainty performers propel themselves skywards then catapult back down to earth to skim the ground, kicking up dust with feet that look like hands in prayer. Almost too special for this world, they flock to Fleur, form a semi-circle, and bow so low before her that their noses could be touching the ground. They like her music! She starts up again as they frolic around her. When she remembers what she is here to do, they leave in a flash.

Scrabbling around in her backpack, she removes and puts on her cardigan, sips water from her water bottle, then yanks out Teddy's kaleidoscope—the heavy-duty ammunition he will find impossible to resist.

She raises the object to her eye, scouts around like a sea captain on enemy watch. But her search is peaceful, for good reasons, on behalf of her best friend. As she adjusts the little tube, her vision is greeted by an assortment of intricate and ornate patterns, especially enhanced when aimed towards the sun. Extraordinary! It would be so easy for her to keep doing this all day, forget about what she is really hoping will appear.

Grace notices unease in her older—by minutes—daughter, who gazes absently out the loungeroom window. Normally, at this hour of the morning, Erin would be with Izzie in the kitchen, having collected just the right vegetables for dinner. With Izzie away, she appears lost, notably flat. Not necessarily because she is craving Izzie's company—Fleur has a closer relationship with Izzie—but Erin surely misses the order Izabella brings to the household. Preparing for the piano, Erin lifts the lid of the stool, takes out her sheet music, and sits down to play. She flexes her fingers before thumping her fists on the keys, dropping her head and sighing.

Grace moves to Erin and gently massages her shoulders, causing her to sit up to attention. And prickle.

'Can't you play later, dear? Come walk with me. The piano will still be here when we get back, and it's such a beautiful day. Those birds are beckoning us.'

The native birds twitter and squawk back as if rounding up the humans.

'They're two courting whipbirds trying to hear one another over the murderous squeals of the lorikeets,' says Erin.

'I hope they meet up.'

'Me too. Finding the right partner isn't always easy.' Erin's matter-of-fact tone.

'So, will you come?'

'May as well.'

Curiosity draws Grace outside to find them, even though neither she nor Erin knows what whipbirds look like. Grace has heard other strange, unsettling sounds this morning, like someone murdering a church organ, and she would like to find the instigator of that murder, too.

She hopes stretching her legs may also help dispel some of her fears about the Harrises. But she doubts it, having just discovered that Carmen abhors the Altons and is probably an abusive drunkard. What will the cost be to her daughter, having that woman as a mother-in-law? Erin would be crushed to hear what Carmen had said of them. Scott must be dying to get away from his mother. What has he been through? Grace feels a tiny pang of sympathy before hardening her thoughts. Can she convince herself that Scott is any better than Carmen?

'Mind if we walk down by the river?'

'Okay,' says Erin. 'I went there several weeks ago.'

'Did you, dear? I'm pleased.'

'Not saying I enjoyed it.'

'Okay.'

Grace fills a thermos with cold tap water, popping it into a string bag for the walk. They hold hands as they amble along, but Erin soon breaks contact.

'I'm trying not to blame the place on what happened there, Mum.'

'You are sensible, Erin, always have been.'

'Hmm, that's what Fleur calls me.'

'It's not such a bad thing, you know.' Getting no response, Grace asks, 'How is everything going with the cottage?'

'Fine. Adding some personal touches, brightening it up. Fleur moving into Teddy's room shows she couldn't wait to get rid of me.'

'I'm sure that's not it. She tells me she likes feeling connected with her brother in his room.'

'Something we never did.'

'You were still close with Teddy.'

'No, I mean Fleur.'

'It's not too late. You are twins. Not identical, but your bond is innate.'

'Innate, not always instinctive. Our relationship is tenuous.'

Fearing the truth of Erin's words, Grace tries steering the conversation from Fleur. 'I guess your dad and Scott had a good time at the pub the other night? Charlie was late coming to bed. Did Scott say anything about it?'

'He was excited. He said it was 'yielding'. When I pushed, he didn't elaborate. I had no idea what he meant, still don't.'

Grace's skin prickles. 'Oh well, probably just men's gossip.'

Erin laughs. 'They do, don't they?'

Grace has floated away. What has Charlie disclosed to Scott? 'What?'

'Gossip. Concentrate, Mum.'

Erin groans, kicking up dirt as they near the river. Naturally more homebody than outdoorsy, she is not enjoying this walk and Grace wonders if the feeling is exacerbated because of her mother's presence. Erin says her boots are pinching, and the stupid uneven ground is giving her grief. With those words she stumbles on a clump of dead grass, somehow avoiding a fall. Cursing, her complaint is answered by those darling little whipbirds rallying them again. Grace is pleased they haven't had to pass *that* tree—the one stained with Erin's sickness—to get to their destination. This thought gives Grace some fresh hope of things improving.

Erin removes her boots and holds them aloft: the silly, old-fashioned things look as though they once had callipers attached. Grace blushes, knowing she must buy her daughter a new pair.

Up ahead, something small and faded red glows in a little patch of sunlight shooting down through the prolific canopy of a large tree. Grace flinches. She had brought it to the house... It is Teddy's hat, it is moving, and someone is wearing it. *Fleur!*

Grace sees Erin break into a wide smile, give a muffled giggle, and duck behind a broad-trunked tree. Reactively, Grace joins her, the smelly old boots digging into her side. Merely catching Fleur outside in daylight hours now is enough of a shock. Grace cannot stop her keenness, and concern, about what her daughter is up to. Why is Fleur standing there with that tube up to her eye? When the sun catches it, there is no doubt it is Teddy's kaleidoscope.

Without warning, Fleur turns towards them. Immediately, they freeze, not knowing if they are on her radar. Grace's heart pounds so forcefully she fears Fleur can hear the boom reverberate outside of her body. Unrealistic, but Fleur's antics are certainly not ones she would want either her mother or sister to witness. For what seems like an eternity, Fleur keeps that kaleidoscope aimed at them, furiously twisting, and turning its end piece. Eventually she rotates her body, not letting go of that silly thing against her eye as though it is a divining rod promising gold. Or is she trying to relive her childhood? Why else would she be wearing her brother's dirty red hat, too small for her head? Grace glimpses Erin's shocked face: she would be thinking her sister shameless.

'There you are!' Fleur bellows.

Erin muffles a yelp as Grace's heart tap-dances.

'I knew you'd finally show it to me,' Fleur cries. 'Now lead me towards it. Come on, Teddy! I promise if you do, I'll put it where you want it. I won't even let Mum know about it, and you *know* I won't be telling *Erin*.'

Grace takes a sneak-peak at Erin, whose bottom lip wobbles as she casts her eyes to the ground.

'Oh, come *on*, I'll do whatever you want. I'll even dance for you. Maybe then you'll show me. But you won't want to watch me, will you? You always said I look stupid dancing, like a frog jumping. I wonder what Tripp would think of my moves. You'd like him. Anyway, it's up to you now.' She pauses. 'Okay, I'm going to dance. Promise I'll stop if you do what I want, but not until then.'

And off she goes. The sight of Fleur frolicking amphibian-like in her big boots, humming and whistling an unidentifiable ditty; the hat; the kaleidoscope locked in place like a strange artificial limb… Under other circumstances it could be funny because, well, what a sight. Unavoidably, tears track down Grace's cheeks. Her poor, pitiful daughter. Now this. Whatever will become of her family?

'Yes!' Wearing a feral look, holding her crazy burden to her eye, Fleur skims across the rough ground towards the river. Grace fears if a cliff were to manifest in her daughter's path, she would gleefully take flight over its edge even if cognisant of the danger.

As soon as Fleur is out of sight, Grace and Erin rush away—Erin's bare feet prompting no complaints from her. Grace's blood pounds in her ears to the beat of her own clodhopping run.

Chapter Twenty-Five

Having tired during their rush towards home, Grace and Erin now pant and stagger. Grace is pleased to have slowed; her chest and leg muscles are cramping.

At a distance they see Scott taking out his frustrations on a giant red river gum. Grace remembers a huge ironbark falling during the wild storm several months ago when life, too, took the worst fall. Whenever Scott lets loose his axe, Grace thinks of the adage 'a chip off the old block' and her thoughts once again turn to nasty Carmen.

Scott is having trouble. Another casualty of the recent storm, the timber is not dry enough. Green timber means problems with shrinking and cracking as it dries. It could do with more months of resting in heat before the build. But the weather is cold, and Scott has told Charlie that he has a deadline to get it near finished by the time Tripp and Izzie return from their journey of discovery. Grace wishes Scott was practical like her husband.

Scott stands tall, stretching his neck and rubbing his lower back. He bends forward and rocks the axe back and forth, trying to dislodge it from a log. Finally, it comes free. He catches his breath and gulps water from his thermos, wincing as he looks at his fingers and palms. The two women move towards him.

Without warning, Erin rushes over and grabs his arm. 'Oh, Scott, I'm so worried about Fleur. We saw her down by the river.'

'So?'

'Erin, you shouldn't—'

Erin shoots Grace an imploring look as Scott places his thermos on the ground.

'Well, you have my attention, ladies.' Scott nods at Grace.

'It's nothing, really. Her behaviour… I'm just… concerned,' says Erin.

'So, what was she doing?'

'Just forget it. She would be mortified if she knew we were watching her frolic about dancing with a toy by the river.'

'And Fleur would be mortified if she knew her sister was telling people about it!' Grace is flabbergasted.

She watches Scott suck on his top lip—as though trying to stifle a grin—as he studies Erin. 'Was it something to do with her brother?'

'Yes, and she was searching for something. She's not been the same since losing Teddy. It probably affected her most because the two of them were so close.'

'Can you talk to her, Erin? About Teddy.'

'Me? No, I don't think I can, Scott. She sees me as a rival. She already is je—' Does Erin want to say *jealous of me?*

'She's hurting,' says Scott. 'Who can she confide in? Grace?'

The thought of Scott assessing Fleur's emotional state leaves Grace cold and bitter. She feels his eyes on her.

'I don't know. I want her to. I'll try harder.'

Such pathetic words. How horrible that she is confirming cracks in their mother/daughter relationship to Scott! Another stabbing pain hits her chest.

'Perhaps Tripp will help her when he gets back? Although, they seem to have been bickering a bit lately,' says Erin.

'Bickering?' Scott arches his eyebrows. 'That's a shame. But I must confess I'm keeping an eye on that one. With the company Tripp has kept over the years, I'm not convinced he wasn't caught up in the abuse of workers at Robinson's.'

'What, Tripp?' Anger rises in Grace. 'Come on, Scott. He was victimised by that man. Tripp's as harmless as a puppy.'

'That's true, Scott,' says Erin.

'With particularly sharp teeth. Just an observation, but keep looking out for Fleur. I'd offer to help but somehow, even with my best intentions, I always cop a cold shoulder from her, as you know.'

'Well, that's just Fleur being Fleur.' Erin flushes red.

After a drink of water, Grace eases herself onto a tree stump—sighing with the relief of being seated yet still stewing in anger—while Erin remains standing with Scott.

As he swings the axe into another log, it once again gets stuck. He growls, twists it out, and stretches to full height.

Grace and Erin stare spellbound as a tall, tanned, blonde woman silently appears by his side.

'You know you're doing it wrong.'

Scott scowls at the woman; her remonstration apparently winning no prizes in his book.

'Well now, hello. Who, may I enquire, are you?' Scott's voice is affected, uppity.

'Apart from being cute?' She beams at him. Grace wishes this woman was wrong in her self-assessment.

'Well, now.' He lifts his burgundy fringe away from his river-deep emerald eyes, gracing her with a twitchy smile.

'I'm Cathy.'

'I'm Erin.' She places herself between the pair like a roadblock. 'And this is Scott—my fiancé—and that's my mother over there.'

'Oh. Pity. Well, I live next door, at the Robinson farm. Just me and my dog at present.'

'What the hell!' Scott balks. 'What are you doing in that place? Don't you—'

'Yes, I know of its history,' Cathy interjects. 'But dark and mysterious suits me.'

'Anyhow, why are you over here?' asks Scott.

'To introduce myself. Doing the done thing. So, can I show you the right way to chop?'

She doesn't wait for an answer. Positioning a large sturdy log lying on its side as a base, she balances a smaller log upright against it, then grabs the axe from Scott.

'Hey!' he warns.

Too late. With a whip-like crack, the axe splits the smaller log perfectly in half, coming straight out when done. Cathy places the tool on the ground, puts her hands on her hips and gives them a side-to-side wiggle.

Grace turns and laughs quietly towards the scenery.

'So, a show-off, too,' says Scott.

'I'll take your condiment.'

'I think you're looking for *compliment*.' Scott is all smiles.

'Will you give me one?'

'Well, I...'

'Whatever. Another thing, your timber's too green.' She shakes her head. 'I can teach you things, Scott. Anytime, just call on me.'

Scott blushes and turns away, looking like he wishes someone would save him from her before he crumbles to dust. Grace imagines he may turn to salt, like Lot's wife, because he hasn't stopped staring at Cathy. Does she talk in this provocative way with everyone she just meets?

As if reading minds, Cathy says, 'Sorry. I get nervous meeting new people and I've been told I'm a bit of a flirt. Tripp lives here too, eh?'

'What of it?' Scott is terse with the mention of his rival's name.

'Did he tell you I said to say hello to you?'

'No! How do you know him?'

'We've met briefly. Anyway, keep your shirt on. Are you always so grumpy?' Cathy opens her gummy mouth and flashes crooked teeth at him.

'Sorry, it's just, well, I'm building this house for him and his mother and, er, his name reminds me of my new blisters.' He gives a guarded chuckle.

'You asked to build it, Scott,' Grace says, throwing verbal darts, her patience tested.

'Huh.'

'You are a strange one.' Cathy eyes him, twisting a lock of shiny hair into a ringlet, before setting it free to fall gently like a feather on the breeze.

'Have to be strange to live around here. No offence.' Scott searches the blank faces of Grace and Erin. 'Anyhow, if you're looking for Tripp he's away for several more weeks.'

'I guess I'll just have to take you instead.'

Erin catches Grace's eye, both startled by Cathy's brashness and zero tact.

'You don't like him, do you?' says Cathy.

'Who?'

'Tripp.'

'What?' Scott wipes his brow, darting his confused look between Erin and Grace.

'Why don't you like him?'

'He worked for Robinson for many years. I advise people to be careful of him.' Scott on his high horse.

'Why would you say that?' Cathy avoids eye contact.

'Yes, Scott, Tripp has always shown himself to be trustworthy.' Grace is surprised by her schoolmarm voice.

'I know he appears honest. But, well, living with Robinson for so many years, the apple not falling far from the tree—that sort of thing.'

Cathy's voice catches. 'I, I think that's about children and parents, if it's true.'

'Oh, right. My mistake, then.' Scott widens his eyes, tapping the end of his nose with his finger.

Having set up the timber in Cathy's 'correct' way, he sinks his axe in, resulting in a clean split, as though he knew all along how to do it. He beams at the women, two of whom are nonplussed.

'Listen, now I've taught you how to chop wood you'll have to return the favour some time.'

'What? Teach you something?'

'Yeah, something, if you can, and if you're up to it. To be honest, Scott, I would love you to do some hard yakka around the house for me. Gardening and stuff. Mum's away up north for months visiting her brother, so it's only me and my little doggie at the property and I've never lived on acreage before. Can you help me? You'll be rewarded for all your efforts.'

'He's too busy here,' snaps Erin, drowning in quicksand.

Scott gives an apologetic, wide-eyed shrug. 'It's true, I am rather busy helping—'

Erin butts in, 'Yes, we're preparing for our wedding.'

'Oh, sure,' Cathy says. 'It's just that I'm all alone there and could really use some help. I was thinking of asking Tripp, but seeing he's away—'

'I might come over in my Jag.'

'Scott.' Erin's dying voice.

'Wow, you sure are flash.' Cathy's hips start up again, somehow reminding Grace of the bobble-headed toy dog Charlie has placed on the rear dash of the Monaro. Half an hour ago Grace had thought Fleur was the only dancer worth worrying about.

'I don't know about that.' Scott pushes out his chest, gives a sniff of the air as a dog would.

'I'll leave you to it, then.' Cathy's eyes take in the little group. 'Bye for now.'

Scott's foolish grin tracks Cathy as she disappears into the bush, like someone who knows where she's heading, like she could conquer the world.

Magic or plain evil, Grace cannot tell.

Chapter Twenty-Six

Every day, Grace sees Erin—sometimes Scott, rarely both—visit the little blue worker's cottage once occupied by another pair of newlyweds: herself and Charlie. Her daughter told Grace that Scott understood why Erin wanted to live there and was keen to keep up the family tradition.

Grace also suspects he cannot wait to get away from his mother. Despite Carmen's overt martyrdom and snobbery, she was—unbeknownst to Erin—even more disagreeable about the wedding. Terrible woman.

Scott also suggested to Erin that living at the Alton farm meant he would be some use to her father. Erin said she had simply laughed and reassured Scott that he is much more than *some use*. Even Grace must admit that when Scott isn't busy building the new—contentious—house, he helps with all sorts of jobs such as taking care of repairs to farm machinery damaged by rust, age, or both.

This evening, having been invited by Erin to check out the cottage preparations, Grace surveys the welcoming atmosphere with approval.

'You've done a lovely job here, darling.'

'Thanks, Mum.'

Grace sniffs the air and shivers. She tries to calm her voice. 'Is that smoke I can smell?'

'That's just Scott. He's taken up smoking. I can't abide the filthy habit and he doesn't dare do it around me. And yet the smoke still lingers.'

'I'm not too pleased about it either.'

Erin fusses about. 'You know, Mum, no matter how drained he is, every couple of days he picks flowers and arranges them here. Aren't they pretty?' She indicates a little crystal vase which seems to be blooming on the coffee table. 'We haven't even moved in yet!'

Today it's gerberas—surely the last of the season—their colour reminiscent of orange flummery. Grace fingers their soft petals, her mouth forming a smile; Nature always makes her smile.

'Scott says it's such a little thing to please me, that no-one needs to know, that it's just a thank you because I make him feel so lucky, a little reminder that he is always thinking of me fondly. He promises that one day he will give me everything I've always wanted, even if he has to dig for it!'

Erin frowns at Grace as though sensing her mother's unease. Is she so transparent?

'And what is it that you want, Erin?'

'Just to be happy, really.' She rearranges the flowers. 'And for you, Dad, and Fleur to be happy also.'

'Does that include Scott?'

'That goes without saying.' Erin's voice is flat. 'Listen, I want to tell you something. Scott confided in me that despite what some people may think, his parents never spoilt him. He says he has never felt as fulfilled as he does now—with us, helping Dad around the property. He supposes that's what has been missing: purpose. No-one ever really expected anything of him, and he's found that painful.'

Grace, too, had never imagined Scott's life to be painful. His parents are hard work, especially his mother, but judging by their lifestyle and houses—Grace hasn't seen the beach house but can imagine it's a gem—she could understand how people would assume Scott's life was charmed. Yet from what she heard the other night, maybe it is all unravelling. Sometimes her heart even hurts a little for what he must have gone through with his mother.

Scott bursts through the door, making both women jump. He balks a little upon seeing Grace, his usual reaction to surprise 'company'. Perhaps he has always needed to be guarded in life? His deep red

Niche

hair appears luminous under the ceiling light, like someone has built a campfire on his head. Grace imagines he would appreciate his dramatic appearance.

'Hello, darling.' He places a quick peck on Erin's forehead. 'Grace.' He gives her a perfunctory nod. 'Well, that's another twelve-hour day.'

'You'll wear yourself out if you keep working the way you do,' her daughter fawns, and Grace cannot help but think it may be for her benefit. 'You don't have to keep proving yourself here, Scott. Dad knows your worth—as a worker, as a fine man.' Erin gives his arm a quick rub.

'I try to believe that. Anyway, there's always something to be done on a farm and I'm not about to let down my future father-in-law, especially when we're short on workers.'

'Hmm, sounds like you could use some extra help. Perhaps after we're hitched, we could somehow conjure someone to assist you, in time, so long as you don't treat him as your slave.'

'A helper, eh?' Scott puckers his mouth.

'Seriously, how would you feel if I fell pregnant?'

'I'm not sure this is for my ears?' Grace summons *beyond*, willing her entire body to escape, to no avail.

'Well, children have always been on the plan, haven't they? Unsaid, but we both know it to be true. Your genes/my genes—they're sure to be geniuses, that's for sure.' Scott is audacious. He dares to wink at Grace, causing her to recoil.

'Don't know about your genes, though, Scott. I may have to think about it further.' Erin clicks her tongue at her mother.

Grace feels bilious. 'Well, I'll just...' *leave you to it? No.* 'see you both later.'

She closes the door on the couple and dallies—with some misgivings—at the cottage doorway, fearful where this conversation may lead, convincing herself she will know when to move.

'I'm waiting with bated breath,' she hears Scott say. 'Show me, Erin, how do you make a baby?'

'I said I needed to think about it, at least until the wedding!' Erin sounds adamant.

'But surely you've been thinking about it since you met me. Show your future husband some affection.'

Muffled noises.

'Come on, Erin.'

'I really want to, I'll try to... experience exciting new feelings. I'm sorry. I can't.'

Poor little Erin. And how much longer can Scott deny his urges? Ashamed, Grace hurriedly tiptoes back home.

The following morning, Marco, and two of his sons, Mario and Paolo, have taken a tractor to service the southern pastures, filling the feed troughs there. In the northern pastures, Charlie, Grace, Erin, and Marco's other son, Cappi, do the same task.

To the troughs, the four have added hay mixed with grain; corn, sorghum, and barley to supplement the grass; and forbs and clover, which usually grows freely on the pastures, but not in this drought. Skirting, swooping—unusually bold today—a pair of glossy black cockatoos make sly grabs at their new grainy banquet below. Their squawks sound the way Grace imagines pterodactyls did, and she loves their eerie calls.

With Grace sitting beside Charlie as he drives the tractor to the next paddock, Erin and Cappi sit side-by-side up back. When Erin drops down and struggles with opening the rusty gate, Cappi jumps down and obliges.

'Thanks for that,' says Erin when she's settled back into her uncomfortable seat.

'My pleasure to help a lady,' he says over the chug of the engine.

Ah, that rich voice. Hearing her daughter giggle, Grace imagines heat moving to Erin's face, creating dapples like red roses. She imagines her sensing some exciting new feelings due to Cappi's charming attention, imagines her smile emerging more sheepishly than the flocks surrounding them.

'Are you still speaking in Italian like I taught you?' Cappi asks Erin.

'I sure hope so.'

'*C'e il sole*.' Surprisingly, a little cohesion in Erin's words, coherent even, despite Grace having no idea of their meaning.

'Yes, it is sunny, you funny thing Erin. You have been practising!'

'*Mi sono persa*,' says Erin.

'*Lascia che ti aiuti*,' says Cappi, a trace of fervour in his voice.

'What?'

'You said you were lost, and I offered to help you.'

In one giant bellyflop, Grace's heart sinks into an abyss.

'Did I?' says Erin. 'That's strange. I knew the phrase but couldn't remember what it meant. Anyhow, I guess it's just something I can still remember.'

'I hope you never feel lost, *cara mia*.'

Grace leans back, eager to hear Erin's response.

'Um, you'll be the first to know if I do. Promise. DAD?' she shouts to the back of her father's head. 'How many more fields?'

Chapter Twenty-Seven

October 1968

Almost midway through spring, the births come in waves. Some weeks little happens, yet on others up to a hundred newborn lambs appear. Overseeing bottles for lambs that cannot or will not suckle from mothers that cannot or will not let them, is a huge job. Fleur adores these little creatures, so looking after them is one job she doesn't have to be cajoled into. Keeping them healthy is exhausting everyone's time and strength, to say nothing of the multitude of current births—something Fleur doesn't want to know about. The local vet, John Wills, helps Charlie when he can, although her father says he doesn't appreciate late callouts to the farm.

Charlie tells anyone who will listen that he is exhausted and wishes Tripp were back to take a bit more pressure off. He is, after all, her father's star worker, to the despair of Scott. Fleur loves such talk, especially when Scott is around to hear of his implied superficiality.

Late at night in the homestead, finding it difficult to sleep after college, Fleur watches television in the loungeroom. When her mother went to bed not long ago – tired, barely able to steer her arthritic legs to her room—Scott was reading a newspaper at the kitchen table.

A labouring ewe has been bleating up a stink all night. When Charlie left for the lambing jug earlier on, as well as the usual growl about the absent Tripp, he said he would call upon Scott if needed, knowing Grace is immobile and Erin has a tummy bug.

Fleur hears her father stagger through the kitchen door, breathing heavily. She hopes the poor ewe is alright, but Charlie returning home, leaving the animal to its horrible yelping, suggests otherwise. He must need help. Fearing the worst, she turns off the TV and joins Scott in the kitchen, his thick head rising from the table, his bleary eyes blinking to attention. The look on her worried father tells Fleur they must hasten.

'One ewe is presenting as breech—a true breech.'

'Breech or true breech, I'm coming,' says Scott, and Fleur imagines he has no idea of what a 'true breech' is. But Fleur does. It is when the lamb is birthed facing backwards, and she has seen the condition before when she used to help her father.

'I want you to come out with us too, Fleur,' says Charlie. 'It's not looking good, and I may need your help.'

'But Dad—'

'Now, don't go complaining, it might just be to phone old Wills. Bugger his sleep; we've lost one too many beasts in the night.'

Terror races through Fleur. She wants to tell her father she will be of no use because it's all too much for her now, all too raw: the blood, the ewe's tormented expression, the cries. And she cringes about revolting Scott being near her during such an intimate and invasive procedure. Yet she steels herself, because if this lamb were to die due to her failings, the guilt would be all-consuming. Fleur and Scott yank on their work boots and they follow close behind Charlie as he hurries to one of the farm's lambing jugs.

Inside the bleak building, strong cold winds create eerie whistles through small holes in the corrugated iron walls. Other harrowing noises come from the ewe. As they approach, Fleur studies her, recognising signs of exhaustion and distress: lying down, panting, throwing her head around as though fitting.

Fleur's father says, 'She's tired, having laboured such a long time. She's straining now.'

'Oh, poor darling.' Fleur sits on the ground stroking the ewe's head, calming her.

'Flossie.' Her father nods as something deep and soulful spreads across his face, bringing light to his eyes.

'Flossie.' Fleur repeats the soft word in a prayer, a slight smile emerging despite her fears. The ewe quietens and Fleur decides the name matches her gentleness.

'What's the score?' says Scott, as though Flossie is all part of a game.

'She has expelled her bag, but it's small, indicative of breech. The lamb's legs are backwards; we need to bring them forward or it will die,' instructs her father.

All tangled up, like the crying tree's limbs. Are its roots crippled too? Or dead?

'Let me. Guide me to do it. Please, Charlie, I want this,' begs Scott.

A pause. 'Alright, but it won't be easy. Come here.'

As the two men kneel on the ground near to where things in Flossie should be happening, Charlie shines a torch towards the ewe's open cervix. 'You can see she is dilated. That's the tail showing there. If need be, you can use ropes. You'll have to cup the lamb's fetlocks, then slip the body out to minimise risk of cord damage and drowning death if it inhales too deeply.'

Gentle Flossie cries and bangs her head repeatedly on the ground. The animal kicks out her hind legs against Scott as he rummages around inside her, causing an excruciating holler at this cruel new intrusion.

'The whole area is slippery,' Scott's burble echoes. 'I can't seem to get a good grip on the fetlocks. Shit.' *Is his head inside Flossie, too?*

Fleur's world spins as she and the ewe become one, knowing that Scott is about to steal something, and it has nothing to do with this—another thing she finds troubling. From far away she hears her father mutter something about ropes again, but Fleur is unwilling to be tied up by Scott, so she decides to distance herself from all the pain and commotion, which is becoming intolerable for her. Fleur has gone to hell. She summons *beyond*.

In one graceful vertical leap she bounds high and lands on a rafter about six feet below the corrugated iron roofing, where it is calmer and less windy. She sits with her legs hanging in the air upon her post, as spiderwebs hang grey and empty around her like lost souls.

Despite her distaste for the stark vision below, Fleur's eyes have become powerful spotlights which focus down and illuminate the birthing scene. When she searches her periphery, she encounters dark nothingness. She dares not look away least it becomes dark below, hampering the efforts of her father. 'I'm up here, Daddy.' Her voice tumbles out of her in a hush. But she can't be seen anyway, which is good; Fleur has never wanted to be in the spotlight.

Protected where she is, she studies the scene below. Curiously, the ewe becomes Izzie—her face startled and confused, hair a twisted nest of sweaty curls from the long hours of pain, from battering her head—under assault and knowing the awful truth that her baby is about to be yanked from her body. Fleur's heart pounds like a jackhammer. 'Don't take him.' But her words may be too late, then Tripp will never be seen again.

Izzie's face morphs into Grace's as seamlessly as when Fleur turns to a new pattern on Teddy's kaleidoscope. What a surprise!

I thought you were in bed. Scott could take from you too, Mummy.

Lying on his back between Flossie's legs, Teddy—*Teddy*—looks up towards his partner-in-crime sister, his eyes and mouth agape in a silent scream reminding her of Munch's evocative painting. Fleur swallows hard.

'Watch out for the red wave, Teddy.' Her shout comes as a whisper. *No, this lamb cannot die again!*

A portent. Fleur's poor mother: which one will be taken from Grace now, Erin or Fleur? With crystal clarity Fleur sees it: Erin will lose everything that has never been for her; Fleur knows her sister is neither the ewe nor its lamb.

Fleur is the ewe, both tattered and torn, awaiting their fate. She knows what will soon be taken, will be more than what has ever been taken from her, much more. Above and below herself, she blinks in attempt to clear away everything, everyone, all the pain. She would suck her thumb but cannot bring herself to release her hold on the beam.

In this rude light, Scott's blood-coloured hair looks to be on fire as he wields a length of rope in his hands. No, it is a cable of sorts with dynamite attached. There he goes, doing something he shouldn't... He seems to enjoy manipulating it because he raises his face and grins, thankfully not at Fleur. As though awaiting an epiphany, he pauses and mouths a count to three before hitting the detonator. Fleur jumps with the boom of the explosion—almost falling on top of him—as a pile of detritus spews through a hole from underground. His thoughts come to her: *Carnage of the captive, what a potent aphrodisiac.*

Fleur hates it but she has become Scott: reverent though God-like, his exquisite contradiction. Her mouth is parched, matching the suddenly dry, dusty atmosphere surrounding her. Heat-induced shimmers of watery mirages around the scene below confuse her. Yet, as Scott, she is invigorated in this new landscape, drunk on the promise of the dancer's undulating ribbons of colours, ready to expose veins of rock waiting to bleed just for him. Both of his arms up inside her now, his adroit fingers locating their prize. A gentle prod, arousal of the virgin. The fragile slither of a captive embryo hibernates, unaware of the forces stirring within its nebula. The gentle hand of this man will ease its entry into the world and entice it to life. Sunlight will shock it to fruition; God is on his side.

Desperately, Fleur shakes her head to eradicate Scott as she looks down to something yellowish and wet now lying on the ground. Meconium yellow. She watches Scott cradle the thing in his cupped hands before lifting it to the light—her light—where it shudders in its nakedness. He rotates his prize—his baby he calls it—marvelling at the now gloriously striated plays of colour in green, blue, gold, and most valuable red. His find, his prize. Serendipity. More than that, Scott has shape-shifted—physically and mentally; stronger now than ever before because she feels his muscles flexing, bulging beneath the fabric of his shirt. Fleur hears his brag: 'Hail Scott: Ulysses of the mining fields.' His repulsive childish giggle. Try as she might, Fleur cannot see the lamb's face, only colours. Scott places his baby—his precious gem—under his shirt and cradles it, understanding its one function is to make him whole.

Fleur weakens. 'Oh no, it's dead. Scott killed it.' Her voice in full volume now. Surprisingly, she has descended from the heights, her body lying on the ground with her head beside Flossie's. The smell of wet straw and livestock is heady. Flossie rises to her feet before Fleur does.

'Give me your hand, firecracker.' Fleur is barely a fizzer. Her father pulls her to sitting position as she picks straw from her hair, attempts to right her dizzy thoughts. She scans the now quiet magical scene knowing she has no need for any more worry tonight. New life: new hope. Her mother knew this all along. But poor Teddy!

Pride comes to her father's voice, 'A healthy ewe lamb.' Lying beside Flossie, the newborn creature gives a tiny bleat, shiver, and a cough to clear its lungs.

Fleur marvels at such innocence. This lamb could never purge any of Scott's sins.

'Alright now, Fleur? Sorry you missed all the action.' Charlie chuckles then pats his daughter's head which she could easily interpret as condescending, but not now that beautiful new life has emerged.

'I wish I had,' is all she can reply, because reaching the moment of new life involved becoming someone she despises. Although not aimed at her this time, Scott's expression is almost carnal, and savage—like that of a murderer following a fresh kill, his thirst for blood remaining somehow unquenched.

Scott grabs a towel and starts rubbing the gagging, disoriented lamb as brusquely as he would himself after a shower. Flossie once again becomes agitated.

'Give it to me,' Fleur commands as she wrenches the towel from him.

'Flossie is special. She knows me.' Flossie settles with Fleur's soothing words as she gently dries the lamb and wraps it loosely in a clean towel.

'Huh, women,' says Scott to Charlie with a frown, a click of his tongue.

Scott has sucked the air from Fleur's lungs although she will get this lamb breathing freely. What kind of life could Scott give to Erin?

Fleur has seen his baby, watched him cradle it, knowing soon he will hide it away. She finds it infuriating how *beyond* randomly connects her with visions that lack sense and detail.

Just like that, Scott gives a hearty laugh, and the men shake hands—sticky with gore—as Charlie asks Scott to christen the newborn. 'Erin Belle', he proclaims.

You own nothing, Scott. Fleur knows he will never have a claim on what is now or what is to come. Especially anything living.

Chapter Twenty-Eight

The ache Fleur endures! Since the lamb's arrival, her sleep has been broken by nightmares about monsters and a blonde woman birthing an unwanted baby. She cannot identify the woman because she always faces away from Fleur. Afterwards, Fleur feels empty with loss, soulless. She remembers the strange cloud she exhaled outside the pub that awful night, the remnants of her remnants. But her current loss is more important and stronger: she misses Teddy and Tripp, both acutely.

They had experienced miscommunication, yet when Tripp left to find his grandmother he and Fleur were on good terms. And Teddy seems to be contacting her at last, perhaps more so because she has now moved into his room. Logic tells her to pull herself together, yet nothing seems to help her current mood of sadness, hopelessness. She is a semi-mobile cadaver carrying weighted funereal thoughts and feelings.

Standing in front of the bathroom mirror, coughing, confirms her suspicions. A ghoulish reflection of a face older than its years with sunken cheeks and a mushroom pallor. She has bronchitis and influenza—she has had a couple of bouts this year—and the latest dose of antibiotics aren't helping clear her skin as they sometimes do. Dark bruise-like shadows smile up at her amber eyes as if mocking; her tiny retinas pierce the mirror—she could shatter it. *Look closely, this is what you created.*

Embarrassed the vision is really herself, and knowing the

feeling will worsen, Fleur closes her eyes as she strips down to her underpants. Taking a deep breath for courage, she lifts her head in nervous little jolts and sneaks a peak at her full self in the mirror. For the first time in months, she examines her body and registers disgust for what she sees, for what she's done. When she tries to put it all together the reality hits hard; her attempts to quell the pain from the outside in are failing. Her rough journey to nowhere shows as a primitive record of wounds and scars. She has failed, achieved nothing. Yet still she persists.

Just a little today, she tells herself. Soon, when Tripp comes home, she will stop. *Come home, Tripp.* She wields the points of small nail scissors and makes a neat little cut on her right breast. Opening it with thumb and forefinger of her left hand she is shocked, as always, by the whiteness of the flesh inside—like tendons in raw chicken—before the blood pools. She replaces the scissors with tweezers, burrowing against the agony to get to the rot. Trying, trying...

Out of the corner of her right eye she catches sight of a figure looming in the yard near the bathroom's half-closed window. She turns her head to see him hovering close by, facing her, his shoulders rolled forward, his arms hanging limp by his sides like he is unaware they belong to him. Sprouting ginger hair, he positions his fat fingers to face her, his fingernails pointing towards the imaginary beasts behind him. He reminds her of an orangutan. He has been watching her.

He has *caught* her.

This new sting is different. A new infection. A new reality. Things have changed. Again.

His burrowing gaze morphs into a strange expression. Embarrassment? No. Shock? Feigned? A lick of his lips. Salacious? Hazy, everything is hazy now as she tries to escape but she's rooted to the floor and his body continues to make its small slow prowling movements. He places the tip of his ape pointer finger over the pucker of his o-shaped mouth, cleverly widening his marble eyes in exact replicas of its shape.

The shape of a lucky strike.

The shape of exaltation.

And then a look of abject pity emerges in the way he drops his bottom lip to pout at her, furrows his brow and shakes his head in an almost *tut, tut* fashion. Poor pathetic Fleur.

She will burn long and slow because of this.

A crippled moan escapes her.

For almost one full week since the bathroom incident, she has managed to avoid him, but her luck is out. *No, not this!*

Fleur almost collides with Scott. She picks up her pace down the hallway and tries to barge past him. She cannot trust that she won't kill him because no-one was supposed to discover her secret. No-one. Ever. Refusing to back up, she tries to edge past him, but he takes up the whole hallway making it unavoidable that she skims his side. She hears him snort, his flaring nostrils hint of barely restrained rage pulsing through him.

He clasps her forearm, wrenching her shoulder.

Guttural howls of a stranger echo in her ears—vile, vehement. She checks his damage, expecting to see her arm hanging at odd angles like the crying tree's limbs, useless as a broken umbrella. A dull surprise: her bones—from the outside anyway—appear intact. Carefully, she tests her aching, throbbing arm. Surely no position would make it comfortable now. All this on top of her cold. She coughs towards her shoulder, the jolt of it heralding bright new pain, making her immediately wish she had spat directly in Scott's face.

So, this is it. She knew that despite his weaknesses—and there are many—that he would possess man strength, especially since she has seen that he will soon find his prize, his baby. Terrifyingly, he is not fit to own such strength, and certainly unable to control it. She knew he'd find a way to damage her further.

'I don't understand, I hardly touched you. Did I hurt you? Oh no, I'm so sorry.' Almost apologetic. 'Let me look. Please.'

'No. Get back.'

'Stop trying to avoid me, Fleur,' he demands.

'You *have hurt me.* Let me pass. Get away.'

As she sidles past him, he grabs her, the keen new pain sharper than before. Can he stoop any lower?

'No, not until you hear me out.' Frantic words. His big burly block to her path.

'Alright, so you're obviously not going to make this easy for me, are you?'

'I can't imagine any of this has been easy for you, Fleur. Look at what you've been doing to yourself. God!' He tugs at his rusty hair before smoothing it down.

'How dare you even look at me, ever! I don't buy your compassion, Scott, or your feeble attempts at caring. I know what you are.'

'And I'll bet you're about to tell me what that amounts to.' Arms akimbo.

She cannot inhale enough breath to curb her dizziness. 'You're a user. You think of no-one but yourself. You don't love my sister.' If only she could stop her voice from trembling.

'I do love her, Fleur. You wouldn't know love if it came knocking. You don't love anyone, even yourself.'

'I'm too tired. I can't play games. What do you want from me?' Bile settles in her throat.

'Shouldn't I be asking you that? I hate to raise this, but why do I believe you seem a little obsessed with me? It's a bit like the way Cathy from next door is obsessed with Tripp. Now *there's* a love story waiting to happen. I wonder if her obsession has been reciprocated, yet? That would be something to explore.'

What? Cathy from the pub? And she lives next door? Fleur is so flabbergasted she can only emit a small bitter laugh. If he is speaking of the Cathy she knows, she may be interested in Tripp, but he couldn't be interested in her, could he? Again, Fleur tries to discount what she saw at the pub, Cathy's body draped over Tripp's.

'Do you know about Tripp's secret past? Perhaps not so secret. I don't want to hurt you, but I know some very interesting facts that may dampen your feelings for him. You need to take care, Fleur, he could be dangerous.'

He must be lying. And what could he possibly know about Tripp, a man who goes out of his way to avoid him? What else does Scott know? How much does he know about her?

'I know lots of secrets. I don't ask for them, but people confide in me. The burden of keeping them is so hard, let me tell you. I know more than you realise, and some information even relates to you and your… relationships. I've seen you being loose at the pub. And now I've seen you in front of the bathroom mirror, carving yourself up in the safety of your home, causing deformities on yourself. Sorry for using that word but I need to shock you out of your silly behaviour. You're worth so much more, Fleur! But I won't hold all your secrets over you like you may think I will; that's not the way I operate. I can't understand your actions but if you want to keep it quiet, your secret is safe with me. I guess we all have them. So, can we stop this nastiness? All I want is for you to be well, to have some fun without hurting yourself, and I want you to accept my relationship with your sister.'

'How? It's not a loving relationship. You have nothing to offer her. Erin is your ticket to stability and security. Without her you're just another loser.'

An inflamed glare. 'You really are, aren't you? You're just like my mother.'

His *mother*. Now *that's* a subject she'd like to explore with him.

'I'm neither a drunk, nor a chronic gambler.'

'What?' Knocked backwards with the expelled word.

'You heard me. Everyone at the hotel sees her gambling and drinking too much. Surely, she drinks at home, too? Surely her wonderful son knows about her problems.'

Fleur watches Scott weighing up her words.

'You think my life has been easy? It hasn't been. I adore my mother, yet she has… weaknesses. Even when I was a kid it was rough. I spent lots of time climbing a ladder onto our rooftop because I felt safe and big like a man up there—the opposite of what I was on the ground. I remember how tiny the wheat silo looked across the river.' His eyes stare down the hallway. 'I escaped there while Mum listened to horse racing on the radio. You see, even then she was gambling. When I'd hear Mum shouting, I thought Dad should climb the ladder more, huh! When the roof wasn't too hot, I'd pretend it was a slippery slide. But I'd always get caught on the rust. I never made it to the edge.'

Fleur now studies the man with the glazed eyes, whose ramblings are now robotic.

'Mum always prompted Dad to get me down, telling him to be a man and do something about it. I thought she was beautiful like a smoky fairy tale princess. If *she'd* have asked me to come down, I would have, and quick-smart.' He gives Fleur a sappy smile. 'When she was nice, I would have done whatever she wanted me to do.

'I remember Mum's words: *That kid has always held me back. How many times have I told you to hide the damn ladder? I've a mind to leave him up there and burn it so the little bugger can never get down.* I thought Mum wanted to burn me along with the ladder. Later, in my bed, the air from the mean broom—that's what I called it—rushed around me and before I could disappear under the bedclothes, I was getting hit and nothing was fair.

'Even at the beach house I'd try to disappear. I'd lie on the sand dunes and pray for a better life. It wasn't romantic: boiling pink blisters on my skin; inviting the harsh, sand-laden wind gusts to sting me like a misplaced penance.'

'Stop playing the card of the downtrodden, Scott.'

He focuses his wide eyes at Fleur as though shocked she has snapped him out of his trance.

She continues. 'So, tell me, how do you treat your mother? Your derogatory tone suggests you're furious with her. You say I'm like her and you obviously don't respect me, so you mustn't respect her.'

'You're wrong. I treat her with respect, I do, because that's what mothers deserve.' His voice catches.

'Carmen? How could you respect that awful woman, even if she is your mother? Or do you respect her but hate her too? Children can be like that.' The scathing words pour out of her without hesitation. *That frightful compulsive gambler, that scourge of a woman!*

'Don't you ever disparage my beautiful, precious mother.'

'So, Scott, in just what ways am I like her? Beautiful? Precious? If I'm so like your mother, do you want to do to her what you want to do to me? Or haven't you *explored* that notion yet?'

What has she said? Fleur has no idea where her repulsive words have come from. Suddenly, she regrets her thoughts have found such an ugly form, especially as Scott's large palm contacts her face. Her head jolts with the impact, the shockwaves of pain returning in repeated assault. She shields her injured cheek with a cupped hand.

'What have you done to me? I've never hit a woman before in my life.' Scott's voice is a hushed whimper. He studies his hitting hand, the skin blooming in shades of mottled crimson.

Fleur silently curses him. His fate: to become as haunted and paranoid as Shakespeare's Macbeth. She will make sure he pays.

'Don't you EVER come near me again.' She says this with as much bite as she can muster through her pain and sadness. What part of her body will he hurt next?

Fleur bolts away, determined to exorcise herself of Scott's presence. Yet she fears she will never be able to get far enough away from him.

Chapter Twenty-Nine

With her emotions as raw as her wounds, sleep did not come to Fleur last night. Every part of her has been exposed. What could be worse than the person she most distrusts having discovered her shocking secret? Scott now holds onto it like a loaded gun.

During the rare, less shattering moments of last night, when her heart settled enough for her to stupidly think she may even sleep a little, she reassured herself he had seen nothing except a girl looking into a bathroom mirror. But then, like a syrup-thick tidal wave, each corroborating detail arrived to demand her recall, to force her to open those sharp little packages of nasty surprises before they smothered her. One by one she ticked off the list of suffocating details she knew Scott saw: a near naked girl who was Fleur, a damaged girl who was Fleur, a weapon used by Fleur on Fleur, a shameful girl who was Fleur.

There was that and here is this: her aching arm, her stinging reddened cheek—lingering results of Scott's slap to her face yesterday. Last night she decided she had a mind to show Erin what he had done to her, to convince her sister just what a monster her fiancé is, but now she is not so sure.

Over and over the pain came. Over and over more pain will follow.

Nothing good can come of this.

'Wake up!' she shouts at Erin, now in the low morning light of her room and sitting on her bed, having kept herself together for too long. She coughs and bounces her bum on the bed. Why should Erin sleep while Fleur is going through all this agony caused by her sister's fiancé?

'What time is it?' Erin's voice is muffled yet terse as she opens her eyes.

'Four-sixteen.' Fleur has been watching the clock all night.

'What's wrong. Are you ill?'

'I need to talk to you.' Her voice emerges with a lucidity she does not feel as she crumples the fabric of her nightie in her fists.

'I'm going into town with Mum and Dad at seven to help them with supplies. Couldn't you have waited until a decent time for this? At least give me another hour of sleep, preferably two.'

'No, I can't wait, I've been waiting all night. This is about the only time we can get a chance to talk privately.'

'So, what is so important that you have to wake me up at sparrow fart to tell me?' Erin blinks at Fleur.

'It's about Scott.'

'No, Fleur, don't start! I know what you think of him. You've made your thoughts perfectly clear.'

'Listen to me. He is not trustworthy. He's unstable.'

'Did you ever consider that Tripp could be the shifty one?'

'What? That's crazy.'

'He may not be as perfect as everyone seems to think he is. What exactly was his role at Robinson's? Scott says—'

'Stop changing the subject. You need to take me seriously about Scott.'

'Look, I've had enough of this. How dare you keep casting aspersions on my fiancé. What exactly has he done to you?'

How can she answer this? She'd hinted about Scott's previous dodgy car fix, at the family dinner before Izzie and Tripp went away. If she tells her sister about what Scott saw of her in the bathroom, and the slap, then Erin will know her secret too. She cannot risk it. Why didn't Fleur think of this before she started this conversation?

'It's the way he looks at me.' She's said enough. 'Alright, I'll stop. But don't say I didn't warn you.' Oh, Fleur, your argument holds no clout, she chastises herself.

'Says the woman who has everyone talking, who has apparently turned into the town bike.' Erin's words may be mumbled, yet to Fleur they come through loud and clear.

'*What?*' Now this. Scott must have said something. Fleur's stomach lurches with indignity as she attempts to leave her body. She has been learning how to do this lately...

Another girl, another time, another hurt.

This new hurt is for today.

'Fleur!' Her name on her sister's lips wrenches her back to the moment. 'You heard what I said. Scott says you've been flirting at the pub.'

'There's a difference between flirting and having sex!' Fleur blushes. Another kick to the guts. 'The *town bike?*'

'Listen, I'm just worried.' Horrid pangs of sympathy ring through Erin's words.

'You should be worried about yourself. Just like everyone else around here, you never listen to me. I might as well not exist. No-one listens, and when something bad happens everyone will exclaim, *why didn't I see it coming?* Well, you were warned, that's all I can say.'

'You talk in circles. What exactly are you warning me about?'

'Scott! My intuition is screaming out to me that he is bad.'

'And what is your intuition telling you about yourself? Because if it held any kind of accuracy, it would be warning you about the massive hole you are digging and about to fall into.'

'I'm off for a very long walk. And don't come looking for me.'

Fleur stifles the urge to slam Erin's bedroom door because that would indicate that her last remark had hurt Fleur, and it would wake the household, so she quietly closes it on her naïve sister—naïve, yet unharmed, for now.

Back in her bedroom, foolish broken Fleur collects her jumbled thoughts as best she can. She does fear for herself, but she would never admit it to her sister, let alone tell her about the cutting. Unless Scott has already told her... She swallows hard. It's no use. Erin is blind to the truth about the two-faced man who will only end up doing her harm. Fleur suddenly realises she is more worried about

Scott than she is about any false rumours of her promiscuity being spread around this hellhole of a place, even if her sister has heard those false rumours from Scott, even if Erin now feels more justified to assert her self-proclaimed superiority.

Should Fleur care?

She moans in frustration. Eyes pinched, she clenches her fists, digging sharp fingernails into soft fleshy palms, wishing her nails were keener today. Somehow, she will compose her wretched self and prove to Erin that she has failed to wound her further. She takes some deep breaths. In slow, deliberate movements, Fleur gathers her watch, torch, dressing gown, slippers. To soften her edges, she snuggles into her warm blue velvet gown, wrapping it around her jagged body in a rare act of self-kindness. Padding her spongy slippers towards the door, towards freedom, she creeps about in the pale dawn light like a lost spectre.

Her father's snores and stark wild-boar-like snorts resound throughout the house. She takes heart knowing they will soon be replaced by the lilt of sweet birdsong from outside, tricking the world of a lyrical household.

Seeking solitude, craving an outlet for her fury, Fleur carefully opens the kitchen door to the colder, private yard.

Chapter Thirty

Such a bite to the pre-dawn air! Fleur has resolved to toughen up and walk the property. As soon as her slippers hit the dewy grass, the wetness seeps through their thin quilted fabric and climbs up her ankles, like an envelopment of sea monster tentacles. Shivering, she discards the soggy shoes, wishing the tentacles would asphyxiate at the doorway, but even without her shoes her saturated bits remain with her. It is darker out than she had imagined, so she turns on her spotlight.

She must be gone long enough for her family to have left for town by the time she gets back. How intolerable it would be to see any of them this morning, especially with the results of Scott's anger surely now stamped on her face. As she sets off, her own anger grips her tight, its clarity as bold and advancing as the unstoppable day.

Scott's moves suggest he has been spending nights alone in the blue workers' cottage—she cannot imagine Erin giving in to her sexual urges, cannot really imagine she would even have any. Is he there now? With her free hand protecting her stomach she sees the indistinct structure hovering in distant mist: a shipwreck doomed before it has even set sail. She rushes away from it.

Fleur strolls beyond the yard's picket fence, across misty pastures. She comes across flowering wattle and native frangipani trees. Their sweet perfume encourages her to linger a while. She stands behind her circle of torchlight which she occasionally aims towards the canopies, in darkness just as she likes to be. But soon the darkness peels back to reveal thin pale morning light, heralding an ever-loudening chorus of waking animals: lorikeets, finches, wrens, and the like—some too tiny and fast-flying for Fleur to identify. They sing to the sun, to rise and warm the world in their frantic fight for the first of the day's nectar, as if neither the day nor its bounty had ever occurred or will ever be repeated. She hears Ringo and Butch barking for Izzie's doggie breakfast morsels, the raucous crows of the rooster. The sound of an engine tells her she can return.

Finally, back in the yard, she watches the sun rise above the eastern plains, amazed as always at how quickly it reveals its full spherical form in the sky, how quickly the light dazzles in a new day, now ripped open for all to see. With nowhere to hide... She cringes, turning off the torch and slipping it into her pocket.

No car in the garage means the family has left for town. This gives her some relief, but what about Scott? No lights are on in the cottage, but his Jaguar is parked outside. She pins all her desperate hopes on the assumption that Charlie had driven him home—as he sometimes does—and Scott spent last night with his parents, or, if he is in the cottage, that he is still sound asleep.

In the herb garden she tears lavender leaves from its bush, crushing them with her fingertips to release the pungent, relaxing oil. Dabs her pulse points in an endeavour to calm herself, purge her feminine odours. The vegetable crops appear healthy in their beds. Even in this cold drought, tender new shoots sprout from the plants, and she wonders why, when the rest of the property is bone dry? She wishes there were a way to watch them unfurl in fast motion while on their steady, unique pathways to fruition. Tops of bright orange carrots crown the soil, catching her eye as they push from their beds. *Don't be in too much of a hurry*, she thinks, *you're bound for the pot.*

Having crept full circle around the house that has taken so little time to circumnavigate, she finds herself outside her parents' bedroom. An empty swallows' nest balances on the rafters above her parent's window – the area covered in bird shit. Below, gritty broken eggshells lie smashed on the ground. Where have the baby birds gone? Did they emerge naturally or were they ripped from their home by predators, like Tripp was taken from Izzie? Like Scott will take...

Everything leaves, everything leaves, everything...

Look, there is the crying tree. The old eucalypt, a spotted gum. She walks over to its mottled green-grey trunk, gives it a hug and a couple of her tears, then backs up to get a good look at the stuff of family legend. The golden sun rising in the background creates a dark silhouette of twisted trunk and branches. Despite its great deformities, its pockmarked skin, the tree stands proud and true, probably more trick of light than gumption. She wishes she could trick herself into thinking she were more than deformities.

'Deformities'. The word tainted, dirty on Scott's lips, poison on her own. Anger prods her. *How dare he!* How dare he know more of her than her loved ones, and deep down she does love them; she has enough left of herself to acknowledge that. And how dare he hit her.

Look at it. That strange towering tree looks magic even without it doing anything. She dares it to perform for her. Yet she knows that no curious show from Nature could minimise her rage this morning. Studying the shadowy tree against the bright sun it occurs to her it could almost be on fire. How bright it would look then, blazing in brilliant fury!

No soft gown will soften her. She is sharp and edgy; she has weapons to help her. She will harness all her anger, see where it leads, knowing she must release it somehow. Scowling, she jabs her finger towards the tree trunk the way her teachers used to point at her in class, didactically. Naughty Fleur.

I will destroy you, Scott! She is a soldier yawping 'pow, pow' like when she played war games with Teddy, but this time it is for real. This time an enemy has encroached and gone too far. Teddy is with her, on her side: she feels his big tugs to her gown in a frantic call to arms.

What is that? A spark flickers at exactly where she has pointed on the tree's trunk, soon growing into a decent flame. She blinks to clear tears and nonsense from her eyes, yet smoke irritates them. But... the tree is on fire!

I have created fire.

Like a mad dog on a chain Fleur rushes around the trunk, weighing illusion against reality. Did she really do this? Can it happen again?

She succumbs to her fervent rage; this is not difficult. Steels herself, glowers, pokes the air—jab jab jab—starting new fires on various sections of the luckless trunk. Soon small sparks become definite orange flames, restricted to where her finger has targeted. No immediate plan to claim her. Once again, she is a firecracker, just as her father used to call her, and now she can really do some damage. The flames follow her as she circles the trunk pointing her gun. Each new fire reaches out in a desperate snatch at freedom; she can relate. She makes fists, growls, hollers, in unrestrained calls that are somehow incredibly old. Unleashing the power within her, letting go of her emotions like this, unravelling her knots, feels so relieving.

She surveys the damage. The fires are contained, yet still they flare. Beyond explanation. *Beyond!* They must be snuffed out before anyone notices what she has been up to. But how?

She is about to run and grab the old hose which should just about stretch far enough, when a sudden understanding of her second task hits her. Stilling herself she focuses on the impressive canopy as though the future of mankind depended on her concentration.

There they are! With each hit comes Fleur's simultaneous jump; they are so precise she could count them. Water droplets hit her face, drawing out her smile against their cold, shocking strikes. The stark clear sky above tries to discount all she is experiencing, but soon she is standing under a torrential rain shower. Moving away, she shakes off water and peers up, confirming the phenomenon has originated in the tree's canopy.

Her mother has spoken of this kind of magic, but Fleur has never been privy to it. Crying tree? This tree is howling! Despite what her mother insists, Fleur thinks Grace has been the only one to have ever seen it. Happening at any time would be weird, yet this is drought, and not one water drop has spilled from the sky since the short but intense storm many months ago. And today relief comes from a tree! It is healing its burns. Can it heal others too?

Still fearing reignition, Fleur creeps towards the soaked trunk where only echoes of its fury remain: lacklustre puffs of smoke and fizzling steam. As she places her hand on a charred yet cold patch of bark, her outstretched fingers disappear in grey clouds.

She slumps against the jaded crying tree, wondering at her power—newly received from her mother—to conjure up its magic, to start little fires. She's seen how powerful objects are, too: this crying tree, Teddy's kaleidoscope. Even before this, an object—a scarf—had something to do with her mother helping get Tripp and Izzie back together. Are objects portals for magic? A faint thrill falls upon her. If she could just believe it… Where could her power lead?

She breathes deeply to calm herself, exhaling tenuous tendrils into the cold dry air. Momentarily, the vapours appear like tree roots, inverted in design and purpose. She steadies herself on the tree which burrows for life deep underground, while she loses a little of her life each day. Have either of them a chance for recovery?

'I hope I didn't hurt you,' she whispers to the wood, touching its wounded surfaces, marvelling at its tenacious grip on life. She feels its connection to *beyond*. Something hidden from her comprehension tingles on the surface of her wounds, within them. A breeze makes her shudder, conflicted by a sense that her wounds could either open further, or even one day heal. She hugs the crying tree now, feeling it soften and mould with her, in—she hopes—understanding.

Where will her strangeness lead? Can this tree work with her?

Chapter Thirty-One

Fleur has decided to keep the magic, the intrigue of the crying tree, to herself, for now. Even though her mother has always known of its potential, Fleur is resolute. Intuitively—even without her mother's cautioning—Fleur understands she must keep any secret power private. And with everyone at the farm probably thinking she's mad, why add more fuel to the fire? She gives an ironic smile, now knowing fire doesn't need fuel to start it, fuel in the conventional sense anyway. Somehow, she must block what Scott saw of her, never let him see her pain. She holds all her hopes on Tripp.

Seized by new, albeit tentative, strength, she prepares herself for the dreaded confrontation she knows must happen today because time has run out. She hopes it won't get nasty yet doubts that outcome since the farm workers are good men. Although, raising the topic will be tricky and she doesn't want to cause any further bad feelings. Tripp returns tomorrow, according to the letter he sent her father. Two months away—not one—two long months apart. She cannot wait to see both Tripp and Izzie again, but this must be done first.

Her father has told her Bene and Luca are wigging the last of the sheep today in the shearing shed, a procedure performed to prevent wool blindness. She thinks of the last time she was at that shed, the evening when she made halting steps towards Tripp's voice, when her thoughts niggled about her earlier heated conversation with him. But it was overhearing his conversation with Bene and Luca that really floored her. Because of her big mouth, Tripp now knows of her eavesdropping. As she once again stands at the open doorway, hearing carefree whistling from the two men she knows are inside, the old fears resurface. Again, an intruder poised to encounter something she should not, yet this time she will not run no matter the outcome.

Sudden bleating of impatient sheep inside; wild, jarring calls of the men. A commotion comes tumbling towards Fleur in an ochre cloud. Her heart pounds as she dodges the galloping animal, its newly wigged face pale like a startled ghost against the backdrop of a dust storm. Scanning the stalls, she sees the haunted eyes of a dozen or so others awaiting their wigging and crutching, resigned to their spooky partial transformation.

'Well now, if it isn't the lovely Miss Fleur!' says Bene, smiling as he strolls towards her, unshaken by the antics of the escapee.

'Yes, that's me.'

'Your sister has a different look.'

Sized up before being sliced up? 'Was that sheep meant to just run out like that?'

'Of course. We get 'em all outside then round 'em up and back to other paddock.'

'Good. Right. Well, hello Bene and Luca.'

'Yes, Luca here is my good worker mate.' Bene indicates the shy man.

Luca beams at Fleur, revealing one missing top incisor, before hurriedly shutting his mouth.

'Good, but not top. Tripp is my top worker, *il migliore*. Top worker is the best worker! We miss Tripp around here. You miss him too, *vieni no*.'

'I'm actually here to talk about Tripp with the two of you. I'd like to hear your thoughts about him.' So far, so good.

'What do you mean?' says Bene. 'Like I say, he's my best worker, top of the class.'

'Yes, I know that. It's just, well, I've been given some mixed messages about him lately.'

'Hah, missy, he just like all blokes.' Bene grins, shaking his head.

'Tripp is coming home very soon—tomorrow morning, in fact, according to a letter Dad received. Did you know?'

'Yes, yes, tomorrow. Charlie told us. Very good news! We will bake a cake!' exclaims Bene.

'Perhaps I will, or perhaps not.' She is under enough pressure. 'Why don't you both come to dinner tomorrow night at the homestead? I'm sure Tripp would love that.'

She did not plan this, but they have indicated positive feelings towards Tripp. Yet now, as the men eye one another, they appear hesitant.

'*Grazie*,' says Luca.

'Shall we say 6 o'clock? It will be great.' She overcompensates with exuberance.

'Okay, yes Fleur, we will come. Thank you. Ripper,' says Bene.

Fleur takes a few steps around the pens, not knowing how to extend the conversation, how to get to her point.

Luca helps her out. 'You say you heard that Tripp was mixed up. What do you mean?'

'I overheard parts of the conversation when Tripp told you both he was like Len Robinson.'

Bene appears aghast. 'What? You heard that?'

'No, no, Fleur!' says Luca. 'He is soft like a gelati. Tripp is a good man.'

'What else did you hear?' asks Bene.

'Nothing really. Just that.'

'You missed the part when he, how you say, stick up you,' says Bene. She blushes. 'You mean stick up for me?'

'Yes, that's it. He likes you much more than other boys,' says Bene.

'Other boys? He doesn't like boys!'

'No, no. I didn't mean... You do, yes, the ones at the hotel. You play up with them.'

'For Pete's sake, Bene. What boys at the hotel? How dare you!' *Three lousy visits. Had they seen her there? What next?*

'So sorry, miss. Stupid stuff. But Tripp, he thinks the world of you.' Luca's words are passionate.

'Really?' Both men nod back at her. 'Well, I guess I should be relieved about that.'

'And Fleur, sorry about saying stupid stuff. My mouth is now shut up like money in a bank,' says Bene.

'Please don't tell Tripp I was here. And never speak badly about me again, okay? I haven't done anything wrong. I haven't slept with any boys!' Fleur turns away, shamed for having exposed such private information to these men she hardly knows.

'Can we still come to dinner?' asks Luca.

'Yes.'

'What will you make?'

'Spaghetti Bolognese. I've been learning how to cook it, Bene.'

'Oh. Fleur, you're a miracle girl! Tripp should marry you soon as he can.'

Despite being the town bike? What more can she say or do to prove herself?

Chapter Thirty-Two

Tripp is back! For so long Fleur's body has felt drained, but today something strange and exciting runs through it—other than the current of her new magic. And it is not tainted with anger. She hasn't even dared face him since he and Izzie returned to the farm late morning; she'd be shattered if he noticed her strange new ruddy complexion that no make-up today has been able to cover. Tonight, she could blame it on the heat of the kitchen, but the fact is, she is overwrought and terrified about seeing him again.

She found a recipe in a *Women's Weekly* magazine extolling the goodness of European food. Continental cooking seems to have become all the rage now. Thank goodness for the family's tomato crop; she has practically decimated it.

Time passes quickly in a working kitchen when one is in a tizz. Being so nervously busy leaves Fleur craving a real—alcoholic—drink, yet she can't risk losing her way with the cooking. But soon she has created a fragrant, garlic-infused Bolognese sauce with steaming al dente pasta. She even managed to find some Parmesan cheese at the local shop which she has shaved for a garnish. What an international dish she has created! One final taste of the piquant sauce and she blows herself a congratulatory—rather Italian—air kiss. Checks the time on the wall clock: 6 pm. No time to spare.

Fleur loses her bearings as the room fills with people. They cramp around the too-small kitchen table with extra seats thanks to the wrought-iron bench from outside, a couple of cushions added for comfort. Cooking is so rare for Fleur—her mother was particularly cautious about her rebel daughter let loose on tonight's meal—and to prove Grace correct she has not checked serving sizes. Fleur is inadequate. The food is inadequate. What if there isn't enough to go around? The diners would surely have gone hungry if Marco and his boys had not declined her dinner offer. They rarely work closely with Tripp anyway, so she was not offended. Although she is sure that Erin would have been excited if Cappi had come. All Fleur wants is to be able to relax and breathe properly. Will that ever happen again?

A gasp escapes her. Scott—having perched himself at one head of the rectangular table like a thinnish Henry VIII awaiting his high-hog feast—is staring at her, unmoved. She tries setting her face in an expression to match his nonchalance. His pale blue shirt adds to his air of coolness. *Why is he here? Of course, he is here.* She braces herself, ready to ignore him no matter what. She will not allow him to upset her tonight.

Tonight is for her and Tripp. He is the one—the only one—she hopes will appreciate her efforts. But will she poison Tripp with her misguided cooking attempts? Why hadn't she thought of poisoning Scott earlier? She stirs the pot with a wooden spoon, chews a fingernail of her other hand, tasting garlic. Rather than setting a large bowl on the table—encouraging the king's gluttony—she manages to divvy up enough food for everyone directly onto their plates. She places the bowl of cheese centre-table next to her father's wine bottle. Nervously, she takes the only vacant seat left, alongside Tripp.

Charlie, sitting at the other head, breaks the silence. 'Welcome to our humble table, Luca and Bene! About time we had you over for dinner. Let's all raise a glass to the great job these two have done while Tripp was away. And welcome home, Tripp and Izzie.'

Yet the glasses are empty. Izzie jumps to her feet then sits, as if seized in sudden understanding that the important job of pouring wine is not hers. She gives a shamefaced grin as Grace pats Izzie's open palm. Charlie pours red wine into everyone's glass and the group raises a toast, after which he gets another bottle and opens it to breathe. Fleur notes it is a Cabernet Sauvignon from a vineyard at Margaret River, a new brand for her father. Her first sip—chocolate, raisins, oak—leaves her warm, sated. Having never seen Izzie drink alcohol, Fleur chuckles with surprising cheer as Izzie slugs hers down in one mouthful, responding with a wink.

'My mother has learnt to drink wine,' says Tripp, with another wink for Fleur. Giggles all around. Fleur is struck by how he has done himself up—in his Sunday best, as her mother would say.

'This food is delicious,' he says to an echo of appreciative murmurs.

'Best food since Italy,' says Bene.

'Even better than my mother's. Many thanks for asking us, Fleur,' says Luca.

For the first time all day, Fleur exhales with ease, letting go of a little fear. She notices Izzie wolfing her food down, no doubt pleased for a night off before starting all over again in the morning.

'So, now that we're relaxing, tell us all about your journey.' Grace directs her question to both Tripp and Izzie.

Everyone is all ears.

Scott butts in. 'Did you see the new house? It's just about done now and looking mighty fine.'

Tripp clears his throat. 'Um, about that...'

'Let's leave this conversation for another time,' says Charlie.

No, let's not, thinks Fleur. *Get it through your thick skulls that they don't want to live in a house that Scott built.*

'Okay. About the trip. Where do we start, *Anya?*' Tripp looks to Izzie for guidance. She extends her open palm for her son to speak for her.

'First we went to Bounty Bay, where we used to live.'

'Were your parents there, Izzie?' says Charlie. Grace elbows him.

'No, they were both gone,' Izzie replies.

Nine pairs of eyes flick from one person to another. Grace covers Izzie's tight fist with her hand.

'My grandfather has passed away,' says Tripp.

'Oh, darlings, we're so sorry,' says Grace, spurring more murmurs.

'What happened to him?' blurts Scott and Erin gives him a distasteful look. Silence.

'Perhaps another time,' says Grace as mother and son cast their eyes to their laps.

Scott is eyeballing Fleur rather than lowering his eyes in pity and reverence, or guilt for what he has done to her. Someone nudges the tops of Fleur's shoes. She cannot tell if it came from Scott sitting to her left at the end of the table, or Tripp who sits on her right—because she is gripping her legs together. She hangs on the latter because the alternative would make her sick and she will not let anyone spoil tonight. She glances at Tripp for acknowledgment of the footsy, yet neither Scott nor Tripp appear culpable.

'My mother is alive!' shouts Izzie.

A roar goes up that belongs at a tennis match.

'We found her in Wagtail! She teach there!'

'At the migrant centre?' asks Grace.

Tripp elaborates. 'Yes. She knew someone working there who thought she could help settle new Europeans into Australia. Cora was a perfect choice for Wagtail. She's learnt to speak English and practically runs the place now. I almost envy her, being able to help so many new Australians. She said we could even work there. Well, perhaps one day. Even now, so long after the war, the world still experiences so much tragedy. This year, a series of earthquakes hit western Sicily. Hundreds killed; one-hundred-thousand homeless. Some refugees have just arrived in Wagtail, having come to Australia to build new lives. We met many suffering—'

'*Anya,* she show me how to knit!' interrupts Izzie, knitting the air with her fingers.

Tripp rolls his eyes at his funny mother.

'Grace once took up knitting. She made me a sleeve,' Charlie chimes in, grinning.

Grace elbows him. 'Well, it sounds as though those people are in great need and your mother is doing a fine job, Izzie. I'm sure you both were helpful, too. But I must admit it's nice to have you both home again.'

'It's good to be back.' Izzie sighs. 'But we will miss Cora, too.'

'Yes, we will,' Tripp agrees. 'One day we hope to revisit her.'

Scott is fidgety. 'You know, I'm ripe for revisiting the subject of genetics, having discovered more about it recently. Although I'd found psychology somewhat irrelevant to engineering at university, I'm now glad to have learnt about what makes people tick. Huh, wish I'd known such things as a child... Do you know that a person's DNA carries heritable information which can transfer generation to generation? And personality traits can be inherited, too. I wonder where I got mine from. Bandura's Social Learning Theory claims people learn by observing, imitating, and modelling.'

'Why are you telling us this, Scott?' asks Grace, fixing Charlie with an embarrassed yet pointed look which makes him turn away.

'Because he's trying to work out if he is the missing link between dinosaur and Frankenstein's monster,' says Fleur. 'I can give you that answer, Scott. Oh, and have you ever heard of Freud's Oedipus complex?' Tonight, she is pleased to impart a little of what she knows from her own psychology books, and she would like to take it further.

As Scott ignores Fleur, she forces herself to stare at him. He takes it upon himself to refill his glass with the fresh bottle. He signals for Fleur to finish what is left in her glass before refilling it, but she refuses—even though she could swig an entire bottle right now—by placing her hand over the top of her glass. She glances at her sister opposite whose scowl shows she notices Scott's game. *What is he playing at?*

It's getting late. One-by-one they leave the table, led by Bene and Luca who are early risers.

As Izzie gets to her feet, Fleur hears her whisper to Grace, 'the little man in the fire was my father.' Her mother gives Izzie's hand a squeeze before she and Charlie exit the room. As Erin moves to leave, Scott smothers his fiancée in a passionate, open-mouth kiss that leaves Fleur nauseous. Erin skips—well, trips—off, but not before presenting Fleur and Tripp with a grin so wide it almost splits her ditsy head apart.

Three remain: Fleur, Tripp and Scott. Stony silence. A knee-knock under the table this time comes from Tripp because he widens his eyes and cocks his head at Fleur, urging her creation of an as-yet-non-existent strategy to force Scott to leave. But there is no need...

'Well, I'm off. No fun around here.' Scott stands, gives a theatrical stretch and yawn, and exits the house with a slam of the door.

'What is wrong with that idiot?' growls Tripp.

Fleur could take all night answering that question.

'What happened to your grandfather?'

'He died in a fire my grandmother accidentally started at the house in Bounty Bay. The house was gone.' He huffs.

'Should I be sorry, Tripp?'

'No. He was no angel, believe me. My grandmother was glad to flee the place and make a new life in Wagtail. And my mum? Izzie is relieved to know that Marcel can no longer hurt anyone. At last, she is free now, free to live as she pleases.' A smile.

'Everyone deserves that right.' Fleur feels like a prisoner. She gulps.

'We sometimes take it for granted.' Tripp's quizzical look towards her is not reassuring. 'So, what's been happening at the farm?'

What can she say? That Scott caught her, hurt her, threatened her? That the entire population of Pig Peak incorrectly thinks she is a slut? That she made her own fire here telepathically? That she confronted Tripp's workmates with fears about him?

'What can I tell you?' She wants to tell him everything, but... 'I went to the river.'

Tripp looks concerned. 'Something to do with Teddy?'

'I played with his kaleidoscope and mouth organ.'

Her information is childish and lame, and this fact is solidified as Tripp raises an eyebrow at her. A blush warms her cheeks. Why does she do this? Her brain goes to mush around this man.

'Well, that's, um, strange.' He smiles widely at her. How can his teeth be so perfect?

'Strange is the word.' A little bubbly giggle escapes her, followed by a loud hiccough. She relaxes for the first time all day. Somehow her strangeness doesn't seem so worrying anymore, now that...

'Now that you are back, everything will be alright.' In a tentative move she squeezes Tripp's hand and is immediately struck by the rush of excitement such a small gesture can generate. Tripp's magic.

'Oh, I got you this.' From his pocket, Tripp gives Fleur a snow globe depicting a bush scene. 'I picked it up in Wagtail. Just a silly thing, really, koalas in the snow.'

Fleur gives it a shake, watching the delicate white particles drift through a liquid Australian bush scene.

'Thank you. And it's not silly. Miracles do happen—they must.'

At last, Tripp is home. And he will look after her from now on. He may just help set her free.

Chapter Thirty-Three

A day at the beach, Stanford Park, October 1968

Grace shakes her head for her husband's naïve bright side. *Hope springs eternal.* Charlie reckons since losing Teddy there has been enough thunder at the farm to bring down the Berlin Wall, and it is about time everyone bucked up. Charlie tells Grace that, despite the hectic births, Tripp and Izzie's return and Erin and Scott's engagement have given him a lift. He has not spoken to her of overhearing Carmen's venomous comments at the Harris's.

Less sensitive to the concept of grieving, Dukie agreed with Charlie that he, and why not, the whole bloody lot of Altons—including Izabella and Tripp—could use a break away with his family to a place on the coast called Stanford Park near their beach house. A little 'jaunt'.

Inviting Tripp? Grace doubts Dukie knows of the rivalry between him and his son. Grace convinces both Izzie and Tripp to come, because they must surely be up to some celebrating since finding Cora in good health and spirits at Wagtail. Put on the spot, they accept. But Izzie recoils. After Tripp's abduction, she was such a homebody at the farm, curbing urges to explore the countryside for fear of being found and persecuted. Who could blame her? Knowing Izzie's story, Grace marvels at the little lady's strength during adversity, her immutable gentle ways.

Grace hears Tripp urging Fleur to come along to the picnic; she suspects it would be both or neither. Fleur has been battling another bout of influenza, but she tells Tripp the antibiotics—which Grace organised—are making her feel better, plus, she is in desperate need of a change of scenery. Erin is wheezy but she would never miss a chance to view her other inheritance, would she? Inheritance? Once again, thoughts of all-things-Harris-unravelling flood Grace's mind.

Charlie jumps at the chance for a short seaside sojourn with his best mate. His excitement about Dukie having asked him is palpable. Dukie couldn't want Grace to come. She knows he is not at all sure about her and probably considers himself lucky for that problem to be his friend's. Her thoughts render her cynical and a little hurt.

Grace knows she will look like a drag if she does not go, but an entire day with the Harrises? Despite the reservations, early one sunny October morning, Charlie, Grace, Fleur, Izzie and Tripp in Charlie's Monaro, follow Dukie, Carmen, Scott and Erin in Dukie's terrain-unfriendly Bentley on a long journey south-east, towards the Harrises' beach house.

However, their little convoy simply drove past it as Dukie shouted back to the Altons to wind down their windows before pronouncing the scenic house on a hill as belonging to their family. The Altons cast one another stunned, miffed glances about not stopping to explore such a grand house and take in what must be an incredible ocean view from the top level. Grace watched Erin sink down in the back seat of the Bentley until she could no longer be seen from behind.

On the walk to the park for the picnic, Dukie, Carmen, Erin and Scott forge ahead along a path bordered by natural massive rock walls. Following them, Grace and Fleur fall into step with one another. Izzie and Tripp lag, captivated by the caves in the area. Fleur continues to turn her head back towards Tripp. Grace turns back too, almost scared both he and Izzie will be swallowed up by the unfamiliar environment. In hush-hush conversation, mother and son saunter past caverns and hollows, touching walls, fingering small shells and debris in shallow caves at ground level.

Izzie stops at a cave approximately ten feet from the ground, its wide mouth caught in an open yawn. Staring up at its cavernous entrance, Izzie crosses herself—a move which heightens Grace's interest and a little concern—as she and Fleur move back to the pair.

'Are you alright, Izzie?'

'Yes, Grace. It is good to be free now. Tripp too. I could sing!'

'No!' Tripp laughs.

'And you are both safe. We can all relax now.'

'Yes. No more bad men. But, Grace, my memory is so strong here that it hurts me. I want to cry too. Seeing this cave, I am in Budapest again. A person's spirit grows in a cave, and I needed spirit back then.'

She's needed spirit here in Australia, too, Grace knows. Izzie turns towards her son.

'When Tripp was a child, we went to together in Bounty Bay, eh, Son? But this one, its—' she makes a high dome of her arms.

'Entrance?' asks Grace.

'Entrance looks like Cave Church on Gellért Hill in Budapest—the church of my childhood. I would go there with my mother every Sunday before war came to our city. Church built up on hill above the Danube River. Such blue waters of our river Danube, and from up high on Gellért Hill, even more blue.' She kisses her fingers, then hugs herself. 'And special waters near the church made people healthy, believe it! In that Cave Church we would hope for miracle. Sunlight came through the hole in roof! It moved down and caught me, made me shiny new, bright with magic. I *was* magic! When war came, the Pauline fathers help people dress like them so they could hide there and be protected with love.'

'I'm sure they needed all the help they could get,' says Fleur, impressed with Izzie's lucidity. Fleur had read to Grace about the cave being sealed off in the church in 1951. The head monk was killed, and the rest of the Pauline order were captured by communist secret police and accused of treason, to curb the progression of the Catholic Church. Grace and Fleur had originally found it awe-inspiring that anyone could build a church inside such a beguiling natural structure. Yet they were sad to learn of its history, its fate. Now knowing Izzie's connection to Cave Church, Grace and surely Fleur are both seized anew in pity.

A faint breeze works its way through the trees from the ocean to the clearing, a grassy spot which Dukie says is perfect for the day's picnic. Around them, rainbow lorikeets feed from grevillea bushes, creating a pleasant yet rowdy scene. Carmen claims—although it was probably Sidney—she has prepared the delicious roast chicken, ham and salad picnic lunch for the group, with champagne and fresh ginger beer to wash it all down. Sitting cross-legged on tartan picnic rugs they tuck in as the sand-flies attack.

Erin wheezes and says, 'Why didn't you pack the insect repellent, Mum? We've become pin cushions here.'

Grace sees angry lumps flaring on Erin's bared arms from sand-fly bites.

'Yes, I suppose it was my fault, but someone else could have thought of it.' Grace scratches her own arms, fixing her eyes on Erin, the default sensible one.

'To tell you the truth, I'm a little worried about all this sun,' says Scott. 'It's the Harris curse. Red hair, fair skin, and freckles are passed down through every generation of Harrises. So, Erin, expect a red-haired baby.'

'I'd love a red-haired baby!' Erin beams as bread sticks in Grace's throat. She swallows with difficulty.

'Being fair, I rarely go to the beach now.' Scott examines a squashed sand-fly on his palm.

'We're in the shade here, Scott,' says Erin, now giving an unsettled shrug as she looks around the group. 'Wait until I get you into the open, away from everything.' She pats his arm as a mother would, an unconvincing gleam in her eye. Grace does not want to imagine what her daughter is planning to do with her fiancé.

Scott's smile is equally unconvincing—about the elements, no doubt—convincing Grace even further that he is weak like his father.

Tripp says shyly but with an undercurrent of a spark, 'I'm excited to see the ocean. I've swum in rivers but never anything big.' He stands and rocks Itchy feet. Fleur smiles at him.

'Same as the girls,' laughs Grace. 'It can get rough in the ocean. It might be best if you just explored the beach or paddled a little. Anyway, what an adventure it will be!' Grace hopes for a little nap.

The four young ones—Erin and Scott, Fleur and Tripp—move in pairs in opposite directions to explore the area, escaping the family hoopla. All day Fleur has managed to ignore Erin and Scott. And now, as she rushes away with Tripp, Fleur must be pleased for her chance to get rid of the pests—both, thinks Grace, glumly.

⁓

As the ocean's roar mimics distant thunder—slyly beckoning the couple—they manage to find an overgrown pathway to the ocean. With difficulty they navigate around tangles of bottle brush, saltbush, cotton trees, sharp bracken. They both wear only shorts, tops, and thin rubber thongs on their feet. Annoying thorns and midges make targeted attacks on arms and legs; plus, they're wary of what they could step on. But the whooshing waves intoxicate them, keeping time with their steps, urging them on.

Suddenly the bush spits them clear to a new exposure—deafening ocean clamour. But the landscape is piquant and pristine; insouciance will soon lift their steps.

On top of a high sand dune, they stop to draw breath as the sea breeze picks up. Tripp tastes wildness on his ruffle of salty hair. Fleur wheezes, coughs a little.

'Hey, are you okay?'

A nod.

'You're not a very convincing liar you know, girl.'

'I do my best. Besides, you seem to be labouring yourself.'

They exchange wide smiles.

Spinifex spiders tumble as they dodge sun-bleached white driftwood. Water-plumped plants claw over the hills, showing a delicate sprinkle of purple pigface flowers. Little heads up, they beam unrivalled colour across the pale dunes.

When facing away from the ocean, the pair notices a semicircular panorama of giant mountains. Turning towards it, a huge cliff towers away to their left.

That ocean in all its grandeur—so much water in one place! Across the sky, seagulls daub white paint onto the blue canvas. Salt and sweat are the couple's own marks of adventure. They have become part of this landscape now, a blight no longer.

She glances to the bottom of the dune, then towards him, grinning.

'It's no problem for me, you know. But you might be sorry; it's a very long way down there.'

'I can do anything today. Watch this.' Ignoring his warning, she jumps over the soft edge of the dune.

Not to be outdone, he follows, determined not to let her know of his hesitance. Their bodies become a smother of gritty puffs as innocuous little tumbles become rough, rushing rolls. They crash-land on the crushed shells, packed hard from the last high tide. They stand, shimmy shake, then rush to the water where their footprints disappear in the wet sand.

A sentry soldier crab takes a tentative peek from its wet sand bunker, then quickly retreats. The girl bends down, then rises, unfolding her hand to present him with a shiny pipi shell. A treat for her budgie, she tells him as she shoves a white cuttlefish bone between her breasts, into the material of her thin cotton blouse.

The ocean displays different shades of horizontal blue stripes—pale aquamarine to deep-water indigo—the water darkening towards the horizon. Little soft white-tops sting, then soothe their feet. The gentle movement and hum of the waves seem to settle the young man's awkwardness. Settled if they stay here, but further out to sea waves crash onto reefs she says are called bommies, having read about them. He is suddenly acutely aware of his reliance on this perpetual girl, more than she knows.

Endless waves break and froth like used toothpaste. The intoxicating allure of this place, of how it would look and smell at night, makes him shudder. Does the performance stop for sleep? Ludicrous, it doesn't. Yet he wants her with him to find out for sure.

'Let's go for a swim,' Fleur says.

'I, I...' Tripp stumbles over his words.

Fully clothed bar thongs, she wades in, and he follows. Even knee-deep their bodies rock a little in the current, lost in the mesmeric waves, understanding the uncontrollable drift of sea creatures that have come to greet them. The deeper the couple go, the more the silver white bait stagger in the cold water's force like they do. The butting waves almost knock them off their feet now that they are immersed up to their waists. A surprise cold spindrift slams his face, yet each acclimatising splash seems to warm him.

Fleur braces herself, then jack-knifes underneath the water. He watches her dark shadow loom across the sandy ocean floor, her jellyfish-like pumping limb movements. Her head breaks through to the air, glistening. She finds her feet, shakes a stream of icy droplets from her hair which hit him fair in the face. Easy to wipe away; she can do what she likes. A toothy grin, followed by a shrill girly giggle, she lets her legs collapse. She jumps up, splashes him, laughing. How could this be wrong?

Around the thin straps of her top her skin is dappled with little red and pearly white patches he assumes are the result of the sandflies. Tripp thinks too much about how easily he could peel those straps away. He resists making a move on her; he couldn't take advantage of someone who's been through so much hurt lately. He will compose himself. Yet the outline of the cuttlebone affixed in the centre of her chest draws his attention. He reckons you could push it and she'd talk, this living doll. He forces himself to widen his field of vision, but immediately regrets it because he encounters way too much pull in her chill-shocked nipples. He knows he's stared too long—any amount of time would be too long—and flushes in shame, relieved for the cover of water. How long can he wait?

The whirlwind gamine: that feisty little bundle of provocation and trouble, lives up to her reputation as she splashes him forcefully. Happy for a reprieve from his wayward arousal, he splashes her back, and so the game continues until they are swirling in tandem, whipped up in a fountain of bodies and pheromones that no ocean could dilute. She pushes him into the water, falls on top of him. He recovers, gives a small push back. Enough now, they wipe water from faces. Standing eye to eye, panting, circling slowly in an unsuccessful bid for calm, caught up in a collision of frustration, excitement, and inordinate confusion.

One that started long ago; one that has yet to come to fruition.

Chapter Thirty-Four

Tripp has come to the river because of Fleur, to find something—just an object, really—which may help fix her a little more, restore her constitution. Objects *can* help put things straight, he knows this from experience. Like a scarf—just a piece of material—at another river, enchanting a child and his mother in its colourful transformation of the sun's rays through it. Tripp felt proud to be able to rescue that object when no-one could rescue him. And afterwards, in the days of not knowing the fate of his mother while he worked at Robinson's, Tripp would tie that pink, aqua and orange material—which faded over the years—around a branch to make a cry for help look like a cheerful flag, as if it would alert her to where he was, and she would come running. Preposterous. Yet that scarf did eventually bring them together in a crazy event he can still hardly believe. Tripp and Izzie are living proof that objects can bring people together.

Tripp stands on a bank above a river in urgent need of replenishment, still on Alton land but near the boundary of what was Len Robinson's property, before the old bugger's blessed death. Tripp smells the aromatic peppery odour of lantana everywhere around him. Its matted roots and tendrils mesh the tops of the jagged and eroded banks, some of which wear deep gashes as though shattered by explosives. Even as they await inevitable collapse, the overhangs tease the bleached beaches below, clinging on in a seemingly delicate—but also desperate—show of persistence and daring.

He looks down to the near-dead winding trench where water used to travel, remembering when it was dark and deep, that water, its flow coursing. Every time he visits this place now, he notices more evaporation; years of drought have taken their toll.

When he lived with the tyrant the workers weren't allowed to swim for leisure, that would be an indulgence. The water was only to be used for self-cleaning of filthy bodies at the end of long, hard working days. And no fishing—fishing was strictly forbidden because the bastard who employed him thought he owned the river, and no-one was gonna steal nothin' from him; his gun would make sure of that.

Today, slime shines up at Tripp like a fresh wound requiring attention, evoking a little misplaced guilt. He never met Teddy, yet Tripp cannot escape the thought that the river probably near dried up with the young boy months ago, so death has been a long, drawn-out process.

He wears thick rubber boots because snakes scare him shitless. It is almost summer, and he knows that they are on the prowl for a feed. He has prepared his mind for this walk, too. Having been surrounded by the ruckus of his mother and grandmother, he needs time alone to think about how he will woo Fleur in a more formal, less chaotic way. And he will woo her. The recent separation from her caused pain like he had only once experienced before. He now knows he can't be apart from her for long again. But is he good enough for her? Where is his pedigree? He hardly knows himself, in any sense.

Descending from bank to beach he sinks into the muddy, feculent ditch. Tripp's boots make sucking sounds with every step as though hissing at him, wishing him to succumb to the same fate. He dodges stones, partially disintegrated fish, other matter of unknown origin. Blowflies swarm above small aquatic corpses. All the action seems to play out above ground; surely nothing living would choose to lie in this muck.

He focuses on his task. Recently Fleur told him she comes to the river looking for Teddy's little blue Matchbox car that may have ended up either on the riverbank or in the watercourse. Tripp knows not finding it has been troubling her, so he walks the trench and searches the bank walls for something of that shape. He stops at a small rise in the ground. With his big boot he unearths a little mud, and then some more, before crouching down to examine it for an elusive blue metal object. Steadying himself on his haunches, the unearthly stink is worse at ground level and the mud is worryingly greasy; he wishes he had brought gloves.

Maybe Fleur will join him today and they can have a real talk. He will tell her more about his grandmother's addictive exuberance about living and working in Wagtail; how one day she hopes her family may live together there; how she wants Tripp to become the teacher he hopes to be. Fleur would like to hear that. She will encourage it because that girl always wants what is best for him. But again, the same old fears strike; he cannot crush the thought that he barely deserves her. *Stop now.* He shakes his head to rid his fears. He is worthy of her and today he will find Teddy's car and give it to Fleur. Perhaps she will come, right here and now. Removing most of the mud around the object uncovers a seashell, of all things.

An undisguised rush of footfalls on dry grass alerts him. A low growl. The barking of either a big dog, or a little one with the usual too much attitude, has him falling from his crouch position into the mud. He hopes the creature isn't feral and hungry. 'Bugger,' he mumbles, then hoists himself upright wiping dollops of wet mud onto his trousers. Something like a giant brown Labrador/Poodle cross comes hurtling towards him, barking as it leaps into the mud and showers Tripp in more. 'Easy fella,' he urges, his hands up in surrender.

'Dippy, get back here now!' bellows a harsh female voice. The dog turns its head towards her but doesn't move from its position of standing before Tripp, wagging its tail.

Its rattled owner arrives to check out the beast's prey before it becomes lunch. The dog looks from Tripp to its owner for approval, a self-congratulatory smile plastered on its open chops.

'Dumb goofball of a mutt! When will you ever learn to come to me when I call you?' she chastises as Dippy jumps up and drapes its huge muddy paws over Tripp's shoulders in an invitation to dance. Rather than lead him in a tango, the giant animal covers his face in slobber as Tripp shoves it away. A dog drool connection stretches and breaks as the dog drops to its rightful stance on four paws. Tripp buries his head in his shirt, smearing the mess. The chorus of the woman's hearty laugh leads him to break out in an irresistible smile. He must admit he likes her lack of ceremony although he is not sure about the dog's. He looks the woman up and down. A recollection.

She assesses him and simpers. 'What are you doing here?' she cries with vehemence.

'Shit. I could ask you the same question,' replies Tripp, one eyebrow cocked.

They smile, knowing they have repeated the words from their initial meet-up at the Criterion Hotel. Same words, different voices. Tripp's mood suddenly darkens remembering his fight with Fleur that night.

'Okay, so now we're even-steven. No more surprises. Deal?' says Cathy. Does she trust her words? He suspects this woman is full of surprises. Tripp wonders at their familiarity—he's only briefly met her—yet he simply cannot deny it.

'Deal. Although, you aren't really keeping your side of the bargain, are you? Why are you here?'

'Just giving me dog a run in the outdoors.'

'Dog? I thought it was a bear. That's some obedient animal you've got there, by the way.'

'Only the best training for my Dippy.'

'At least you got the name right.'

'Named for his love of swimming.'

'If that's what you say.'

'Anyhow, what a lovely day it is. It's been so nice having my walk interrupted by a gungy stampede—no offence to you. Tell me straight, Cathy, what are you doing here? Don't you have enough control over that, that monster, to stop it bombarding other people on their private property?' Tripp casts his eyes towards the dog which fervently assesses the mud with loud sniffs.

'Go play!' Cathy sings, at which it dashes off into the bushes.

Tripp wipes himself down. 'Is trespassing your hobby, Karen?'

'Very funny. I'm no trespasser. In fact, you're about four yards short of trespassing on my land.'

'What the hell?'

'I live next door to you. My mum and I have moved from Perth. She'll arrive in a few months, after I get the place in decent order. She's charged me with that fun task.' She rolls her eyes.

'What?' A sour taste comes to his mouth. 'At Robinson's old farm?'

'That's correct,' she snaps, then sighs and looks to the heavens as though sick and tired of eliciting the same reaction from whomever she tells.

'I can't help being shocked. I just had no idea that anyone... so soon after...'

'It's okay, really it is. I know some bad things happened there. I dunno, Mum and I might live there for a while before deciding what to do.'

'What do you mean by that?'

'I mean we'll decide whether to put the place up for sale, or keep growing wheat, or grow fruit trees which is what I'd really like to do, if not here then somewhere else. Staying in one place makes me nervous.'

What is she running from? 'Well, whatever you decide, good luck. I hope your time there is happy.'

'Having a friendly neighbour can't hurt, can it?'

'Guess not.'

Cathy paces, eyes scanning the scenery. 'Say hello to Scott for me. You didn't do it after I asked, though, did you? Don't worry, I've met him now.'

'A dubious pleasure.'

'Call it what you want. I met Grace and Erin too.'

'Good for you. So, are you out here now trying to catch a glimpse of Scott?'

'Don't be ridiculous.' She clears her throat.

'I have to ask, why and how have you ended up living there? Don't you know what Len Robinson did to... to those people?'

'I know he's been implied in a number of crimes, yep.'

'Implicated, not implied. Including murder. Did you know that?'

The woman looks drawn, her colour fading as rapidly as it appeared. 'Word is there were shootings, yeah,' she answers quietly.

'Sorry, Cathy, I'm just finding it hard to understand why anyone would choose to live on a property with such a sordid past, where such an odious man lived, until recently.'

'I don't even know what odious means. Does it mean smelly? Struth, are you some hot shot intellectual or something?' She rolls her eyes.

'Hardly! I read a lot, that's all. And it means nasty.'

She gazes at him fair in the face, chewing on her bottom lip, weighing something up. 'If I tell you why Mum and I are living there, you *must* keep it quiet. Promise me!' Desperation in her words.

So that's it, the reason for the nerves: a secret, something she needs to get out of her system. He fears what is coming next.

'If it's for the best, I will.'

'It is for the best. And well, I've got no-one else to talk to. But if people get word about it...'

'Stop worrying. Just talk.'

'We were left the property. We inherited it. My mother was Len Robinson's wife.'

'Dot?' Tripp is flummoxed, remembering the haggard woman who waited on Robinson like a servant. He didn't think they'd had any children.

'No. My mother is Elena—Elena Robinson, but she never uses that last name. She was his only wife.'

He scratches his mud-caked head. 'So, Len and Dot weren't married?'

'No. Never. My mother was married to Len before Dot ever entered the picture. As gorgeous as I obviously would have been in the outside world 'cos I still am and in fact glow with beauty and charm, as you can see,' she winks at Tripp, 'my dear old daddy Robinson didn't give a hoot about my big potential, couldn't handle the responsibility of a pregnant wife, so he took off.'

'Oh, Cathy, I'm sorry.'

'Sorry he took off?'

'No! Sorry you had such a dud of a father.'

And Tripp would know. He considers telling her he had lived with the bastard for near fifteen years, having earned the right to call him that, but thinks better of it.

'Dud is right. He was hopeless, evil, tight as a prawn's bum in cold water. Can you imagine how I've felt, hearing about his cruelty, knowing that I came from that monster? Imagine if people around here found out who my father was. I couldn't bear the shame, Tripp. I've learnt something: when I have children, I'll make sure the father has money, ambition, and is generous. So, then I could feel secure for once, you know? My husband will be nothing like my father. The only thing Len Robinson gave my mother was a sore heart.' She searches the skies.

'But what about the farm? How did you end up with it?'

'Apparently, when they were first married Len made a will leaving everything to my mother. She thought nothing of it 'cos he was always crying poor so she assumed things would never change for such a loser. They separated, never divorced. Then Len's parents died and left him the property where he lived out his days with Dot. Dot wasn't left a penny, but I hear she couldn't wait to get out, to go live with her sister in Sydney after my father's death. She wanted nothing more of the place.'

'I... knew Robinson, and I know he was a cruel and calculating old codger. He treated his workers poorly, and Dot was used like a slave. Poor woman. Poor *women*.'

'Like I said, he only gave my mum pain. Thank Christ I never knew him, the bastard. Take, take, take, he took what was hers even though she never had much of anything. When she came to Australia, fleeing Italy in the heat of war, she brought only a few things, but they were precious to her, you know? And Robinson was quick to swoop like a vampire or something. He took every little thing of hers: a few books, keepsakes. He took her jewellery and sold it. He even took her scarf when he left her up the duff to go live with Dot. Preggers and all alone. Poor Mum. She used to tell me about that scarf: a beautiful thing, colours like a fierce sunrise. Robinson probably gave the scarf to Dot.

Or another European woman Mum heard he had on the side while he was with Dot. A reffo from Hungary or Greece. There was talk my father got her pregnant too, and he ran off, just as he had done with Mum. Tiger never loses its spots, right? Bloody loser. Liked to spread himself around, did my father. He used to go to the pub and brag. My mum was pleased to be rid of him.'

Silence. Stunned silence. Was that 'reffo' his mother?

'My mum,' Cathy repeats.

Tripp's stomach churns. He is rooted to the ground like a big, goofy, open-mouth statue. He feels Cathy's eyes on him as she resumes shuffling her feet.

'That's strange,' he broaches, having found words again. 'I was just thinking about a scarf. Your mother's one sounds beautiful. Tell me what colours were in it so I can picture it.'

She looks sceptical. 'O... kay, although I don't know why. Pink and orange, and greenish blue, and it had some embroidery around its border. Why? Are you thinking of buying your girlfriend one like it?'

Memories once again come flooding back, of days at the river with his mother, both staring in awe at the sun through the aqua, pink, and orange material, through tiny water droplets glistening like a multitude of stars.

She smirks. 'Or do you wear women's clothing yourself?'

'No. Nothing like that. You were saying?'

'Give me a call if you ever need a cup of flour, won't you?'

His heart has jumped to his neck and ears, pounding fast. In a vague fog he sees her back away, looking perhaps a little afraid. Tripp hears her call to the dog, hears its swishing and thumping through the bush.

He looks over his shoulder. 'What?' He has hardly registered Cathy's last quip. 'Yes, I will,' he agrees to God knows what, to God knows who, because she seems to have, indeed, left.

Tripp walks home in a daze.

Chapter Thirty-Five

Tripp and Izzie lie in their beds awaiting sleep. For Tripp, the day has been an awakening and his thoughts are throwing off sparks, warring in his head. After only fifteen minutes he turns his bedside lamp back on.

'Did we really get rid of that scarf, Mummy, the one my father gave you?'

'What's wrong, Tripp? You don't sound right.'

'Am I right or am I wrong? Only you can tell me that.' He knows his voice is monotone and creepy and he can't get any life into it. And his gait and stride have taken on an oddness as though someone else is walking him around, and it has been this way since he discovered the truth about his parentage. Even at rest he is two distinct entities, both dead in the water. He is both puppeteer and puppet, and the strings, which were tangled before, have come right off now.

'Right or wrong, what is all this? What about the scarf? You know we *burnt* it, Tripp! We did it together.'

'When I was a child, we used it like a filter to see colour and light in this world. But it wasn't real. Nothing can mask what is real. I can't help but feel that it's not done with us yet.'

'What do you mean, Son?'

'I met Cathy from next door. She's a little older than me. She and her mother have moved into Robinson's property.'

It seems a pang of pity has seized his mother as Izzie sits up, frowns, shakes her head, and clasps her small hands to her breast.

How awful it must be to live there after all that's happened at that ghastly place, she'd be thinking.

'Poor people. Did they pay money for it? Do you think they know what happen there?'

He guessed right.

Tripp sits up, studies her. 'They didn't buy it. They inherited it. Robinson left it to them when he died.'

She raises her eyebrows. 'What funny word, *inherited*. How that happen?' The default broken English when she's been cornered.

'Robinson gave it to them. He was married to Cathy's mother before he lived with Dot. Cathy is his daughter.'

Someone cuts Izzie's strings too as she crumples in a heap back onto her bed, her eyes shiny, wide, and desperate as she scans the room for someone other than her son to help her.

'Len Robinson left Cathy's mother because he couldn't handle the responsibility of a child. Now *you* don't look right, *Anya*. Do you want some water?' *Perhaps pouring it over you would be suitable?*

A nod leads Tripp to lift a jug from her bedside table, half fill a glass, and pass it to her. He notices how awkwardly she moves to sit upright, the shaking of her little hands as they encircle the glass then lift it. She empties it in one gulp.

'Apparently, he and Dot were never married. Cathy told me of the way Robinson took everything of her mother's, even her pink, orange and blue-green scarf, with embroidery around it. Sounds like yours, doesn't it, the one we used to play with, the one we burnt? She told me she heard that Robinson gave the scarf to a little Hungarian or Greek woman he was seeing when he lived with Dot.'

His mother clasps a trembling hand to her mouth. 'I, I...'

'He's my father, isn't he?'

She drops her hand into her lap. 'You need to understand truth!'

'Understand? I was so bloody careful not to ask you why you never came looking for me, not once, while I was missing for all those terrible years. When all along you probably knew I was next door. Right there next door with a monster, getting beaten and starved and being terrified and fighting for the lives and sanity of myself and my mates—'

'Stop it! Stop now! I didn't know you were there all those years! When you taken from me, Altons found me on road. A snake bit me and they saved me, bring me here. Robinson—Joe, he call himself to me—he say he kill me and family if I take baby away. But I did! Away from him. But still you were taken from me as a boy, so I think you with him or police or bad Hungarian friends of my bad father! Please, Tripp, it wasn't my fault you were stolen. And I didn't know where you were for all those years.' His mother's tears are flowing now, and Tripp admits to feeling a little sorry for her. Sorry and indignant.

'And what? Charlie and Grace just magically knew I was your son, and I was working next door at Robinson's, so they brought me here to you?'

'Teddy found my scarf at Robinson's and bring it here. Until then, I not know you were there! Believe me, Son!'

'You know, I used to wonder why the old bastard Robinson was so strange about the scarf. It was the only thing of mine he allowed me to keep. Then again, it was all I ever had. Perhaps he was planning on giving it to his next woman. He made sure everything else was taken from me: my dignity, freedom, my grandmother, a name I could be proud of, you...'

Abruptly, he stands. 'Since meeting Cathy and piecing together the truth—no, even before then—I've wondered if I'm half rotten. Now I know I am.'

He grabs his coat and leaves the room, preparing for another cold night-time walk around the property before spending an uncomfortable night on the scratchy hay floor of the shearing shed.

With Tripp out of the house all night—Grace heard him leave and not return—Izzie spent the long hours making terrifying howling noises, like those of the wild dogs they sometimes hear in the bush at dawn. Izzie's awful wailing continues this morning. Grace supposes that they must have had an argument.

The crying tree has been shedding tears lately, and Grace has tried so hard to stop her fears of upcoming trouble from overwhelming her. Unable to wait another minute she knocks on Izzie's door.

'Tripp?' Izzie's broken voice.

'It's me, Grace. Can I come in?'

'I, I not know.' Izzie sniffs and shuffles around to prepare herself.

'You've been up all night, crying. Please let me in.'

'Alright.'

Realising Izzie is not moving, Grace enters and draws the curtains on the new day, then sits next to Izzie on her bed. The little woman looks wretched as she squints against the light, wipes sweat from her forehead, releasing a heavy sigh.

'What has happened, dear?'

'Tripp, he knows.'

'Knows?'

'Yes, yes! He has found name of father.'

'No! But Izzie, we haven't told anyone.'

'It was girl living on next property now.'

'Cathy?'

Izzie nods. 'Yes. Her mother, she was married to Joe before he met Dot. Joe had child all along!'

'Married to Len Robinson? But what about Dot?' Remembering the crumpled woman in Robinson's decrepit kitchen, being dismissed like a dog when talk between the Altons and that horrible villain got tough.

'Dot and Joe not married. He give farm to Cathy and her mother after he died. In his bill.'

'What?'

'Bill. Paper after died.'

'Will? Is that what you mean?'

'Yes. Bill, will, would, won't. I so confused, Grace. And now Tripp thinks I put him with that bad man. Now Tripp think he bad inside like old apple. My fault.'

'No, surely not.' How can Grace reassure her? 'He must remember how excited you were when you saw him again. He would never think that you betrayed him.'

'I think he hates me now. He loves me, now hate. What am I to do?'

'Oh, Izzie, he'll come around, you'll see.' Grace gives her a rousing cuddle, resting her chin on Izzie's hair that seems to be turning grey as she rocks her—wondering, fearing what all the lies and deception have led to.

Tripp had decided to try to settle his mother, to try giving her the benefit of the doubt. But in the stark morning kitchen light, she clattered dirty cooking utensils from breakfast in thinly veiled anger that Tripp absorbed like a warning, leaving no room for him to get close to her. He couldn't stand seeing her like that—that little ball of fury—so he left her to her rage. In the garden, he vented his own anger by digging up weeds and ruthlessly pruning shrubs, sneaking into the kitchen for an occasional drink or snack. Then he moved on to his farm chores and—despite his tiredness—found the distraction of being physically occupied all day relieving.

Late afternoon, when Fleur returns from secretarial college, Tripp waylays her in the kitchen. He has vowed not to be angry with her; his ancestry is not her fault. Together they sit sipping lemonades at the kitchen table as he hears—without really listening—to stories of her tutor making some appalling spelling mistakes. This genial scene belies what he is about to tell her. Still more inflamed than he supposes, he doesn't start well.

'It may be for the best if we just take things slowly.'

She coughs on her lemonade. 'What the hell are you talking about?' She thumps her glass down on the table and swipes her palm over her mouth. 'Did Bene and Luca tell you I spoke with them while you were away? Is that it?'

He scowls. *What exactly had they spoken about?*

'So, they didn't believe me?'

'No, that's not it, Fleur.' *What did those mongrels say to her?*

'You know, Tripp, at least they were honest. You've all been talking about me. They thought I was sleeping with boys at the pub.'

'No, Fleur. You don't understand. I defended you.'

'I defended *myself!* I don't need your protection.'

Tripp's stomach knots. 'God, Fleur, can't you recognise affection?'

'Does your affection include doing this, dumping me?'

'I'm not really. I just need some time to think things through.'

'About me because you are ashamed of me.'

'No, never—not you! I suspect I might be ashamed of myself.'

'You are making absolutely no sense and I really don't need this now. You've been away for so long. Surely you had enough time to think about us then? How can you be so cruel to me, after all we've gone through?'

'Now I know why I avoid looking in mirrors, I've been scared to see what I really am. Truth is, I'm also scared of what I may become.' He hears the tremble in his feeble voice—how pathetic.

'Well, that makes two of us, Tripp. Now, if you don't have anything nice to say to me you can just piss off!'

As Tripp slumps away to shower, he turns and watches Fleur opening the drinks cabinet. She brings out a dusty bottle of unopened whiskey. Tripp shudders, because she unscrews it like she's breaking someone's neck.

Chapter Thirty-Six

In the loungeroom after dinner, Grace struggles with a magazine crossword puzzle made more difficult because she is acutely aware of Erin and Scott sitting wordlessly opposite her. How can Scott stare at one page of a newspaper for many minutes?

'Hey, Erin,' he says, angling his head towards her, 'there's an article here about Blackstone Ridge. It says there's an opal rush. People are coming all the way from Europe to Australia to strike it rich on black opal.' He stops to draw breath, then grins at her.

Erin heats up. 'That's an awfully long way to go to mine with no guarantee of a strike.'

'That's the pull of it, I guess: the possibility. Can you believe that in 1935 they found a 170-carat black opal out there? The Southern Cross, they called it. That'd be about this big.' He extends his arms to the size of a small loaf of bread. 'How would you feel if I took a little trip out there, just to case it out?'

'What, now? Leave me—leave us—here? But you said you couldn't bear to be apart from me, especially since… the picnic.'

Grace clears her throat, wanting to escape. 'What's a seven-letter word for *harmony?* Not *harmony*.' She chews on the end of her pen.

'I want to be with you, Erin,' whines Scott, 'but we have our whole lives to discover one another. It would only be for a few days.'

'Why, Scott? Can't it wait?'

'That's it, *balance*.' Grace writes her word.

Scott shakes his head. 'I need to prove myself to you, to our families.

I must make it on my own, can't you see? Please see that, sugar.'

'But you are proving yourself every day here, to all of us.'

'My parents don't care. I suspect they'd rather I just sat on my arse all day watching the share prices rise. Excuse the French, Grace.'

'But we need you here—I, I need you here.' Erin's words sound hollow.

'We're just talking about a few weeks.'

Weeks now?

'Please let me try to make a go of it. It's for you. I could find you something pretty, something to put around your finger, and your wrist, and here.' Scott plants kisses on Erin's neck, making her giggle. Erin doesn't giggle when upset. Things are changing, her oldest daughter is losing control.

'You know, I do like pretty things. Just don't stay any longer.'

'Bother, I just remembered I said I'd do a bit of gardening this week over at Cathy's, at Robinson's old place.'

'Why you? Can't they afford a gardener?'

'I know, Grace. It's a bother. Cathy told me that there's a hole in the roof and she's scared of possums getting in. Since I'm a builder and I like climbing roofs, I thought I could help. Perhaps I could drop in over there tomorrow.'

'You like climbing roofs?' Erin knots her brow.

'Rooftops are safe places.'

Grace and Erin exchange unsettled looks.

Scott spends all the next day, and evening, at Cathy's. Two days later, he gathers a few essentials, gets a lift from Charlie to the train, and travels to Sydney—where he stays at some swishy hotel for a couple of nights—en route to Blackstone Ridge.

In the blue worker's cottage, Grace, and Erin—who has barely said a word—sit shelling peas for dinner, bringing a routine task into the cosy little place. Grace notices the vase sitting empty on the coffee table, just as it was for a time before Scott left; its presence is loud and distracting. Grace wonders if it will ever hold flowers again. Erin said it was just a little thing, but the life has left it now; that is not a little thing. The air feels unnatural and tense. Erin's mood almost stifles Grace.

'Do you think Scott is "finding himself" in the wilderness? We're not even married yet and he takes off.'

Grace struggles with her words of reassurance. 'He has been working like a trooper. Dad is forever speaking of his work ethic. But Scott's priority is you.'

'Leaving someone is not prioritising them.'

'He wants to make his fortune for you both, on his own. Although your dad has tried to keep it from everyone, Scott must know by now that our farm is in a bit of strife.'

'It's not just about him going away. If only it was that simple.'

'Is it really that complicated, darling?'

'I've stopped bleeding, Mum. I haven't had a period since we lost Teddy.'

Grace flicks her eyes around the room, searching for an answer. 'Yes. Stress can do things like that to your body.'

'I saw that cantankerous Doctor Gibbs, quite the charmer. He poked around a lot and ran some blood tests.'

'That was sensible.' That awful sensible word again.

'Sensible, right. Mum, I've just found out that I'm barren.'

'What?' Did she hear right?

'As the Simpson Desert.'

The heaviness in her daughter's words! Grace's blood runs cold, her breath flooding her lungs like setting concrete.

'His diagnosis, I cannot believe how dispassionately he delivered it. Premature menopause, he said. He gave me a prescription for hormone replacement. Apparently, I've been through the change, at my age! Fleur was right, she always told me I was old.'

'This cannot be real.' Especially if Gibbs—known for his ineptitude—told Erin the news. Grace scans the room to make sure she is not having a nightmare.

'The tests confirmed it to be true, perfectly imperfectly true.'

'Oh no, darling, not you. If anyone deserves a baby, you do. You've always wanted children so much.' Her tears are building but she must stay strong.

'And now we may never get a male heir for the farm. Imagine Fleur having a baby? Perish the thought.' Her daughter's cruel words are unlike her.

Grace reaches for Erin's chilly hand. 'Now don't do this, Erin. You girls are the heirs to the farm. You're quite capable—both of you.'

'Until we're no longer around. Oh, Mum,' Erin pulls away, 'how did everything go so wrong? Heirs to an impoverished farm, no children. This must be my punishment, for failing Teddy.' Erin's filmy eyes threaten to spill.

'You didn't fail your brother! How could you think such a thing? You were so ill that when you were in hospital, at times we wondered if you'd make it. I'm the one who should feel guilty about all the fallout from that day. And if anyone should take the blame for what happened to Teddy, it's me.'

'Well, this new fact is just another cross for me to bear, and I'll suffer it as best I can. But being told so bluntly that I'll never be a mother is really, really hard to take.'

Erin grabs tissues from her pocket, furiously rubbing away her tears as she would clean a blackboard, as though trying to erase any trace of her emotions.

'I beg of you, Mum, promise not to tell *anyone* about this. I'll work out how to handle it.'

Erin retires to the piano and spends the next two hours playing what seems to be every concerto, symphony, and sonata she knows—dragging out her lament for all to hear.

Recently, in confidence Fleur told Grace she was having baby dreams. *Beyond*. Grace couldn't mention it—Erin's private matters are not for Grace to divulge—but she suspects Fleur's dreams were an omen predicting the family will be meeting no newborns here on Earth.

Grace stews on Erin's infertility as she and Charlie sit reading the previous day's morning newspaper together in bed. Erin has been uncharacteristically cantankerous and sullen for a while now, and it's been worse since Scott's unpredictable journey. And now this! Grace is powerless to do anything about any of it. Something else would need to change. As usual, Charlie has said nothing of Scott's absence, so she must. She whacks her section of paper down on Charlie's leg.

'Woah, easy!'

'I just don't understand why Scott felt the need to leave his fiancée. Shouldn't he be spending every spare second with Erin? It's not natural, unless he has employment out there, which I suspect he doesn't.'

'It's only been a week so don't jump the gun about anything long-term. And you know Scott—he's his own man, Grace. He loves Erin and just wants to do things in his own way.'

'At the expense of his fiancée. Erin has been unhappy for a while. Everyone can see it. Tripp told me that Cappi is worried about her.'

'Cappi is a thoughtful man. But I hear Erin playing piano—that must mean something, love?'

'Don't you know by now that she plays when she's upset? It's therapy for her. Can you have a word to Scott when he comes back? He needs to know how unhappy she is.'

'Good God, Grace, I can't meddle in other people's relationship woes!'

'It is your daughter we're talking about, Charlie. Our daughter. If you won't say anything, I will.'

Led to confrontation yet again by Grace, he reneges: 'Alright. Leave it to me. I'll see what I can do.'

'We have an unhappy little family at present. And Izzie and Tripp are troubled because neither wants to live in that new house Scott built. They've both confirmed this to me on separate occasions so don't be surprised if they approach you about alternative living arrangements.'

'I'll take it as it comes.'

Why can't she just flippantly not care like her husband?

'Charlie, there's something more pressing: Tripp knows who his father was.'

Grace looks outside towards the crying tree, sensing it cringe.

'What? I told him not to...'

She barely hears Charlie's words but notices that he, too, turns to face the window.

She makes eye-contact and continues. 'A young woman named Cathy lives next door at Robinson's place now. Apparently, Cathy is Robinson's daughter from an early marriage. She told Tripp this, who then confronted Izzie about it.'

'An early marriage?'

'Yes, Charlie, but that's not the biggest revelation. This all means that Cathy is Tripp's half-sister.'

'So, *Cathy* told... But this is ludicrous!' Charlie comes to life. 'Another Robinson marriage, another poor suffering woman.'

'Not "another" marriage, just the one. Len and Dot were never married.'

'Well, at least Dot must have had some sense. That's one up on that slime ball.'

'Small mercies. And not profitable because he didn't leave her a cracker.'

'Gracie, I hope Tripp isn't too cranky with Izzie.'

'He will understand, even if it takes time. He will see that no mother would ever choose to leave her precious son with a no-gooder like Len Robinson. Especially a mother as caring and loving as Izzie. But, Charlie, we shouldn't get involved in this. Never say a word about it to anyone.'

'Yes, yes, you're right. Of course, yes, you're right.'

'Settle down.' She pats his leg. 'What's happening with Fleur and Tripp? Things should be better now he is back, but he has found this out... Poor Fleur. Those days of coming home at dawn, saying it was college when I know her classes are during the day... I thought we'd made a breakthrough in our relationship but whenever I come near her, she rushes off. I'm terribly worried about her, Charlie. I can't talk to her properly because she's still blocking me out.'

'And you are hurt because of it.'

'Me? I guess I am.'

'She's still suffering over Teddy, love.'

'Her partner in crime, yes. We are all suffering. I know at first, I was confused about the whole situation, but I hope she doesn't think I blame her for what happened to Teddy. I don't—not in the least.'

'She must know that.'

'And I've told her!' *But you blamed Fleur initially, didn't you, Grace?* 'It's as if she has no-one to talk to, and I was so hoping Tripp would help her. By the way, thanks for organising the trip to Stanford Park. I mean it, everyone seemed refreshed afterwards. Though it's all suddenly gone pear-shaped since then, again. I truly fear for our girls.'

'It was generous of Dukie to ask us; I can't take credit for that.'

'Then give me something I *can* give you credit for.'

'That's harsh.' Charlie sounds hurt but she's in no mood to give him compassion. 'So, the truth's out,' he continues, 'you don't admire me.'

'I didn't mean it like that. I'm speaking about our girls.'

'Have I let you down?'

'No, not at all. I always admire you. Your heart, your work ethic, your soul, everything. For the love of God, do I have to spell it out?' She could cry. *This is not about you, Charlie Alton!*

'It's just sometimes I need to hear how wonderful I am.' His wink is met with her unresponsive stare; she is too flustered to jest.

'You could try and help Fleur.'

'Alright, tell me what I can do.'

'Involve her, Charlie. She's always wanted to help more around here than you've allowed. Sometimes you wouldn't let her when she was young, and now you don't even have that excuse. Come on—she can do anything, that one, and you know it. Give her some responsibility.'

'I'll see to that then, too, shall I? Looks like I'll be busy. Do *you* have any awkward conversations to look forward to?'

'Don't call speaking with your daughter "awkward". And I've had my share—trust me. I'm not letting myself off the hook, I know our family needs healing. If things can work out as well as they did with Izzie and Tripp—finding each other, finding Cora—I'll be the happiest lady alive. And you'd better watch out for me when I'm happy, Charlie.' She manages a wink of her own.

'I can hardly remember,' he mumbles. Chucking the bedclothes off as though they were filled with vermin, he rises and leaves the room.

'Ah, just the girl I want to see,' shouts Fleur's father, sneaking up behind her as she downs a glass of water at the kitchen sink. She splutters, relieved to have managed to swallow her contraceptive pill, just. She needs a real drink, but her new urges must wait—at least until she gets some time alone.

'Whoa! Settle down. Morning, Dad.' Her voice is shaking, can't calm it. 'Where's Mum?'

'Still in bed and better bleeding well get a move on soon.' Charlie shuffles his bulk awkwardly around her.

'Well, you sure sound happy with her today!'

Her father grunts. She steers around him and returns to the table to finish her meagre breakfast. He makes himself a tea, then joins her.

Suddenly Grace appears in the kitchen and without a word, heads outside.

'Love you too, Mum!'

'You've been on my mind.' Charlie casts Fleur a serious look across the table.

'Sounds scary.' She winces. Her father doesn't usually talk like this, and she is in no mood to answer anyone's questions, even his.

'Wonder if you'd be up to helping a bit more around the farm. The sheep need to be dipped soon. We could use all hands on deck.'

Not as scary as she had imagined. 'Sorry, Dad, but I can't. I'm snowed under with study.'

'What study? Typing?' His tone is sarcastic and patronising, and he averts his eyes; so he should.

'I don't study typing.' Some deserved anger in her voice. 'But I do study shorthand and I have an exam coming up.'

'No need to get upset, Fleur. I understand your work is important. I was just wondering if you could help your old man out.'

'Like I said, I can't now. I've still got this damned chest infection, too.'

'Do try to look after yourself, love. Mum's worried too. It looks like you're run down, with that greasy hair, and those circles under your eyes make you look like you've been branded.'

'Thanks for the pep talk, Dad. But branded? Not me. I don't belong to anyone and never will! Don't worry, you can tell Mum I'm taking tablets for my chest. Pity they won't help my ugliness.'

Charlie simply shakes his head at her. *That ugly, eh?* Does he wonder if he's left everything too late with Fleur? There is nothing she can do; she lacks any strength to placate him with words he may want to hear.

She rushes outside hoping for some peace. In silence she passes her mother and Izzie crouched over the vegetable garden like animals meeting at a waterhole.

Not a care in the world.

Chapter Thirty-Seven

Monday morning. Scott returns to the farm. Grace—sitting beside Erin at the kitchen table—balks as his enlivened body tumbles through the homestead door. His flash of movie star teeth, slick Brylcreemed hair. Peeling sunburn. He has been gone little over a week.

'That place is *buzzing* I tell you, Erin.' His grinning face is rubicund. He plants a kiss on his startled fiancée's forehead.

'Well, *you* certainly sound as though you enjoyed yourself,' says Grace.

'I did, very much. Met an honest chap named Colin who's been out there for a few years and built up quite a reputation in the area's mining circles. Sorry, sweetheart, I didn't find you the big one this time, but I got you a few scraps to whet your appetite.' From his pocket he removes a handful of opal nobbies, flaunting them in his open palm before Erin's face. He catches Grace's stare, smiling and nodding as though she is his confidant.

'Such bright colours,' croons Erin. 'What's this about whetting my appetite? What scheme are you planning, Scott?'

'Oh, don't sound so dire. I've merely said to Colin I'd be back in a week or so to help him.'

'What, again? And without consulting me.'

'Look, darling, there's so much possibility in the mining fields for a man. I'd never dream of taking you there. Honestly, it's only smelly men, flies, dirt everywhere. It's hot as Hades, everything is rough. I wouldn't want you to go through it. You understand, don't you Grace?'

She is speechless. The Scott she knows prefers indoors; this one looks like it's been on holidays.

'We missed you here. I... oh, don't worry about it,' says Erin.

'So, how is everyone here? Have you been working with Cappi again?'

'What? Not lately. Why?'

'All good. How is your sister?'

'Fleur? Dire as ever. Why?'

'It's nothing really. I worry, that's all. Just look after her.'

Grace flinches. *You have no right to even be thinking about Fleur, Scott. Worry for your fiancée.*

'I do my best, Scott. Always.' Erin's mouth stretches but the smile doesn't come.

⁓

Carefully so as not to get scalded, Grace plops chopped potatoes into a stew brewing on the stovetop for tonight's dinner. Izzie is outside picking tomatoes, beans, and cucumbers, for a salad lunch. Grace would rather have joined her, but Izzie said she needed some fresh air, meaning time alone. Grace is worried about her; she wants all of Izzie's moments to be only happy ones now. Grace has waylaid Charlie to talk more about Fleur before he feeds the horses this morning. But suddenly Scott hurries into the kitchen—interrupting their conversation which has hardly begun—saying he hopes to grab a quick bite to eat before helping Charlie with the chores outside. He appears more edgy than usual.

'Good to have you home, Scott!' Charlie says, rousing.

'Good to be home, Dad.'

Grace stirs the stew with her wooden spoon, ignoring them both. Glancing sideways, she sees Scott sniff, scouting the room for food like a mongrel dog at a barbeque.

'Grab yourself something from the fridge,' says Charlie. 'You're looking thin; sunburnt, too, I see.'

Grace turns to assess the damage. 'Looks nasty. It could peel. Turn patchy. Like— Charlie, what's that bad skin condition?' She is pleased to point out the damage. Stir, stir, stir.

'Really?' Worriedly, Scott gently pats his cheek. 'I'll be tanned in a day or two. Thanks, Dad, to be honest I'm ravenous.'

Scott whips open the fridge door and makes a sandwich, making himself more at home than Grace wants.

'So, tell us, how have things been going out there?' asks Charlie.

'It can be rough, believe me.' Scott takes a bite from a celery stick and talks through the stringy mess. 'Snakes, dingoes—and that's just the miners!' He pauses for a reaction. Grace is surprised not to hear Charlie's laugh at the lame joke. 'But my mining mate, Colin, thinks we're not far off the big one. He had a spill with his former partner who recklessly broke his agitator and refused to cough up for repair costs. But after citing my qualifications, my building prowess, my ability to learn fast, Colin was impressed and has gladly shown me the ropes. Colin usually restricts himself to mining only the Bridge, but the mad crowds—the Bridge's "maniacs"—have spread their activities, so we went further west to Cobby Creek where Colin has leased a claim. He started me on noodling: sorting rocks on the surface.' He takes another bite of celery, focusing on stacking his sandwich. 'We've moved on from that to the old-fashioned way of mining: shaft sinking with pick, shovel, and dynamite. It's a blast, let me tell you! Ha! Imagine how those glorious rocks came about. Hundreds of millions of years ago, silica filling underground cavities and eventually creating something amazing.'

'What is it you're mining for again, Scott?' asks Grace, knowing full well what he is mining for. She keeps her back to him.

'Opals! Blackstone Ridge is the home of black opal, Australia's most highly prized gemstone.'

'Well, we hope a strike is on the cards. But you must be relieved to be back with Erin again,' says Charlie.

Grace turns at this, noticing her husband assess Scott's blank gaze at his food on the benchtop. Curling his tongue over his top lip, he slices his sandwich into two halves.

'She misses you when you're away.' Grace now stares at Scott whose throat makes a grunting sound. He bites into his sandwich. Smiling weakly, he walks over to Grace and wraps an arm around her waist. She focuses on the food. Stir, stir, stir.

'Yes, I know she does. I'm afraid I'll be going away again soon. But Erin says she's glad I'm trying to succeed, and I'm working on a trip to Sydney for both of us at an opulent hotel when things at the Bridge ease up. After we're married, of course. It'll be something special, believe me.'

'Do they have a bridge there?' asks Charlie.

'No, it's just a contraction of Blackstone Ridge the locals like to use. Perhaps it's a bridge to the Emerald City, or rather one brimming with opal. Utopia to my mind anyway.'

Grace prickles. 'Or the locals might just sit around playing bridge all day. Does Erin know about this trip to Sydney?' Feeling Scott's tension, Grace dislodges herself from him to get to the sink for a glass of water, suddenly very thirsty.

'Not yet so please keep quiet about it, okay?'

Urgently, she guzzles the tepid liquid. Why would she say anything? A trip with Erin? Grace doubts it.

Dread-stricken, Fleur watches as Scott moves to sit at the kitchen table next to Erin as the family await dinner. Fleur retracts her feet because he is opposite her and his touch could well be lethal. Erin looks like she's been crying. Fleur doesn't blame her—Scott is back. Izzie keeps elbowing her son as if to prompt him to perform something of crucial importance. Fleur catches Tripp's unease. She doesn't know what to make of all this sickness.

'Perfect shepherd's pie, Izzie dear.'

'My pleasure, Grace. Everyone, please eat, I made plenty.'

Everyone picks at their food, even Charlie. Fleur takes a long slurp of her wine. Her fork is a cricket bat: she nudges peas, watching as they roll across the plate and catch in a mashed potato practice net. She flicks one pea onto the table by accident. 'Six!' she yells. No reaction.

Another Izzie prod to Tripp's ribs. He twiddles his thumbs and clears his throat, but his words emerge as a rasp. 'There's something Mummy and I have been wanting to speak with you all about.'

'Haha, *Mummy*,' chortles Scott. Fleur wants to kill him.

'Gawd, this sounds serious. At least we're all seated,' says Charlie.

Tripp seems to inhale all the air from the room. 'We've decided not to move into the structure Scott built.'

Fleur spurts out red wine, chuckles, and wipes her dribbling nose on her linen serviette. Catching Izzie's eye, she indicates the red-splotched fabric and mouths 'sorry'.

Scott shuffles about on his seat, breathing audibly through his nose due to obviously gritted teeth. 'You wait to tell me this now, in front of everyone?' He glares at Tripp. 'Have you even seen inside? And it is a *house*. It's all ready to become a home, and it's glorious.'

'I'll probably go see it sometime when you aren't around. Make sure it's structurally sound before anyone decides to inhabit it. Don't want people getting hurt. But it won't be my mother and me living there, Scott.'

'After all my hard work? I spent weeks on that thing, weeks of backbreaking slog!'

'Charlie, if you want us to leave the farm, so be it,' says Tripp. 'With all the lies and deceit around here, I may even go alone.'

Fleur loses more of her appetite. *Don't leave me.*

Izzie looks fit to explode. 'No! You're not leaving me, never again.' Izzie bows her head, shakes it from side to side. Tripp takes her hand and pats it.

'Bally rot you're leaving!' Charlie bellows. 'Neither of you are going anywhere if I can help it.'

Izzie beams.

'Tell me, Tripp,' says Scott, staining his white serviette brown with gravy from his top lip, 'isn't it good enough for you and your mother? Is that it? Because I tell you, you won't find a more solid piece of architecture in the country.'

Fleur laughs out loud at Scott's preposterous brag.

'We have had so many changes, Scott. Too many. So hard. You not understand.' Poor Izzie, trying to make peace.

'Oh, I understand alright!'

'Scott!' Grace chastises. 'They've made up their minds so please just let things be. Izzie and Tripp, you are most welcome to continue living on in the main house if that's where you feel most comfortable. Please don't contemplate leaving. This is your home, for as long as you both want it to be.'

'Thank you, Grace,' mother and son say in unison.

'Right, so that's settled.' Charlie rubs his palms together.

Scott is fuming, his eyes flick around everyone yet fix on no-one, lacking punch. 'In that case, Erin and I will move into the new house after the wedding. So, Tripp and Izzie, you can then move into the little blue workers' cottage, can't you?'

The group sits immobile, startled, Scott's idiotic comments raising their anxiety once more.

Erin looks puzzled before shooting Scott a death stare.

Who does he think he is, trying to organise the household? Fleur feels some smugness as Scott buries himself deeper with his ramblings.

Picking up on Erin's wrath, Charlie gives a defeatist slow head shake. 'Well,' he manages, 'there's plenty of time to consider all options. Scott, I'm sure you'll be wanting to speak with Erin *in private* about where you're going to live. Tripp and Izzie, Grace is right, you're always welcome in this house, or wherever you decide to rest your weary bones. No more talk about leaving the Alton property, okay?' Charlie nods at Tripp.

Glances all around. Tripp opens his mouth as if to say something that does not emerge.

'Yes,' snaps Scott, 'but I'd say those two would agree most of the time anyway. Minds thinking alike. Mother and son. Father and son. Funny how family members are usually so in tune with their thoughts, words, deeds. The apple doesn't fall far from the tree, eh Tripp?'

Indulging his self-proclaimed omnipotence, Scott cannot, or does not want to, hide the thing festering inside him. Whatever it is makes Fleur shudder. Another slurp of wine.

Charlie gives a nervous laugh. 'Don't know what you're drinking,

Scott, but you're about as lucid as a llama.'

'Lunatic,' mutters Fleur.

'Speaking of drinks, isn't it time for a top-up?' Abruptly Scott stands, almost toppling his chair. He grabs the wine bottle and pours himself a large red. 'Anyone else?'

The room has fallen deathly quiet.

'Fleur, you're not one to knock it back,' declares Scott, making Fleur want to hurl her dinner from her stomach for his inuendo, and hurl her glass at him.

Her eyes are grog-bleary, but she manages to grip the top of her glass just as Scott pours a waterfall of red wine over the back of her hand. It rushes onto the tablecloth, and Fleur imagines a part of her haemorrhaging with the spill, once again losing more of herself, losing something this time that may never be replaced.

All eyes now blank stares. Innocent bystanders to a crime, a crime she knows will soon...

Chapter Thirty-Eight

One week passes. Tripp's presence without his affection has made the days drag for Fleur. Yet Scott has been away mining again during that time, and the days without him have sped by. Now he is back; here comes the rot again. It is late at night. Earlier, Fleur watched on with some satisfaction as Erin bitterly banished Scott—with his broad grin, his filth and stench—to the shower, after demanding he eat the scrambled eggs that she had burnt for him. He did both.

Something about the full moon on this mild, dry night makes Fleur remain outside with the crying tree for a while. The drought drags on, yet as she predicted, the tree is beginning to spit water, to weep. Soon, very soon, will be its time; Fleur knows this. What she doesn't know is whether to be excited or wary.

'I know you will show me your magic soon, old tree.'

With her arms wrapped around its damp trunk she spies Scott creeping across the yard. He is about to hide something he has stolen. She knows this because she saw his prize at the lamb birth. She has been waiting for this moment, and for just about the first time in her life, she trusts her intuition fully.

The beam of light from Scott's torch snakes across the grass, announcing his appearance—to Fleur, his serpentine appearance. Unlike her, Scott enjoys the spotlight. Yet the moonlight envelops him in a kindlier way than it should—that thief. He is heading towards the newly built structure, which now has its cladding up. No-one wants to call it a home, let alone live in it.

Scott carries a knapsack on his back, and Fleur is certain it is filled with tools. Stuffed under his shirt he cradles his recently birthed colourful prize which he carries like a newborn. She hears him call it his baby! Awkwardly carting his bundles front and back, Fleur reckons he looks a little like Linus from the Peanuts cartoon with his security blanket, or an upright pregnant camel.

Crickets provide background chirping as Scott nears the new structure. Fleur scuttles after him and hides behind a nearby tree which allows for close, unobstructed viewing of the house. She sees him approach its entrance, turning off his torch before opening the stiff door.

She scans the darkness, searching through the windows for his form to appear. The house illuminates as Scott pulls a cord of an electric lightbulb pendant hanging from the ceiling. The bulb swings—knocking his head, causing him to curse and Fleur to snigger—casting spotlights around him. Fleur half expects police sirens to follow, perhaps even a fighter aircraft to bomb the place.

Her eyes follow Scott to the kitchen where she hears the whoosh of a valve being released. He turns and walks away. *Idiot! If he is testing the gas, why leave the area?* From another room he eventually returns to switch it off. Fleur smells the eggy, noxious gas as it floats from house to yard towards her.

As Scott moves about, Fleur hears a couple of floorboards creak underfoot. He bounces, testing them for looseness, then crouches down, vanishing from her sight. She hears Scott jimmy then lift those floorboards, hears the rip of them breaking free. When he stands and turns on his torch, Fleur is aware of his muscular arms as he aims its light down into the abyss underneath the house. From his shirt he removes his prize, eases it into the hole, then presses the boards back down.

Secrets buried for now, Scott will sleep well tonight.

Chapter Thirty-Nine

Two days after Scott's latest return, Grace barges in to accost Fleur in the lounge room at midday, thumping down upon the couch beside her. Is there anywhere in this place she can hide? The last thing she needs right now is her mother's accusatory, or worse, condescending words.

'Did you stay out late last night?'

'No, I didn't even go out.' *I stayed on the property.* 'I haven't been out for ages. And stop, please just stop. I'm in no mood to be interrogated.'

Another of her mother's dramatic sighs. 'Alright.' Fleur sees her stewing on something. 'It's just I haven't seen you with Tripp much since his return.'

'Haven't you got a wedding to plan or something remotely meaningful to do?'

'Yes, that's right, the wedding. I've barely thought of it, to be honest. Erin seems a bit down lately. Have you noticed?'

'I'm not surprised. Have you seen who the groom will be?'

Her mother droops her head. 'Listen. Perhaps it's time we tried to…'

'Now you listen! I have enough problems of my own to start worrying about my pampered sister.'

'For goodness' sake, Fleur.'

'No, I'm not biting any further. Now if you'll excuse me, I have homework to do. Talk it out with her. Do you really think she'd tell me anything? Ever?'

'Fleur…'

'See ya later, alligator.' Arms towards her mother, she claps her palms together as the reptile would snap its jaws.

Homework, what a joke! She hasn't been to college for weeks. Suddenly feeling enormously tired and burdened, her room beckons.

Lying in bed, she hears her mother stomp down the hallway, her footfalls heavier now that she is too. Funny how Fleur can predict the owners of family shoes and feet treading their merry way to nowhere. Plods, scuffs, shuffles, tippy toes. Fleur is drifting away now, lost in this funny little thought. When suddenly she sees... her hand covered—near seeped—in red wine that gushes over the white linen tablecloth. She is remembering what happened after dinner the other night. Everyone leaving the table. Fleur at the kitchen sink. Scott huddled up behind her watching as she tries to wash away the sticky stinking red from her hands and sleeves. Voices in her head. Had she died and gone to hell? For real, that time?

Fleur looks around the empty bedroom; she can't even sense Teddy with her here— not now anyway. Attuning her ears, she hears nothing outside her door or window. Yet, word for awful word, a voice—a smug whisper—comes to shatter the peace of her secure room, a bullish intrusion to her private thoughts.

'You just don't get it, do you? Len Robinson was Tripp's father.' Scott's hyped-up voice. 'Izzie told your mother who told your father, then me. So, you'd better smarten up. He's probably carrying a genetic predilection for criminal behaviour, so if he were to spawn, his offspring would be delinquents. My genetic map, on the other hand, is perfectly clean. Now, I didn't ask for this information about Tripp, and it's been weighing me down, I tell you. Should I feel better about sharing it with you? I don't know, but I may just have saved you, Fleur. Charlie also explained that Izzie is terrified of Tripp finding out and I'm sure you don't want to hurt her, do you? There's nowhere for you to go with this, is there? But I'm warning you, if you let on to anyone that I told you this, I'll go straight to Tripp and tell him everything. Listen, we don't want anyone to be hurt by this, do we? We both love Erin and don't want her to suffer.'

'What's it got to do with Erin?' Fleur had asked, pink water dripping from her hands.

'Erin will always play a key role, Fleur, and if she found out we were close enough for me to tell you, well... I know you won't tell your perfect little Tripp that his father was a common criminal. Listen, I'm willing to take the secret of Tripp's murderous heritage to the grave with me, if you keep your end of the bargain by shutting up about it. You're obviously good at that.'

'Or what?'

'You don't want to find out. I'm sorry, Fleur, but what I've told you has come from a place of wanting your protection. Forgive me.'

The barrage stops. She lies still, silent amidst the screams in her head, fearing Scott is lurking nearby, second-guessing the validity of her memories. If what Scott said is true it could explain Tripp's recent strange break up with her. But Scott doesn't think Tripp knows of his parentage. If he does know, who could have told him? Not her parents, not Izzie, but so many people knowing this! For how long have they known? Surely not while Tripp was being abused at Robinson's property—that would be despicable.

How is it possible that Tripp's father was the abomination, Len Robinson? How could he treat his own son so cruelly for so many years and never even acknowledge his paternity? Scott is right about one thing: she would never tell Tripp the truth, because it could kill him. His life has been too hard already. *But is it too late? Does he already know?* How can Fleur pack this away into a nice, neat compartment in her brain like her mother continues to do with Teddy's precious things? It may work for her mother, but Fleur knows this revelation will eat away at her.

Her family found Izzie years before Tripp came to them. But Tripp's father having lived right next door to them? Fleur understands Tripp arrived because Teddy found Izzie's scarf at Robinson's—the scarf Teddy told Fleur was going to help their mother with something—and Tripp's release involved some deal with the offspring of her father's prize ewes. Izzie's reaction of bliss upon Tripp's return to his mother was something to behold, so she couldn't have known he had been living there—none of them could, surely. But how could Izzie have fallen for someone like Len Robinson?

Fleur fears for herself. What will she do? She cannot tell anyone about what Scott told her. Not even Tripp. Scott now has another thing over her—he whom she despises the most. One thing she understands a little more now is why Tripp and Scott separately warned her not to get close to the other. Yet Scott's warnings about Tripp somehow being affected by evil fall on her deaf ears. What Fleur now knows changes nothing about her love for Tripp; she just wishes she could ease his worries and tell him of it.

But another thought niggles at Fleur: perhaps Tripp's previous shafting of her—the warning to back off—had nothing to do with his father at all. Perhaps it had more—or crushingly, everything—to do with her.

***

The following night. Like a woman possessed, Fleur flings herself around her bed, ragged thoughts competing with their restless host. Perhaps her body is attempting to expunge her heart, to set it free to go join her soul in the ether. *Let me out.* Fleur's twisted heart rattles and leaps about under her ribcage in alarm, demanding she take notice of a body which can no longer remain still and quiet. Where is magic when she needs it most? Where is Teddy?

More copious alcohol at the dinner table—always more with Scott around refilling her glass, and she feels woozy. Fleur almost wishes she had gone to the late session at the pictures tonight with her parents and Erin.

She has felt especially tormented since Tripp's cruel words weeks earlier. Yet perhaps he has rethought his ridiculous stance and will come to her tonight. She knows only Tripp's presence could suppress her fears, calm her. She doubts he would come here; he has barely spoken to her lately. A stab as another thought takes hold. Her incubus may come to her tonight, should she fall asleep, should she not fall asleep, having waited in limbo long enough.

She hears breathing. Tripp?

She scans the dark room, hoping—not hoping—for her fear to take shape and form which would at least give her some proof of her sanity, tenuous as it may be. Yet she understands not every force is tangible. Teddy would help her escape, from what she doesn't know, but… How would she escape? Her bedroom window won't open properly anymore, she'd have to break it. Either that, or she must leave through her bedroom door. But she cannot because he is out there.

Footsteps padding down the hallway, weightier than hoped for, too halting and hesitant for family. Not her mother's. She doesn't recognise them as Tripp's. Her heart falls.

Through the invisible door she sees his shifty form. The brass doorknob screws around ostensibly on its own, turning as Fleur imagines a torture rack would. She is on that rack, every inch of her coming apart with every excruciating little turn of the metal, on the receiving end of his infliction before he even arrives. Eventually predictable, yes, he is, coming here like this. *You can't trick me.*

But you can find me.

Over there. He is in her room now. She pulls a sheet up under her chin, fearing the conspicuous look of her shadowy head as it sinks into her white pillow. His hulking shadow blots her vision. In the moonlight his hair is infested with blood-red sickness; *take care not to catch it, girl!* In a flash of flames her last hope of the vision being Tripp has extinguished.

Scream, run, flee, stupid nothing girl.

She cannot move, having fallen down the rabbit hole into the fire below.

Heft and sudden stink beside her. On her. Hot wine and onion breath—the opposite of Tripp's sweet, honeyed exhalations. She feels sick. *Don't breathe.* She cannot breathe properly anyway, but by God, her heart can pound. She jams her mouth shut before closing her entire body in on itself. He tugs her sheet away, saying he has come to take away her pain, as he causes more with fat ginger finger prods to each one of her scars. Reverently counting them. Singing some silly nursery rhyme while scratching her, starting new ones.

'This is what you do.' He tells her so.

Yes, you do this to yourself, Fleur. You hurt yourself. Why shouldn't he?

He says he loves her imperfections because they are a part of her. A faulty message: she does not buy it, but she is too tired and afraid to argue. Every part of her being screams danger and hate for this man but she cannot move. She is stoic now, like her stupid sister. Her body knows what to do. Close the gates. Stop the tide. Block her primal hunger—the hunger she cannot even name—because it is not for him, it will *never be for him.*

Scream. Run. Flee.

'You shouldn't have asked me to come here tonight.'

Did she do that, ask him? She can't remember. She is so muddled.

'This is what you do.'

This is what you do, slut. Yes, she knew he would say it again, and with his clever new meaning his words are now dirty, carnal. He is in her now. Broad hot shoulders pin her chest so that each increasingly frantic pump pushes more air from her lungs, leaving just enough to sustain her for the act. His body is clumsy and rough, soon it will tremble with unbridled ecstasy as she flounders in sickness.

Time to leave. She squeezes herself out, floating to a safe place above her body where she stares down and regards herself, dispassionately at first. In the dark room, below and beside the shadow of his blood-haired head, a shock of white contorted face suddenly comes into focus; Fleur can just about catch the hurt in her eye. Her face matches the sheets! No use hiding now anyway. This face—shut up, shut down, screwed up, pinched, cringing—contracts into a road map of worry lines with no way out. She feels sorry for this person.

His broken voice asks if she is alright, bringing her back to become the thing she has been looking at. Raw and dirty, she is not alright. Scott stands on the bed, emitting a high-pitched giggle as he stretches up to retrieve the underpants that he threw on top of the cupboard.

She is aware of the nail scissors on her bedside table. How easy it would be for her to stab at the parts of his body that have hurt her the most, his places of worship. Because he deserves scars, too. He would fall back onto the bed and crush his underpants over himself. In horrifying wonder, he would notice the small taint of blood mushrooming as it spreads across the ashen fabric.

'If you ever touch me again, I'll finish the job.' She would take pride in her surprising calm voice.

She *is* pleased for it.

Does she catch him groan?

'Why did you do this? Cruel little bitch. By the way you were moaning, you enjoyed our lovemaking as much as I did.' Was she? No! Her cries for help.

'I wanted you to be Tripp.'

'What? Yet calling out my name as you—'

'No, I didn't! Not yours, I would never call for you!' She yells and punches him, determined to stop his further filth.

But then, 'Tripp, where are you?' whispering his name, because it is too late to save her, and she would be horrified for him to hear or see her, here, like this. Fleur will pack this night away in a neat compartment, forever trying to rid herself of the key.

'I just want… Leave me. Go!' She sounds like a ten-year-old.

Scott drapes himself on the bed beside her, inhaling poison through the cigarette clasped between his teeth, offering her a smoke too. She flicks his hand away and closes her eyes.

Fleur has never felt lonelier. A balloon ready to burst, who will release her pressure?

Can she do it herself? Her rage now flares more intensely than the fires of hell. She may have some power left, and with Teddy's presence, and this new magic from her mother that has somehow infiltrated her—even if it lets her down at times like this—she may just realise it.

Come show yourself!

Fleur notices that Scott has left, but not the cigarette smell. She opens the window. A faint sound alerts her to a brown bead moving across the floor. Freddy's remaining eye! Did he see the awful act? Has it caused Freddy's sudden blindness? His last vision ever. She picks up the smooth bead and brings it to bed with her, rolling it around in her fingers as she weeps for the soft little toy, despairs for herself.

She runs to the toilet and vomits, brushes her teeth until her gums bleed, then showers, scrubbing herself furiously in the steaming hot water before collapsing into bed.

She hears her family return, each person hushing the other as they dissect the film they just saw. They sound happy. She hears Tripp and Izzie back at the house too. Where have they been?

Fleur is certain that Scott will leave the farm. He would blame her for making him do, 'Something despicable, something I would never do, to any woman. Only a demon would have such power; you may have even cursed me.' She hears his words in his own affected voice. Naturally he will never touch her again. He will tell himself that he is not too worried about his injuries, surface wounds really. And what he did to her: he will reason that he did her a favour—bringing it closer to home, filling a void, boosting her confidence during traumatic times.

She will not say a thing. She is used to keeping secrets and has too much to lose. Lying on her bed, another conversation with the bastard comes flooding back to her, from where and when, she does not know.

'Can you honestly believe I'm not attracted to you? You've seen it, haven't you? If something comes of this, I will never take our relationship lightly. I'm a good man, Fleur, just like you are a good woman. We both come from fine church-going families. I only want to do what's best for you.'

'We have nothing together. I don't want you and never will. You're delusional.'

'Don't you see? I'm falling for you, Fleur.'

'You're an idiot. And why? My sister is much more your style. I have nothing to offer you.'

'That's not what I see. I see a beautiful girl who needs someone to love her. I know you've been hiding secrets you don't want your family to know about, things you've been doing inside and outside of your home. You need to trust me. Look at this.'

He took a crumpled brochure from his trouser pocket, gave it to her.

'See this—it's The Pimm's Point Hotel. Five stars—in Sydney. I stay there when I go to the big smoke. Management knows me and says I can stay long-term if ever I need to. I want to take you there with me one day. The Pimm's Point can be our love nest, somewhere no-one will ever bother us.'

'You're crazy. You should take Erin there, but then again—'

'It's not her I can see lying on that bed, drinking champagne. I knew the minute I set eyes on you there was something between us, and something tells me you felt the same way.'

'You're not reading me. How damn clear must I be? I'll never be your whore, or anyone's for that matter. I have absolutely no reason to trust you.'

'You must because you need me. I'm the only one who knows the woman you are. Others wouldn't understand, but I do because in a way we're both the same. We both know why we do what we do, and we can help each other. Neither of us wants to cause trouble, we're just… inordinately misunderstood. Take your time to think about what I've said. You might just get lucky.'

'Over my dead body, Scott. But I doubt I'll be first to go.'

Here, now, Fleur opens her bedside table, turns on the lamp, and studies the hotel brochure Scott had left behind.

She hears Teddy's sweet little boy voice in her ear, urging her on, as the shame she should never feel for this wicked night begins to dissipate. She listens to her brother's words with care; they were always good together.

Chapter Forty

Fleur will not be working alone. Teddy will take the lead because he knows exactly where the bounty is, having pestered her throughout the previous night about it. She was relieved to find him happy, and eager to move on this important task.

Tools in hand, she follows her brother—a spring to his step—outside into the cool night air. With a torch to light their way they scurry across the yard to the new structure she couldn't bear to be anyone's future home. She has deliberately kept her feet bare to dull their patter as the two of them creep through the house. Teddy's footfalls are as light as air. Lit in bright torchlight, Teddy turns to her and grins with teeth missing when they hear the sudden creak of floorboards underfoot. Understanding her task, she returns his smile and nods to him, watching as he fades away.

Wielding a hammer to loosen the nails, she jimmies the planks and removes the parcel from its mooring. A prize—finders keepers. Stuffing the load under her nightgown—cradling it as a heavily pregnant woman does her belly—she tiptoes back to Teddy's room and unburdens herself, the load coming out much easier than she knows a baby would. She opens a cupboard, pushes the object to the back of a high shelf, where it will stay safe and sound.

Until needed.

After little sleep, Fleur rises at dawn, wraps dressing gown over nightie, dons her tennis shoes, and sneaks outside. She knows Scott is still at the farm because his car is parked outside the workers' cottage. There are no lights on, but he may have left on foot. For how much longer will he stay at the farm? His next flight may not be so fancy. Fleur swallows against bile. Perhaps he will leave today, perhaps in a way he had never contemplated…

She strolls past the crying tree—weeping rivers today. With its omniscient hold from its stationary reach, it knows what she has been through, has seen all the signs, heard all the truths, the lies. In soothing words, she calls to it, prepares it for what she is about to do, sensing a corroborative nudge of agreement.

Fleur's tension eases as she walks the dimly lit yard. She experiences the first gifts of the day: chirping birds, cautious rays of dawn. Cumulus clouds hint at a sky eager to absorb any blue and break to an afternoon storm, if God is kind to the Altons today. When did she last think of God?

She will not be swayed from this crucial step, her purpose for this day. And Teddy is once again by her side. He will help Fleur to harness her energy, absorb all the world's rage, remain strong. She senses little creatures stir, supposing they will frolic more today with the faint promise of rain. They are at her beck and call, although she already has everything she requires.

Lights are on inside the newly completed broken-down structure—another half-house to be enjoyed by no-one. She is pleased Scott started work early; he's an early riser when it suits him. In stealth she skirts the creepy eyesore, noting the pathetic crooked beams, skew-whiff tin roof. She imagines its similarities to Izzie's former haunted half-house at Bounty Bay, which she told Fleur about. From outside *this* half-house, she smells Scott's pungent cigarette smoke which seems to have permeated the timber, another thing making her want to run. Yet she will not be frightened off. And she refuses to imagine that Scott will confront her this morning.

Standing tall at a distance but facing the front door, raising one pointed finger to the skies, she summons all her energies, all Teddy's energies, all her mother's energies, and all the crying tree's energies, to help her along. She hears the tree's wail, or cheer—the signal she cannot decipher.

Something infiltrates her—like the electric current originally passed to her from her mother—rendering her strong and invincible, bringing her enough fury to destroy every plan of the wicked. She raises both arms now to hug the sky. In her embrace the clouds rush to converge and darken, yet no rain comes; they have another purpose that Fleur and her army of one have commanded.

A faint whiff of gas emanates from inside the shack house. All at once a little flicker becomes one big one, and Fleur's world becomes deafening, as a rod of lightning— straight, swift, lethal—shoots down from the heavens to take away the house no-one ever wanted.

Awkwardly, Fleur rises to her feet, having been knocked to the ground with the force of the lightning bolt. She feels lightheaded and spent, yet overall, okay. She watches—with some satisfaction—as the fire takes hold of the half-house, knowing its upwards-surging fury will bend the tin roof as effortlessly as the act of unwrapping foil from a stick of chewing gum.

A blood-curdling wail from behind Fleur causes her to spin around and see Izzie rushing to her side.

'My boy. My boy. No! He can't be the little man.' Her earnest words make no sense.

'What?' The word hangs limp and pathetic on Fleur's mouth. *No, don't worry Izzie, it is Scott inside. Scott is inside and he will run out soon because bad things stay bad.*

Izzie flaps her arms about then grips herself. 'Tripp! In there,' she points towards the burning structure, 'checking the gas leak!'

'WHAT?'

From inside, a man coughs and moans. Fleur throws her dressing gown over her head—as if this will protect her.

A primal scream rips from her throat as she rushes inside towards the fire—into the impossible heat, the smothering smoke—attempting to wave it all away as a loud trail of family voices cry out behind her. Her eyes sting and she blinks manically, repeatedly calling out Tripp's name through her coughs. In the smoke haze she locates him—bent over, grim, staggering towards her. Together they move outside, far away from the inferno. With difficulty, Tripp sits down upon a tree stump. Fleur sits next to him on the ground, noticing that for some reason she does not feel burnt.

What has she done?

She takes charge. 'Izzie, I know you want to stay with Tripp, but you would do better to grab a blanket from the house, wet it, then wrap him in it. Please. Now!' Fleur will not leave Tripp.

'No water. Kaboom!' Izzie throws her arms in the air.

'The strike took out the power and the water pump,' Charlie's voice comes in jolts, his body trembling, overwhelmed.

'Okay then. Izzie, get the outside bucket and fill it from the crying tree.'

Fleur watches Izzie bolt away, somehow understanding its magic.

'You alright, Tripp?' asks Charlie. *Stupid comment, Dad.* He circles the scene uselessly.

'Better than I've been,' he whispers. Guilt stabs at Fleur's heart.

Charlie wrings his hands. 'How the hell are we gonna put this out? No water from a tree will kill this bastard of a fire. The bloody hose is too short. Pity wonder-boy Scott didn't think of that!'

'Dad, Erin, round up the workers, take buckets, get water from the crying tree. Believe me, it will give us more than enough.'

'Do it, Charlie, it's crying, a lot,' says Grace to her stunned husband. He and Erin comply.

When Izzie returns to Tripp's side, Fleur wraps him in the blanket his mother has brought from the house, soaked in the crying tree water the others continue to fetch. All the while Fleur sits beside him like a faithful mutt.

'I'll phone the doctor,' says Grace, moving towards the homestead.

A pause. Fleur jumps to her feet and rushes to her mother's side. 'No, wait, I won't keep you.' Together they walk towards the house. 'I did this, Mum, through some strange, awful power. I caused lightning to strike! That day when I found you'd moved Teddy's hat... What the hell have you given me? Did you know something like this would happen? I could have killed Tripp.'

'*Of course* I didn't know, darling. My God, if only I *had* known... All this was my failing. Now I see that I should have warned you to treat it—this strange, formidable force—with awe and care.'

'Strange, formidable. Stop trying to make it sound romantic.'

'I'm not, and it's anything but romantic. I'm sorry. Its powers are unpredictable and I didn't stress this point enough to you. I failed you like I failed Teddy. Don't you think I would have protected your brother if only I'd known to heed the warnings?'

'So now I'm doomed forever, am I, because of some stupid curse you put on me?'

'Oh God, Fleur, no. And I didn't curse you. I'm sorry if it chose you like it chose me. It's not too late for you. Just have faith that good things can happen too. It can redeem itself.'

'How awe-inspiring and impressive.' Fleur's small spiteful voice. 'And what of me, Mum? How can I redeem myself? You can't separate a consequence from the owner of the action. What have I done? I've hurt Tripp.' Fleur's tears spill as she quickens her pace.

Grace pulls her daughter to a stop, sighs, then fixes her eyes on her daughter. 'Have faith, Teddy will help you.'

Fleur *is* letting Teddy guide her, but she will not tell her mother about that yet.

'Help me?' says Fleur. 'Do you seriously think I can even help myself?'

'You can.' Grace strides towards the door to the house, as Fleur hurries back to Tripp's side.

Scott suddenly appears on the property running towards the scene. He is followed by the large dog the family now knows belongs to Cathy, leaving no-one in doubt about where Scott has been. Panting, the man bolts directly inside the burning building, ignoring everyone's screams to do otherwise, muttering something about rescuing his baby. The sound of timber planks shifting. Scott's high-pitched cries.

An explosion precedes a sudden burst of flames in brilliant, near-blinding light.

On his feet now, a sodden Tripp shouts, 'The gas. Get that idiot out of there!'

Barely waiting for the latest flames to subside, Tripp pulls away from Fleur's grip on his blanket and, dodging people carrying buckets of water, rushes inside. At least he is covered by the wet blanket, she tries to console herself. Her attempt to join him is stopped by her father who tugs at her dressing gown. She ricochets back. Imploring, she searches her father's face. 'Settle down, love,' he instructs.

Soon—perhaps in an aeon—Tripp reappears, his actions belying his fragile state as he drags Scott outside by the arm. Both men sooty, choking, raw. Scott's clothes seem to have melted onto his skin.

'What the hell were you doing in there?' Erin implores Scott.

'Our child is missing, it's been stolen!' Scott's muffled, befuddled, troubling reply. A reply that only Fleur understands because she has seen the meaning of his words.

'You're crazy! Why the hell didn't you come home last night?'

Fleur is relieved her sister has asked this; it is about time she saw through her fiancé.

Scott grabs a bucket from Grace and pours the last trickle of water over himself.

He groans, clearly in agony. 'She did this, she destroyed my house.' Scott wags a fat red finger at Fleur. 'That witch, I saw her start a fire on a tree the other morning without even touching it! She cursed it, just as she cursed my house.'

Fleur hopes Scott's incoherence is sufficient for everyone to think he has finally lost his marbles. Better he, than she.

Chapter Forty-One

Dukie told Charlie that Scott—having suffered second degree burns—is recovering yet will need to spend a week in hospital before returning to the Harris property.

Tripp spent only two nights in hospital, his burns first-degree—widespread, yet superficial, for which Fleur is thankful. Overwhelmed with guilt and grief, Fleur has avoided him, barely spoken a word to him. This has not been difficult as he spends most days in his bedroom with Izzie by his side. Once again, Fleur has put the life of someone far too precious in jeopardy. Due to her stupid curse and reckless actions, she may have lost him forever.

Fleur has taken to some hard slog around the farm because work she can control. In the stables, she looks up from filling the horse troughs with fresh water. She freezes, holding her pail mid-air as water drips rhythmically from its base to the dirt below. Tripp stands before her with both arms bandaged, smiling.

'You work hard, girl.'

'At least someone appreciates it. My God, Tripp, I'm so sorry! How are you?'

'Sore. Sorry too. Better for seeing you.'

She frowns. 'Show me your arms.'

He lifts one bandage to expose pus-laden reddened skin. She feels heat in the air around it.

'Don't worry, I'm on antibiotics.' He seems concerned, for her!

'I didn't mean for this to happen!'

'You had nothing to do with it. It was lightning.'

What can she say? Now is not the time to tell him of her madness.

'The doc said if it wasn't for that wet blanket you wrapped around me, I'd be one hell of a lot worse. What was all that about getting water from the crying tree?'

Yet this question of his... What can she lose by telling him? 'The tree is magic.'

His eyes narrow. 'Magic?'

'It has warned us of trouble before. This time it helped extinguish fire.'

She places her pail on the ground as naturally as the shock of this meeting will allow. When she searches his eyes, a sudden fresh understanding comes to her. 'It knew you were inside. It wanted to help save you!'

'Save me? It's a tree, Fleur.'

'An incredibly special tree. One day I will tell you all about it. Just trust we are all on your side.'

Tripp doesn't appear convinced.

After completing her chores—all the while preventing Tripp's help—they walk outside through magnolia trees to sit on the wrought-iron bench. Its black paint flakes like burnt skin shed from someone stricken. *Everything reminds me of pain.*

Suddenly she becomes gruff, remembering their encounter before the fire when he dumped her. Or was he trying to protect her from the secret of his father?

'Why are we even speaking? I thought you didn't want anything more to do with me.'

'You probably just saved my life, girl.'

'Your gratitude is the last thing I deserve.'

'Come on, it warrants a thank you, even though I'm hardly worth saving. One good thing has come of my accident, I've had time to myself. I thought of you.'

She braces herself. 'Great, more time to analyse me. Should I run yet?'

'No.'

'After what you've heard about my *liaisons*?'

'Forget that shit. In hospital, all I did was fear for you. Seeing you now doesn't reassure me.'

Instinctively, she fixes her unkempt hair. 'That bad, eh? Thanks, Mr Lanolin.' She catches his smile. 'Well, just don't look at me.'

'How? Even when you're not around you're somehow inside of me demanding that I care for you. You look tired. And you mustn't have been eating well because it shows on you. Going out late at night won't solve a thing.'

She almost wishes she could highlight something disreputable or unhealthy about him. 'Aren't you meant to be focusing on your recovery? And I've stopped going out!' *Mainly for you!* 'It wasn't something I enjoyed. No-one acknowledges I exist until I'm not around.'

'You're wrong. You have this strange sentience, an uncanny ability to rattle, Fleur Alton.'

'Is that some back-handed compliment?'

'Up to how you interpret it. Just remember that even in Pig Peak monsters exist that can pounce on you.'

'Don't I know it.' She looks away to examine flecks of black paint on her fingers as a horrid vision of Scott chills her. *Oh God!*

'Know what?' His stare towards her is unreadable. He probably thinks the same of her silence. 'I hope you've never encountered monsters, Fleur, and never will. I know I haven't helped you though.'

Correct, your indecision and downright cruelty have made things worse. She is the bud on the gardenia bush beside them, withered before its time in the unforgiving elements of drought. There was some promise there... His arm around her shoulders now brings her to tears.

'You're right, Tripp, you're confusing me all the time. Where do we stand? You're almost as crazy as me.'

'Moreso without you.'

'The curse of the evil twin! And I *cause hurt*.'

'You know it was an accident, and you did all you could.'

'So you say. Lightning. But with some added spark. At least Scott's structure has gone now.'

Her coy smile hurts her because she has caused Tripp harm. Perhaps one day she will tell him of her new power, but not under these circumstances.

He raises an eyebrow. 'I'm not speaking of the fire, although you were mighty brave throughout that situation. The accident, at the river.'

She does not want to revisit that day. 'Accident. I know if Teddy were here now, he would be ashamed of me.' *He must hate that Tripp got hurt.*

'He wouldn't. No-one is ashamed of you.'

'But they should be. *You* should be. Don't you see?' She takes a huge breath. 'I cut myself.'

'What?' She hates his quietly contained statement.

'I can't seem to stop doing it.' Her words seep out like deadly gas.

Tripp tenses. 'What are you talking about?' Why can't he just scream?

'I didn't want to get into this.'

'Come on, Fleur. We're past secrets now. I won't judge you.'

'These scars.' Cringing, she stands and lifts her top, enough to expose skin above and below her bra displaying patterns of shiny scars and sores at different stages of inflammation and healing. She barely glances at Tripp because she imagines him screwing up his face in horror and could not bear that. She lets the material fall as she sits back down upon the flaking bench.

She turns to him. 'I only meant them for me. I'm ashamed of myself and ashamed to make you look, but I must, because I want you to try to understand. There's a term I've read about called self-flagellation. Is that the type of thing this is? I don't know. What I have done doesn't discipline me, and it never gets to the real hurt. It's somewhere hidden, somewhere silent. I can't reach it. I want to get rid of the pain, but I can't, Tripp, it just won't go away. Oh, I didn't want to tell you this.'

'Harming yourself won't change anything.' His sigh. His head shake.

'I know I can't change the past. And although pain tells me—just for a moment—that I'm real, ironically, I'm not even sure that I want to be real. I know cutting only makes things worse, and it makes me uglier.'

'You'll never be ugly. You are beautiful.'

She takes a deep breath. 'Listen, I can hardly say this, and I have to keep talking before I can't, but Scott found me naked in the bathroom when I was using scissors.'

Tripp turns away from her. Is this the time for his judgment?

'When you hurt yourself?' His guarded voice.

'Yes.'

'What was his reaction?'

'He came to my room another night, not long ago.'

'What do you mean?' Tripp's words quaver.

'I didn't want it! I was terrified. I couldn't move, couldn't escape. And that lunatic, he told me he wouldn't tell if I didn't tell. He said he loved my scars, told me he wanted me to go to Sydney with him. Tripp?'

Silence.

'Tripp? Did you hear me?' she cries.

For several infinitely long seconds he clenches his jaw, his fists. 'Did he hurt you?'

She nods.

He punches a fist into his hand. '*Bastard*. So, he's bargaining with you now, playing you.'

'Yes, he is. And you know me, I'd never believe him. I'm not a total idiot, just a scared and confused crazy person. And poor Erin. I know we haven't seen eye to eye, but she's my sister and I love her.'

'Keep away from him, Fleur. He'll get what he deserves.'

'Will he? At least Erin might now see through him—she must after he returned from Cathy's the day of the fire. I always try to stay away from him! He's rotten, always will be. I tried to make him pay... but he's like some unstoppable force. I hate him! What about Erin?'

'She can't marry him. Just be there for her, I guess.'

'Be there for her like I never have before? She'll probably have me locked away. Is that what you want?'

'No. Calm down now. Take some slow breaths. He will never hurt you again.'

'Can you be bothered with me anymore, now that you have more reasons to judge me?' Bold words, petrified about his response.

He eyes scan the sky for an excruciating amount of time. 'Oh Fleur.' He makes eye contact with her. 'You are not the problem here. I judge Scott. And myself. I should have protected you. You can't keep hurting yourself the way you have been.' He takes hold of her hands. 'Promise me, for God's sake.'

She exhales, pulling back to wipe her eyes. 'Promise.'

Tripp shuffles on his seat. 'I have a secret of my own. Brace yourself, Fleur, this may come as a shock.'

Nothing could scare her further. 'Go ahead.'

'I learnt from Cathy next door that I'm Len Robinson's son. She is my half-sister.'

'What?' *What?* 'Cathy from the pub?'

'Yes. Len Robinson was married to Cathy's mother, and he took off when she got pregnant with her. When he died, he left the property to them both. My mother only found out that I'd lived all those years with Robinson after I came to the Alton farm. So there, Fleur, now you have one hell of a reason not to care about me.'

Tripp has a half-sister! And Fleur cannot stand a bar of her. And yet, she is part of his family. Tripp knows about his father now; Fleur will play it cool and not let on she already knew this disturbing fact.

'I can hardly believe it!' *Cathy is related to Tripp?* 'But it makes no difference. How could I not care about you too? You have your mother's precious traits.'

'So do you, Fleur. Grace's.'

'What? Perhaps, but they've been hard to find lately. Someone will have to get me back to my shiny best.'

Softly, she punches his arm, before remembering the burns. 'Oh God, have I hurt you?'

He shakes his head in a *no*.

'I'll try hard to be more thankful for my mother, promise.' The thought of Fleur repairing her relationship with Grace is freeing.

Relief hits Fleur for disclosing such sensitive topics that have plagued her for so long. But the main reason for her lightness is Tripp's reaction. He has not blamed Fleur for the damage she has done to herself or to him. He did not question her about the specifics of what Scott did to her—Tripp knows he is evil. And he cared enough to tell her about his father—such a brave disclosure. Once again, he has given her more reasons to love him.

No more secrets.

Chapter Forty-Two

Fleur reasons she should feel better since her candid conversation with Tripp. Emotionally, she probably does, but physically? She runs to the toilet and vomits. It is worse because she has no food left in her stomach and is throwing up bitter green bile. Is this the price she pays for not eating enough? Foggy brain, her body rebelling. She walks with care to the kitchen—because she cannot trust her jelly legs—and sits alone at the table.

Izzie appears, ready for a new day, holding her head a little higher since Tripp was released from hospital, not dragging her body behind her like an afterthought.

'Good morning, Fleur! Happy to see you, girl.'

Fleur realises it has been some time since they have spoken. She wonders if Izzie, in her quietude, has noticed Fleur's odd behaviour. At least Fleur is proud she can finally call it that.

'It's always very good to see you too, Izzie.' Although speaking the truth, Fleur's jocularity doesn't come easy because she feels like shit.

'Oh yes!' On her merry way, Izzie collects cups, bowls, and silverware for the breakfast. 'How is that school, Fleur?'

'Oh, you mean college. Okay, I guess.'

'You don't like it there, I can see.'

'It's not really what I want to do.' *Please don't ask me what I want to do. At one point I wanted to be a farmer, but now I have no idea.*

'Have you had a nice talk with Tripp after hospital? He likes being with you. Special.'

Fleur smiles at Izzie, thrilled by her words, thrilled to see her content here with her son after all she has been through.

'I have seen him, and it's good that he's getting better. Now he is home from hospital, you are like a bright and shiny new lady.'

'Yes, I am. Tripp and I, we fight but now we're good.' Izzie's smile fades quickly upon studying her. 'But, Fleur, you look sick. I will make you a big breakfast, okay?'

Before she can stop her, Izzie is preparing something huge and fatty, something Fleur will eat if it kills her.

Fleur has been considering what Tripp said about her having Grace's traits as though they were something to aspire to. She knows if she could let a little of her mother shine through in herself, she would surely benefit, be a better person. To find those traits means sometimes doing what her mother wishes. So, when she insisted Fleur see the doctor—managing to slot her in despite his 'hectic' schedule—Fleur allowed Grace to drive her.

Doctor Gibbs ran an obligatory blood test then arranged for a second appointment to discuss results.

Today, Fleur lies fully naked—unnecessarily, to her mind—under a cold, stiff white sheet on a narrow slab of an examination table, awaiting the inevitable roll towards the mortuary. Gibbs prods and pinches her scarred body as she stares at wall posters showing diagrams of people with their innards on display. Is this her fate?

'And for how long did you think you could keep this a secret, without seeing a doctor?'

'It's private.' *Or once it was.* 'I can manage my skin myself, unless you're saying it's getting infected.'

'Infected? Ha! Is that what you call it?' asks Gibbs smugly.

She is in no mood for games: 'Just give me a diagnosis, prognosis, prescription, and I'll stop wasting your time.'

'Diagnosis—pregnancy. Prognosis—baby. Prescription—obstetrician. And start looking after yourself, you're going to be a mother.'

Having escaped a trip to the morgue, Fleur travels home, her mind awhirl. A tummy bug, she tells her mother.

Pregnant? Surely not her? How could she be? Although the way she has been administering her contraceptive pill—without breaks for bleeding—would explain how she did not grasp the possibility of pregnancy. But she had understood that The Pill was safe, that it would work!

In her room, she pulls herself up, gets the little box from under her mattress, and carefully reads the miniscule words typed on the pamphlet inside. One warning, or *contraindication*, has her panicked: *Certain antibiotics may reduce the effectiveness of this product.* She reads the list of offenders, the tablet she has been taking sitting proudly at the top. No! Who can she tell? She has no friends. Her mother would die of shame.

Could she tell Erin? No. Her sister need never find out who the father is.

⁓

Erin is finally waking up to Scott. Fleur is proud of the way she tackled him on the day of the fire which could have claimed his life. Proud enough for Fleur to take a risky chance with her sister and hope like hell she will keep her secret, because she has no-where else to go with this. Just before midnight, she creeps into Erin's room and sits beside her sister who lies belly-up on her bed. Fleur smirks at the lady-like delicacy of Erin's snores, until her pathetic crescendo wakes her with a start. Fleur bounces on the mattress to make sure of it.

'What's going on?'

'It's me.'

'I can see that. What on earth are you doing?' Erin stretches her arms above her head. A shoulder clicks.

'I'm sorry to startle you.' Fleur cannot stop shaking. 'Please, I really need to talk.'

Erin lifts the covers. 'Here, get into bed.'

'Are you sure?'

'Come on.'

As Fleur climbs in, she sees her own sharp hip bones protruding from her cotton nightie. She rolls a palm over the crest of one, despairing of her hidden plan to sharpen her weapons for battles. Fleur never invited them, never wanted any of those battles. The sisters roll to face one another.

'Now, what is it that can't wait 'til morning?' asks Erin gently, wrapping a lock of Fleur's dull blonde hair behind her ear.

Fleur has prepared her speech. 'Okay, confession time, though I don't know where to start. I've been seeing some local boys at the hotel, well, sleeping with them. It was only one time, but... I let them.' Her words have an unnerving bright curtness in their determination to vocalise without her eyes crying. What would hurt more? The lie or the truth? Now, she cannot tell.

'Oh, Fleur, why ever would you lower yourself? From what I've seen of the type who hang around there, they're scum.'

Her hackles rise. 'Can't you stop judging me like a mother? Don't you think I know they're idiots? I'll never do it again. But it hasn't stopped there.'

Erin sits up and swings her legs over the side of the mattress, turns on the bedside lamp. She places a palm over her breast. 'What do you mean?'

Fleur joins her so they sit side-by-side. 'They've left a... stain on me.'

'No, not VD?'

'No, not that. Shit, here we go...' She jiggles her body, causing the mattress to rock. 'A baby, Erin. I'm pregnant.'

'What? You! I feared something like this could happen.'

'Did you? I think I need to get away.' Her voice is monotone.

'Why? To have an abortion?'

'I think it's too late. Even if I could, I probably couldn't.' Fleur can hurt herself, but she would never hurt a child. Clutching her stomach, she weeps.

'It's alright, my dear sister.' Fleur feels a squeeze to her shoulder.

'I'll help you.'

Having succumbed to her own tears, Erin wipes her eyes on her nightie. Her sister is emotional with the news, but Fleur wishes she knew what Erin really thought of all this.

'I know where Scott hides a little money,' Erin whispers, 'if he hasn't already taken it.' Her voice loudens. 'I can give it to you! You've been on your own for way too long. Your sister is here for you now.'

⁓

As organised, after dinner the following night the twins meet with their parents. Fleur sits before them in trepidation, still unable to read her sister's true feelings about her news.

'Mum and Dad, you know I've been down in the dumps lately. But you needn't worry, I think I've found a way to fix things.' Fleur jiggles about, her voice jolly with feigned enthusiasm.

'That sounds good, firecracker.' For how much longer will her father use that term of endearment for her? She feels another part of her soul rip away, as she dies once again a little more. 'What have you got planned?'

'I want to study animal husbandry, to be a farmer, just like you, Dad.'

Her mother's eyes widen before she bows her head.

'And you, Mum, naturally.'

Grace's smile is thin.

Charlie claps his hands together. 'Now, that's what we want to hear, eh Gracie? Though, how are you going to work that?'

'Well, I've discovered a university course in Sydney. I know it's a long way from here, but you have Izzie, Tripp, Marco and his sons, the other boys. And Mum and Erin, of course.'

Fleur reaches out and taps her sister's arm, producing a quick smile for Grace. Fleur will not let Scott's name tarnish her lips. She hopes he has taken off somewhere far away. No-one has heard anything about him since his parents told Charlie that he had returned to them following his hospital stay.

'Won't that cost a lot of money, Fleur?' Grace flashes red.

Thanks Mum, for being more concerned with the money than with your daughter leaving.

'Oh goodness, I didn't mean that.'

'Listen, I've been working some nights at the hotel, and I've saved up some money.'

She pats her dress pocket which houses the money Erin confessed to have grabbed from Scott's wallet—*before* the fire.

'Sorry I didn't tell you, but I didn't think you'd like the idea.' Fleur braces herself, determined not to be stung by her mother's reaction.

'Well, no, we certainly don't, do we Charlie?'

He grunts.

'But we do like you studying, don't we Charlie?'

He smiles, nods.

'How do you know you'll get in?' asks Grace.

God, she hadn't thought of this. Erin comes to the rescue. 'They've offered her a scholarship.'

Fleur sinks as she watches her parents' confusion grow.

'Because she works on a farm.' Erin ensures the puzzle is almost complete.

'Yes, yes. I need to leave soon though.'

'How soon?' her parents say in tandem.

'Next week. After I've sorted out somewhere to stay.'

Her mother says something unexpected: 'I'll try harder, Fleur.'

'So will I, Mum, if I'm able to.'

Grace gives her youngest daughter a cryptic gaze which softens and leads to faint mutual smiles.

Chapter Forty-Three

'What are you going to do with the baby, Fleur?'

The two sisters again share night-time secrets in Erin's bed, times redolent of rare childhood disclosures when they were not fighting. Fleur cannot bear being in her own bed now.

'Adopt him out, I guess.'

Fleur is a bundle of confusion. Whenever she considers adoption, she thinks of the horror Izzie must have endured, at an awful time when she was prevented from thinking for herself.

'Him, eh? I have a plan. You may not like it, but it might just be another way to go about things. I could help you Fleur, help raise the baby here at the farm.'

'Why? And how do you think our parents would react to that?'

'I think they'd love another child here and once they saw him or her—'

'Him.'

'Okay, they'd love him.'

Erin flicks her eyes about as though she holds some crucial secret.

'What?'

'I, I can't have children, Fleur, according to that arsehole Doctor Gibbs. I've had all the tests.'

Something hits Fleur's stomach with force, hits her heart with grief, causing fear for her baby. *And did Erin just swear?* 'I'm genuinely sorry. I know how much you've always wanted a child.'

'True, and so does Scott. He'd be heartbroken if he found out the truth.'

'Would he though, Erin? He seems too selfish to ever want to be a father.'

'Not long ago I would have slapped you for that comment. Now? I'm just confused. He doesn't mind sharing himself with Cathy, I know that much.' *Cathy: the daughter of a murderer. Scott could one day father a child with a 'genetic predilection for criminal behaviour'.* 'Which should tell you there's a problem and you should rethink your future.'

'I can't believe you're actually giving me advice, Fleur, but I'm not angry about it. And I'm considering my future very carefully, especially since… But back to my point, Mum and Dad want the farm to carry on, but what happens after we go? Only a family line will ensure it continues to bear the Alton name. There's no chance Kitty will return now she's gallivanting around England. So, what do you think of my plan?'

'I can't answer that now! I have too much to worry about with this new life growing inside me to be stewing about the future of the farm. I'll consider what you've said.'

'Just remember there's a way other than adoption. In any case I can stay with you when the baby is due. Could you handle that?'

'Um, yes, but I'm not even sure about keeping him.' *What will my sister's reaction be to seeing the baby—the red-haired baby.*

Armed with her hurriedly packed Samsonite suitcase, some money from her parents, and a little of Scott's cash from Erin to tide her over, Fleur is driven by Charlie to the train station, where she departs on her journey to Sydney.

Fleur stays at a bed-and-breakfast within walking distance of Darling Harbour. She soon discovers the decrepit red brick building holds transient derelicts and drug addicts, and the stench of mildew hangs in its walls like yet another unwelcome tenant. At night, Fleur lies on her uncomfortable single spring mattress shielding her eyes from the glare of flashing neon signs outside. Loud voices, thumping, and crashing sounds throughout the night make her wish she were back at the farm, but only if Scott has fled for good, forever. She refuses to dwell on that louse. She is fretting for someone infinitely more important, and she misses him deeply.

Fleur has found a job waitressing at a cheap cafe which 'specialises' in toasted ham and cheese jaffles, and milk shakes, the menu termed 'gold star'. Wonders why they bother. Her work shift is 5pm until midnight, with Mondays off. She is not pulling in much money, but enough to keep her from having to beg her family for more.

Her womb is coming to life, and in the early mornings, just when she is dozing off to sleep, her little boy starts up his dancing. A boy for sure, judging by his punches and stomps. She asks God to help her with her decision. How can she take Erin up on her offer, suspecting the baby is Scott's? His hair will surely be red like Scott's, and his mother's real colour under the brassy blonde dye. It would give the game away to everyone at the farm, even to Tripp. She dismays, imagining more days and nights of pure anguish, worse than the anguish she feels now.

Overcome with worry, she sometimes phones home, or talks to her baby while rubbing her taut tummy. Then she gets angry with herself for becoming emotionally attached to the thing growing inside her, the creature planted with nothing like love. Adoption would probably be the best option.

In any case, she has stopped cutting herself and her body seems to have miraculously come alive again for the first time since losing her brother. She sees old scars over her belly widening and lengthening, like shiny leaves stamping their reminder that a new abundant season will soon arrive. She cannot bear to think the scars show something else, that she has been branded for life.

Chapter Forty-Four

Ferocious barking outside from the Alton's two normally placid dogs, a budgerigar screech, followed by three loud knocks. Grace opens the squeaky, weathered front door to the kitchen, puzzled about who the visitor could be, angry because of the lack of warning.

'Can I help you?' Charlie moves alongside her, surveying the lanky dark-haired stranger on his doorstep.

The man clarifies with them that he has arrived at the Alton farm, before introducing himself as Colin, an acquaintance of Scott. 'Is he here?' he asks.

'I'm Charlie Alton. No, Scott has gone, and you might have some trouble catching him.'

'Oh.' He dallies about.

'His father says he's left their property. He's not next door either where he's been doing some yard work. I think the place is empty now 'cos we haven't heard the dog barking lately.'

Grace knows Charlie will not mention the fire, the last anyone at the farm saw of Scott. She stands back.

'Well, I'm Colin Turner.' He extends an arm to Charlie, and they shake hands. 'I've been working the mines at Blackstone Ridge for over ten years now. A few months back I met Scott. He said he was new to the business, begged me to show him the ropes, so I took him under my wing. Don't mean to offend you and your daughter, his fiancée, I believe? But it was the worst mistake of my life.'

Charlie throws his shoulders back and frowns. 'You'd better have something to substantiate your accusations, young fellow.' Charlie is upset about this stranger's words, his confrontation. Grace could rub her palms together in relief.

'My proof is my word. I'm proud of my longstanding record at Blackstone Ridge, my damn near perfect reputation, and I wouldn't jeopardise it for the world.'

Charlie edges out the doorway, scanning the yard for eavesdroppers. 'You'd better come inside.' Charlie leads him to a chair at the kitchen table opposite himself and Grace.

'Okay, spit it out, mate. What has Scott supposedly done to rile you?'

'He has not kept his part of an agreement. He's stolen something from me, something worth a lot of money.'

'What in the blazes are you talking about?' Charlie sets his mouth in a line. On his shirt, Grace thinks she detects his heart pounding, stretching the fabric with each quick little leap.

'I had to leave our mine for a day or two, to renew supplies, get some machinery fixed—broken agitator. While I was away, without my approval Scott blasted our site and removed from it a large black opal. I mean huge, and valuable.' Colin widens his arms and eyes, nodding in quick jabs to prove his point. 'I saw the results of his pillaging on my claim. He's taken it alright and denies doing so.'

'How do you know it was Scott who found it?'

'Small towns are no places to keep secrets. He blabbed about it to someone in the town's only hotel. Scott and I had a 50/50 deal meaning I own half of what he has discovered. Doesn't matter who found it—me or Scott, it's all the same. Rules are rules. I am a man of my word. I expect anyone I take on as a partner to be as honest as me.'

Charlie sucks air through his gritted teeth. 'Well, you won't be getting a chance to sink your boot into him today.'

'Apparently not. Has he told any of you about the opal? I don't suppose it is here, is it?'

'Well, I'm not sure how true any of this is, but I know nothing about any opal.'

'What about his fiancée? Do you think she would?'

'I doubt it, but I'll be the one to ask her. I don't want Erin being interrogated by someone angry that Scott wronged him, if that's really what happened.'

'That's exactly what happened, Sir, I assure you.'

'Well, if that's all.' Charlie rises.

'One more thing, please don't tell Scott I was here.'

'I won't. Then again, he's about as likely to turn up here again as it is to rain.'

Colin appears intrigued.

Charlie trails a finger down the cleft of his chin. 'But you've left me in a right bloody pickle.'

'Sorry about that, but it's best you know the truth about him. He is not to be trusted. He's capable of doing the same to you and your family.' Colin removes a piece of paper from his trouser pocket and hands it to Charlie. 'This is the phone number of the hotel I'm staying in at Pig Peak. Call me if you hear anything. I'll be there for two days. Underneath is my address in Blackstone Ridge. Just in case something comes up later.'

Charlie pockets the note.

As Colin makes to leave, he pauses at the doorway, then turns back. 'It's annoying. Scott used to rave on about some lavish hotel where he'd sometimes stay in Sydney. I thought he might be there, but he's taken the brochure he showed me, and I can't for the life of me remember its name.'

Later, Charlie tells Grace he has questioned others at the farm about Colin's accusations and the puzzling whereabouts of some mysterious opal, but without revelations. Erin—bursting into tears, poor girl—said she knew nothing. Fleur, on the telephone, also denied any knowledge of it.

Grace is also unaware of any expensive rock lurking about, and strewth, she would be the first to tell Charlie if she was!

She could have predicted all along that someone outside the family would finally, thankfully, turn on Scott.

'Fleur told me she was going to college in Sydney, but I think there's more to it. She's been gone for many weeks now with no contact, I just wish I knew what was going on,' says Tripp to Izzie as they sit together on Izzie's bed.

'She knows how you feel, Tripp.' He knows his mother is trying to reassure him, something she has done a lot in response to his moodiness since Fleur left.

'Everyone is behaving so strangely around here. Have they told you anything?'

'No-one tells me nothing, son.'

'Scott hasn't been around upsetting everyone. But there are secrets, for sure. Why did Fleur leave so quickly?'

Izzie shrugs. 'That girl has had big problems. Let her go for now, Tripp. You know people find each other again.'

'I thought things were finally alright with us, *Anya*.'

They both jump with the sudden ring of the telephone, its loud, persistent bell. They hear Erin's voice as she answers it. Guiltily, they look at one another as neither of them moves to shut the door which is ajar. The young woman's voice slices through the gap.

'What is it, Fleur? Stop, take a breath. It's alright darling, really it is. No, he hasn't been around here for weeks. Waitressing? What? Sacked you? Okay, now listen. The time has come for me to visit. I know you think you can do this on your own. You're stubborn, but you shouldn't be alone at a time like this, no woman should be. Look, I'm sorry but I'm coming, like it or not. Now, calm yourself down and give me the address.'

They hear the phone hang up and Erin moving away.

'*Anya*,' says Tripp, 'is Fleur pregnant?'

Chapter Forty-Five

An enormous weight lifted from Grace's chest because of Colin's visit, and last night hearing of Dukie's revelations to Charlie on the phone. Yet both encounters had pained her husband, she saw it in his face, heard it in the unsettled waver of his voice.

Charlie told Grace that his old friend disclosed that Scott has taken off for the huge rabbit warren of Sydney in his Jaguar which—unbeknownst to Scott—Dukie was about to sell to pay off some debt. Scott took a substantial sum of Harris cash—the near last of the Harris cash—that was to be used to help finance Scott and Erin's wedding. Grace had tried to meet Charlie's news calmly, with a suitable degree of compassion and empathy, resolutely ignoring the distraction of her insides doing cartwheels. She felt some sorrow for the effect the news had had upon her husband. But mainly her hurt and worry concerned Erin, a lot, because this news would come to her daughter as another dream-shattering, life-altering blow.

Now, as Grace stands watering plants and pondering the situation in comforting morning sunlight, Erin appears by her side.

'Mum, I've decided to visit Fleur. You won't mind if I stay with her for a few weeks, will you?'

What perfect timing. She only hopes Erin doesn't bring up the subject of Scott's whereabouts because Grace doesn't want to talk about him.

'Give me a sec.' Grace turns off the hose tap and together they sit on the old wrought-iron garden bench.

'I think you already know my answer. Yes, please, go to her. Have you two spoken lately?' asks Grace.

'I did speak with her yesterday afternoon. She's missing us.'

'Us?'

'Yes, she did mention you, Mum.' Erin pats Grace's arm.

Could Fleur really be missing her pesky mother? 'Well, I haven't heard from her in some time. When we last spoke, she said that as well as going to college, she has been waitressing in Darling Harbour. She sounded worn out on the phone, poor dear. I don't see why she needs to work so hard. Even if we're not flush, we can always send her money if she needs it, somehow. I've told her that.'

'You know Fleur, Mum, she's proud and stubborn. The more we push, the more she'll back away.'

'Unfortunately, that's Fleur: reactive, and sometimes prematurely. I love her so much and worry about her living on her own, in an unfamiliar big city. Plus, she hasn't been well lately. It's just not right, everything is wrong. To be honest, I wish she wasn't even studying. She should just come back home to us, where she belongs.'

Grace wipes away two tears—one from each eye, both for Fleur.

'Don't worry. I'll stay with her until she finishes her course then bring her home. I promise you, Mum.'

'I'm grateful for that. Oh, and Erin, we'll pay for the train. And I hope you don't mind company.'

Grace has weighed things up. She was expecting Erin's shock about a travel companion, but her daughter appears petrified.

'It's alright. Just you and Fleur will be staying together.' *Not me.*

'But you don't understand.'

'But I do.'

Stand back, Grace. You are not needed at present.

As hard as Tripp has been working, Grace knows he cannot get Fleur out of his mind and her being so far away is tearing him apart—once again being pulled from someone he loves. He wears it like an ill-fitting, unwanted outfit. Hasn't he had enough pain?

Tripp appears—as if having been conjured—and sits with Grace in the kitchen. She lifts her eyes from her magazine.

'Can I get you something?' she asks. 'Cup of tea?'

'Me? No. You?'

'I'm fine.'

Tripp takes a deep breath. 'It may not be my place to say this, but I'm worried about Fleur.'

'It's alright you know, we all are. Even Erin is, and I say that ironically because those twins have never gotten along much until recently. But it doesn't quell our concerns for Fleur.'

'It must be contagious.'

'I knew you'd be affected. Come on, Tripp, open up.' A welcoming smile.

He gets himself a glass of water from the sink tap, and downs the lot before returning. 'I thought we were starting to work things out, when suddenly she's gone.'

'Perhaps going away to college is what she needs to take her mind off things.' Lying doesn't sit well with Grace. She knows distance will not help her daughter but being close to the only person she misses—the man sitting in front of Grace now—will. Also, she knows Fleur is not at college.

'Please believe that I never intended this. I really do think the world of her. I hope you don't mind.'

'Why would you think I'd be upset? Feelings should guide us; they hold more logic than we give them credit for. Fleur needs someone with stability. She's better with you.'

'That's very kind. Thank you.'

'What do you want to do?'

'I'm not sure. I just miss her, I guess.'

His eyes to the ceiling in awkward embarrassment, this openness with Grace is difficult for Tripp. He probably thought long and hard before coming to her. The pull of Fleur must be too great for him to ignore any longer.

'I appreciate your honesty. Would you like to visit her?'

'What? Yes! I really would. But how can I? What about Charlie and the farm work?'

'He'll be happy for you to go. They'll all be fine here for a while. Remember, they've done it before. Although, perhaps you shouldn't be away for as long as you were last time.' She winks. 'We've had too much sadness here, with Scott and everything.' *Scott, be gone!* 'It will do you good to get away. Could you use some company?'

'Who? You? Sure! *Are you sure?*'

'A mother should trust her instincts. But no, I won't be going. You and Erin will be travelling by train to Sydney, return tickets. She will stay in Fleur's apartment with her. You can share a taxi with Erin from the station and the driver will drop you at the hotel I will book for you. I hear Fleur's living quarters are cramped, and all the other rooms are occupied anyway. Charlie will pay for the expenses. I suggest you stay around your hotel. Erin will call you when Fleur is ready to see you.'

Grace cannot see Tripp catching a train on his own and was relieved—but unsurprised—that Erin suggested going herself. Just as Grace knew Tripp would want to go to Fleur. Grace holds faith that Erin and Tripp will deal with whatever happens in Sydney. Grace hopes she can remain settled at the farm with the upheavals she knows will soon come. She also hopes to visit Fleur herself.

She can stay alert. *Beyond* is still perched upon her shoulder—weightless, not worrisome—whispering timely instructions into her ear.

'I'll be going on a train to Sydney? Wow.'

'Wow indeed.'

'How do I explain being there to Fleur?'

'You can explain when the time is right. Trust me.'

'Why would you do this for me, Grace?'

'Because she needs you now.'

'I suppose she just might.'

Grace is gaining strength—ready to put her pride aside for what lies ahead.

Chapter Forty-Six

Sydney, July 1969

Erin stands before Fleur assessing her. 'You're huge!' She drops her suitcase. Tentatively, she reaches out and pats the protrusion straining from her sister's middle.

'I am, aren't I.' Fleur arcs her back, smiling down at her belly full of baby.

Erin holds the look of someone mortified because her sister wears the blatant sign of having had sex. She gives her head a quick shake before taking a good look at her younger twin: unruly hair, dry skin, panda eyes. Mess. The infernal eternal martyr, Erin must be convinced she did the right thing by coming to Fleur's rescue, to set things straight. Her way.

'I'm sorry, darling.' Erin pouts.

'Sorry?'

'Come here and give me a cuddle.' Condescension. Arms out towards her with palms raised as if to keep space between them. The two sisters embrace like rusty robots.

Erin now weighs up the Darling Harbour apartment with similar distaste. A floral chenille bedspread covers a single corner bed. Grimy oven and stovetop, dirty cream refrigerator, lack-lustre wardrobe, small wooden table with two metal chairs, a waste-paper basket which could never cope with all the rubbish around here. Proudly, she identifies the source of the musty smell: rising damp clawing up the walls—as if Fleur hadn't yet noticed it. She has tried cleaning products, and even the open window cannot dilute the stench of mildew which seems to have invaded every square inch of living space.

'You really should be home at a time like this.'

'I don't think I'm in much of a state to be at home, do you?'

'Can I make us a pot of tea?'

'Yeah, sure. No, don't worry. I'll do it. I know where things are.'

Fleur shuffles her bulbous frame to the almost-kitchen, eventually producing two steaming cups of tea in chipped mugs, with two bendy Anzac biscuits—emptying the packet. They sit at the rickety table.

'I'll get the landlord to put in another bed for you.'

'Thanks?' Erin gazes around like she's wondering where on earth he'll put it—a justifiable concern Fleur can't work out either. 'Have you been seeing a doctor, or going to a hospital regularly?'

'I've been taking a bus to the women's hospital in Glebe every month. Don't worry, everything is as it should be, in terms of a single pregnant woman having no clue what she'll do with her baby or future.'

'Have they been treating you okay though, Fleur?'

'If I don't dwell on the disapproval.'

Erin tries to stifle her own disapproving look with a biscuit she shoves into her mouth.

'It's alright, they do as well as they can, I guess. But I know things would be better if I had a wedding ring on my finger.' Fleur hates this admission, sipping her tea for calm.

'Have they discussed with you... options?'

'You fluffed the word; I think you mean adoption. Why don't you just spell things out, Erin, rather than dancing around the subject?'

'I'm not. I'm just trying to be, I don't know, sensitive I guess.'

'There's nothing sensitive about the options you speak of. They have discussed that "option" with me. But I don't know if I can, and I don't want to talk about that please, not yet.'

'What about the plan I put to you about bringing the baby home with us?'

The plan I put to you. Because Erin thinks she is in charge, even of this. Fleur wishes she could charge her sister with pushing a baby out.

How can Fleur admit to the depth of her love for the life growing inside her? So many nights she has spent lying awake chatting to him, imagining the sound of his voice, promising them both a new, safe, and secure life together. Despite her fears. Some part of her hates giving in to sentiment, the weakness of pregnancy. Even with all the time in silence to think about what she will do, no solution is coming to her. If only Teddy would make contact and help her with her decision. One thing is clear: with each passing minute, the thought of giving away the only thing that has ever been truly hers gets fainter, becomes less likely.

'Fleur?'

'I have nothing to say.'

'Right. So, the reason you have told no one about the pregnancy at home is? I'm sorry to bombard you, but decisions must be made, and I'm here to help you with them.'

'Of course. If it benefits you.'

Erin appears extremely composed in wanting to kill her sister.

'Is he still at the farm? I couldn't bear to see him again. Honestly, I'd rather die. And Erin, he's going nowhere near this baby, ever!' It could all happen without Scott's knowledge, couldn't it?

Erin straightens her back against the rusty chair. 'If you mean Scott, no, he's not at home. You have some strong opinions about him, don't you? Always have. I tried phoning the Harris place, but they tell me nothing other than he is not there. We haven't heard from him since the fire.'

Her sister rises, unsuccessfully smoothing wrinkles from her linen skirt. She moves to the open window for a dose of the fresh air that is dodging this room as stubbornly as a sensible solution to all this. Fleur joins her, placing a tentative arm around her waist, because she guesses it was good of Erin to come. Also, she feels less guarded now knowing that Scott has—she prays—disappeared into the veritable ether.

No glorious harbour from this outlook, just a back alley. Together the twins absorb the sorry sight of a young mother dragging her screaming child along a footpath, a bursting-at-the-seams string bag hanging over her other arm. Fleur imagines the marks it will leave—circumstantial evidence of her load, her burden. Is Fleur's pregnancy like that? Will the marks made—and there will be many—be only temporary or will she forever carry them around as her burden? Her brand…

'Fleur, if you want me to go, just say it.'

'No, it's alright. Please stay. I just don't for the life of me know what to do.'

'Do you want to keep it?'

'Keep him? Sometimes I want to.' Too tired now to chastise for the gender thing.

'Well, there's your answer. Options, yes, I know, before you scold me, there's that word again. You could adopt him out, or you could tell Mum and Dad that you've been sleeping around, well, been loose enough to get knocked up—pardon my bluntness—went away, had the baby, then brought it home.'

'Him, bloody hell! *Sleeping around?* They would be so proud! Nothing you've said sounds like much of an option.'

'Or you could say it was an immaculate conception, but somehow that doesn't seem to fit with you.' Erin arches her eyebrows, purses her lips, wobbles her head.

'Careful or I'll strangle you with my rosary.'

'I'm surprised you've even heard of such things.'

'My halo may be choking me, but I still have some life left.'

'You sure do.' Erin looks at Fleur's over-inflated body.

'And I will always have my secret weapons. I could crush you, for one.'

'Fair enough. We're even. Seriously Fleur, I don't hear you coming up with anything better. One thing is for sure, if you keep the baby there will be rumours.'

'Ah ha, so that's it. What would the community say? Oh, my God, an illegitimate child in the Alton family, the sheer horror of it all!'

'That is not what I meant, and you know it.'

'Do I?'

'I just mean you need to get your story straight. Because realistically, you should be proud to have a baby.'

'Would you?'

'Yes, I would love a baby more than anything.' Hurt in Erin's voice.

'Sorry. But surely not Scott's baby?' Those awful words, *Scott's baby.*

'What do you mean by that?'

'He's unstable, the way he runs off all the time, spending time with other women. He's untrustworthy too, you must know it.'

Fleur's revelation shouldn't shock Erin, but she wears that look. Fleur has a fleeting thought, wondering what their parents now think of him. Deep down, surely Erin would hate to raise Fleur's baby as her own, knowing the fragility of her own relationship with Scott. Imagine if the child Erin raised was Scott's! Fleur swallows at a lump wedged in her throat like a baby refusing to be born. *Bring out the forceps.*

'Well, it's either we bring the baby home with us, or give it up for adoption. Only two real choices.'

'Erin, for God's sake stop calling him "it". I swear... Look, I don't know how I'll cope with anything anymore. Satisfied? No? Of course not. Because you haven't been able to brag about being the only one who could bring Fleur to her senses. Keep going the way you have been, and I'll soon be on my knees.'

Fleur pushes past her sister and drops her heft onto the inadequate bed, its springs shrieking under pressure like something haunted.

Chapter Forty-Seven

Like a gaggle of ghosts, doctors and nurses huddle round a television set which has been placed hurriedly in the corner of the hospital delivery room. Fleur suspects it is the only one in the entire hospital. They struggle to get the two rabbit ears of antennae positioned well enough to stop the static being beamed into, and out of, the box. So, they take it in turns to play with them but never quite get it right. Even though Fleur is the only labouring woman here, the impending birth is secondary to the thrill of the satellite newscast—obviously.

Her worst nightmares are coming true. She twists her limbs against the unbelievably painful contractions. *Is the poor crying tree always in pain like this? Is that why it is so twisted?* This pain of Fleur's is much worse than she had read or been told about in her birthing classes where, snickering at her single status, the nurses lied that the whole thing would be a breeze. She could kill every one of those bitches, stick them repeatedly with a scalpel or the pins of their nurses' watches, either way extinguishing them in slow painful deaths. The other nightmare—the one where Erin sits holding her hand during the labour and birth, aghast as the wet shock of blood-red hair that won't wipe away makes its appearance—is well on its way to eventuating, too. But the big question remains. Fleur still refuses to tell anyone what she wants to do with the baby because she doesn't know herself.

Against staff's—and Fleur's—wishes, Erin talked herself into the delivery room. Fleur didn't have the strength to argue. And now Erin is sitting on a chair next to the bed straining to watch television too. Everyone seems to be succeeding in ignoring Fleur's cries of agony.

The nitrous oxide and oxygen do nothing but make Fleur sick. Some nurse asks her to wriggle her toes while she sticks a large needle into her leg and pushes in a nasty shot of pethidine. When the next contraction hits, predictably stronger than the last, Fleur wonders when, more crushingly if, the drug will kick in. It does not. And here she is in her moment of dread—dread, pain, and exhaustion. She does not care anymore. She cares.

'The Eagle has landed,' announces an American voice from the television.

Gasps ring out around the room. Around the world.

'God help me!' *No-one here will.*

A nurse begrudgingly comes to her, looks between Fleur's legs and says: 'You're almost there.'

'I can't do this anymore. Just let me die.'

'For goodness' sake, you don't want to die. Now, do you feel as though you want to push?'

'YES! Help me, this is too much.'

'It's alright darling, I'm right here.'

Erin screws up her face, surely ecstatic she cannot have children.

'That's one small step for (a) man, one giant leap for mankind.'

'Ah. Did you hear that? How profound! This is incredible!' One doctor cannot contain himself.

'Aahh!'

'Shush!' commands the doctor to Fleur.

'Shut up yourself!'

'Hush now. Okay, when I say push, push. Push!'

'Aahh!'

'Okay, almost there, Fleur. You're doing fine. Now push!'

She feels the head has crowned, and she pictures it stretching her fragile skin—in its now shaven frame—with each push. That sting!

Relief as his head emerges. Shoulders, body slipping out. Fleur falls back, exhausted.

'You can stop watching TV now, the baby's here,' says Fleur, to the room. Waiting for the placenta to be delivered, she hears an indignant infant scream when someone plonks her newborn on a set of cold scales.

An adult scream. 'He's a big fella. Nine pounds, ten ounces!'

Fleur cranes her neck to watch someone wipe his body before wrapping him snugly in a white blanket.

'Let me see him,' whispers Fleur.

A chill in the atmosphere. 'Have you decided what you will do, Miss Alton?'

'Let me see my baby.' Downtrodden, confused.

The nurse reluctantly places the baby in Fleur's arms.

And she knows exactly what she will do.

∽

The new mother sits in bed nursing her newborn baby. Her sister perches on the edge of a chair by her side. Having taken the colostrum from Fleur's left breast, she turns the baby and attaches his mouth to her right nipple. As if he'll get more by doing so, he takes the areola, too. As the electric shocks of letdown flood her body, tears well in her tired eyes. Looking up to the bright lights does not prevent their spill. Erin grabs a handful of Kleenex tissues from the side table, gives them to Fleur, then gently pats her leg.

'I have to tell you what happened. I didn't want to but now I know I must,' says Fleur.

'Whatever it is, darling, it doesn't matter. Look at what you've been through!' Erin peers out the window and shakes her head as if trying to dislodge an insect from her ears.

'Get away from him, Erin. Scott can't be trusted.'

Erin returns her gaze. 'Don't fear, Fleur, I'm getting that message. I can't believe I've been such a fool.' Erin's turn to cry; she reaches for her own tissues.

'I don't know how to explain what happened,' says Fleur. 'I was cutting myself and he saw me. I was ashamed. Then he came to my room and, well, it felt like he was bribing me. I wanted no-one hurt, you must believe me.'

'Cutting yourself? Where, when? More to the point, why?' Is Erin more concerned with her sister's welfare than her fiancé's infidelity?

'Why does anyone do anything? I've stopped. I know it wasn't normal,' says Fleur, haltingly.

'Even strong people wear down when they're pushed enough.'

'Or we can rise up.' Fleur reaches over and taps her sister's leg.

'We can.' A smile for her. 'For such a long time, I've wished you'd let me in. I knew something was going on. And poor Mum, so full of self-blame, especially when something bad happens to you. She adores you, Fleur.'

'I know she loves me. I just wish we could tell each other that. Mum said some things she didn't mean, and I never wanted her to feel bad about me. I just don't know how I will explain... him.' She stares at her suckling baby.

'Don't assume things. We'll just take one step at a time. Now you have someone new who needs you, every part of you, all your attention. That's all that matters.'

After burping the baby, Fleur calls for the nurse who takes him back to the nursery; he has seen enough tears for now.

The twins sit in silence.

Fleur's mind takes her back to the conception. She understood that water could not dilute passion; she didn't know it couldn't prevent new life.

The sisters nod off. But not for long. They awaken with a start to the commotion of someone entering the room.

'Mum, what? How did you know we were here?' Fleur's frantic voice sounds accusative.

Crack hardy, Grace, her father used to instruct her in the face of adversity. But this is her daughter, not her enemy. She pulls up a chair.

'Oh, Fleur, why didn't you tell me—tell Dad and me—you were pregnant?'

'I was...' Fleur's words fade to stunned silence. She adjusts her bed sheet.

'We didn't know you were here. We went to your apartment and ran into a lady who said she thought you must have gone to the maternity hospital to have the baby.'

'Oh no. That must have been a shock.' As Fleur takes some shaky breaths, Grace notes her daughter has not asked who, exactly, 'we' are, because surely, she must realise her father has remained at the farm.

'To put it mildly, yes. Darling girl, why couldn't you tell us rather than running away?' pleads Grace, yet she can't help but wonder what she would do in the same situation.

'So many reasons, you have no idea how complicated it has been. But it is time I stopped keeping secrets from you, Mum, from all of you.' Fleur—eyes foggy due to a probable cocktail of drugs—flicks her gaze from Grace to Erin then back again.

'Where's the baby, dear? Is he well? Or did they, did they... take him from you?' Grace's words falter. Another boy lost; she couldn't bear it again. Fleur couldn't.

'How do you know he's...? Yes, he is a boy. But no, no-one took him from me. He's with the other babies in the nursery. Bouncy, healthy, big. Nine pounds seven ounces. Though it was confusing when I first saw him, we've decided to keep him.'

'You say 'we', as if Erin has helped you make your decision,' says Grace hopefully, yet wondering about Fleur's 'confusing' comment.

'She's been helpful, haven't you, Sis?'

A new beginning? Grace hopes so with all her heart. And Erin deserves to share the joy of a baby, even if not her own.

'It's been traumatic for Fleur. I'm just pleased I came,' says Erin.

Grace feels herself flush fire engine red.

'It's alright, Mum.' Fleur pats her mother's hand. 'I know you would have helped.'

'I only wish I could have done something. I was a nurse, you know! And once a nurse, always a nurse!'

'I know. Sorry.'

'And Tripp has been worried sick, haven't you Tripp?'

Grace scans the room, catching her daughters gawping, Fleur murmuring to Erin, 'What?' Grace finds him standing outside the room, appearing terrified, diasporic, painfully out of place.

You need to be with her. 'Now is the time to see her, Tripp.'

In the little hospital room of wonders, Fleur and Tripp hug one another tight amid unstoppable tears, plenty enough to rival the crying tree's outpourings.

⁓

The old arcane tree is frail. Try as it might, it cannot seem to shoot what is left of its water into the sky to fill the clouds, which could start healing the land and its inhabitants. Its twisty roots and branches ache from their continual search for sustenance. It feels it could die if help fails to come soon.

Chapter Forty-Eight

Fleur's baby nightmares will not abate. She fears someone is in trouble. Yet today, she can push this to the back of her mind to the point of almost feeling sanguine. She vows to repair two important relationships—with her mother and sister—while fostering another two: with Tripp, and a bright new one in the shape of her miracle baby.

Back at the farm, she opens the front door to an atmosphere inside throbbing with promise.

Extending his arms towards Fleur and the baby, Charlie welcomes them like long-lost friends. 'Give him here. Oh, my little soldier.'

'Of course.'

Fleur passes the baby to his grandfather. The baby mouths his fist before Charlie lets him trace a tiny finger down the cleft in his chin. Charlie laughs.

Cappi—unusually, waiting inside the house—greets Erin with a shy smile. Saying his name, she giggles like the girl who was always somewhere inside her, like a girl suddenly once again blissfully aware of her youth. Cappi remains composed as he speaks a few Italian words to Erin, eliciting more laughter from her. Will she at last get her chance to give in to her feelings for him, ones she has harboured since childhood? As she—uncharacteristically—hugs him vehemently, his astonishment seems to settle into something mellow and comfortable. At long last Scott isn't around to suck all the life from their world.

Tripp takes Fleur aside. 'You will like me as a father.'

Love surges throughout her body. 'There was never a question of that.'

'Listen, my grandfather, even my own father, disowned me.'

She gently pats his arm in reassurance.

'Now you have given me my own son, Fleur, you must know that I will be nothing like them. I will be the man that they should have been for me. I swear this on my life.'

Framing Tripp's face in her hands, she smiles into his eyes, sighs, then kisses him with passion. 'You are the man of my dreams.'

Tripp has become a father, and a fine one he will be. He wears his pride like a suit of love visible for anyone to see. He will love his child with the ferocity of a tiger and the gentleness of a lamb. He gives his promise to always be strong enough to hold his boy no matter how big he becomes, no matter how wild his adventures.

The couple returns to the others. Fleur notices that, except for proportions, father and son look almost the same: olive skin, mops of black curls, twinkly smiles, star-filled eyes. Mini-Tripp blows a fountain of giggly bubbles towards his father. *Isn't he too young to be smiling?*

Izzie makes a grab to take the little one from Charlie, laughing at his antics as he tugs at her abundant hair. She exudes a natural exuberance, because she now has both her son and grandchild, and Fleur knows that soon she herself will be part of Izzie's family too.

'Do you have a name for him yet, dear?' asks Grace of her daughter.

'I spoke with Izzie a couple of times on the phone before leaving hospital. She's been helping me choose a name for him.'

Izzie beams at this.

'I wanted all of us here before telling you. But only if it's fine with you, Tripp. You will naturally get the final say. Go on, tell everyone, Izzie,' urges Fleur, smiling at her in reassurance.

Izzie passes the baby back to Charlie, as though the thought of doing two important things at once is too much for her at this moment. She fixes her eyes on Tripp.

Izabella says, 'Ervin: it's Hungarian, because Budapest is a beautiful place, and it is where his grandmother—that's me!—and his great-grandmother lived. It means friend of the sea.' She beams, proud of her smooth delivery.

'The name is perfect,' says Tripp, winking at Fleur, understanding the circumstances of their union, making her blush. New life conceived in water. A miracle! Fleur blushes as the warm feelings continue to surge through her body, proof that she is indeed a sentient creature: flesh, blood, and soul, all in one package. She has spent far too long imagining otherwise.

'I wish all the family were here.' Grace's mother's voice trembles as she gives Charlie's hand a squeeze, his adoration apparent in the reassuring face he gives to his wife.

'We can try,' says Charlie.

'When the time is right, we'll introduce him to Cora,' says Tripp.

'When Tripp is a teacher at Wagtail,' Fleur is safe to announce, as if having had his baby has enabled her to grant all his wishes. And hers, because, unexpectedly, she now feels fulfilled. Also, something at the back of her mind tells her that in the future she could be a teacher, too, and a fine one.

'One day at a time,' says Charlie. 'For now, there's too much to do around here, especially since everyone left me alone and went off having babies.'

'Has anyone heard anything from...' Erin swallows. 'Scott?'

'Nothing I'm afraid. Sorry, love,' says Charlie. 'Dukie told me the fire really affected him, his mental state I mean. After hospital, he only spent a week with them before setting off to God-knows-where in his Jag with a stash of their money. There's something else: Carmen was arrested for assault and battery. She punched up the manager of the Criterion, even bit him! Can you believe it? A woman!'

Fleur muffles her giggle with a forced cough.

'Dukie was terribly humiliated,' her father sets his piercing eyes on her. 'So, we must keep this between ourselves. Mind you, around here...'

'No wonder Scott is the way he is, with a mother like that,' Fleur blurts out, before realising she could just as well be comparing Tripp with Len Robinson. Embarrassed, she adds, 'But everyone has choices about how to behave, don't they?'

'Is Cathy still next door?' says Fleur, hoping the two have run off together. Or does she?

'Don't believe so,' says Charlie, giving Erin a sad smile.

Fleur's baby dreams have continued. Is someone else in trouble?

'More importantly, while we were away, Dad made something for the baby.' Grace kisses Charlie on the cheek. He beams. 'It's in Teddy's old room—your bedroom, Fleur, perhaps not for long though? Anyhow, come, we'll show you.'

'I can't wait to see this mysterious object, Dad. Please come with us and show me,' says Fleur.

'I might leave you to it,' says Cappi.

'I'll make sure they behave,' says Charlie to Cappi, handing Ervin back to his mother to carry him over the proverbial threshold.

'I'll tell you about it later,' Erin calls out to Cappi as he turns, returns her smile, then moves outside.

Grace, Erin, Fleur, Tripp, Charlie, and the baby move to Teddy's old bedroom. Fleur had grand plans to put her stamp on this room, yet she knows it will never be anything but her brother's room. But for now, it is also for her and Ervin. Especially as she sights—with astonishment—what lies inside a bassinette in the corner, inside the wooden object crafted by her father with so much love and attention.

Fleur's mother waylays her. 'See, darling, I told you I'd show you the rainbow painting Teddy did for me.' Grace indicates a painting on butchers' paper stuck to the wall opposite the new bassinette, reminiscent of a naive Van Gogh's *Starry Night*. 'I thought you'd probably both stay here for now and would like a precious reminder of Teddy.'

'It's beautiful,' she replies truthfully as its colours flash before her eyes. But her voice is flat. She has barely glimpsed the artwork.

'Or I could take it down,' mutters her mother.

'No, don't! I love it. And the bassinette. Oh, Dad, thank you. I can see you have really put your heart into it. But where did this come from?' Fleur moves to the crib, the volume of her voice softening to little more than a whisper.

'What?' Grace looks to where Fleur points.

Her father steps over and looks inside. 'I didn't put it there,' he says, in a bit of a flap.

'Do any of you understand? No, how could you? Teddy showed me where it was on the riverbank. I saw a little snippet of blue metal. It was stuck underneath a heavy log there was no way I could lift. Erin?'

She shakes her head. 'I know nothing about it. How could I anyway? I've been with you.'

'Tripp? Mum?'

Both shake their heads in a *no*.

'Teddy wants to play with Ervin,' says Fleur decisively, locking eyes with each person, finding no disbelief reflected in any of them.

Fleur cradles the clean, shiny Matchbox car that Teddy once so loved. She strokes it before placing it up on a high shelf facing the window to outside, between Freddy the bear – both eyes now intact and beaming – and where her mother's china animals have also claimed their spot. Other animals reside on the shelf, too, in the form of koalas in snow.

'See, Ervin: Mother and baby koala, tiger, bear, dog, rabbit.' Grace points to each object, giving him a fresh smile as she identifies each one for him. She has no need for them now. 'Carry them with you, my little darling. For as long as you need, they will share with you all the secrets of the universe.' She has no doubt they will.

Fleur places Ervin in his new bed. He giggles, kicking up his legs, surrounded by love bubbles.

'Now I have a surprise of my own for all of us.'

Standing on tiptoes Fleur stretches her arms up to reach the back of the top shelf in the wardrobe. Locating the newspaper-covered parcel she exhales with relief and brings it down. She unwraps it and holds its contents towards her family. Her parents gasp at the extraordinary beauty of the magnificent opal, glowing in sunlight, carefully cradled in Fleur's hands.

'This is the opal Scott stole from Colin,' Fleur presents it to her family.

'But how?' asks Erin.

'Teddy helped me move it.'

Erin widens her eyes, appearing aghast. 'What do you mean?'

'Teddy will always help us.' Grace widens her arms to indicate the extent of her boy's compassion. Fleur cannot remember her mother looking happier than she does now.

'Without doubt, Scott has no claim to this gemstone,' says Charlie decisively.

'But do we?' asks Erin.

'More than he does. But perhaps someone who Scott wronged deserves it more,' says Fleur.

Charlie says to his concerned looking family, 'I have Colin's address. Don't worry—it will all work out fine.'

'Just the way Teddy wants it to,' offers Fleur.

'Thanks, love, for all your gifts.' Fleur feels her mother's warm embrace as she angles her head towards the outside view.

'Mum?' Fleur's voice is suddenly high-pitched and tremulous. Her tears of joy are quick to come.

'What is it, dear?'

'Look.' Wearing an easy smile, Fleur points outside. 'It's raining!'

She watches as the crying tree drinks up, at long last becoming renewed. She sees its branches flexing, straightening, tiny leaves and buds beginning to form on its harrowed habit. 'Isn't it magic?'

This is Fleur's life: one of here, there, and in between. She is learning not to be afraid of herself or of anyone else, to trust in her instincts.

She may just have found her niche.

Chapter Forty-Nine

In a desolate town such as Blackstone Ridge, the best place to ask for directions must be the local pub, Erin and Tripp have decided, as many would have realised before them. After only a few questions, they soon discover Colin's whereabouts. A miner has even offered to take them to him, and they're happy to accept.

'We think it only fair for you to have this,' says Erin to Colin as she places a parcel on a small table, 'after the trouble you've been through with Scott.'

Colin asks, 'May I?' indicating the parcel.

'Of course,' says Erin.

Colin unfolds the soft cotton material Fleur had used for wrapping, to reveal the dazzling giant. Tripp notes that the distinct lack of light in the cabin cannot pale the huge gem which illuminates the room in blues, reds, greens, and golds on black. The colours dance merrily as Colin examines the opal with an eyepiece from his pocket—for play of body colour, pattern, and clarity, he says. Lots of reds: according to Colin, the most desirable colour in a black opal. Importantly, no imperfections.

'Dear God! It's perfect. Just as I imagined it to be. I knew it must have been there, and Scott took it after all, the bastard. Sorry, miss.'

'No offence. I totally agree with you.'

'Scott is a cruel man who has hurt both Erin and her sister, Fleur,' adds Tripp.

'So how did you end up getting the opal from him?'

'He fled the farm without it,' says Erin.

'So, he doesn't know that you have it?'

'I'd be surprised if he wasn't suspicious about where it was, but he wouldn't dare come anywhere near the farm again, let alone set foot in the house.' Erin's fingers tremble as she scouts around. 'He's not here, is he?'

'Scott is long gone. He wouldn't turn up here again, wouldn't be game. In case I find out where he is, I have someone here in town who'd like to give him his just desserts for wronging me. Just rough him up a bit, enough for Scott to think twice about messing with miners. In the meantime, I also know someone who'd be willing to buy this beauty at a decent price. And if you agree, I'd like for you and your family to have half of what I get for it,' says Colin.

'But why would you do that? You hardly know us.' Erin is shocked and impressed by this man's incredible generosity.

'Why would you come all the way out here to give me this if you weren't good people? Let's just call it a fair deal. I'm sure you've all suffered at the hands of Scott.'

'You have no idea,' confirms Erin sadly. 'We can't thank you enough.'

'If you leave the opal with me, your family can soon expect a cheque for around $20,000. I'll put this in writing before you leave. And when it's sold, then I can make a new life for myself in Melbourne.'

Erin removes a fold of glossy paper from her handbag and gives it to Colin. 'I almost forgot, Fleur gave me this with the opal, said to give it to you. She was adamant about it and said you'd know what to do with it. Perhaps she thought you'd sell the opal, then go on a nice holiday?'

As Colin unfolds the brochure, his wild eyes suggest he is brewing something darker. Seeing photos of the luxurious decor of the Pimm's Point Hotel in Sydney, Colin's face breaks out in a smile of what appears to be relief, and recognition.

'Bingo! Found him. Your sister has played her trump card.'

'Just be careful,' says Erin. 'There's likely to be a tall blonde woman with Scott. Her name is Cathy. She deserves no more harm than what she has likely been through with him. My sister says you must speak with Cathy alone and—I say this verbatim without having had a chance to clarify things—please tell Cathy that she has new family and the Altons will never judge her. Tell her Tripp needs to speak with her urgently and will always protect her. Main thing is that she leaves Scott and comes home immediately because he is dangerous. Fleur says not to tell Cathy this, but she could be pregnant.'

Chapter Fifty

A day at the beach, Stanford Park, October 1968

Fleur watched Tripp's wonder as he discovered the ocean's secrets. She imagined bringing him back there at night-time, imagined how entranced he would be by the pulse and glow of iridescent plankton specks on waves and shoreline. A fallen Milky Way—God's gift of a night sky to the sea creatures in their briny home. A show like that could happen, just for Fleur and Tripp. During that reverie she studied his face and realised she loved him. And she knew that she wanted him at that very moment, in that very place. Holding him close, using every part of her being, she asked him to take her.

The ocean took them as its own.

'What are we doing?' he asked—not in guilt, but in wonder.

'How can it be wrong?' she replied with certainty.

Collaborating, concurring, the waves approved the bond. They changed pace to keep time with their rhythm, rocking them along as passion heated salt water to the boil. Two became one, both at one with the ocean too, as their flesh and bones, their spirits, created another.

Ervin—one born of love. Friend of the sea.

Acknowledgements

Heartfelt gratitude to everyone who has stuck with me throughout the various interpretations of this series.

A huge shoutout to Alana Lambert from Book Burrow, who assisted with my second editions of both *Emigree* and *Niche*. Your professionalism and support have been immeasurable.

Immense thanks to my two exceptional editors—Lauren Daniels and Daniel Car, whose generous feedback challenged me to find some sweet spots in my manuscript. You both exceeded my expectations.

I doubt I would be as enthusiastic about my writing without the support and feedback from my talented, eclectic writers' group—Writers Rendezvous in Dayboro. Thanks doesn't quite cut it, especially regarding Vicki Stevens, prolific author, inspiring friend, and steadfast writing partner, who brings out my best. I also credit George Johnston, for helping me find that forest through the trees in my story.

To my darling husband Lew, aka the typo spotter. Your support and tolerance for my writing obsession is commendable. Bless Tom for his honest assessment, and David, who I know will read this book with generosity of spirit. For Sam and Bec, thanks for always wishing me well. Your love, family, lifts me constantly.